Against Impossible Odds

RORA

A Novel

JAMES BYRON
HUGGINS

LION'S
HEAD
PUBLISHING

RORA

ISBN: 1-891668-08-0

Published by Lion's Head Publishing, 3 Coray Court,
Little Rock, AR 72223.

Literary development and cover/interior design by
Koechel Peterson & Associates, Minneapolis, Minnesota.
Manufactured in the United States of America

Dedicated to
my beloved son,
Gabriel

Remember your strength,
your faith, and your love,
and you will overcome,
in the end . . .

❧ FOREWORD

HAVE YOU EVER HEARD THIS STORY BEFORE? Have you or your children ever heard, read, or spoken the names Gianavel, Pianessa, the Duke of Savoy, or Incomel? Have you ever, even with your imagination, touched upon a world in which cruelty could be so real, unbridled, and unaccountable, and faith so gallant, unshakable, and transcendent?

Then it is time to hear the story of the Waldenses of Rora, for it really happened, and the players must be remembered, some for their soulless cruelty, some for their weak indifference, and some for their immovable, valiant faith.

In what could be his most significant and profound work ever, author James Byron Huggins has resurrected this story from the yellowing and dusty records of history, robed it in flesh and blood, infused breath and spirit, and created a vivid saga that is part poetry, part painting, part cinema—and a great part *question*.

Question.

The answer is never quick and easy in coming, but the Question never fades from era to era, place to place. It lurches to the forefront in places like Masada, poses itself again on the beaches of Normandy, condemns the watching world during the Holocaust, demands our attention with television images of Tiananmen Square. It disturbs, it challenges, it interrupts our personal peace as, from our so far safe haven in the "free world," we read about innocent people in faraway places being slaughtered for their faith.

In a world ever tainted with an audacious evil, we stand on a timeline littered with the bodies of martyrs and have to wonder, What if it were me? What would I do? What *should* I do?

We dare not think our day to decide will never come. How sturdy is that paper wall that separates us from the legal precedent, the judge's ruling, the officer's nightstick? If our church door should ever be padlocked, our prayer made a felony, and the Gospel punishable as hate speech, how will we answer? Keep in mind that we are never alone with the Question. Our neighbors come into it. Our loved ones. Our children and their children. The kind of world they will live in will begin with what we do.

The story of Rora places us within the actions, the conversations, the very thoughts of real people who had to weigh the Question from wherever they were standing and whatever character they may have lacked or possessed: the wavering, politically vulnerable ruler of a country, the heartless, ultimately practical commander of an army, the deluded and incomprehensibly sinister Inquisitor, the politicians and church leaders who had the luxury of watching from a distance—and the fiercely committed patriarchal leader of a people who chose to live only if religiously free. The Question was unavoidable. It mattered.

The Question still matters as much for us as for them.

The answer is in the story, forged in battle, found in loss, victorious even in death.

Relive the story in the eloquent word painting to follow and consider the answer you find.

Frank E. Peretti
March 7, 2001

⟳ PROLOGUE

HARVEST WAS APPROACHING BENEATH a gray sky brushed with crimson between and beyond the craggy peaks of mountainous Vandalin, a sight that lasted long as dusk faded into night. A cool breeze, fresh with the scent of snow, flowed down the gray granite mounds, across the swaying wheat, and through the thin, wispy smoke of chimneys. And it seemed as though these things had lasted forever, and that they should.

Stone, sharpened by ages of ice, led upward to the crest of the peaks—a hard path that led across the summit and down, down into a valley of rolling hills of bloom and heather, of chestnut and oak and cherry, and quiet streams.

This was his home, his life—the place he had stayed to raise and protect his family. And beneath the dunes of deeply caressed wheat he knew where the graves lay of those who had settled here before him—his mother, father, and sister. He had helped bury them, marking their graves as his people marked all their graves, with reverence, with respect, with confidence, knowing that their souls had already ascended to a land far better, far greater.

He scanned the distant peaks of towering Monte Visto, its titanic gray slate as smooth as silver, to the running crest of Angrogna, whose snow-clad peaks cast such ponderous shadows across the valley, and finally to gigantic Castelluzo that dominated the landscape like some brooding guardian of the gods. All the fortresses of the world together did not equal their strength, their magnitude, their defiant might, though he feared it might not be enough, in the end.

They would come here, too, as they had come to the valley known as the Pelice, so far below, where only the wind carried the horrible tale of sorrow and woe.

Like an eagle he scanned the peaceful slopes and saw only what he had seen each day since the earliest days of his life. And for a moment he wondered what it would be like to shed blood on those familiar and comforting mountainsides, then turned his mind from it and closed his eyes, feeling the wind, listening and praying as men pray when they know that death is near.

When he opened his eyes, head bowed, his mouth was turned in a frown, and the gently swaying grass beneath the rock seemed suddenly restless. Then he dropped from the rock, through the cold and gathering dark, only dimly aware that his hand found his sword as he fell to the Earth.

1

MOUNTED UPON HIS HEAVY STEED, armored in black, the warlord Marquis de Pianessa frowned over the smoldering bones and ashes of those who had begged for mercy. He did not bother to count the dead. Monks commanded by the pale, soulless Inquisitors saw to that, though his own scribes checked names against bodies to insure he was not cheated for his pains. In any case he was not a man prone to pondering dusty tomes. No, he was a warrior, a general, and a monarch. It was what he did best, and all he cared to do.

Though he heard nothing, Pianessa was keenly aware of the black-robed Inquisitor as he approached. It was an acute sensitivity he had long ago perfected so that he was constantly aware of the position of everyone and everything—a man, a shadow, the flight of a sparrow however distant, however meaningless. He would not be taken by surprise on the field of battle.

The Inquisitor halted sparse steps apart and stared up. His hands were folded, as if Pianessa should speak first, but Pianessa, hostile and moody, said nothing. It was the old, familiar game, and Inquisitor General Thomas Incomel inevitably surrendered to the marquis' grim apathy.

Incomel glanced serenely at the smoking ashes heaped about fire-charred stakes. "Those who renounced their witchcraft and heresy have been sent to El Torre. But according to law, as you well know, they have lost all claim to their lands and possessions."

Pianessa's black eyes—eyes that revealed the faintest sharp crescents of red—blinked but once. Beneath his low, broad forehead, his down-turned mouth was framed by a thick beard and mustache as black as his mane, allowing the impression of a man grimly comfortable with any manner of death, any number of dead.

His sword, long and heavy and with a two-handed hilt, protruded high from behind his right shoulder—the image of a barbarian, which is how he fought, fierce and direct, sacrificing grace for power, finesse for bearish strength that shattered armor and flesh alike.

And yet Pianessa was also a soldier of his age. His hand lightly held his long rifle, and a belt of three flintlock pistols crossed from his left shoulder to his waist, where he bore a long, broad-bladed poniard almost eighteen inches in length.

A god of war, black and armored and angry, the Marquis de Pianessa sat his horse unmoving and unmoved by all but himself.

"Children," Pianessa muttered to the Inquisitor and turned his brooding gaze beyond the smoking village where butchered bodies lay twisted upon trampled ground.

"Children, Inquisitor," he repeated. "They will not live long enough in the dungeons of El Torre to serve your God. Not that that was ever your intention."

Incomel grimaced. "Do you have a full account of those purified by flame, Monsieur de la Marquis?"

Pianessa's laugh held neither mirth nor melancholy. "Six thousand are dead, Priest. I care nothing how they died. A dead man is a dead man. They are all the same in terms of my reward."

Incomel's smile did not reach his eyes. "Some decisions are not yours for good reason, Pianessa."

Pianessa gazed down again, seeming to separate even farther from the Inquisitor with a vague, sullen deadness that many, to their doom, mistook as an indication of simplemindedness.

With a cautious bow, Thomas Incomel turned to rejoin his cadre of bodyguards who were plate-armored, though musket balls had long made the armor obsolete, and vanished behind a wall of smoke and flame.

Pianessa stared after the Inquisitor with the gaze of a man set to kill a wild dog. Then, frowning, he turned his steed toward Turin and vanished into the smoke and flame as well.

><><

She turned toward him as he quietly shut the door of the cottage, and he was again reminded of her unearthly, almost spiritual, beauty. For as some men dreamed of wealth and power, he dreamed of her. But he had no time for this pleasure as a host of small forms rushed forward to embrace him, holding fast.

Laughing, Joshua Gianavel leaned his rifle beside the door and responded in kind before lifting his sword belt over his shoulder, hanging it with his cloak.

The warm smell of stewed lamb in the crock awakened Gianavel's hunger, but he lifted a three-year-old boy high in the air as his three sisters laughed.

"Finally decide to come home, did you?" Angela smiled. "I'd hate to see what hours you'd keep if you had an orchard to tend instead of watching for criminals in a valley that doesn't have any!"

Gianavel laughed and sat wearily beside the fire. He looked into the surrounding faces, then Jacob began sternly, "I-I-I was winning barrel slip but they cheated on me!"

Gianavel held the boy's shoulders and stared solidly into the transparent gray eyes. "Cheating on you, huh? And just how did they cheat on you?"

Jacob stared, very serious. "They made me fall first, and I didn't do anything."

Gianavel nodded gravely. "Ah, they *won*...Well, I tell you what we'll do tomorrow, then."

"What?"

"I'll teach you to beat your sisters at barrel slip!"

Somehow, that didn't seem to be the answer Jacob sought. He glanced with suspicion at his larger, older, sisters, who smiled back at him sweetly and without mercy.

"And now," Gianavel said, reaching for the bowl of stew that Angela had ladled for him, "I want to taste what your mother cooked for me!"

With a sigh he savored the first warm measure so heartily that he almost forgot how good it felt to be home in their quaint cottage with the lulling heat of the fire. After a moment he glanced up to Jacob sitting in Angela's lap, helping her knit a sweater that he recognized as his. It was the same off-white as the freshly shorn wool of the sheep they herded in the valley and had loose, generous shoulders, wide sleeves to accommodate his heavy arms, and a wide, deep cavity for his chest.

The cottage where they resided had stood for two hundred years, witnessing the births and deaths of Joshua's line. Built from stone and poplar by those who came first, whose names were carefully recorded in his hand-copied Bible, the cottage had been strengthened and hardened by experience and time so that the walls were as solid as the cliff walls of the Castelluzo itself.

Angela's loving gaze caught his attention, and Gianavel held it with a faint smile.

"Nice to have you home, husband," she spoke and smiled.

Gianavel laughed and turned to the hearth. But as he stared into the flames of orange and crimson streams rising against ashen stone, the smile began to slowly fade. Today he had watched columns of smoke rising from the valley of Piedmont. He had heard the sound of cannon and seen armies roving the field under the flag of war. And he had seen no one escape the slaughter to climb the mountain to safety.

And, most tragically, he had not expected to.

✕✕✕❖✕✕✕

Gianavel leaned against the frame of the bedroom door, watching Angela smooth the last blanket over the girls. She blew out the candle with a familiar whisper and kissed them once more before she half shut the door and stood before him.

They moved to a velvet-covered, lushly cushioned couch, and Gianavel pulled her close to his chest while shadows danced about the room like dark harbingers of doom.

"What's happening?" she whispered softly and did not turn her gaze from the hearth.

Face bent slightly forward, Gianavel's forehead hardened. He released a deep sigh as he whispered, "We might be able to escape to Geneva."

Angela was silent and still.

Finally Gianavel tilted his head to kiss her softly where a tear glistened beneath her sky-blue eyes. He caressed her unusual, lightly tinted hair—

17

unusual because their people, the Vaudois, were an olive-skinned mountain race. Of the children, only Jacob had inherited her unique complexion. All the girls were raven-haired, like Gianavel himself.

"War," she whispered, and he knew she had closed her eyes. "War after war...They never stop killing us."

Gianavel said nothing, held her more tightly.

"Perhaps we should leave now, Joshua. Perhaps there's a chance we can cross the mountains before they come."

Gently lifting her chin, Gianavel gazed into her eyes. "We have a treaty with the Duke of Savoy. Charles Emmanuel is young, but I don't think he will attack above the Pelice."

She was quiet; then her voice rose in a whisper. "The righteous are as bold as a lion...but even lions can be killed."

Gently stroking her hair, Gianavel sighed. "It's already too late to run, my love. They've closed all the roads to Geneva. Perhaps you and I and the children might be able to slip across the mountains. But not our families, and not the village."

Angela gazed at nothing.

"All we want is to live in peace...to worship in peace. But, like before, they will kill us for it." She bowed her head. "It's madness. All of it— madness."

Gianavel sighed, closed his eyes as he leaned back. He pulled her tightly into his chest, and their breaths were regular, together.

"Yes," he said.

2

A LL OF THEM?" Charles Emmanuel II exclaimed from his throne
in the fortress-city of Turin. "You killed all of them? That's six
thousand of my people, Pianessa!"

Pianessa did not respond. He had only reported what transpired in the
past week when he laid siege to the valley of Piedmont. He had burned villages, destroyed churches, executed pastors, and killed those who refused to
accept the authority of the Catholic Church. He had fulfilled his duty as he
was ordered by the Inquisitors, just as Emmanuel's ancestors had done.
History was merely repeating itself.

But Emmanuel, only seventeen years old, had only been named the
Duke of Savoy, Supreme Lord of Piedmont, upon the death of his Regent
Mother, the Duchess Christina, when he was sixteen. He had never experienced war or so much as religious purification. Indeed, since Emmanuel's
tenure, Piedmont had been relatively unmolested by Spain and Germany, so
it had fallen upon Pianessa to educate the young prince in the more brutal
responsibilities of his crown.

"War is a simple thing," Pianessa muttered as he poured himself a chalice of wine. "I've killed men and I've killed dogs—they all look the same inside."

Coated in riding dust, Pianessa had not yet deigned to discard his weapons. He still bore his sword, poniard, and bandoleer of pistols. His leather cuirass, doubled folded to refuse or at least slow a musket ball, was gray with ashes. His forearms were covered with thick gauntlets, and chain mail was visible at his wrists. He was the image of a warrior to be feared—the purest survivor, the fiercest fighter—an image enhanced by his dispassionate aspect.

Emmanuel stared sullenly and shook his head. "It seems incredible to me, Pianessa, that you would equate killing dogs with killing my people."

Pianessa's gaze did not waver. "Killing men is how other men gain wealth, my prince. Would you look poorly upon your ancestor Phillip while enjoying the rich rewards he provided you?" A laugh. "Strange that men can criticize others who insure their freedom when they are willing to do nothing themselves."

Emmanuel watched Pianessa refill his chalice, then gestured curtly to his four bodyguards. They departed without hesitation, obviously accustomed to the vague command.

Noticing the abruptness, Pianessa picked up his chalice in a broad, strong hand and strolled imposingly toward the Duke of Savoy.

Even at seventeen, Emmanuel possessed an aura of self-possession that emperors would have envied. He was not physically large—not half so powerful in appearance as Pianessa—but he presented a far stronger impression of intelligence in aspect and even in his dress. He tended to deign stockings and sleeve-bloomed blouses for tighter-fitting trousers and shirts of leather and wool. His boots, also, were out of place on the throne—high and sturdy, more suited for hunting than dancing.

Meeting the marquis' amused gaze, Emmanuel spoke with distinct pique. "Do not forget, Pianessa, you are only a general in my army. I am the Supreme Lord of Piedmont." He paused to let that point be established without dispute. "I warn you; be cautious how you address me in front of my subjects."

Pianessa's face was a caricature of a smile. "I forget nothing, My Lord," he answered without fear. "*You* should not forget who trained you in the art of war."

"I do not forget," Emmanuel admitted without praise. "You also taught me that I should tolerate no rebuke. And that I should measure the cost of a battle before I commit myself."

"I did." Pianessa nodded. "So what do you see as the cost of this battle?"

"My conscience."

Pianessa made no attempt to lessen a deep, amusing laugh. "How piquant…I should have also taught you that a monarch cannot afford a conscience."

"But more practically speaking," Emmanuel continued, "the cost is the lives of virtually all my subjects. Tell me, who will tend to the crops and the villages, the herds and orchards and vineyards, when you finish with your purification of the Waldenses?"

Pianessa was dismissive. "The valley of Piedmont will not go uninhabited, Charles. Immigrants will resettle the land of the Waldenses once we have destroyed them."

"And when will that be?"

Pianessa indulged himself again, wiping the wine from his mouth with a forearm. "Soon enough," he commented finally. "The main of the valley of Piedmont has fallen. Only the Waldenses living above the Pelice remain."

Emmanuel stared long at the huge warrior before him, who always appeared so comfortable—even more comfortable than he was—in the Throne Room. And he knew that if the throne could have been claimed by strength alone, it would have been Pianessa's to claim. But it was an inherited right, and not something that could be won. Besides, Emmanuel had learned that thrones easily won were also easily lost.

"Those above the Pelice," Emmanuel repeated and paused. His saturnine features appeared even more aristocratic with the expression. "You mean those of Rora?"

"And Lucerna." Pianessa belched, then rubbed his chest angrily. "But, yes, mostly those of Rora. They also refuse to join the Catholic Church, so the Inquisitors have sentenced them to death."

"For what charge, exactly?"

"For heresy."

A moment of stillness followed.

"Heresy," Emmanuel muttered, then chuckled without humor. "You never cease to amaze me, Pianessa."

The marquis' dark eyes brightened with the amusement of a man who spied a monkey bearing the robes and crown of a king, lifting high a jeweled scepter. He laughed.

"Yes?"

"You are a warlord to be feared. You gained your rank by the power of your sword and your own cunning. Yet you bow before these Inquisitors."

A pause, and then a frown slowly settled upon the marquis. He stepped closer, upon the very steps of the throne, and stared down over the once boy-king. The marquis' face darkened, eyes hidden beneath the shadow of his brow.

"Hear me, boy," he rumbled. "You hold your throne by the grace of the King of France. If you were to displease him in any manner, he would send a hundred thousand dragoons over the border tomorrow. And the day after that, you would be as dead as any of those fools I left in the valley."

Pianessa poised dangerously close, as if daring a response. "Cardinal Mazarin, the regent of Louis, has not interfered with the Inquisitors, who have sentenced to death all the Waldenses who will not renounce their faith."

Pianessa's countenance became heated, fierce and hard with the rule of war. "Not one out of a thousand Waldenses will renounce. And since we cannot imprison them, we must kill them. It is as simple…as…that."

Finally Emmanuel found the courage to answer. "Inquisitors don't have the authority to kill, Pianessa. They can only deliver the Waldenses to secular authorities for disposition."

Roaring in mirth, Pianessa threw back his head, his laugh thundering across the huge beams of the high ceiling. He was still laughing when he looked down over at Emmanuel. "Did you learn nothing from me?" he continued. "The Inquisitors decide the fate of this nation and all within it! What would happen if you contested the authority of an Inquisitor?"

Emmanuel remained silent.

Pianessa's hateful strength was like a physical force. Gazing down like some angry god of war, dancing flames inhabited his eyes. His beard shone gray with human ashes.

"Hear me, boy. You sit upon your throne only because the Church has not judged you a heretic. If the Inquisitors decided you were sympathetic to the reformed church, I would be ordered to enter this hall and take your head."

Emmanuel stared up at the beastly black image. His voice was barely audible. "And would you?"

In stillness, Pianessa stared a moment longer. Then with a flash of his arm he cast the chalice aside. It struck the steps and tumbled end over end, as a head would do, until it fell ominously still.

"Some questions should not be asked," the marquis said as he turned away.

—————

Gianavel quietly closed the door of Descombie's cottage and stared through the dim light of a single lamp to see the old priest writing, always writing at his small table.

In his fifties, Descombie was a big, heavyset man who appeared even heavier in the gray robe he had retained from his years as a Dominican monk. Now one of the most ardent "barbes," or pastors, of the Waldensian Church, he had never completely shed his severe aesthetic appearance and manners. After living among the villagers of Rora for seven years, he possessed little in the way of material comforts.

Gianavel laid his musket beside the door and walked quietly forward. As Captain of the Guard of Rora, it was his habit in times of danger to visit the pastor late in the night. "Speak to me, Descombie."

Descombie regarded Gianavel's tall, powerful figure grimly and without surprise. He waited until Gianavel stood before him, presenting no indications he would sit. "It has begun," he said, watching Gianavel closely. And when the Captain of Rora did not reply, he continued, "Six thousand in the valley are dead."

Grimacing, Gianavel turned into the darkness of the room. "Why now?"

"Inquisitors," Descombie said simply and without tone.

Turning, Gianavel acutely studied the pastor's expression; there was little.

"Rome has launched a new war to bring all of Italy under a united church," the barbe added. "Everyone who belongs to the reformed church—those who are not Catholic—have been declared guilty of heresy. They are to be imprisoned or killed."

"They're not taking prisoners," Gianavel said calmly.

"No," Descombie agreed and was silent a moment. "No, they are not taking prisoners."

The barbe stared at the letters before him, then after a moment rose. He leaned against the mantel, staring down. He did not look at Gianavel, who had become as solid as a statue.

Darkness dominated the room, more powerful, more permanent than both of them together. The barbe stared closely at Gianavel. "So," he said finally. "Even you are frightened."

"For my family," Gianavel confirmed. "For the children, the old ones." He paused. "It is my responsibility to guard Rora. I do not intend to lose any that the Lord has given me to protect."

Descombie revealed no surprise. "All roads leading across the Alps have already been closed by the Marquis de Pianessa. It will be…difficult…for anyone to reach Geneva."

Gianavel stared into the flames as Descombie continued, "I think they took the north passages first so that none of us could escape. Then they took the towns and villages in the valley. And they will come here, too."

"When?"

"After today? Perhaps days…hours."

Raising his face toward the ceiling, Gianavel closed his eyes. He shook his head once, then bowed it again. "Can we send an emissary to the Duke of Savoy?"

"We can," Descombie judged. "But you must remember the Council of Constance. They consider all those of Rora to be heretics, and no faith—no promise—is to be kept with heretics."

"And yet we must try to negotiate, Descombie." Gianavel was visibly agitated. "At the least we might gain a respite. If there is going to be war, I need time to prepare."

Finally Descombie nodded. "Yes, subterfuge will gain us time, perhaps. But they scent blood, and killing becomes easier every time a man kills. They will not wait long before they climb above the Pelice."

Gianavel's countenance lifted, though not with relief. He nodded as he turned to the flames. "Dispatch letters to Captains Jahier and Laurentio. Tell them to recruit as many survivors as possible." His face became grim. "Tell them we'll make a stand at Rora."

"Here?" The barbe seemed surprised. "Why here?"

Gianavel spoke softly, "The mountains where Lucerne, Angrogna, and Rora meet form a natural fortress stronger than any in all of Europe. There are only two means in or out—the Pass of Pelice and the Ravine of Turin. And if we…if we can, we might hold each of them against their greater numbers."

The old man's eyes revealed no fear, though he spoke words a man should speak with fear. "They will attack with twenty thousand men, Gianavel. At the most, we might raise a hundred."

"It's enough," Gianavel said and walked to the door. "We make a stand here, or die. There's no place to retreat to, no place to hide. And they'll kill anyone who surrenders. Just like they killed those people in the valley below."

There was no dispute, but Descombie had a final question. "Do you think we can possibly win?"

Gianavel stared upon the old man with eyes suddenly shadowed and pained. It seemed that he was considering a hopeful reply, but then without a word he turned away...

And was gone.

3

PIANESSA HESITATED IN THE COURTYARD of Savoy's palace to study the severed heads spiked atop the battlements of Turin and the buzzards that soared in the gathering dark. He was still watching when the war wagon containing the Inquisitors—a square, fortresslike black carriage built from the heavy timbers of a ship—thundered through the portico. From where he stood, he regarded Inquisitor General Thomas Incomel as he descended, lifting his robe to avoid soiling it upon the likes of the earth.

Incomel spied Pianessa almost immediately, smiled with satisfaction, and walked forward. He cast a single glance at the battlements before he halted beside the monolithic marquis. "You do excellent work, Pianessa. I wondered what suitable use you would make of those you butchered."

Pianessa shrugged his thick shoulders with indifference. "Hardly a new thing, Inquisitor."

"No," the Inquisitor agreed, "but effective, nonetheless. Actually, it's hard to conceive of a more daunting defense of the Church than putting the heads of one's enemies on a pike. Was that your intention? To defend the cause of the Church?"

Vaguely threatening, Pianessa's dark eyes roamed back to the Inquisitor. He smiled slowly. "Of course."

"And so, have you made arrangements to deal with those living above the Pelice?"

Startling the Inquisitor, Pianessa raised his hand to his forehead and bowed his departure. "Something I must attend to forthwith, Inquisitor. I bid you good night."

Incomel said nothing as Pianessa walked across the courtyard to the stables, sharply returning a salute from soldiers who were drinking outside, and vanished within. Then the Inquisitor looked a last time at the buzzards feasting upon the castle wall, and smiled.

xoo◈oox

Charles Emmanuel II, standing beside the banquet table, was speaking quietly to visiting dignitaries when shadows of the Inquisitor's bodyguards stopped at the entrance, allowing Incomel to proceed into the Throne Room without the unseemly display.

At the approach, the Duchess Mary Elizabeth, Emmanuel's cousin, regarded Incomel politely. Nor did she move as Incomel closed the final few strides and spoke.

"Your cousin has done great things this day, Duchess. We have pacified the valley, and tomorrow we will climb above the Pelice to deal with those at Rora."

The Duchess Elizabeth folded her hands and replied without either haste or emotion, "History has shown that those at Rora will fight to defend their freedom of conscience, Inquisitor."

Emmanuel's tone was despising. "Those who live above the Pelice—those at Rora—are protected by the ancient treaty, Incomel. They legally

30

possess freedom of conscience and are not subject to the laws of your church."

"Ah yes." Incomel smiled graciously. "You refer to the treaty made with your ancestor, Phillip, which grants all those living above the Pelice freedom of faith." He lifted his hands. "I'm afraid that I have judged that ancient pact to be abrogated, Savoy. No secular authority has the power to overrule the divine edicts of an Inquisitor."

The smile that masked Elizabeth's face was as pale and thin as her skin. "The treaty with Rora has existed for three hundred years, Inquisitor. Are you certain you do not exceed your dominion?"

Incomel bowed. "God has all dominion, Duchess."

Emmanuel poured the duchess a goblet of wine, which she accepted with a minute nod. He clasped his hands behind his back as he turned fully toward Incomel.

"Since my valley is already crippled," Emmanuel began with considerable charm, "tell me—exactly—how you intend to deal with those of Rora. Surely you don't expect *me* to work in the fields and gather the crops. Or did you forget that the vineyards and orchards of Rora comprise the agricultural wealth of Piedmont?"

"Forgive my timing," Incomel replied as he accepted a goblet of wine, "but it would be impossible to move above the cliffs in winter. And, please, do not unduly concern yourself. God will see to your crops, as He sees to all things. Even birds of the air have nests, as evidenced by the sanctity of these castle walls this very day. And does God not care more for us than for them?"

Emmanuel said nothing.

The duchess smiled coldly. "And what of the vast lands acquisitioned

31

during your recent purifications, Inquisitor? Does the Church also raise its flag over these?"

"The Church is beneficent, Duchess. The land and the king are one. But as long as the king is subject to the rule of the Church, the land is also the responsibility of Rome." Incomel laughed alone. "We can't allow heretics to poison their land as they have poisoned the minds of their children, can we?"

"And how many children did you rescue today, Inquisitor?" Emmanuel muttered.

"Over a dozen were sent to El Torre for proper care." Incomel responded, lifting a benevolent hand. "They will be harbored there until more suitable quarters are arranged. Unfortunately, they will not be able to return to their homes because…well, what with the tragic conflict of recent days, many of their homes are…no more."

Emmanuel glanced at his cousin, whose contempt for the Inquisitor could not be concealed. He knew that if the decision had not already been made, Elizabeth would have denounced the merciless cruelty of the powerful priest.

"Victor Amadeus was also forced to attack above the Pelice because the Church ordered him to rid Piedmont of heretics," the Duke of Savoy commented. "He said afterward that every skin he took from Rora cost him fifteen of his best soldiers."

Incomel smiled tolerantly. "My Lord, these people are farmers, not warriors."

"They are friends and family," Emmanuel muttered with a severe frown. "And they are wise in the ways of war because this world has forced them to become wise. Besides, the mountains surrounding Rora are a natural fortress. Ten men could hold off a thousand in one of those ravines. The problem with persecution, Inquisitor, is that sooner or later the persecuted *will* fight back."

Emmanuel waited, but Incomel did not reply.

"Do you dispute me, Inquisitor?" the young monarch pressed more loudly, an action that drew the attention of attendants. "Why do you think the Waldenses settled above the Pelice in the first place? They have inferior numbers, it's true, but any fool of a captain will tell you that they have more than a fair understanding of battle. They know every rabbit trail on that mountain. They have powers of communication we cannot match. And they have...other advantages."

Incomel's laugh was the bark of a dog. "What advantages would those be, Savoy?"

"I understand they have a captain...this man, Joshua Gianavel."

The Inquisitor stared. "And...?"

Emmanuel's frown was a mask of contempt that made even the Inquisitor take pause. "They call this man 'Great Lion of God,' Priest... I have heard my captains speak of him." The Duke of Savoy grew more composed. "I am young, Incomel. But I am not a fool. If the peasants of Rora regard this man so greatly, perhaps there is a reason. I do not wish to see my army decimated by this war."

The Inquisitor laughed. "That is ridiculous, Savoy. We all know that heretics are a cowardly lot. Which is why they use witchcraft for their powers."

Lifting his arms, Emmanuel agreed with enthusiasm. "Ah yes! Which is why their children have two rows of black teeth! Why their children have a single eye in the middle of their foreheads! And are born with fangs like dogs!"

Incomel did not blink as the Duke of Savoy almost snarled, "Yes, yes, we certainly remember what your predecessors told us, Inquisitor! How the

Vaudois were half-demon and half-human with six fingers on each hand and ears like bats! Or, at least, that is what they maintained until Victor Amadeus *sent* for these children! Then he discovered, *mon Dieu*, that they were normal children! Precocious and wide-eyed and full of amusing chatter!"

Emmanuel's smile vanished as he closed his arms to his sides. "Which is why he *banished* your colleagues from the palace, Inquisitor! I mean, the great Victor Amadeus could not very well tolerate Inquisitors incapable of telling five fingers from six, could he?" The reigning Duke of Savoy leaned into his words *and* his meaning. "*Heretics* seem a bit too popular around here if you ask—"

"My *Lord*," the Duchess Elizabeth said suddenly, touching his arm. "If you will pardon me, my guards have been waiting to speak with you about my journey to Pinerola."

Bending his head, Emmanuel settled. And Elizabeth leaned closer, grasping his arm more firmly. "Thank you, cousin.... Now, would you be so kind as to insure that my guard is prepared?"

Without any semblance of fear, Emmanuel regarded the Inquisitor. Then, with a tight smile, he bowed. "Another time, Inquisitor."

Incomel was ice. "At your service, My Lord."

Emmanuel strode across the hall and began to instruct Elizabeth's bodyguards. More impatient than usual, his voice carried as the duchess gazed upon the Inquisitor, who seemed not to notice the glacial regard.

"It would be unfortunate for your cousin, Duchess, if he seemed to contradict any of my—"

"He is the Duke of Savoy, Inquisitor." Elizabeth's words and her tone were unmistakably firm. "He is the Supreme Lord of Piedmont, and you will hold him as such."

Incomel bowed. "Of course. And I do apologize, Duchess, if the Duke of Savoy finds even the faintest displeasure in dealing with the Waldenses. I'm sure you realize the dangers of a house divided?" He paused to silence. "Well, the danger is that any house divided against itself cannot stand."

Mary Elizabeth de Medici smiled at last. "We are alone, Incomel. You have no image to protect."

The Inquisitor stared. "My substance is what you behold, Duchess. I have no image at all."

"Really?" Elizabeth's eyes widened mischievously. "The Duke of Savoy's serving girls inform me otherwise."

Incomel would have started if there had not been others watching. Even as it was, he stared with ferocity at the duchess. His jaw tightened as he spoke again. "You would be burned alive if another had heard those words."

Elizabeth's smile was sweet; her teeth were steel. "I suppose you will want Maria again tonight? She seems to be your favorite."

Incomel's breaths were short and sharp. He seemed unable to speak, and the silence would have lasted forever had not Elizabeth closed it with her words. "Your secrets are safe with me, Inquisitor. Only remember one thing." Her eyes were shards of ice. "My cousin is not a boy, though he is younger than me, and I am not old. You may do what you want with the Waldenses; they are not my highest concern. But you will not threaten Emmanuel."

"He cannot deny my orders, Duchess."

"He *will not* deny your orders, Inquisitor. But with this man, Gianavel, leading them, the people of Rora will fight for their freedom of faith. And Emmanuel knows it is a battle his treasury can ill afford. So I advise you: Express no pleasure at his loss."

A still pause.

"I foresee no difficulties," Incomel stated. "I will leave the attack upon Rora to Pianessa. He is a ruthless barbarian, a man or war. And I trust… things better left unsaid…shall remain so."

"Of course."

Incomel was a statue as the duchess turned and walked across the hall where Emmanuel was tersely instructing her guards, clearly in charge of his kingdom.

Pianessa's rugged face reflected the fire of the furnace as he watched the last blows of the hammer forge his new sword. The blade was fully four feet in length and carved down the middle with a deep groove for blood flow, which allowed an easier draw when embedded in flesh. And although it was two inches wide, the edge was finely tapered for lightness, allowing him to wield it one-handed with the grace and agility of a rapier.

Unlike the two-handed Scottish claymore, whose true strength had been its massive weight that was easily capable of denting plate armor to shatter flesh and bone together, Pianessa's weapon held the finest razored edge. From steel smelted again and again and beaten thin and folded and beaten again, it had also been forged with tin so that it could strike another sword, bend without breaking, and retain its edge. Indeed, Pianessa had painstakingly overseen every aspect of its creation, from the deep angle of the edge, which greatly eased sharpening, to the two-handed hilt.

The blacksmith laid the glowing steel upon an anvil, hammering again to flake off the carbon. And with each blow the steel resounded with a sharper ring. Even now it appeared perfect, the blade running smooth and straight. But it would not be ready until it was sharpened and polished and wrapped with the micarti and leather hilt that had been carefully carved to accommodate Pianessa's broad grip.

"How much longer, blacksmith?" Pianessa shouted to overcome the bellows of the furnace.

Sweating and grimacing, the blacksmith lifted the steel before his face, staring along its length. "It should be ready by the morrow, My Lord!" He examined it from every angle, allowing light to shift along the angled gray edge. "A finer blade I've never forged! It's light as a saber with twice the size and strength!"

Fortunately for the blacksmith, Pianessa was clearly pleased as he walked out of the stable and was soon in the militia tavern. Smoke from herbs smuggled from the East floated in heavy halos over couches and tables, making everything formless and without depth. Drunken gamblers slouched in crude chairs, muddy boots stretched before them as dice and coins rattled and dropped to be raked in a pile amid loud curses and harsh, pitiless laughter. Men with eyes like sharks watched from pillows thrown against walls. Some lay as the dead, while some lay wary and indistinct amid mud and weapons as others stumbled over their prone and unmoving shapes.

Ignoring them all, Pianessa approached a grease-faced, stoutly built man seated near the rear exit. Wearing a double-folded cuirass, the man seemed prepared for battle even inside the tavern. Then he seemed to sense Pianessa's monolithic image separating from the gloom and raised his face. A smile split the wild red beard as he leaned back.

Pianessa was the first to speak. "Captain Mario!"

After a halfhearted salute, Mario gestured to the wine, women, and games. "Care to share the spoils of heretics, Pianessa?"

Pianessa cast a small sack of gold upon the table. Its sudden, dominating presence seized Mario's attention.

"You ride tomorrow!"

Unable to restrain his greed, Mario stood as he tore open the bag. He didn't finish counting the gold coins before reckoning it enough. When he raised his face, the Marquis de Pianessa was already departing.

"Pianessa! There's no one left to kill!"

Pianessa spun on his heel. "There are those above the Pelice, Captain! Those at Rora!"

Mario scowled. "The sheepherders?"

"Heretics!"

"Heretics!" Mario erupted with laughter that continued for a long moment before he sobered. "You have lost your mind, Pianessa! Those fools at Rora are not heretics!"

"The Inquisitors have promised fifty pieces of gold to the captain who leads the attack," Pianessa pronounced.

Mario stared with confusion; it didn't last.

"Really," he muttered and raised a single gold piece to examine it in the dim light. "Well, then, heretics they are."

><><><

Dawn broke the color of silver, silhouetting Gianavel alone in the open doorway of the cottage. He stared over scattered rags of snow and tiny pebbles that cast long shadows like knives from the low, rising orb that looked like the head of an angry god gazing over a sea of shattered ships littered upon a reef.

Frost gave white hair to the earth, then began to glow gold and crimson as the moment stretched. The cold wind was low, but no dust rose to its caress, and the planet was still and quiet before him. His eyes were crescents of ice around sad wells of black that fell into the depths of something unseen.

Then a sound behind him.

Small shuffling feet...

Gianavel smiled as he turned and saw a tiny figure standing alone in a nightshirt splashed with gold from the rising sun. He shut the door and walked forward, lifting small feet from the cold floor, warming the body with his own. Then he sat upon the couch, pulling Jacob's head into his chest.

The fire was ablaze again, feeding on the chunks of dry wood Gianavel had cast upon the glowing red embers from the night before. The cold retreated at the color of flame, and the room was wrapped in walls that contained a combined safety.

Jacob's voice was quieter than the harsh sound of vanishing wood, but it was heard. "I'm scared, Papa."

Gianavel's hand settled on Jacob's neck, softly stroking his light brown hair. His voice was low and strong. "Don't be scared, son. I'm here with you, and your mother, and your sisters. We won't let anything happen to you."

Jacob didn't remove his eyes from the hearth.

"Soldiers," he said.

Silently Gianavel wrapped both arms tightly around his child and rubbed the small back. He bent forward to kiss his forehead and whispered, "You're going be all right....Things happen, sometimes. I don't understand it, either. But the Lord is Lord of all the Earth, boy. All things belong to Him, in the end."

In stillness, the child asked, "Will you ever leave me?"

Gianavel felt his throat tighten and kissed his little boy again before leaning his head back. "One day, yes, I will have to leave you—but only when the Lord decides. And you'll be stronger, then. The Lord will make certain of that.You won't need me so much." Gianavel laughed, hugged him again. "You'll probably have your own children, then, and you'll love them as much as I love you. But you will always be in my heart, my boy. And you will never be alone...."

Closing his eyes, Gianavel shook his head—a hope, a prayer. "You will *never* be alone...."

Jacob said nothing, and in the silence that followed, Angela stood in the door of their room, smiling. She rubbed her shoulders as she walked forward and kissed Gianavel, then Jacob, and settled in close to them both. And together they were silent as the windows whitened with day, and Gianavel rose and walked quietly, solemnly, to the wall. He lifted his coat and heavy cloak and wide-brimmed, Puritan-style hat. Then he looked back to see them where they had been, watching his every movement. He smiled as he lifted his musket and weapons, winked at Jacob.

"Remember what I promised we'd do today?"

Jacob nodded eagerly. "Barrel slip."

"That's right," Gianavel laughed.

"Joshua..."

He waited.

Angela's eyes spoke more eloquently than words ever could. "Be careful, my love."

With a quiet nod, Gianavel walked out. He ignored the frost that crunched beneath his steps and the cold that lifted his cape as he bent into a long, loping run that he could hold for miles and miles. Trees grew nearer and nearer and passed, and the slope rose before him until a lonely, vigilant rock stood alone against the distant blue-rimmed cliffs—the Roc de Doc, where he could observe every approach into Rora.

He climbed to the crest and searched the valley but saw only orchards and empty roads. The land was without danger, the people were safe, and yes, he would remain here until nightfall—watching, always watching, until the people were safe for the night.

Knowing it in his heart and soul—in what was deepest within him, the place where his deepest strength was born, Gianavel knew he would never move. No, as long as the Lord called upon him to stand upon this hill, he would never move.

Nor would he *be* moved.

4

NIGHT PASSED, AND MORNING CAME AGAIN....
And Gianavel returned to his place, watching.

He was weary as he gained the height once more, a fatigue greater than what was physical assailing his limbs because the strength to endure vigilance now was worn by worry and fear. He knew what was coming, and his hands were solid as they gripped the rocks as he climbed. But the grimness that marked his grip was also light with the touch of battle—battle dreaded but no longer denied.

No more than sixty miles in circumference, the valley of Rora was thickly fielded with orchards and vineyards that prohibited view from the ground, but from the Roc de Doc, Gianavel could gaze over the verdure to view the entire valley.

There were only two entrances through the encircling walls of sheer white cliffs that stretched thousands of feet into the sky. The first, and most difficult, was a deep ravine that broke through the mountains toward Turin. Climbing the ravine was not perilous, but descending in foul weather or in haste was a treacherous affair.

The second entrance was the Pass of Piedmont itself, which cut across the summit of El Combe after rising from the valley of Lucerna. It began with a long climb from sea level, swung left past the jagged cliffs of the Castelluzo, then down and across the Pelice by way of a single, narrow bridge before rising again through the mountains that formed the wall of Rora. Only a four-hour walk for a strong man, it required a day's travel with oxcart or herd.

As a consequence, the inhabitants of Rora had become almost entirely self-sufficient with cattle, sheep, crops, and an abundant water supply channeled past brownstone chalets that were exactingly maintained by craftsmen, farmers, and townspeople. Nor was the valley considered a poor slice of Charles Emmanuel's kingdom. Rather, because of its agricultural exports, it maintained widespread wealthier quarters.

Rora was ruled by a civilian council, and disputes were settled by moral laws and codes founded upon precepts of the *Lingua Romana*, a translation of the New Testament written in Romaunt, the common dialect of Southern Europe. Although the Roman Catholic Church loudly proclaimed that any layman possessing the Scriptures was to be arrested and punished, the Waldenses had, with precise attention, patience, and dedication, translated the heavy, illustrated tombs of Latin text into small, plain, portable volumes that could be read and understood by all.

Those who lived in Piedmont already declared that the Waldensian Church was older than Rome, and the Romaunt translation was theirs by preeminent right. Others said the book was the product of a rebel faction of faith that found criminal refuge in the mountains during the eleventh century. And, then, many deemed the matter to be of no importance; dead men alone knew the answer, and dead men would not speak. It existed, and none could dispute that it did.

And so the Romaunt version stated that every man, woman, and child had a right to read and interpret the Bible themselves. And as the Vaudois—another name for the Waldenses—read the Old and New Testaments, they had come to proclaim many beliefs that were contradictory to the official doctrine of Rome.

They did not believe in the infallibility of the pope or the necessity of a priest to mediate God's forgiveness. Even more disturbing to the Catholic Church, they declared that prayer offered in a barn was every bit as sacred as prayer in a church as long as it came from a sincere and contrite heart. But, most alarming, the Vaudois stated that the "bone relics" of Rome were most likely the bones of God-only-knows-who and had little or no value before the Lord.

Such blasphemy could not be endured....

And at the heart of it, the Waldenses believed that the atoning death and justifying righteousness of Christ was the cardinal truth, and that only the Lord had the power to forgive sins. They believed in the Trinity, in the need for divine grace to do works of righteousness, in the resurrection of the body, in heaven and hell. And they believed that the Lord, and not man, was Judge of all the Earth.

Yet because of the scarcity of the Romaunt Scriptures, both laymen and barbes were asked to memorize large sections so that the written books might be distributed outside the valley to people everywhere, that all might know what was written in God's Word and decide their own minds.

As the Captain of the Militia of Rora, Gianavel was responsible for confronting those who invaded the valley. His militia, if it could be so termed, was exceedingly small, unless war was declared, and then every man fought as they had fought in the past, father passing to son the heart and courage to stand in the gap, to defend the weak.

None were perfect, but courage breeds courage. Some things, even the world cannot deny.

Gianavel squinted against a wind sharp with cold. But he knew the cold would fade quickly as the sun was already above the cliffs, thickening shadows into a semblance of what cast them. He could still not discern every detail in the distance, but the pass and ravine were clear enough. And if anyone, whether alone or with an invading force, crossed the snowcapped Alps, he would see them. Nor was he defenseless, though he was reluctant to use weapons.

His flintlock rifle, which had replaced his old cumbersome matchlock, was effective to more than a hundred meters, and he could discharge a second shot in twenty seconds. He also carried his saber, four feet in length with a full handguard, a flintlock pistol, and a forthright poniard that was eighteen inches long and double-bladed for the entire length down to the oval-shaped hilt and spiked pommel.

Altogether, the weapons had cost him forty doubloons, but Gianavel was practical. He was the marshal of a small valley surrounded by forces that sometimes seized Waldenses, even today, when they ventured outside Piedmont and tortured them to death without trial or even an accusation of wrongdoing. Many wars had been waged to destroy them completely, and though Gianavel prayed each day for peace, peace had never come, and he had no illusions.

When Gianavel was only fifteen years old, Rome had executed the sentence of death on all the Waldenses because of their faith. The army of the Catholic king invaded and massacred the inhabitants of the valley from end to end, leaving forests of crucified skeletons in the trees and pyramids of skulls to witness their glory. Over half the population—sixteen thousand men, women, and children—were burned at the stake, drawn and quartered, hanged, crushed by stones, disemboweled, decapitated, thrown onto pitch-forks, or fed to hungry dogs. They were set afire and extinguished only to be set afire again or hideously tortured in ways Gianavel still saw with bright red horror even when he shut his eyes in the dark.

His father had been among the first to fall, fighting bravely but futilely to save his family. And although his mother and brothers and sisters had died, Gianavel managed to escape into the mountains, where he evaded the troops who scoured the snow-covered trails for those who had escaped the sword. And through the first frostbitten months, he learned quickly how to move without being seen or heard, how to pass through a forest without leaving a sign, how to forage food or steal what he needed to survive.

Gianavel had watched over and over how the battalions maneuvered, deployed, attacked, and counterattacked. He studied how weapons and cannons were used, watched how men killed with dagger and sword. And when the war was finally over, he descended from the mountain to see who else had survived...and then came the plague.

The Black Plague was brought from France by the Catholic soldiers themselves and reduced the valley of Rora to smoldering funeral pyres surrounded by starving survivors who had no strength to dig more graves. The black stench that rose and crowned Gianavel's brow for a year and a half held the blood and bodies of his father and friends. It soaked into his head, his ragged clothes, and his lungs as he worked from nightmarish dawn to dusk disposing of worm-eaten bodies until he finally understood the dark heart of war, the frailty of the flesh, and the terrible power of the sword. And somewhere in the long night, lying awake, watching the mounds and dunes of bodies burn beneath a cold, haggard moon that grinned like a skull, he knew that he could never again run from evil, for there was no place to run.

And as Gianavel grew strong, he grew wise.

With each year his skill increased with the rifle and sword, listening to old Descombie recount the fabled stories of David, the greatest king of Israel, as he defeated the enemies of the Lord. And, even in the old stories, Gianavel could see David's gift of attacking while retreating, of striking while avoiding, of stalling while confronting, to contest a grim battle of truth. When he was cold, he would build a shelter to weather the night like the squirrel built its home—leafy and small on the inside yet covered with bark to resist the dew and rain. And when he hunted, he hunted as the wolf, exhausting the prey until it simply fell to the ground, ultimately defeated by its own fear.

And…he read the *Lingua Romana* until he could recite entire gospels and epistles by heart, searching every word for a deeper understanding of life and death—of living in peace, surviving in war, and honoring God throughout.

And, in all this, Gianavel learned more than he ever expected. He found his mind retaining more, remembering more, so that memory became a vast repository of knowledge—of nature, science, philosophy, and cunning—that he could recall effortlessly.

When he reached manhood and could take a respected seat in the synod, his growth had not escaped the attention of the elders of the barbes. At the request of his kinsmen, Gianavel had been called forth to be Captain of the Militia in a valley decimated by war after war, a valley surrounded by enemies—madmen and tyrants and fools that executed their ambitions upon a foreign land simply because the land was weak and thin with peasants. But Gianavel, head bowed, had solemnly accepted the responsibility, and since that day, now twenty years past, had maintained his lonely vigilance.

Standing upon the sentinel's rock, Gianavel recalled untold encounters against bandits, against wandering bands of mercenaries and marauding deserters of the German or French kings. He was thankful that he had rarely been forced to violence. He had confronted, yes, had sometimes wounded men, when he had no choice. But he had only, with the greatest grief, executed that fatal action only when all other actions had failed. And the pain he had borne from the battle was far greater than the battle itself.

Yet the drums of war had sounded again. Nothing was new, and men did not change even as slowly as the land. The heart of man was a lake broken by bladed crests lifted on dark winds hidden by whitewashed walls. Each man, alone, was aware of what secret winds moved behind the white veil. And each man, alone, could alter its course.

He had no illusions.

Gianavel had fled once from war, it's true, when he was a child—when he felt himself upon a precipice with so little strength left to fight—but he would *never* flee again, not after the Lord had so greatly delivered him. No, not now—not without the lives of his family, his neighbors, and his friends safely borne within his cloak where he could bear them over the mountains into Geneva.

Death held no terror—the Lord was Lord of life and death and whatever was beyond....

Yes, he sometimes feared death, though much less than most men. And he pondered death much more than most men. But death, after intimate years, had become to him only a darkness he knew would end. It would come to him, and he would pass through it to the other side, and whatever lay there would be his love.

It was a twig of shadow rising upon the distant pass that caused him to return to the moment. His eyes had never stopped searching the valley, and he focused on the Pass of Pelice but did not move.

Movements, he had learned by watching creatures of the forest, were what betrayed a man—what made him separate from the shadows and trees and stones. He had learned that when the trees moved, he could move. And when they stopped moving, he stood motionless until they began to move again, using the shadow, the sound, to mask his own.

He bent his head forward only an inch so the wide brim of his hat shielded his eyes, and he saw an alien army emerging upon the ridge. Though still miles away, their number could be estimated, and it was great. And then there was no more time for thought.

Gianavel dropped from his rock, hand on his sword and rifle raised for balance. And when he was in the trees, he began running, the grassy plain rolling away beneath him as his legs flashed dark, stretching and striking, devouring the ground.

It was time.

✕✕✕◈✕✕✕

Gianavel threw open the door of the cottage and stood unmoving, framed by the whiteness of the morning.

Angela took one glance at him and moved without a word. She threw her shawl over her shoulders and quickly turned to the children. "Shoes! Coats! All of you! *Now!*"

Only little Jacob stared in wonder and surprise at what had interrupted his breakfast, and then Gianavel snatched him up, wrapping him in a warm wool blanket. They were quickly out the door and into the small two-wheeled wagon used for traveling the valley. Angela had the reins, and Gianavel placed his hand on her leg, staring up.

Her face was vivid with fear, but she was doing what they had rehearsed a thousand times. Nevertheless, Gianavel heard himself say quietly and calmly, "You know what to do."

She nodded and struck the reins. The wagon violently broke from the frost with a crunch, moving from the cottage toward a series of caves. She would alert every house on the way, and within minutes everyone would be afoot with whatever food and clothes they could carry.

Gianavel ran back inside the cottage and emerged in seconds carrying three extra matchlock rifles with a bag of musket balls and two horns of powder. He heard the alarms of nearby bells, and then he ran deep into the orchard, where he came upon six friends—men he had known since his youth—pruning an orchard.

Turning toward him, one man with a greasy black beard cast aside his ax, understanding instantly. He strode forward as Gianavel tossed him a musket, and then the rest gathered.

"They're coming across the pass," Gianavel spoke quickly and passed out musket balls. "Does anyone have a rifle?"

Heads were jerked, no, no, though the big bearded man reached behind himself to the wagon and a sword—a broadsword of two hundred years' antiquity—rasped from beneath the straw. He lifted a hatchet and slid the handle into his belt.

"Bertino stands beside you," he rumbled.

Gianavel smiled, turned. "Follow me!"

Though they were all in their forties, the men kept apace of him easily enough as they traversed the six-mile run to the lowest section of the trail that descended from the path. And when they arrived, the sun was starkly high in the blue cobalt dome of sky. Gianavel estimated that they had mere minutes before the army was upon them. He laid his rifle upon the ground as he knelt—the others followed his movements, breathing heavily, wordless, staring close.

Gianavel drew two lines upon the ground that spread into a wide funnel. "This is where the pass narrows before it enters the valley. We'll station ourselves on both sides of the ridge, and when they're directly under us, we open fire."

"You know we are outnumbered," Bertino rumbled.

"Yes. But *they* don't know that."

All nodded.

"Listen closely," Gianavel spoke sharply. "Don't shoot for the soldiers— to kill a soldier means nothing! Shoot for the captain, the lieutenants, and sergeants! Shoot once, then move, and shoot again! Don't shoot twice from the same place! And don't let them see you move! If they see us moving, they'll know our number!"

Bertino stared down. "Strike them with confusion and fear."

Raising his face, Gianavel continued, "Yes! We must make them think we're a hundred! Shoot for the officers, move, and shoot again! And use solid cover—rocks and trees! They don't have to see you to shoot you!"

Bertino lifted his rifle without invitation. He whipped out his knife and severed the wick, twisting it quickly with his fingers to loosen the powder. Now it would light with the faintest spark, but he didn't seem settled by the odds. "This is an old weapon," he rumbled, "but good enough."

Gianavel passed out the flintlock pistols and spread a handful of musket balls on the ground where he'd drawn the trail. "Brothers, if we fail to turn them, you know what they'll do. The great massacre of twenty years ago will be repeated! They will slaughter our children! No one will live!"

Dark eyes of men inured to suffering gave no surprise.

Gianavel stood and pointed to three of them. "Go with Bertino to the west ridge of the trail! Stay inside the trees! When I fire, all of you open fire."

"If they retreat?" Bertino questioned.

Gianavel glared. "Don't let them escape!"

"Why?"

"Because they'll be back!" Gianavel gasped, then calmed for a moment. "Once blood is drawn, there can be no mercy.... Mercy is what you show before the battle begins. In battle there is no such thing as right moves or wrong moves. There are only good moves and bad moves. Good moves kill the enemy. Bad moves get you killed. Fight like the bear defending her cubs—no questions, no mercy." Gianavel bowed his head, grimaced. "May the Lord judge me if I am wrong!"

"We'll be judged together!" Bertino declared and turned to the three. "Come!"

They trotted up the slope, rifles swinging rhythmically in their hands, and Gianavel loped toward the east, his breath already hard and fast, his body preparing for what it had prepared for all his life.

5

GIANAVEL DROPPED TO THE GROUND beside a huge oak tree that spread a late penumbra of night through the forest. He was already charging his musket as they arrived behind him breathless.

"Remember," he whispered, listening for any sound of the approaching force, "shoot for the officers, then move and shoot again. Keep shooting! Keep moving! But don't let them see you move! If they retreat, follow them and hit as many as you can!"

"What if they break into the valley?"

"If they break through us, then let them spread out and follow them into the orchard! But don't be seen!" Gianavel studied their faces; some were following, some not. "Just do what I do!"

The ridge was thickly wooded and hid them easily, offering an abundance of solid cover against counterattacks.

Gianavel rechecked the plate to make sure none of the powder had spilled—a common fault of flintlocks—but very little was lost. As he leaned over the rifle, he wondered what it was that he was fighting for. Wondered if Angela and the children had reached the safely of the caves. Wondered if he had missed a secondary approach of the enemy, if the rest of the valley had been alarmed, if they had enough weapons to defy the attackers, and what might happen if they failed.

But even as he wondered, he knew it was too late to doubt. He had to concentrate on the fight at hand. He heard the faint, distant clink of a canteen, bowed his head in prayer for so few against so many. He could only hope that it was enough.

And as he prayed, he was grateful that he was stronger than he had been in his youth. He was aware of the strange but very real sixth sense that often warns a man of unseen and hidden dangers. He had trained to hone the edge of his greatest strengths—his mental alertness and pure physical strength, skill, and endurance—because he knew that something so basic could often decide life or death.

Now he was stronger than he had been in his youth. He was almost as fast, though age had indeed claimed a step, but experience compensated for its loss. Nor did he strike with the hectic energy of youth. Rather, he struck direct and with a sense of calm purpose that he'd never possessed in his youth.

Clink…

Frowning, Gianavel turned his head.

><>><><

Mario scowled as he stepped over the pedestal-slab trail that led down toward Rora. To maintain balance he was forced to lean back, jamming his toes deeply into the hard points of his boots. His legs visibly trembled at the strain.

"Curse this!" he rasped. "These Waldenses aren't worth the trouble!" He looked to the stoic man alongside him. "Sergeant Major! How much farther do these fools live?"

"A half-league, My Lord," was the answer, and the red-bearded man pointed to where a long, level dirt trail bordered an orchard. "Their homes are not far beyond that field."

Mario grunted as he moved his canteen farther back around his hip. His rifle strap was cutting a deep line in his shoulder, and he kept moving it to another worn position. His anger projected a heated vehemence as he shouted, "Kill the children *first* so their mothers and fathers can watch! Then rape the women, take all you come near, and savor the pleasure of spilling heretic blood!"

A chorus of joyous agreement flooded the ravine, and Mario shifted the rifle strap again. He turned to ask the sergeant major another question, and it took Mario a moment to understand that the paint-red splattered across the officer's head looked like...*blood!*

The sergeant turned in a slow, light pirouette, eyes glassy, brains protruding through a ragged hole in his head over white fragments of skull dangling on tethers of red flesh, and fell to his face.

A plume of smoke rose from the ridge as the report of a rifle boomed in the canyon, and then Mario saw the hillsides erupt all around him with thunder and smoke. He staggered back, then forward, turning, shouting, screaming as chaos erupted around him.

※

Gianavel had heard the name and identified the commander in chief—Captain Mario.

You're next....

Almost instantly Gianavel found another tree. He quietly raised aim at Mario, who had stupidly drawn his sword and, even more stupidly, was bellowing commands.

Even as Gianavel pulled the trigger, the standard-bearer stumbled into the path of the bullet, and the captain was saved by the unintended sacrifice. Gianavel's shot hit the man dead center of the spine, and he fell forward, knocking the captain back across a boulder as the soldiers fell frantically into columns, aiming at either ridge.

Gianavel twisted behind a tree as they fired—a single thunderous discharge of white that hit the hillside, but only the hillside, in a voluminous rain of lead.

Almost before the sound struck the leaves about him, Gianavel moved again, keeping high on the trail for swiftness. When he reached his third shooting position, he saw that the column had reloaded and leveled once more. The second enfilade ripped through the foliage and bored into trees as Gianavel twisted back and reloaded.

Gianavel fired in the heartbeat to kill another sergeant, and then he moved again, listening to know where each of his men was firing from the slopes, knowing exactly where they were inflicting damage. He positioned himself to hit what they were missing. Gianavel smiled, for they were doing exactly as he had instructed them, hitting and moving, hitting and moving, and it was having a cumulative effect.

With four commanders struck down already, the ravine erupted in chaos. Gianavel saw no sergeants standing, only one lieutenant. The standard-bearer was also down, leaving no one to coordinate the musketeers who were leaving large holes in their firing pattern. A few men with crossbows were also firing bolts blindly into the thick skew of leprous-white boulders that littered the walls, and the firing continued from Bertino and his men.

Every one of the Waldenses was an accomplished marksman, taught by their fathers at a young age because both farming and hunting were skills that every man needed to know in order to survive. And now they were using those patiently taught hunting skills to save their lives in another way.

The first mistake of Captain Mario was that his men were so thickly crushed into the narrow trail that marksmanship wasn't vitally necessary to hit them. And, often enough, a single shot dropped more than one man. Although there were at least five hundred soldiers in the half-regiment, five fell every fifteen seconds as the defenders of Rora moved like lightning up and down the slope, always firing and moving, only to fire and move again.

Knowing that the others were doing the heaviest damage, Gianavel attempted to inflict the most effective strikes by taking that extra second to discern whoever seemed to be bellowing orders and then drop him from sight. He claimed twelve men with thirteen shots before he saw Captain Mario once more.

Covered with blood, but not his own, Mario broke from the wrecked formation waving his sword wildly above his head. His eyes were feverish and unfocused, and his steps were off balance as he ran through the broken formation toward the rear. Only by chance did his words carry above the howls and screams of the wounded.

"All is lost! Save yourselves!"

Rifles were cast aside like kindling as soldiers spun as one and charged back down the trail, heedlessly crushing the wounded and climbing, climbing to escape the death raining down upon them without mercy from the ridge. Like men freed at last from a cavern where some hellish plague had been melting flesh from the bones of the living, the untouched fled the battle they had so earnestly sought. Blindly, they cast off whatever weapons they had borne to facilitate escape from these demons that fired on them from the shadows.

The cry echoed throughout the valley everywhere and at once.

Retreat!

But Gianavel had no intention of letting them retreat. They had brought this fight to him on their terms—terms they considered well enough when they thought they would be slaughtering defenseless victims with no fear for their own lives.

No, that would not stand.

Gianavel would finish it on his terms.

Followed by his men, the Captain of Rora raced along the slope, firing again and again to drop ten more before the chaotic flight from the unexpected ambush reached the first switchback. And to the very last, at the farthest limit of what the rifle could reach, Gianavel dropped his final man, using elevation to throw the musket ball in the high arch of a rainbow, before the panicked soldiers were frantically gone.

When it was over, the air was thick with gunpowder, and the barrels of their weapons were hot to the touch. Gianavel looked down through the ravine to see the wounded writhing on the trampled frost, howling and pleading and screaming in agony and fear. He raised his face to see Bertino step from hiding on the distant slope, the stock of the matchlock hard against his shoulder.

Bertino looked at the wounded. At Gianavel.

Frowning, Gianavel stared across the wounded. Rora had no prison to hold them. To take them into the village would occupy half the population with tending the wounded, and their people and resources were already too few.

This was *the* fundamental truth of men who terrorized men: They considered mercy and compassion to be weaknesses of their victims until they themselves were met with terror and stopped cold. Then they begged for mercy, hoping the compassion of their intended victims would be their salvation.

Stoically, sadly, Gianavel drew his sword. He turned to those around him, head bent, and they repeated the movement. They stood sword in hand, waiting for the command. Gianavel's voice was cold and controlled and tragic.

"Be merciful.... Do it quick."

✕✕✕✖✕✕✕

Gaping, Pianessa stared in silence at Captain Mario's ravaged figure. Bloodied and bruised, his face swollen from contusions, the captain held his cap with uncharacteristic humility as the marquis had absorbed the details of the battle. It took Pianessa a long time to decide upon a suitable reply, which sounded not so suitable when spoken.

"*Fifty?*" he asked. "They killed fifty of my men?"

Mario nodded tightly.

Pianessa was silent, then, "And they wounded forty more?" For some reason he was compelled to repeat it: "They killed fifty and wounded forty more?"

Mario held out his hands. "It was an ambush!"

"How many *were there?*"

"Perhaps...a hundred."

Pianessa stiffened. "*A hundred!*"

Mario gazed about as if someone would help him, but no one came forward. His voice was tentative. "They must have hired mercenaries."

"Mercenaries!" Pianessa scoffed, and jerked back angrily. "And what would they pay them with? Sheep?" He stared away and fell to brooding,

61

gazing at nothing. "No, not mercenaries…no…what did those peasants call this man?"

A second Inquisitor now accompanied Incomel—a heavyset man whose gray robe stretched taunt over his expansive gut. He was totally bald and also seemed to have no hair on his hands or face or eyebrows, as if he was completely shaved or totally hairless from some unnatural means. It was certainly a strange appearance—even disturbing.

Mario searched the queer, dolphinlike image for a long moment before looking again at the marquis.

Pianessa continued to gaze into shadows with a peculiar fixation. He did not seem as confused; he was merely astounded. He mused deliberately, "I killed over fifteen thousand of these peasants without losing a single man. And this man has already cost me fifty…."

Incomel spoke, "Should I inform the Duke of Savoy of your casualties?"

Pianessa's eyes were like blackened coals, smoldering with a heat beyond white. The threat of violence burned there, deeply fed and closely banked. "Thank you, Inquisitor, but I shall inform Savoy with what he needs to know…. Do you understand me?"

Incomel bowed. "Of course."

Now that the Inquisitor had spoken, Mario focused on him openly. "Fifty pieces of gold was promised…"

Incomel laughed. "That was for an attack, Captain, not a retreat."

Mario stared bitterly.

A guard appeared in the distant portal of the hall as Pianessa continued to contemplate. Then the marquis finally recognized the shadow looming across the hall and raised his head.

"Yes?"

The guard spoke loudly enough for the Inquisitors to hear: "Ambassadors from Rora, My Lord! They humbly but urgently request your attention!"

The Inquisitors moved gracefully toward a corridor and exited the hall—no words, no gestures, no questions. Pianessa stared after them until they were gone, then made a slashing gesture for Mario to follow. When he was utterly alone upon his throne, he nodded to the guard.

In seconds two men stood before the massive black marble throne, and Pianessa stared over them. He seemed surprised at their dust-cloaked condition and weapons and scowled as they knelt.

The one who appeared to be a pastor spoke first. "My Lord Marquis de Pianessa, I am Descombie, and this is Sergeant Michael Bertino. We come as peaceful ambassadors for the valley of Rora, one of Your Lordship's territories."

Whatever anger had vexed Pianessa's face moments ago was replaced by the indulgent suffering of a benevolent monarch as he stared over the heavily armed sergeant. But Pianessa displayed no shock that the pastor also bore rifle and pistol and saber.

"Rise," Pianessa said sullenly. "Speak."

Descombie took a single step forward. His tone was calm and restrained. "My Lord Pianessa, we are ambassadors for Rora, your land above the Pelice. And we come to ask why you would launch an attack on our village."

Pianessa allowed an impression of great fatigue. "That is answered easily enough, Priest. I did not order any such attack on your village, nor have I considered one."

Utter silence prevailed. Descombie looked at Bertino.

"Priest," Pianessa continued wearily, "those were not my men who attacked you. Those were bandits who have been pillaging Piedmont." With a questioning glare, he scowled before he leaned forward. "Are you so ignorant of what is happening in your own country, Priest? Do you not know we are at war?"

Descombie opened his mouth, but Pianessa pressed, "Well? How many of them did you kill? Surely you have done *some* good!"

"We counted fifty-five dead, My Lord. We wounded, perhaps, thirty more."

For a moment Pianessa seemed to weigh whether that was a meaningful contribution. With tactical analysis he muttered, "Can you lead my forces to them?"

"No, My Lord." Descombie noticed Bertino searching the corners of the hall. "They fled the valley in discord! We do not know where they are encamped."

Pianessa was not utterly disappointed. "Good, then they are at the mercy of my patrols in the valley." He continued to nod with satisfaction, an overburdened commander brought back to the moment by concern for his people. "Ah, forgive me—the troubles of war. Were any of your people injured?"

"No, My Lord. We suffered not a single man, wounded or killed."

Pianessa's initial response was silence. "Not a single loss?" He stared longer. "Not *one?*"

"No, My Lord."

Pianessa chewed a corner of his mustache—an uncommon act for nobility. "Tell me," he continued, with a certain craftiness, "how is it that your people managed to fight off these bandits when the entire valley of Piedmont lies in flames?"

At that, the one named Bertino stepped forward. "There is no need for My Lord to worry himself. We are heavily armed with cannon and rifles and are prepared to repel any attack. We have food and water to endure a lengthy siege, and the will to last."

Pianessa gazed brutally upon the big-bearded farmer.

Frowning, Bertino held the gaze without blinking.

Silence…

"Yes," the marquis muttered.

Pianessa looked upon Descombie. "Which of you is in command? I would like for him to remain with me and discuss coordinated responses to this threat."

"Neither of us," Bertino said loudly.

Pianessa blinked, sullen or angry. "So who commands your militia, warrior?"

Descombie broke the tense atmosphere between Bertino and Pianessa. "That would be our local marshal, My Lord! Captain Joshua Gianavel!"

Brooding, Pianessa took a moment in thought. His brow hardened, recalling—remembering. "Gianavel…Yes, I…I *know* this man." He took a moment longer. "Did this Gianavel not fight beside Savoy to repel the Spanish?"

There was no reply, and Pianessa answered for himself, "Yes! I *saw* this man at Pinerola!" A moment passed, and Pianessa grew strangely still. "Is this the Gianavel you speak of?"

"Yes, My Lord."

The words that rumbled from Pianessa were subdued, as if spoken against his will. "This Gianavel…he is a warrior."

Descombie answered, "Gianavel is a great friend of the Church, My Lord. In battle he fights like a lion, it's true. But in domestic life he is humble as a lamb. He is merciful without weakness, and pious without excess."

Raising his eyebrows, Pianessa commented, "It seems your merciful captain was not so merciful today, barbe."

Bertino interjected, "Gianavel understands war, My Lord. He reveres all life and will not provoke a fight. But if the fight is forced upon him, he strikes quickly and ends it quickly. He does not strike to wound."

Pianessa studied Bertino as if measuring the intent hidden beneath the words. Bertino did not blink as he grimly held the marquis' gaze, and within Pianessa's a somber malevolence surged like a black tide beneath a moonless sky—thunderous, deceptive, dangerous.

Finally Pianessa muttered, "My guards will see you safely to the pass."

They spoke as one: "Your servant, My Lord."

In a moment they disappeared through the glowing gateway of the hall, and then the guard quietly closed the massive doors. The huge iron rings struck once and fell silent.

Pianessa did not need to turn his head to see the ghostly outline of the Inquisitor emerging from the corridor.

With steps almost instinctively silent, Incomel approached and halted at the steps. For a moment he studied Pianessa's glowering visage, then spoke with uncommon friendliness. "Surely you understand Machiavellian subterfuge, Pianessa."

Pianessa turned slowly to the priest. "What I understand, Priest, is that I have lost a hundred men."

A dismissive wave. "They were soldiers, Pianessa."

"Soldiers cost money, Priest. Money to train, and money to equip." Brooding, the Marquis de Pianessa stood. His entire form seemed to swell in his wrath. "If others follow the example of Gianavel, I will soon have nothing to rule."

Incomel had not moved but spoke with obvious caution. "Rest assured, Pianessa, your throne is ruled by the Church. And the Church has declared war upon these heretics. You have no need to be troubled…or wrathful."

As if the Inquisitor were a strange insect that Pianessa had never seen, the marquis stared over him. "How curious that you declare war and cannot lift a finger in the fight."

"It is not my place to fight, Monsieur, but to pray."

"And so God gives you a cause for war, and yet He prevents you from risking your life to fight it?"

Incomel held his words, as if contemplating. "My place is to pray, Pianessa. I am God's minister to insure that the war is fought for the proper cause."

There was a dark interlude, and Pianessa shook his head. "Convenient, Priest, that God does not ask you to die for what you believe. My only question is…would you?"

Incomel hesitated.

"Die for what I believe?"

A frown, and Pianessa leaned closer. "Yes…"

The Inquisitor had stepped back. He recovered.

"Of course, Pianessa…I die daily."

"Indeed," Pianessa murmured, and the pause that followed was the longest yet. "Pardon me, Inquisitor, but I see a world of difference between you and this man…this Gianavel."

"Oh?" Incomel retorted. "How so, Pianessa?"

The Marquis de Pianessa laughed. "I have a world of whores, Priest. There is a world between denying yourself whores and dying for what you believe." With a grim laugh, Pianessa turned away. "Perhaps I am too practical, but to watch a man drawn and quartered, his arms and legs torn from their sockets, and yet he still refuses to renounce his faith, is a remarkable thing. For one thing, Inquisitor, though you have never experienced it, arms and legs do not break easily. Have you never attempted to twist a turkey's leg from its carcass? Yes…it is difficult. You must break it, twist it over and over. You must tear it to shreds before it separates."

Incomel snorted, half turned.

Pianessa laughed. "Does leaving your whores trouble you more than that, Priest? What kind of spiritual pain would be so great that a man would even endure having his arms and legs torn apart before he renounced his faith?" The marquis seemed moved at the thought.

Head bowed, he continued, "Make no mistake, Priest. Whether Gianavel is right or wrong makes no difference to me. But yes, I see a difference between the Vaudois and you. This Gianavel…he is willing to fight, and even die, for what he believes. You are only willing to have others fight and die."

Without another word, Pianessa stepped from his throne and strode quickly past the long red tapestries that hung between windows filled with darkness so thick that there seemed no stars in the moonless sky, no wind moving in the soundless night, and was gone.

⋙⟐⋘

What happens after a battle is almost always as difficult as the battle itself, Gianavel remembered as he moved through the campfires of the pass, observing and encouraging.

The men were understandably joyous at victory, but this was not the hour for joy. It was the hour for discipline, for cold thought, and even colder action. But such vigilance was difficult to maintain, so Gianavel only gently reminded his men that the battle was not yet finished. He urged them to remain prepared but let them rest as they could.

None of Rora's defenders had been wounded in the short but intense battle, mostly because veterans like Bertino had kept those with less experience close beside them. It was something done naturally and without a word from Gianavel. And he was grateful for it because, in the confusion of establishing a quick defense, it had not occurred to him.

To have lost even a single man would have weakened them, but to strengthen them even further, thirty men had arrived from the valley. Having heard of the battle, they had come from their hiding places in the caves and forests of Piedmont. Wounded and starving, they pleaded for sanctuary. But there had been no need to plead. The defenders of Rora had outdone one another in bestowing blessings, taking each of them into their own homes where they were clothed and fed. And those who had the will and strength to fight were provided with new flintlock rifles, all the ordnance they could carry, thick coats, and boots from the slain soldiers of Pianessa.

It was a hard choice; it had been made.

In only a few hours, with hot meals, warm clothes, and fellowship, they had become different men, once again strong, encouraged, and willing to fight for the right to believe. And Gianavel knew they would be needed—this war had only begun.

He passed another fire where women ladled out wide, deep wooden bowls of soup for the troops and approached a much older man. Bearing a cap of wild white hair, the man noticed his approach and grinned widely with amazingly strong teeth, teeth white as snow and evenly squared despite his seventy-something years.

"Ça va, Gianavel?" he asked as he stacked another rifle on a table heaped with rifles and pistols and powder horns—enough weapons for a hundred men.

"It is well," Gianavel said as he studied the ordnance. "What's the count?"

"It must be easier to retreat without a rifle," Hector surmised, looking over the bounty. "We gathered one hundred thirty-five muskets and scavenged four demicannon and six four-pounders. Small, of course, but deadly effective if you're using grapeshot."

Gianavel placed a hand on the cannon and looked into Hector's clear brown eyes. "Prepare grapeshot for the demicannon, too. We're bringing down men, not a wall. And remember; never fire grapeshot at a target more than a hundred feet away—it scatters too much to be effective."

"I'll man one myself. Bertino will take the other." Hector hesitated, more solemn. "Do you think they'll return, Joshua?"

Gianavel paused, gazed away. "They'll return. But not until they prepare a little better." He twisted his neck, as if the earlier action had left sore muscles. "They didn't expect a fight, but they won't make the same mistake twice. Next time, they'll bring more men, more cannon. Maybe even cavalry."

Scanning the men and women of the camp, Hector revealed neither dismay nor confidence. "Brave souls to a man, but they don't have any experience. Most of them have never seen a battle, much less fought in one."

Gianavel selected three flintlock pistols to replace the ones he'd lost. His tone was somber. "There are things more important than experience, but make sure that the younger ones are teamed with a veteran. How many are resolved to fight?"

"Forty-seven men and enough reloaders to charge ten rifles per minute for each man. We can keep up a well-directed fire without interruption."

"Good. We'll train in the morning."

"You don't expect Pianessa to attack tonight?"

Gianavel turned to gaze over the pass, a river of black beneath over-arching trees white with moonlight.

"I expect nothing, and everything. But we've got men watching the ravine to Turin and the pass, so we can't be surprised. We'll hope for the best, take every precaution against the worst."

"C'ais azzez."

Gianavel stared over the heap of confiscated rifles with a sudden, faint disturbance. Then he turned and walked back toward the steadily rising battlements.

"We have weapons," Hector said after him, and Gianavel turned, staring back. "But they have more weapons, Joshua. They will always have more weapons."

Gianavel frowned, shook his head.

"Our strength does not lie in weapons."

And was gone.

THE BEARDED IMAGE OF HENRY IV, one eye slightly larger than the other, gazed ponderously from its rest above the mantel. Dressed in pantaloons and bloused shirt, the king stood slightly off-center, a huge pit of darkness carefully positioned over his right shoulder beyond his peacock-feathered hat.

The Duchess Elizabeth looked over the countenance of her boorish relative and wondered if he ever realized the open contempt with which the artist immortalized him. Then she turned her head as a distant panel on the wall swung silently open. There was the glimpse of a torch-lit corridor beyond, and then the light vanished as a huge form emerged from the hidden passageway.

Pianessa walked forward without a smile or sound, and Elizabeth lifted a glass of wine that he accepted stoically before collapsing in a cushioned chair. The gray ash that lay upon his armor was as heavy as the gloom that surrounded him. He said nothing as the duchess walked to where she could observe his face more clearly.

Releasing a deep breath, Pianessa shook his head. "It seems my late wife's reward grows further away by the moment," he muttered. "I knew the Vaudois might be difficult to kill, but nothing like this."

The duchess dipped her finger into her chalice and spoke over her shoulder. "The Marchioness de Pianessa knew how to stir your strength, my love. But the treasure she bequeathed cannot be claimed until you've killed every Waldensian in the valley."

"Yes," the marquis muttered. "Even in death she molests me."

Elizabeth chuckled. "But she is dead now, my dear, and the valley is yours to rule."

"Beneath your cousin, of course."

With only the slightest clink of glass, the duchess refilled her chalice. "France supports the kingdom of the House of Savoy in order to prevent war with the Spanish, so Emmanuel must rule."

"True," Pianessa replied, "but Emmanuel is too young to deal with the Waldenses."

"Really? How so?"

Pianessa gestured wearily. "Too many wars against the Waldenses have made them wise. If I attack, they will retreat along the trails and caves—their rope bridges and secret lifts. And the mountains provide a strong defense—narrow approaches where men must be bunched together with no good means of retreat. Once it begins, retreating will be ten times more difficult than advancing."

He paused, mumbled, "I once saw an entire battalion caught on the Castelluzo after dark. I was with them, but I secured myself to a crag with my belt, remained awake, and weathered the night. But almost a thousand men perished in falls before sunrise.... The mountain has killed more men in this valley than in all the wars combined."

"Do I sense fear, my dear?"

With a grunt, Pianessa continued, "It's not like the old days, Elizabeth, when the Vaudois only threw rocks and stones, or shot arrows at us from the trees. Now they have cannon and muskets. And ten good men with cannon can defy a thousand in one of those ravines." He became grim. "In many ways, they have the advantage."

"My love, you have never been defeated. How could the Waldenses possibly withstand your siege?"

"Sieges are won by thirst and starvation, my dear, and the Waldenses have plenty of food and water." Pianessa debated. "Yes, if they are in a strong position, this captain of theirs—Gianavel—can hold off ten times his number for months. Even years."

He leaned back into the couch, more pensive. "A hundred years ago, cannons could reduce any wall. But then the Italians, and then the Spaniards, learned how to build angled bastions with walls forty feet thick that can resist ten thousand shots. And the Waldenses have walls of solid stone hundreds of feet thick. They have the mountain itself." He took another sip, stared into the flames. "No...brute force will not conquer the Waldenses. Especially not with this man to lead them."

There was a long silence as Elizabeth read the marquis' face. Her eyebrows raised slightly. "You know this man?"

Silence lasted for a moment, and Pianessa frowned. "I encountered him three years ago at the Battle of Pinerola."

"Emmanuel said you commanded brilliantly in that battle."

"For a time, yes. But the Huns finally broke our line. We were too scattered, and they had depth—depth is always preferable to length." He sighed. "They crushed a single section of our line and cut us into two armies. In truth, we might have lost the day if the Waldensian reinforcements had not arrived when they did."

"My cousin also said that you gave the Waldenses credit for turning the tide of battle," Elizabeth said, watching the marquis carefully. It was seldom that the feared monarch shared credit for his victories.

"Yes," Pianessa muttered. "The Huns attacked through the Monté del Cuerpo—twenty thousand dragoons on horseback. All our positions were overrun. I myself was almost killed." Pianessa's brow hardened. "And then a man came over the barricade with only a dagger and sword, but I knew from his coat of arms that he was a Vaudois."

For a long time, Pianessa was silent. He sighed, shook his head once. "*Never* have I seen a man fight as he fought. He killed Huns like dogs, dropping them where they stood, one after the next, and somehow retook our demicannon. Then he swung them around to fire into our own position."

His eyes opened wide. "I thought he was either a traitor or a fool until I realized it was our only hope. The battle was lost. We were going to die anyway, if events didn't change. So I joined him, and we fired blast after blast into their rear guard."

"Why would you do that?"

"A basic rule of war, my dear. If your enemy outnumbers you, separate them and fight one piece at a time." He nodded. "Yes, the Vaudois is wise. And even in the chaos of battle he does not forget wisdom. He is…a worthy adversary."

Elizabeth was listening intently. "This is the same man who defeated your troops today?"

"Yes."

The duchess waited a moment more, then strolled with flowing, aristocratic poise across her bedroom.

"Can this man be bought?"

Pianessa shook his head. "Doubtful. The Waldenses refuse to betray their neighbors even when we torture them. They have been raised to endure persecution. They prepare for it their entire lives. So when one is captured and…questioned…they are fully resolved to die with their secrets. I've seen it time and again. Today we burned six hundred of them at the stake, and not a single one renounced." He seemed truly stunned as he took a deep breath. "Incredible…"

The duchess cradled her wine in both hands. "But, surely, even Rora has criminals imprisoned at El Torre. If you promised them full pardons, they might prove beneficial as spies…or, even, as assassins…for the right price."

Pianessa smiled wryly. "My dear, you think I have not considered this, also?"

She broke into laughter.

"Yes," Pianessa continued, "I've dispatched a rider to El Torre with orders to search for anyone familiar with the mountains." He gazed moodily into his empty goblet, as if suddenly uncertain what he beheld. "I will destroy the Waldenses. But I must do it quickly."

"Why?"

"Because if others see that my throne can be successfully defied, I'll soon have no throne to rule. And neither will you."

Elizabeth turned and stared. Her voice took on a sudden edge. "That will never happen, Pianessa."

"No?" Pianessa steadily held her gaze. "Who will you lead, Duchess, if no one follows? A king is only a king, my dear, as long as the people allow him to be king."

Her dark eyes remained controlled, but her voice was subdued. "Then what is your plan?"

With a sigh, Pianessa replied, "Tomorrow I will send a thousand of my mercenaries up the mountain. Before I commit myself, I want to further test the resolve of these people."

"You do not expect to win?"

"No, my dear, I expect to lose. But it is a necessary sacrifice in order to know their strength. And I would rather lose a thousand men than ten thousand."

Elizabeth laughed with mock anxiety. "A guilty conscious?"

A corner of Pianessa's mouth hooked in a smile. "Hardly, my dear. The mercenaries are doomed with or without my assistance. If not in this battle, then the next, or the plague. Or in some drunken brawl over some diseased harlot." He chuckled. "Few soldiers are worth more than the horse that bears him."

Elizabeth came closer. "Of course not, Monsieur de la Marquis." She placed her goblet on the table. "Any fool can be one of your soldiers. But only a stallion can carry them into battle, and a stallion has needs that must be satisfied."

Pianessa stared over her.

"Indeed."

＊＊＊

Howls—hideous, rhythmic, and horrifying even to him—ended as Incomel descended into the depths of the Prison House of Turin, a subterranean world crowded by those accused of heresy.

Prisons for heretics were termed *murs* and were distinctly different from formal prisons. For one thing, they were remarkably lacking in structure and schedule. Prisoners, men and women, were generally free to roam about the grounds unsupervised and were largely prisoners only in the fact that they could not leave.

Interrogations were done chiefly with carefully orchestrated questions and documents meant to deceive the prisoner. If the prisoner could be "led," as it was described, into an inadvertent admission of guilt, then that was taken as evidence of a crime. It made little difference whether the accused understood the pattern of questioning or even the questions themselves. And those who bandied words more wisely than the Inquisitors were encouraged by the use of physical pain to not be so circumspect and careful. But even torture had limitations; it was commonly accepted that a prisoner resolved to die for his faith could not be coerced by physical suffering, however hideous.

False testimonies were another tactic.

Seated before the prisoner, the Inquisitor would lazily leaf through a thick manuscript of "confessions and witness reports" as the prisoner watched. The Inquisitor was to remark, quite casually, that the abundance of evidence clearly supported all accusations against the prisoner, so why did the prisoner continue to refuse cooperation? Denial, it was ominously inferred, would only lead to great physical suffering.

The danger in this involved the prisoner requesting names of witnesses or specifics of a crime. Since the testimonies were false, any answer by the Inquisitor would betray the ruse.

Also, the Waldenses, in particular, should never be allowed a quick death, for they were grimly resolved to die for their faith and considered their death martyrdom. Killing them only gave them what they were willing to accept and encouraged the rest to resist. So the most infinitely painful torture chambers were utilized.

The Prison House of Turin contained perhaps the most terrible of all Inquisitional tortures—the Fosse.

Coming into wide usage during the fourteenth century, it was originally a series of cells in the dungeon of the Paris Chatelet. But, in effect, a Fosse was a single room in the shape of an inverted cone without fresh air or light. Prisoners were lowered into it by rope through a hatch in the floor. Half-filled with water, a Fosse was so small that one could neither stand nor lie down. Submerged hip-deep in the fetid cones, it took only a few days before the prisoner's flesh began to rot, leaving bloody rags that soon turned black with gangrene. Then fever and delirium would infect the brain, and the prisoner would erupt with wild and incoherent statements until they purposefully drowned themselves in their blood or their hearts failed from the strain.

There were fourteen of the cones in the dungeon, and they were all filled.

Glowing red braziers held pools of fiery coals across the full width of the underground chamber. The bellows were worked by prisoners chained to walls. Severed limbs were heaped in a pile amid wide sheets of skin that had been stripped from the living, and bodies not yet destroyed were stacked like wood against the far wall.

Incomel was sweating almost instantly in the smothering atmosphere that burned his nostrils regardless of how shallow he breathed the noxious air heavy with the stench of charred flesh. He avoided limbs that had been torn, not severed, from at least a dozen prisoners and moved gingerly aside as Corbis finished with another. As the broken man slumped forward, he reached out to Corbis with blackened stumps that had been arms—arms that erupted with fresh blood at the fall. His hideous shriek was cut short by Corbis's boot.

Sweating profusely, Corbis wore only a short smock and the tight, sleeveless harness of a blacksmith. It was obvious that his enormous girth was not comprised of copious fat like so many other monks, but rather that his arms and legs were unnaturally hard and thick, like the quarters of a bull. His belly, straining against the thick leather harness, revealed only a tight curving gut that hinted of great power stored between the thick thighs and wide, barreled chest. His neck was a wide stump that supported his strangely bald head.

Corbis's face should have naturally reflected fatigue at the onerous work. Instead, it reflected only a rising pleasure. "More prisoners?" he spat, peering from hairless lids.

"No," Incomel responded placidly. "But Pianessa attacks again tomorrow."

"Good. These will not last the night." He waved roughly and guards dragged another prisoner from the crossed bars of a cell, strapping him to the chair.

"Have any renounced?"

Corbis looked across, as though in a daze. "What?"

Glancing at the guard as he stepped discreetly away from the chair, Incomel blinked at Corbis's flat stare. "Have any of the prisoners *renounced* their heresy and rejoined the Church?"

"Oh," Corbis grunted. "No...they died."

Incomel paused. "I see."

His gaze passed over the dozens of prisoners huddled in small, motionless positions against the farthest wall, dark eyes gazing at him in various modes of defiance—some strong, some broken. Several of the adults still walked, tending to the wounds of those who had survived Corbis's interrogations. One child lay still in the corner, his eyes covered with a bloody bandage. He did not move.

"There were fifty," Incomel remarked. "I count only thirteen. The rest?"

Corbis shrugged. "Were heretics."

Incomel stepped forward, his face flushed and glistening with perspiration.

"Hear me," he whispered, and at the tone Corbis's dull eyes froze, gazing at a distant wall. "I will *not* report to the cardinal that I have not a single reformed heretic to show for our labors! So you will satisfy your bestial pleasures elsewhere, Corbis. *Not* with every prisoner I bring to this palace!"

Corbis blinked but said nothing.

Incomel turned and walked away, hands folded plainly within his cloak. Moving almost too quickly for the dignity of his station, he had almost reached the door at the top of the stairway when the screams began again.

✕✕✕✦✕✕✕

Long shadows stretched like pyramids across ground hairy with frost, and the scintillating white yielded with a slight crunching as the men of Rora prepared their weapons.

Gianavel had not slept but had moved throughout the camp during the night, encouraging and instructing. He did not wonder that he was still awake and alert when morning rose. He had never slept well in battle, had risen every day of every war to watch the sunrise, to meditate on the execution of grim action, and to accept the end of it before it began. And he had long ago come to peace with one thing. The greatest tragedy was not fighting. It was not having anything worth fighting to keep—no faith, no freedom, no hope.

Gianavel had only to remember the faces of his children and Angela, the peace he knew in his heart when he served God, the freedom he possessed since he would not bow to a man. It was all he needed; he was ready.

Today he held an even newer rifle than the one he'd borne yesterday—a French-made flintlock with better accuracy. He'd cleaned it by pouring warm water down the barrel and swabbing it with a rod and rag. Then he'd cleaned his pistols, four in number, all the same caliber. He was perpetually armed now, and would remain so until this ended. Also, he carried flint, oil-skin, a canteen, and other small items he'd need if they were overrun. The intention was to remain prepared to either fight or flee with a split-second's notice.

A line of twenty men stood approximately fifty paces from rock targets placed on a nearby slope.

"Load," Gianavel ordered and watched as they carefully measured and poured powder from the hollowed-out staghorns. They inserted a patch of paper beneath the ball and rammed it tight against the chamber with the rod. When they appeared ready, Gianavel walked slowly down the line, studying each man.

"The first thing you must understand," he explained, "is your weapon. The second thing is yourself. And the third is your enemy."

Gianavel knew that most of them were already accomplished marks-men. The older ones had been forced to defend the valley in more than one war against Germany. But shooting was a skill that dulled easily, and shooting men was *never* easy.

"There's only one way to learn," he said and angled past the far end of the line. "So pick your target, and see what you can do."

Gianavel did not watch the targets, but he watched the men to see which ones set the stock tight against their shoulder, which ones steadied their breathing and, consequently, the barrel. He also determined which ones jerked the trigger, moving the barrel so that they ineffectually hit the slope. After the smoke cleared, he determined that the oldest were the steadiest—no surprise.

"Reload!" he called out and studied to see how they had positioned their powder horn and ammunition pouch.

The older men carried the horns and pouches high and tight so they wouldn't waste energy searching or even reaching. Nor would the horns bounce when they moved, revealing their position in the dark. The younger carried them on long, fashionable leather straps that rested the horn on their hips, clattering across canteens.

Yes, there was nothing like experience to teach a man that strength in battle was an expensive commodity. Once spent, it was hard to regain; the best remedy was not to expend it.

Veterans had already prepared rucksacks that they kept close at all times. They also kept their weapons with them at all times, and they bore long poniards at their waist even when they slept because they knew a good knife was *the* indispensable implement for a soldier. If a man lost his rifle or food, he could always regain them with patience and a knife. But if he lost his rifle *and* his knife, he was as good as dead.

And there was the most important rule of all—always keep it simple. Always, *always* keep it simple—a simple means of foraging, of building a fire, of navigating. The less complicated it was, the less that could go wrong. The rule, alone, was simple to remember, and it applied to everything.

As Gianavel passed one young man, he pulled a red bandana from the boy's pocket and spoke sternly. "Wear nothing with color! Dress like the forest! And wear only leather! It makes no sound when you brush against branches and leaves! Remember the difference between cover and concealment! Concealment means you can't be seen! Cover means you can't be shot! Always use cover! Always! A man does not need to see you to kill you!"

Some eyes widened with fear as Gianavel walked the line. Then he focused on the youngest—a boy of perhaps fifteen who tightly clutched his rifle, fingers white with tension. Gianavel paused before him, his voice loud enough to carry. "Put on your gloves!"

The boy started. "Sir?"

"Your gloves!" Gianavel said and waited while the boy struggled to pull gloves over each hand. Then, fingers stiff and insensitive, he trembled as Gianavel walked behind him. "Load and fire!"

Fumbling with the heavy stockings, the boy managed to uncap his horn, poured far too much powder into the barrel, needed twice as long to work the rod, and spilled even more powder charging the plate. He was fumbling awkwardly with his grip when he fired, and the shot went high and wide, completely missing the target.

The boy staggered, waving at the huge cloud of smoke that blocked his vision. Then, coughing, he stepped back in line. It took only a glance to know he was humiliated.

Gianavel firmly gripped his shoulder, no condemnation. "That's how you'll feel when you fire a shot in battle." He patted the boy on the back, then filed past the rest of them.

"In battle *nothing* will feel as it feels now. Your fingers will feel like sticks! Your feet will feel like blocks of wood! Everything will seem dull and thick! Like you are fighting underwater!" He paused, insuring they were listening closely. "It has nothing to do with fear! It is only your body preparing itself for battle! Don't fear it and it will fade! But if you fear it—if you think something terrible and strange is happening to you—then it won't go away! Your fear will keep it with you!" He looked at each man in turn. "I have seen a hundred battles, and I have felt the same every single time! Every time! But I know what it is and it does me no harm! Be strong! Remember what it is, and it will fade!"

Gianavel glanced again at the hill, back at the boy. "It's a better shot than I made when my father made me do the same thing," he nodded.

The boy smiled, still uncertain, as Gianavel continued, "How do you fight a hundred men?" He waited until Bertino shouted from the far end, "One at a time!"

Gianavel gave a hearty laugh. "Exactly! *One at a time!*" He walked on. "You think they are like the elephant! And they are! But even an elephant can be eaten one bite at a time!"

He spoke louder, watching them closely. "If ten men attack you at the same time, you must move quickly, hit fast and *keep moving*! Make it so they can only come at you one at a time! If you're fighting outside, put the sun at your back! If that's not possible, keep the sun on your right! Make them retreat! Make them back up! And don't give them time to look around! Try to gain the highest piece of ground and shout when you strike! It frightens your enemy and encourages you!"

One man spoke, "What about fighting inside buildings? Going room to room?"

"In buildings," Gianavel answered, "always fight with the door to your back or to your right! Make sure there is nothing behind you and that there is free space to your left! Chase the enemy to your left and don't give him time to look around to see what's in the room! Make him trip! Make him fall! Use the entire room to your advantage!"

He could see their spirits rising. "What do you see coming against us? Siege engines? Cannons? Brooms and dragoons and cavalry? A dragon?"

No one answered.

Gianavel paused, his voice falling low and controlled. "Once you have had one or two clashes with the dragon, you will know that they are but men. They live like you. They bleed like you. What will hurt you will hurt them. Yes, they have siege engines—mortars and cannons and cavalry. So do we! They have men with rifles! So do we! They have their cause! So do we! But they fight for money! We fight for our families and our freedom to believe! For a salvation no man can take from us!"

Standing before them, the Captain of Rora said slowly, "Only if a man fears death...can death conquer him."

Along the line there was silence, stillness.

Bertino's stout visage lifted slightly, watching Gianavel with hard eyes, a grim frown. The others, too, were solemn and unmoving, watching steadily.

Slowly Gianavel nodded. "Take a platoon into the pass," he spoke to Bertino. "You know what to do."

"Oui!" Bertino caught his rifle. "Come," he said to those around him. "We have work to do."

In a moment they dropped over the crest of El Combe, moving for the forest where they would drop trees and boulders into the pass itself, making it more difficult to climb. They had prepared avalanches and half-hewn trees that could be dropped on entire battalions as well as powderkegs that could destroy dozens at once.

Gianavel knew they would need every advantage when this battle was joined. He had overlooked nothing, he hoped, but there was no way to be certain. Nothing was so small that it could not be used to an advantage; a man needed only to keep searching. But all he could do for the moment was continue to search.

"Again," he said and stepped through the lines to stand behind them. "In battle you'll only shoot half as well as you shoot in practice, so practice must be perfect! Again and again and again!"

Steadily, they fired.

Steadily, targets fell.

BROACHED PHEASANT WARMED before the hearth as Gianavel leaned his rifle beside the door and entered their cottage. He caught Jacob in his arms and lifted him high as the girls also rushed forward and embraced him. When he looked at Angela again, he was stunned to feel how her smile made this moment seem as though it was all there was in the world, and that the rest was only a bad dream from which he'd awakened.

Unaware of how tired his legs were until he sat, Gianavel wearily stretched out his arms and embraced the children again. Then, smiling, Angela walked forward and collapsed on the couch, crushing the girls against Gianavel's chest. Muffled screams and laughter lasted until Angela leaned back, feigning surprise.

"Go," she said to the girls and Jacob. "I need to talk to your papa for a minute." She silenced their remonstrations one by one, and in a few minutes they were alone.

Gianavel softly touched her hair as she gazed at him. Neither of them hurried to speak and break the moment. They were alive and that seemed like everything.

"How is it," Gianavel spoke quietly, almost reverently, "that you don't seem to age?"

Angela's look was a portrait of innocence. "Hector came by. He said that I need a real man around the house, so he proposed."

Gianavel chuckled and his eyes brightened.

"What did you say?"

"I said, 'of course.' So he said he'd come back tomorrow with a horse and buggy and that he'd take us to Geneva." She stared close; her smile faded. "But I told him I would stay beside my husband, no matter what."

Gianavel touched her face, traced a line. Then he reached and pulled her close and held her as the burning logs crackled in the hearth. Finally he noticed the children collecting in the open doorway, staring, uncertain, and frightened. He stretched out his other arm, and they came forward slowly, sitting at his feet, beside him, holding him.

More than at any moment in his entire life, he wished he had something to say. But there was nothing to say that could not be said better with silence.

Emmanuel strolled across the Great Hall of his keep, arms folded across his chest, head bent, mouth turned in a frown, brow hard in concentration. He was not alone—he was never alone—but the few servants who stood close to attend to his needs were silent and still. And his personal body-guards, who'd long ago learned to read his moods, were tactfully obscure.

The fireplace, a relic from an age when fire itself was some unspoken means of protection against forces beyond man, was as long as a wagon. And, contrary to growing custom, had no hearth or mantel. It was simply a gigantic pit of roaring flame, a pronouncement of man's ability to control his destiny.

Emmanuel knew something of that because his mother had lacked the insight, when she appointed him a tutor, to eliminate all those who disagreed, in even the smallest parcel, with the Church. Indeed, she had, in the end, appointed someone who was the complete antithesis to the cold, barbaric ruthlessness of Pianessa.

Her choice, which she'd deemed so innocent, had been a man who prudently kept his own counsel yet had quietly exposed Emmanuel to the works of the pre-Socratics, to Plotinus, Augustine, Dun Scotus, Ockham, Bacon, and Descartes. He had taught Emmanuel the value of being modest in the demonstration of piety, so as not to insinuate moral superiority. He had taught him the wisdom of remaining austere in private observation and to keep his counsel and speak little, for offenses were unavoidable when one multiplied words. He also taught Emmanuel to lay his plans deeply and with great foresight, then to pursue them with strict secrecy and an inveteracy of purpose that allowed no rest or mercy until they were accomplished.

It was advice Emmanuel had taken to heart because he had watched his father endure the patronizing and insensible Inquisitors who presented their ideological wares in terms that cost both soldiers and wealth. He had watched army after army destroyed for a cause that benefited no kingdom that he knew, and he had yet to discover what virtue was satisfied by blood. He was deeply into thoughts of it when he turned at an approach and saw the source of his pondering.

Smiling mildly, Emmanuel said nothing as Marcelus Simon, his tutor, drew near and stopped, arms folded within the warm easement of his priestly sleeves. Simon had been discreetly scarce in past weeks, wisely avoiding conversation with the Inquisitors or their retinue as he studied and learned. His eyes, a shade strangely beyond blue, revealed little, nor did he speak.

Quietly amused, Emmanuel expressed no surprise. Dull greetings were beneath them, and Simon was forever the teacher, waiting for Emmanuel to explain the situation. It was a tactic of Aristotle, which the Catholic monk revered for his ethics and poetics.

"And so," the old man said at last, "what do you see?"

"Only that there is nothing new under the sun," Emmanuel replied with a faint, and somewhat sad, smile. "Again the Church uses my house to make war against the Waldenses. Again the treasury of Savoy is spent in a doomed attempt to drive them from the land. And, again, the Church will fail as they have failed before."

Simon's august head bent thoughtfully. Although well into his sixties, the old monk revealed little physical weakness and had made his own contributions to Emmanuel's training in the arts of fighting, and more importantly, the art of not fighting. Some might be shocked that a monk would teach treachery to a young monarch, but young monarchs untrained in treachery did not become old monarchs—a lesson Simon had been no less astute in teaching than the poetics of Aristotle.

The Master of Arms had taught Emmanuel to wear a sword of great quality at his waist. Simon had taught him to conceal a disposable ice pick in his sleeve. The Master at Arms may have taught Emmanuel to dramatically draw his sword as a bold warning, but Simon had taught him to hide his weapon until he struck. The Master at Arms instructed Emmanuel to terrify his enemy, but Simon had taught him to smile and strike with words of friendship. The Master of Arms had taught the Duke of Savoy the rules of war; Simon had taught him that war has no rules.

"Expect everything," Simon had said, "reveal nothing. Always be prepared to defend yourself against your family, your friends, your allies, even against your own bodyguards." His eyes narrowed slightly. "*Especially* against your bodyguards."

When Emmanuel had protested that such vigilance would be tiring, Simon replied, "Does a man enjoy the warmth of a fire without also suffering the cold to fetch wood for it? If you lack the will to maintain your kingdom, you should become a monk."

The old monk was far more than a teacher—he was guardian of Emmanuel, body and soul. And on more than one occasion rumored colleagues of some subversive plot against Emmanuel's throne had mysteriously disappeared from the face of the Earth. The full intent of the conspiracies was never revealed. But when she who prepared meals for Emmanuel was found dead, killed with the same poison she intended to use on the prince, Simon dryly remarked, "The danger of not richly rewarding conspirators is that they betray you for so much less."

And now Emmanuel was being tested, he knew, because the time had come for him to use all that he had learned. He glanced at the distant servants who were certainly listening—eavesdropping was an art in the palace, a means of maintaining not only one's career but their life. No, of course they did not appear to be listening, he noted, as Simon had taught, but neither were they speaking, which was more revealing. He gazed at his friend and mentor.

"You taught me that I should become wise before I became old," he remarked quietly. "But, in this, I see little place for wisdom. I do not rule my kingdom."

Simon pursed his lips as he bent his head slightly. He rarely spoke until he carefully considered his words. A man's folly, he often told Emmanuel, is that he answers a question before he truly understands it. "There are two means of ruling a kingdom, My Prince. Through your own hand, or through the hand of another."

"I do not see how I can rule through the Inquisitors."

"Do you see how you can rule through others who, perhaps, rule the Inquisitors?" Simon gave Emmanuel a long, searching look. "Remember what you have learned, boy. You must appeal to a higher authority."

Emmanuel was silent, then replied bitterly, "I lost my temper. They see a weakness."

"Even a dog can see fear." When courage was the question, Simon had no mercy. "You are wiser than this."

The young Duke of Savoy stood quietly for a moment, studying his hand. "Can you not help me?" He stared into the old man's eyes. "You are the closest thing to a father I have ever known."

Simon's eyes lit with quick understanding. "I know, my son." He waited. "Yes, I will help you. By reminding you of how great is your own strength. By reminding you of what you already know."

Emmanuel's entire body seemed to shrink and he shook his head. "It seems very little now, my friend. This is a contest of giants. I am the small monarch of a small land that is ruled, and you know this to be true, by another king of another land."

The silence that followed disturbed Emmanuel because Simon almost always revealed to him what he did not see, unless...

Emmanuel looked again. "By another *king*..."

Simon smiled faintly.

The Duke of Savoy smiled widely.

"Be careful of your countenance," Simon said without inflection. "What is not said is—"

"—more important than what is said," Emmanuel finished. "Yes, I remember." He turned his face to gaze into the flames of the hearth.

As if speaking of ubiquitous scandals, Simon added, "I would hate to imagine what trouble this is causing Cardinal Chigi, who is currently in Pinerola to discuss trade with Cromwell's committee. We must be sure to include him in our prayers."

As Emmanuel stared into the flames his eyes narrowed. "Oliver Cromwell has heard of our little unrest?"

"Oh, certainly." Simon folded his hands behind his back. "I understand England's great Lord Protector has sent petitions to Cardinal Mazarin, the mentor of King Louis, enjoining him to intercede on behalf of the Waldenses. One of England's poets, John Milton, I believe, has written a very moving letter in an attempt to usher in a peaceable settlement. But Cromwell has not excluded a forthright invasion of your kingdom, if hostilities are not suspended."

If Simon's words were overheard and repeated, they were crafted to only reflect the nervous concerns of a poor priest for his life—a purely selfish interest the Inquisitors would well understand. Of *course* he was concerned for the outcome of the war, Simon would declare! It was an old man's *right* to be concerned with his diminishing health and security, especially an aged priest too enfeebled to relocate to some desolate missionary outpost. Yes, Simon would declare, he hoped the war ended quickly and successfully and that all the Waldenses should be utterly destroyed from the land, including their cattle and sheep, and then the bodies must be burned and the ashes scattered so that not even their memory remained.

In a loud, droning monotone that could lull even the most attentive spy to sleep, Simon hoped the details of the increasingly fierce war did not reach the revered Cardinal Fabio Guigi, for the cardinal would certainly want to know what great victories had been won by the Inquisitors for the sake of both God and man, yes, yes…

Emmanuel suppressed a smile, but it took little effort. He was already formulating a plan: carefully, silently, as he had been taught. It was the first lesson—plan your victory in secret, execute your enemy in darkness, and take no credit for the victory. But, rather, give thanks only to the omnipotent hand of God who has *obviously* chosen you to lead this kingdom. Then wipe your dagger clean, hone the edge, and sheath it for another day when God will preserve you once more.

"Well," Simon said with some fatigue, as if the dull conversation had been nothing but worrisome, "I have selfishly hoarded your presence once more, My Prince." He stepped back, bowed humbly. "I must return to my administrations."

Emmanuel did not move or acknowledge the comment or stare after the harmless priest as he departed. There was no reason to stare after him, much less thank him, for, after all, nothing of importance had been said.

Upon a high white ridge crested by wisps of cloud and blue and sun, Gianavel stared over the mountains. His face was peaceful, and he seemed to see something, though no others saw anything upon the winding trails beneath them. A moment more he scanned the snow-slivered crags and ravines of the Alps as a cold wind lifted his long black hair; then he tilted his head to Bertino.

"Everything is prepared?" he asked.

"Oui," Bertino nodded. "You expect them to come today?"

"I expect nothing."

Bertino squinted at the Pass of Pelice. He shook his head, as if denying some kind of physical pain. "Why not tomorrow? A delay of a day or two might lull us into complacency."

"No," said the Captain of Rora. "Pianessa knows I will not be deceived by his words. And to delay an attack only strengthens me. He will come quickly to measure our resolve."

The words provoked Bertino to a worried countenance. "Pianessa will not expect to finish us with the next battle?"

Gianavel continued to search the pass. "You must understand our enemy, old friend. Pianessa does not rely upon the grace of the Lord. He trusts only in the strength of his sword arm. He is wise in the ways of war, and the first rule of any war is to know your enemy—know his weaknesses and his strengths. Strengthen yourself to endure his strength, and prepare to strike his weaknesses. That is what he is doing."

With weary, unseeing eyes, Bertino stared down over the pass. "How many men will he bring next time?"

"More than he needs," Gianavel said simply. "Ten…perhaps fifteen thousand. They'll divide, attacking on two and maybe three fronts." Gianavel's quiet, steady words held no fear. "He will try to stretch our line, knowing we only need a few men to hold a pass."

"But they'll have to attack us through the pass."

Gianavel's widened eyes lined his forehead. "Why?"

"Because it's too hard to climb the cliffs."

"An army can attack anywhere a man can climb or walk," Gianavel frowned. "Expect nothing, old friend, and everything. If a man can climb a cliff, he can attack from a cliff. If he can climb a tree, he can attack from a tree. And if Pianessa stretches our line, we'll be too thin to resist his superior depth.

Yes...depth is always preferable to length. We'll slow them, for certain—we have too much of an advantage not to—but they'll eventually swarm the walls."

Bertino growled, "Like locusts."

Listening, Hector said, "He might try to feint an attack, Captain. Just to see if we're prepared."

Gianavel shook his head. "We have the terrain, Hector, so Pianessa will trust in the depth of his line. He'll sacrifice his men like sheep, throwing them at us, so that we can't kill them fast enough. It will be a flood, dead men charging over dead men. He'll be trying to make us use all our ammunition because when a man's out of ammunition, he's out of options. And when they take one wall, they've taken them all."

Bertino was still displeased. "You say he will come with thousands. But he used only five hundred yesterday."

"Not so great a mistake, my friend. Pianessa was hedging that we might not be on guard. But now he knows we won't be caught by surprise." Gianavel pondered a moment more. "Also, he underestimated his mercenaries."

"How so?"

"Mercenaries will kill for a victory," Gianavel said. "They won't die for it. Come. There's much to do."

They proceeded down onto one of the ubiquitous ridges that combed the peaks surrounding El Combe. Every field and creek and orchard and field was barren of movement.

"There," Gianavel said, pointing, and the rest shielded their eyes from the glowing sun. "If we lose the pass, retreat through the Valhenza. Once you're inside, remember to maintain a rear guard of your most experienced men. Don't run. Don't reveal panic. If you do, Pianessa's troops will rush in and overrun us."

"What's the best defense while retreating?" one asked.

"Make them too frightened to pursue," Gianavel said as he descended. "Have men chop trees and tie them off with ropes. Drop them on those that are chasing you. Have your rear guard composed of marksmen and shoot back often. If Pianessa's men are moving cautiously, they'll be moving slowly."

"Is that so important?" asked one man.

Gianavel's mouth became a grim line. His eyes narrowed, utterly lacking in sympathy. "If the people panic, they'll lose formation. If they lose formation, they'll break into small groups, then smaller groups, and finally they'll be running without a weapon across an empty field. Their fear will have killed them. *Never* retreat with an indication of fear! Never! Retreat as if you dare anyone to pursue!"

Hector muttered, "Not as easy as it sounds, Captain. It's a bit unnatural to fall back with discipline."

"Many things in war are unnatural," Gianavel gently rebuked. "The ability to remain calm in the midst of exciting events will, alone, make you a great soldier."

As they carefully picked a path down from the ridge, they analyzed elements of resistance and withdrawal until they reached camp and dispersed, each man carefully instructing his squad for every conceivable complication, although they realized that every complication, by the time-tested rule of war, was inconceivable.

⋊⋊⋈⋉⋉

"Spies," Pianessa grumbled, staring at a small black snake he had lifted from a field. "I need…spies."

Incomel frowned over the poisonous reptile. For whatever reason, he seemed to have little tolerance for serpents. He roughly shouldered the other Inquisitors aside as he stepped forward.

"I don't understand why you don't simply march up the Pelice and kill these heretics," he demanded. "You act as if you are planning to invade France, Pianessa." He gestured with irritation. "Simply send a thousand men up the pass, kill all you meet, burn their homes, and send the children to El Torre."

Pianessa's face split in a smile of genuine amusement. "Why don't *you* lead them, Inquisitor?" He lifted his heavy arms toward the mountains and laughed. "You seem to understand these heretics far better than I."

Incomel's sullen pause was meant to affect Pianessa; it didn't. "God's calling on my life is not in the field, Pianessa. It is in my charge to rescue the Church from these heretics."

"Yes," Pianessa sneered. "A holy man, I almost forgot." With a tired sigh he stood and walked forward. He leaned on the table, studying the map. "How fortunate for the Waldenses that you have only their salvation in mind, Inquisitor."

As the Inquisitor began to retort, Pianessa spoke sharply to his sergeant major—a tall, red-bearded man who rivaled Pianessa himself in the appearance of primitive strength.

"Have pikemen and riflemen advance six abreast in the pass. At the first engagement, flank them and move up the cannon. Then reduce their battlements to ruin." He hesitated. "You should need no more than five hundred shot, I think."

"Yes, sir," was the quick reply.

"Then," the marquis continued, "you will simply enter the village proper and kill everything that walks or crawls." Pianessa seemed as if he were searching for something he might have missed. "Make no mistake, Sergeant,

Gianavel is wise. If you consider a tactic, assume that Gianavel has also considered it. Nothing will cross your mind that has not already crossed his."

"Yes, sir."

"The Pass of Pelice gives us no advantage," Pianessa observed. "There is little cover, and the Waldenses will be heavily protected. Watch for ambushes and feints. Do not rush forward—*especially* if you see an opportunity."

"A tactic of the Moors," the sergeant muttered.

"Yes," Pianessa replied sullenly. "Gianavel knows all the tactics of the Crusaders, Sergeant. His ancestors fought in them. Just as he knows why the Crusaders failed."

The sergeant paused. "Why did they fail, My Lord?"

"The Crusaders knew how to take a city, Sergeant. They didn't know when to surrender one. If the cost of holding his position is too high, Gianavel will fall back in an orderly fashion. He will do nothing precipitous, so don't rush forward as though the battle is won. If you do, it will be the last attack you lead."

"May I ask what else you know about this man, My Lord?" The sergeant stared coldly.

"Nothing of consequence, Sergeant. But one thing is certain: Gianavel will make few mistakes."

The sergeant grunted. "I saw his kind in the valley. I will use every precaution."

"Do that," Pianessa said slowly, "but you have rarely, if ever, seen his kind, Sergeant."

"What do you mean, My Lord?"

"I mean"—Pianessa raised burning dark eyes—"this man does not fight like your mercenaries, or even those Waldenses you slaughtered in the valley.

This man knows war as his purpose—his destiny—put upon him by God." Pianessa let his words settle into his listeners.

Incomel's frown was terrible, but the marquis did not seem to care. He added, "Gianavel does not fear death because he knows something greater than death." Pianessa bent his head, staring to the side. "My best advice, Sergeant: You attack a lion. He will not care for pain, or horror, or loss. He will ignore any wound that is less than mortal. He will kill more coldly than your coldest mercenary, and if you make the smallest, single mistake, he will kill *you*."

The sergeant shifted. "I see."

Pianessa looked back up. "This man believes God's purpose for his life is to defend his people. He has seen war and he has trained for war. He will maintain lines of communication. He does not need a map because he knows every footpath. He knows we're coming; he is prepared. The only hope we have is that we can overrun his cannon fire. If we can breach their line, if we can close on the Waldenses with hand blows, we can take Rora by overwhelming force. But to get close enough to accomplish that will be expensive."

Frowning now, the sergeant said nothing. Pianessa finished gazing around the hundreds of mercenaries assembled on the plain. "What of these Irish you mentioned?"

"Cromwell's criminals," the sergeant major answered, still staring at the map, and his mind seeming very far away, somewhere above the Castelluzo. "There was no room in English prisons, My Lord, so Cromwell banished them to the Continent."

"What are their crimes?"

"Murder, rape, thievery, and whatnot."

Pianessa nodded. "Very well. Put Cromwell's criminals in the first wave. They can exhaust the bulk of cannon fire. And don't follow too closely with reinforcements."

"Why, My Lord?"

"Dead mercenaries cost nothing," Pianessa said without hesitation and fell more somber. "And there will be plenty of dead."

×oo×⊗×oo×

Staring down, Gianavel said nothing. He had returned to the stable to see if Abraham still prayed.

Yes, Abraham still prayed, his knees wet with wet ground and his head bent in eternal petition to God. Nor did he remove himself from his petition for a long time. But finally he lowered his hands, looked at the warlike Captain of Rora.

He smiled. "You are well, Gianavel?"

Gianavel was silent a moment. He nodded. "I am well, Abraham. I came only to see if you might have received any wisdom. If, perhaps, you knew another way."

The old man laughed quietly. "No, Gianavel. I have received no great wisdom. I have only faith and hope. Those things a man clings to in darkness and confusion."

As if he wanted someone to give him a reason for why he should not fight, Gianavel waited, head bowed. But every reason had been given, and they were not reason enough.

Abraham understood. "You and I are different, Gianavel," he said with a smile.

Gianavel raised a dark gaze.

"You think fighting is the means to defend your people," he continued.

"I believe that giving our lives as a living sacrifice to the Lord is our defense."

At that, all that could be said was said.

Gianavel's face hardened in a grief that had no answers. And now the questions had reached the backwater, where unrest overflowed familiar peace.

"I would be a fool," Gianavel said at last, "if I let Pianessa come into my home and murder my children, my wife, my friends. Perhaps you do know peace in laying down your life, and all the lives of those you love. But I can't do that. It defies everything I am. I *must* fight."

Abraham nodded his head sadly, as if at a sad truth. "Sometimes it is better to sacrifice a finger than to lose a whole hand."

Gianavel frowned more deeply. "Perhaps there is a greater truth," he answered. "Perhaps God, in His wisdom, appointed some to be priests, and some warriors, so that all the world might know that the end belongs only to God."

Abraham said nothing, nor did he move as Gianavel walked away.

∞◈∞

Emmanuel was almost stunned when he walked into Pianessa's command post and saw the marquis reclining on his hunting chair, staring morosely at the distant mountains of Rora.

He waited, curious, until Pianessa spoke.

"Do you know what I think, Savoy?" he said mildly.

Cautiously, casually, Emmanuel continued forward. "You are the general of my army, Pianessa. I would like very much to know what you think on the eve of a great battle upon which the future of my kingdom hangs."

Pianessa sighed deeply. "I think…that the Waldenses are not meant to depart from those mountains."

A solid silence.

"The will of God, Pianessa?"

The marquis shrugged, tired or depressed—a rare moment. "I know nothing of the will of God, Savoy. I am a soldier. I fight where I am sent to fight. I kill whom I am sent to kill. But the Waldenses have been attacked again and again. They have been dispersed, scattered to a dozen countries, massacred by the thousands, and still they return to these mountains, like Moses to Sinai."

At the young Duke of Savoy's silence, Pianessa looked over. "You think I have not read the Scriptures, Savoy?" His voice, even for a moment, lost its cold brutality. "Yes, the Waldenses remind me much of the Israelites. They are killed over and over, and still they return. This land, to them...it is sacred ground."

The aura around Pianessa was something Emmanuel had never sensed around the general before—a persona of defeat. "Do you doubt victory?" he asked cautiously.

Seconds passed before the Marquis de Pianessa rose and walked slowly back to the map. He leaned across it, shook his head. "I will kill them all, Savoy. I was only...musing."

Whatever comfort or even information Emmanuel had sought when he first entered the tent was completely trampled by Pianessa's grim mood. He backed away quietly and turned to leave.

"One thing, Savoy."

Reluctantly, Emmanuel turned back and waited.

Pianessa was grim. "What will you win if you take these mountains from Gianavel?"

Fear—actual fear—enveloped Emmanuel's heart. It was one thing for Father Simon to warn him that God might be against this war. It was another for a pagan general to warn him that God himself might fight beside Gianavel.

Without a reply, or even thinking of a reply, Emmanuel moved to the stables.

>oo☙oo<

Gianavel knelt and thirty-four men followed, listening closely.

"Our defense is as good as we can make it," he said quietly and calmly. "But the hardest aspect of any battle is changing your defense to meet changes in the attack. The side that changes the fastest will have the advantage. More the reason to take out their commanders quickly. Make sure you're far enough down the slope to target them. They won't be at the front."

"I wouldn't be either," commented Hector.

"Have men with mirrors stationed on the slopes above your positions. If you have to retreat up the slopes, use quick flashes. What one side does, the other does as well."

"As Joab and Abishi did," grunted Bertino.

"Exactly," said Gianavel. "None of us have the advantage of a military education. We have only our experiences and the stories of our fathers. But we know what David, Joshua, and Gideon did when they fought against their enemies. Their tactics were sound. We will do the same things."

Hector laughed once, nodded.

Faces grim and resolved met Gianavel as he gazed at them all in turn. "You are men," he said, and the words strengthened them as no accolade ever could.

Gianavel nodded, lifted his rifle.

"Let's go," he said.

>oo☙oo<

The last of the heavily armed battalion disappeared along the highest switchback that curled around the farthest height of El Combe as soldiers struggled to drag the reserve cannon over the narrow, rocky ledge. Dust cyclones swirled in their wake like a storm leaving tatters of itself on the mountain.

Pianessa suddenly erupted with a laugh, drawing the attention of a lieutenant who sat beside him on horseback. The merciless guffaw seemed to have nothing of human pleasure within it, but there was harsh pleasure, nonetheless.

The lieutenant studied Pianessa's barbaric countenance, asked, "Something you see, sire?"

Pianessa settled back into his saddle. His huge hands closed on the flat, wooden horn, reins held easily. "Nothing, Cassius," he commented. "I was simply wondering if the Vaudois have any idea what is going to befall them when that regiment descends on their village."

Cassius, tall and lean with an aquiline face that gave him an almost aristocratic air, shrugged. "I expect they've heard what befell the valley, sire— rape, murder, pillaging, burning." He paused. "It doesn't matter if the Waldenses renounce their faith. The Inquisitors have issued orders to kill them all."

"Indeed," Pianessa murmured and was silent for so long that the lieutenant was watching curiously when he spoke again. "But tell me, Lieutenant. Would you lead that battalion knowing that Gianavel and his people are waiting for you?"

Cassius took a deeper breath and leaned back, stiffening as he gazed upward at the slope. He said nothing, but a sudden, frozen paleness in his face answered for him.

Pianessa laughed loudly and spurred his stallion toward the field.

"Neither would I."

×∞∞∞×

Bertino spun as the runner, a scout, arrived at the camp breathless and sweating heavily. He staggered the final few steps, and Bertino caught him by the shoulders.

"What is it, boy?"

The boy gasped, "A battalion. At least a thousand! They're coming!"

"How long?"

"An hour!" the boy cried. "Less!"

Gianavel lifted his rifle and walked forward. His poise was calm. There was nothing about him that matched those who surged quickly and nervously to don weapons and equipment. His voice was cold as he spoke to Bertino. "Keep a close eye on signals. The more chaotic the battle, the more important are our communications."

"Oui!" Bertino nodded and turned to a small platoon of ten men. "You know what to do!"

Hector walked quickly past the Captain of Rora, his men close behind the elderly man, though he said nothing and didn't glance to insure they were following. When they were gone, Gianavel lifted two extra rifles that he slung across his back.

He, alone, had no one to reload for him. He would attack the most critical, and most heavily guarded, elements of the battalion, striking at the head to kill the body. To take out the general was a mission best suited for six coordinated men, but he would risk no one else in the attempt. So he would run the gauntlet himself. He had only to seize the opportunity when it was there and execute with precision, then retreat quickly without a single mistake.

It was possible, Gianavel knew, because it would be at close range, and everything at close range was chaotic. Shots fired from ten feet easily went wide. Men swiped wildly with sabers, afraid they would lose their own head if they struck a second too late. And their fear would be his advantage because he had no fear. No, he had no fear, for he knew what was awaiting him—death. And the victory he would claim would make all the rest seem as nothing.

With a last impulse, he slid two more poniards into his belt, which would be quickly discarded because he would be too close for rifle or pistol with no time to reload and no time to retreat. It was the only way to do it. For, if he failed, he would be the one to pay the cost.

When all were gone, Gianavel paused. Though he revealed nothing, the fire was in his blood—the sunlight was bright, brighter, his blood fast, his hands tingling. Everything about him was white and dangerous, even the leaves that swayed beyond the camp. It was the mind he would keep until the killing was done.

With long strides he vanished into the trees.

8

CAPTAIN MARIO BRUSHED A TREE BRANCH ASIDE, glaring warily at the boulder-strewn slope Pass of Pelice. He saw only deep forest almost black beneath the overlapping crests of trees. There was no sign of Rora's defenders, nor was there any sound. He paused a long time, searching, but saw nothing in the distance, where the trail leveled across the valley. No, nothing...

It was as if Rora had been abandoned with uneaten meals still warm on tables, open doors swaying in haunting silence, open curtains at empty windows with dogs scurrying sideways on dust-devil trails utterly hedged by mountains ominous and silent as gravestones.

Mario looked to the side. "Sergeant!"

The red-bearded man turned his head. His face, also, reflected a sweating tension. His voice was quiet. "Yes, sir?"

"Why haven't they attacked?"

The sergeant major scanned the impenetrable forest once more. "I can't say, sir. If they're lying in ambuscade, they have the patience of devils."

"You're certain that men march parallel on either flank? I don't want to walk into another trap."

"Twenty men march parallel on either slope, sir."

Mario glanced at the size of the regiment. "Is that enough to fight off an ambush?"

The sergeant, too, appeared to be moving at a pace convenient for passing. "Oh no, sir, the fools will be murdered without a survivor. But they'll still sound the alarm."

"If we're attacked, will you charge the slopes?"

The red beard moved almost imperceptibly. "It's foolish to charge uphill against a fortified position, sir. It's like being caught halfway across a river. You can't advance and you can't retreat. The Spaniards are wizards at it, but, then, they're adulterous devils." He continued, quite businesslike, "No, sir, if they hit us from the slope, we'll retreat and barrage their positions with cannons. Beat them down a bit before we charge into their rifles."

Mario slowed his pace even more. "These people are wise, Sergeant. If they see that battle is unavoidable, they'll strike without warning and strike to kill."

"I'm confident the flanks will provide a warning, sir, however abrupt. And a warning is all we need."

Mario's eyes lighted nervously from bush to bush. His voice was quieter than the leaves that rustled above him.

"Yes...a warning."

◇◇◇◇◇◇

As silent as a breeze, Gianavel ripped his poniard from the chest of a soldier that marched on the flank of the regiment. Strewn behind him, the soldiers' comrades, twenty in number, lay in a long scattered line.

The Captain of Rora raised burning eyes at Captain Mario, now so close.

No, there would be no warning.

As he'd anticipated, the first company was comprised of mercenaries and a rank sergeant. But it would do little good to kill expendable mercenaries and a low-level commander. He had to target a commander whose sudden death might throw them into confusion.

Just as with his own men, Gianavel knew that as long as they retained their discipline, they would be difficult to defeat. But when they lost their discipline, when they began fighting like individuals instead of a team, they were already half-defeated.

Silently sheathing the poniard, Gianavel angled through the thick stand of poplar until he moved parallel with the standard-bearer, who traditionally stood beside the commander in chief. After Gianavel killed the sergeant, who truly controlled the riflemen, Captain Mario would be next, and then the standard-bearer. He turned his head, gazing across the narrow ravine.

Within one hundred feet, Bertino would open the first volley. Then events would move quickly, and there was no way to predict the enemy's reaction. To charge uphill was certain doom, but to dig into a bad position was little better.

Bent and silent, Gianavel moved alongside the center battalion, his eyes darting from the detachment to the path before him with each step. He avoided twigs and stones and only lightly moved branches that brushed silently over his wool shirt and pants.

He heard the first volley.

Plumes of white smoke erupted on the slope as men began shouting in terror and confusion, and Gianavel's musket rose as he fell into a crouch, searching over the sights for the first man who dared to shout a command and die.

)oo(◈)oo(

Mario drew his sword as the sergeant major spun and thundered for the men to—

With the sound of a meat cleaver smashing through ribs and flesh, the sergeant staggered.

Mario stared for what seemed an amazingly long moment as the sergeant's face relaxed, eyes glassy with redness flooding over his face through a white portal of brain and bone where his forehead had been. Strangely, his sword seemed to make no sound as it clattered on the stones, bouncing soundlessly beyond a boulder.

Dead?

In shock Mario searched the slope and saw for the most fleeting fraction of a second a shadow racing high through the woodline. He shouted and pointed frantically for those around him to *do something,* but they were firing in every other direction. When Mario looked again, the shadow was gone and another shot—a lot of them—erupted from the ridge to drop men by platoons.

Pointing with his sword, he cried, "There, you fools!"

Uncoordinated, they fired high and low and wide, strafing the forest with a blistering barrage that tore limbs from trees and vaporized leprous white rocks of the slope while the slope above them still thundered with rifle fire—they had hit little or nothing.

"Devils!" Mario shouted and found himself retreating with others who had thrown their rifles aside for the advantage of speed. He raised his saber to—

The bullet that struck his saber snapped the thin blade in half and sent it spinning end over end.

Mario was not even aware he'd dropped the jagged grip as he staggered back in shock.

If Gianavel's concentration had been one iota less, he would have been amazed that the commander's sword deflected his bullet before it reached his forehead, but there was no time for thoughts of anything but action. Moving deliberately but quickly, Gianavel recharged his first rifle and didn't waste a second to replace the rod.

Captain Mario, eyes wide and wild, had cast the broken sword aside and held pistols in both hands.

In the same breath that Gianavel sighted, he fired. Mario shouted as he fell back, disappearing behind a boulder. The Captain of Rora ducked back as others saw him and opened up.

The bullets that struck the tree could be felt to the other side, and Gianavel waited to let the second volley pass harmlessly through the woods about him. Then he dropped his second rifle and launched himself forward, running toward the front of the battalion. He had killed the captain and sergeant major, but there would be others who might rally the force.

Everything was fully alive—every leaf was distinct with its own shade and motion, every branch was skeletal and clear before him, outlined to the faintest twig as he ran. His breath was without effort or thought, and he was aware that everything was vivid to his eyes. He knew how many steps he would need to reach his destination, how much strength it would require, how he would drop, where his hands would be reaching—powder and ammunition and patch.

It was the kind of mind speed that comes only when the mind instinctively shuts out all emotion and worries, forcing everything not vital for survival to the sides, dominating with a power that only emerges in dreams or death.

Gianavel felt sixteen—*sixteen, his mind counted*—shots tear through the trees about him, most missing widely but one sailing inches behind his back—no threat. Then he dropped beside another oak, uncorked his powder horn, scanning. In seconds he reloaded and saw a man carrying a sword. He aimed, waiting to see if the man was in charge. He was.

Gianavel fired.

Another down, and then Bertino's thick form was visible on the distant ridge, not so far by the yard but a long path if one climbed up from the ravine. The huge farmer threw a small barrel.

Burning fuse!

Gianavel dove behind the tree and opened his mouth to the tremendous concussion of the powder keg, and then smoke billowed like a wheat field afire with oil. Huge plumes of black blotted out the sun in seconds, night beneath day.

He didn't need to look to know that the third company, largely untouched by the battle and led by at least two captains and a half-dozen sergeants, was stampeding up the pass, fiercely determined now to charge the slopes. And although they would certainly incur heavy losses, they would more than likely reach the ridge.

Gianavel saw Bertino's thick form on the opposite slope and hailed him, dangerously exposing his position. But Bertino was unaware that the third company was charging.

Dropping to a knee, Gianavel aimed carefully and fired, hitting a tree trunk. The big man shouted at the impact and then bellowed to those around him. But even as they aimed, Bertino recognized Gianavel and shouted for them to hold fire.

Gianavel gave the sign to retreat.

Bertino obeyed without question. With only a terse word to the others, he turned and vanished into the trees.

Gianavel raced down the slopes, ignoring the dead and the wounded and the smoke and the flame, knowing they had to prepare a secondary defense to hold the village against these last three hundred who would be upon them in seconds.

✕✕✕◈✕✕✕

Mario glared about angrily, his hand reflexively grasping his upper arm where the bullet had struck. He didn't remember being hit, only falling back. When he finally reached his feet, the entire ravine was black with smoke, and the company was racing forward with pikes lowered.

He staggered into the wave not because of courage but because he was less a target among many than alone. They didn't slow as they passed the remains of the first company, nor did anyone offer aid. Then they were rushing down the slope toward the village that loomed beyond, riflemen already firing.

Chaos was visible as the third company climbed a slope that seemed stunningly difficult to Mario, and then they reached the farthest outskirts of Rora—scattered clusters of huts that were being quickly evacuated but not quickly enough.

The greater portion of Rora stood within reach, if they could quickly make their way through this poorer section of the township and take the bridge. Victory was within his grasp.

Mario saw his men killing everyone not quick enough to gain the bridge—young, old, women, children, babies, strong men. All fell alike under sword or rifle or bayonet, but he wished for the company to move forward far more quickly. He bellowed orders to leave the dead where they lie and to continue the assault.

117

Obviously, these people, perhaps two hundred, would not abandon the village unless all hope was lost. Which was wise; they stood far less chance of reaching one of the caves than of holding a fortified position, and many were too old and feeble to even make the attempt. Yes, they would retreat only when they had no more chance of holding this ground—their very homes.

They neared a bridge that led into the better-built section of the township when suddenly Mario felt the hairs stand on the back of his neck and saw the same shadow—*the same man* he had seen on the slopes—the man who almost killed him.

Alone, sword in hand, the man boldly stood on the far end of the bridge. His countenance and his stance made it clear that he would not let them pass. He stood, watching.

Waiting.

✕∞✕◈✕∞✕

Gianavel did not even blink as the three hundred men charged through the already burning remnant of the village, closing quickly on the bridge. He looked at Bertino, concealed within a doorway, and nodded once. Bertino also nodded. They were ready.

With no time to devise an elaborate defense, Gianavel and those with him had reached the bridge only seconds ahead of their attackers. Unable to reinforce the poorer section of the village, they had been unable to stay that massacre. But all was not yet lost. If they could stop them here, then the larger portion of Rora—including all the field hospitals—would be saved.

Unmoving, Gianavel watched as the infantrymen narrowed like sand through an hourglass, crossing the bridge. When they were less than one hundred feet away, he raised his sword, and windows above him erupted with rifle fire.

Pikemen sprawled face first across cobblestones, but those in the rear did not hesitate. Trampling down the bloody bodies, obviously electing speed as the greatest element of safety, they threw themselves into a frantic charge.

Gianavel leaped to the side as they rushed toward him, and baskets stacked behind him were cast aside. The Captain of Rora could only imagine what the attackers beheld in that instant.

Grinning and holding a torch in one hand, Hector was bent over a demi-cannon. On his flanks, two forty-pounders were aimed dead into the heart of the regiment.

What Gianavel did see were twenty men dropping pikes and turning to retreat, only to be pushed backward, since those behind them were slower to arrive at the sight.

Then the street exploded with the force of a volcano, and entire buildings vanished behind roiling clouds that reached almost to the face of their disappearing attackers. Gianavel gazed out to see heaps of bloodied corpses strewn across the entire length of the street and bridge rails.

On the far side of the creek, commanders instantly began bellowing furious commands to attack, to attack, to overwhelm by sheer superiority of numbers. But no one wanted to be the first into that horrendous grapeshot that dismembered men like insects, leaving arms and legs scattered unrecognizable amid bodies split and torn.

Bertino raised his rifle in the air as those in the windows erupted in taunts and jeers, and Gianavel grabbed the big man's arm.

"We don't have enough cannon fire to hold them!" Gianavel shouted above the din. "We'll take them twelve at a time with rifles as they advance!"

Bertino nodded and grabbed men close to him, repeating the instructions as Gianavel reached a stairway. In moments he was on the second floor, positioning men behind overturned furniture that strengthened the walls against muskets. He assigned them to specific angles because each man had only a limited view of the street.

"Each man has an angle, like a pipeline, on the street below! With all the angles together, we have the street covered. Each man must shoot only what is within his pipeline! Do not pursue a man if he gets past your pipe! Don't try for a man who hasn't reached you! Shoot only what's in front of you! Do you understand?"

They nodded together.

Gianavel turned to the window.

The battalion was advancing twelve abreast, but there was no space between rows. It was like a solid black snake flowing across the bridge. In the background, commanders had mounted horses for a better view of the conflict.

"Be ready," Gianavel said sternly. "Don't shoot until they're across the bridge."

They waited as the men neared.

Nervous eyes glanced at Gianavel.

"Wait," he whispered.

The drum of boots was muffled as the soldiers strode over the bodies of those who had fallen, and some of the bodies cried out painfully. Then they were over the worst and continued steadily.

"Fire!" Gianavel shouted, and every window and doorway hurled musket balls into the ranks, dropping those in front, who were replaced instantly by those behind. Then another volley was fired and another, and another, and still they came, shoulder to shoulder with rifles and pikes held high.

"Fire!" Gianavel shouted again and again, and musket balls were redoubled. But still, the army grew inexorably closer.

Then a single man, young and covered in soot, began to rise, and Gianavel grabbed him forcefully by the shoulder, pressing him back into position at the window. If one broke, they might all break. And a retreat was difficult to stop once it began.

Gianavel snatched a rifle against the wall and shoved it into the boy's hand. His words sliced through the tension, making all of them more afraid of him than their enemy.

"We hold them or we die! Look! Your wives and children are behind you! How will you take them with you?"

No one answered as Gianavel stalked across the window to see the column advancing against the death that plummeted the ranks like rain. But behind them, beyond those who, doubtless, already reckoned themselves dead, the troop thinned, hesitated.

Every window and door continued to erupt without pause to drop five, six, ten men at a time, and the column was shortened with each stride, rising higher on the bodies of the slain. Then a single man broke and ran, fleeing for the far side of the bridge. The fact that a sergeant killed him in stride should have affected the rest, but either they didn't see or didn't care. In a moment more they overwhelmed the sergeant as he struck fiercely with his sword to cut down all deserters. At the last it was a full rout with rifles tossed aside and pikes cast into the river like so much kindling. Amid shouts of victory, Gianavel raced to the bottom floor of the tavern.

Bertino turned to him, a smile creasing his face—a smile that instantly faded as he saw the black rage masking their captain's face. Bertino needed no words but snatched up his rifle and called out to the others, "It's not over! Come on!"

Gianavel paused only a moment, but it was necessary because the last, and most difficult, task would spread them over miles of forest, and it would be impossible for him to oversee their actions.

"They'll try for the ravine to Turin!" he shouted and slung three rifles over his shoulder. He paused for the briefest moment, staring over them. No one flinched.

"Come!" he shouted, and as they cleared the door, they broke in a long, loping run that took them at a right angle to the ravaged remains of the retreating battalion.

Bertino drew parallel to him, a flintlock in each square fist, arms swinging the stocks like a man thrashing wheat. In less than thirty seconds, his face was twisted with exhaustion. "What's the plan?"

Gianavel said nothing as he leaped a log and continued without a break in stride. Finally he yelled, "We catch them in the ravine and kill as many as we can!"

Bertino fell back and passed the word, and they closed quickly on the ravine. They heard subdued shouts in the distance, the bellows of dying men who were afraid to die. Then they arrived at the ravine, staring down at the path below.

So completely was the ravine hedged by rock that an antelope could not have found a quick path to evade the destruction delivered the battalion from above—more men were killed by boulders than the hail of bullets that descended point blank.

As Gianavel lifted his rifle, they heard the shouts of men coming quickly, frantically, stumbling headlong with injured shouts, and they moved to the edge to see them streaming below, shoving one another aside to race for the front.

Gianavel twisted his head to Bertino and nodded.

"Now!" the big farmer shouted and set his shoulder against a boulder.

Almost instantly it broke from its mooring and rolled down the face with a cascading sound of granite crushing bush and stone alike. Only at the last, seconds before it crashed murderously into the ravine, did those beneath it understand. They had time for one howl of terror before they were crushed down.

And then there were more howls, more pleas for mercy as more boulders, rocks, and logs descended in a cascading avalanche of fury that drowned out all petitions for peace, and dust rose from the pit like a flood of steam unleashed within hell itself.

When it was over, Gianavel stood stoically at the lip of the cliff, dust rising past him in pillars and plumes, hiding what carnage lay beneath.

Bertino moved beside him, shook his head. "We killed them all."

Gianavel was implacable. His face was pale with fatigue, and his hands were open and relaxed. Only his eyes revealed the fierce fighting mind that had commanded the day.

"No," he said. "Not all."

He pointed at distant figures, astonishingly few in number, staggering across the rolling plain of wheat that led to Turin. They were wounded, weaponless, and easy prey should Gianavel decide to overtake them.

"Should we finish them?" Bertino rumbled.

"No. It's enough."

"Enough for what?"

Hesitating, Gianavel seemed to carefully weigh his response, as if he knew it would be laid on a scale where God would judge the violence of his hand against a measure unknown. "Enough to establish justice," he said and then sighed, holding it a long time before raising his face to the sky, eyes closed.

Now, indeed, a fatigue greater than the mere physical was visible. The pure fighting fury so inspiring only moments earlier was banked—something he shut down at once to leave only a white pallor, a sickness of the soul. He was no longer a deliverer of justice in a land besieged by evil men but simply a man—a father, husband, friend.

"Let's go," he said somberly and turned away. "We've killed enough men for the day."

⟩⟩⟩◈⟨⟨⟨

Cloaked in the habitual black suit that he wore even in private, the man stood with a single arm folded across his chest, staring pensively out the towering window of his private chamber. Uncommonly, he was alone and unguarded. Not even a servant stood in the arched entrances that gaped on the far side of the utterly silent chamber. Nor were there the distant sounds of cavalry, guardsmen, carriage, or the din of transit.

His face was decidedly militaristic—stern, disciplined, deeply lined by pain and determination. His physiognomy was half a head less than six feet, but he was solidly, though not heavily, built. A carefully maintained goatee and mustache framed his frown, and his eyes were like heated stones with the thinnest sheaths of ice. And not much was required, it was well known, for the eruption of volcanic heat that would blast the ice into shards with fearsome rage and imperious will.

He turned as boots thudded on the far side of his chamber. His face revealed nothing but calculated assessment as the man walked forward; then he dropped his arm and extended his gloved hand.

"We have much to discuss," he spoke, as if there had been no question of the man's arrival. "Please pardon me if I proceed quickly past pleasantries."

Oliver Cromwell, the Lord Protector of England, walked to the hearth, and the man followed thoughtfully. As formal in private as in public, Cromwell began, "Understand that I have prayed a great deal over this mission. It is quite dangerous and…important in a manner that is difficult to describe."

"I'm humbled," Sir William Lockhart said to the uncrowned King of England.

Lord Cromwell's mind, both in war and diplomacy, was difficult to anticipate, and even more difficult to endure, though the old man had mellowed considerably over the years. His greatest strength was his sincere conviction that God created him to fight a truly righteous war. His greatest flaw was searching for it.

Lord Cromwell stared over Lockhart as if he could somehow divine his thoughts. "Tell me, my son, if you are fearful. My final mind will be established by your words."

As England's greatest monarch, Cromwell's native genius and imperial will had saved the island in a dozen desperate battles. His daring night-march to win the battle of Dunbar—outnumbered ten to one with no chance of retreat if the tide had turned—was already the rubric of legend. As well as his cataclysmic rage, which had once dissolved Parliament in a single memorable confrontation.

It occurred not so long ago when Cromwell suspected betrayal by select members of the body. Still wearing his nightclothes, he stormed into the midnight meeting of England's ambassadors and seized command to send a hundred horrified and appalled emissaries fleeing for their lives. The next morning, a quick-witted secretary hung a sign in the front window: "Building empty, open for Lett."

And thus was born yet another epic tale to be told and retold in the chronicles of Oliver Cromwell. How much was truth and how much was enhanced by enemies was impossible to divine, but safe to say that the Lord Protector had, almost single-handedly, altered the course of England. And, as ever, his rage was born from his most deep-seated commitment—a commitment even greater than his patriotism. For even as Cromwell's devotion to England was titanic, his devotion to God was equally so. And for years, it was well known, the great Lord Protector had sought a final war so that he might die as he'd lived, fighting for a righteous cause in the name of God.

None of Cromwell's exploits or convictions were unknown to the Scotsman as he shifted the Spanish sword at his waist. He rested his hands on the cushioned scarlet arms of the chair and measured the wrath that boiled not far beneath the surface of the great commander.

"I would only like to know why you requested my services and not those of another," Lockhart asked calmly. "I am primarily a soldier, not a man of intrigue."

Cromwell paused to light a cigar—despite judgments of those outside their religion, Puritans relished their tobacco and port—and dismissed a long stream. He held the ember delicately, more like a priest than a soldier. Then he leaned back, seeming to form his entire dialogue before he spoke the first word.

"Sir Lockhart, you were taken into my protectoral family through your marriage to my niece, Robina. But make no mistake—many are within that circle. I choose you because you have proven your courage and fidelity and worthiness on the battlefield. You are a Scot of an honorable house and respected by both commoner and nobility for your wisdom and physical courage. You are also a man of great native intellect and gifted with powers of intuition that I consider invaluable. And most importantly, you have earned my trust."

Sir Lockhart nodded. "Honored, My Lord."

"Three weeks ago," Cromwell continued as if that were obvious, "I received alarming rumors of war in the valley of Piedmont. Are you familiar with these people—the Waldenses?"

"Yes, My Lord. I know of the Vaudois, as the French call them. They are an ancient people and, despite persecutions within Italy, well respected and received by our Church."

With a satisfied nod, Cromwell explained, "I do not know what grim tragedy may have befallen these people, whose only offense is refusing to renounce the Christian faith that they have held for centuries, but my best reports indicate severe massacres and slaughters of almost biblical proportions."

Lockhart did not mask his concern. "For centuries the Catholic Church has striven to destroy the Vaudois, My Lord, because they do not accept the regency of the pope."

"I have told Admiral Blake to design a plan of invasion," Cromwell said flatly.

Sir Lockhart's eyes flared before he managed to suppress the bad form.

Standing solemnly before the hearth, Cromwell folded both hands behind his back in a composure that would belie the most believable tale of his infamous wrath. He spoke with profound somberness and quiet conviction. "This is your task, Sir Lockhart. Catholic France is losing her war with Spain. Meanwhile, the Catholic Church is winning its war with the Waldenses. I propose that we change the destinies of both wars with a single gambit." Cromwell stared down his prominent nose. "A gambit that you, alone, must play."

After a pause, Lockhart glanced over his shoulder.

"Never do that," mumbled Cromwell. "If you wish to become invisible, move to where everyone can see you and smile at everyone you greet."

Lockhart smiled. "Of course, My Lord."

"Your task is to journey alone to France. You are to make acquaintance with Cardinal Mazarin, who is both mentor and master of the boy-king, Louis XIV. You are to *somehow* convince Cardinal Mazarin that he must intercede on behalf of the Waldenses and force the Duke of Savoy to end his war."

Sir William Lockhart didn't blink. "Somehow?"

Cromwell's outburst of laughter lightened the atmosphere like the sun breaking through clouds. "Yes, my boy—somehow. But I shall not leave you marooned. Let me tell you how to achieve this."

"Please."

Hands once more at his back, Cromwell began to pace. "Mazarin was defeated in his bid for pope by the Italian cardinals, who jealously aligned against him. He has no love for Italy.

"His recent war against the nobles of France during the Frond also gives him no love for his country. So Mazarin's first and greatest loyalty is to Louis, whom he loves like a son. Therefore his chief concern is the security of his throne. And this is what you will use to our advantage."

After a still pause, Lockhart ventured, "You propose an alliance with France to defeat the Spanish?"

Cromwell paced steadily. "France does not possess the fleet to defeat the Spanish Armada. Mazarin is no fool. He has negotiated enough peace settlements to know he is doomed. Therefore, he will consider what England's Royal Navy can achieve for him."

"For a price," Lockhart offered.

Cromwell waved off any concern. "The good cardinal is a practical man; he knows he must give if he is to receive. And this is what we shall offer. If Mazarin will exert his considerable influence to persuade the Duke of Savoy to end this war against the Waldenses, England will align with France to defeat the Spanish Armada. We shall have what we want, and the good cardinal shall have what he wants."

"What if Mazarin objects because the Vaudois are not the children of France, and technically not his responsibility?"

"They are children of *God*," Cromwell said more sternly. "Think of what has befallen these people! And if it befalls them, it can befall *us*! There is no reason why this religious persecution cannot spread beyond the borders of Piedmont, and that is a danger that threatens us all.

"Think, my boy; the Crusades began with a noble cause, but that cause was quickly lost amid competing interests for land and dynasties. And after they betrayed God, the Crusaders were struck down and strewn across the desert like chaff, obliterated by the combined hosts of the South." He became abruptly still and delicately touched his forehead. "I am not reluctant to admit, Sir Lockhart, that even many of my own campaigns have been impure because of questionable national interests that I had to oblige in the course of political process. Even worse, I remember the guilt and regret that engulfed me the morning after the Battle of Drogheda when I saw a living baby at the breast of its dead mother."

Like a tide trapped within a cove, churning the surface white with competing currents, Cromwell's face flushed with conflicting emotions, and his eyes glazed with a faraway vision or memory. "Believe my words, boy: What a man bears from the battlefield can be tenfold the horror of the battle itself."

In utter stillness, Lockhart followed every grimace, even seemed to follow every thought that plunged through the dark and fiery mind. Finally he spoke as soldier to soldier. "Even when a man bears the sword for God, My Lord, only God knows the destiny of it."

Cromwell smiled wryly, then leaned forward, staring across the polished floor to the Scotsman. "But never, my son, have I ever seen a more righteous cause than what is before us today. The Waldenses have surrendered their land and their allegiance to the Duke of Savoy. In all ways, they are his loyal subjects. Only their faith remains, and for this…men will kill them."

Lockhart revealed nothing as Cromwell added, "How, pray tell, can you destroy a man's faith?"

Morose, Lockhart shook his head.

"You cannot," the Lord Protector of England intoned. "You can only destroy the man, and then all those who know him or know of him. Then you burn his home and hope you have completely erased his memory from the land. And yet this is not a single man. This is an entire nation—an entire *nation* sentenced to death simply because they refuse to surrender their faith to the Catholic Church."

Silence hushed the room as neither man moved. Then Cromwell spoke gravely. "So what will you do, my son? What must be done must be done in secret without history to honor the true measure of your sacrifice. The wounds you may suffer will not be rewarded by pensions. Your courage will not be rewarded by advancement. No, in this, the only honor you receive shall be from God."

The muscles in Lockhart's jaw tightened as he turned his face toward the flames, considering. Then, as if in amazement, he shook his head. But Cromwell was smiling when he raised his gaze.

"I accept," he said.

9

INCOMEL'S AGITATED PACING PROVOKED a sadistic laugh from Pianessa. Replacing the wine bottle on the banquet table, the marquis seemed far less disturbed by today's defeat.

Torches outside the Duke of Savoy's palace burned the pale color of frost in a soundless, utterly black night without sky or stars. Rather, it was as if the darkness began here and expanded infinitum to swallow sound and light without returning even the faintest echo or shadow in response. While within the Great Hall itself, the least sound seemed fragile and false, and every torch seemed to flicker for strength.

It was a mood that suited Pianessa. He smiled as he sipped from a tall glass of red wine that cast shifting scarlet hues—a complex, alternating spectrum, all the color of blood.

"You seem surprised, Inquisitor," he muttered to Incomel. He nodded also to Corbis, who also stood in his usual mute, piggish posture. "Rather unbecoming for a man of war."

Incomel's anger was transparent. "I am not a man of war, Pianessa. I am a man of the Church. And you are the general of this idiotic campaign. What are you going to do?"

One side of Pianessa's mouth curled. "I was waiting for you to give orders. Is this not a holy war?"

"It is a war fought by men for the glory of God," Incomel answered bitterly. "The Waldenses must be destroyed because they corrupt the entire valley with their witchcraft and Manichaean doctrines. Already we have lost members of the Church to this madness." He walked farther. "And now we have lost a thousand men."

"At least," Pianessa commented mildly. "But that isn't the worst of it, Inquisitor."

Incomel froze. "What's the worst of it?"

Stone sober, Pianessa lifted the wineglass and tilted it before his face as if searching for what else might lie within its scarlet hue. "The worst of it, Inquisitor, is that now I must order the entire militia of Piedmont into the field."

"What is so terrible about that? Perhaps that's what you should have done from the beginning."

The smile faded slowly from Pianessa's face. "I thought," he spoke slowly, deliberately, "that it was a shepherd's responsibility to defend his sheep against wolves. But you sound more like a wolf."

The Inquisitor's chest rose with indignation.

Brooding, Pianessa muttered, "You know something, Priest?"

"What, Pianessa?"

"I don't believe that I believe in your God."

Incomel's eyes flared; Corbis turned his hairless head toward the Inquisitor General.

Pianessa laughed. "Oh, I believe in God, Inquisitor. I just don't believe in the God you profess. In fact, I would say that you are much more a politician than a priest."

What the marquis had said, if there had been three witnesses instead of two, was punishable by burning at the stake. But, though peasants could be executed without legal procedure, the same could not be done against a monarch. Calm, Pianessa waited as Incomel's instinct for self-preservation bitterly censured his words.

"You are a heretic, Pianessa," the Inquisitor said finally. "You are a godless man who will drown in his own blood. That is the portion of your cup in this."

Pianessa pursed his lips, considerate. "The portion of my cup... And what will be the portion of your cup, Inquisitor?" He waited; Incomel said nothing. "What will be your reward when the Waldenses are slaughtered from one end of this valley to the other? What great treasure will you find, Inquisitor, on Gianavel's mountain, when you roll away the stone?"

Incomel's jaw tightened.

"Let me tell you a secret, Inquisitor. You will find nothing but those Scriptures you quote so often." The Marquis de Pianessa waved vaguely. "Yes, yes, Gianavel will die, and you will claim the land. But the land will be here long after you and I return to dust, and who will possess it then?" Pianessa's eyes narrowed, calculating and merciless.

"Why don't you tell me," said the Inquisitor coldly.

Pianessa laughed out loud at Incomel's pale expression. "The Waldenses will possess it, Priest. Kill the Waldenses until your hand freezes to your sword. Kill them until the hills are bleached by their bones, and they will return, Priest. They will always return."

"How do you know this?"

"How do I know?" Pianessa laughed. "Your church has tried to destroy the Waldenses for centuries, and for centuries the Waldenses have endured." He gestured to the darkness of the ceiling. "You would do better to forbid the stars from the sky than to forbid the Waldenses from their land. Some things are and will remain so. And a wise man knows when not to kick against stones."

Incomel's gaze was like crushed ice sliding into the sea, flowing out to smother everything about it. "On my word, you will die a horrible death, Pianessa," he pronounced.

"By your hand?"

"No."

"By God's, then?" Pianessa lifted both hands as if in supplication. "Tell me, Inquisitor, why does your God not strike me down as I speak? Is it because He does not have the might? Or because the words I speak are true?"

Frustration was checked, but Incomel's words were openly venomous. "You are a barbarian."

Pianessa's laugh was like a demon's bark. Then he cut it short as Corbis stepped forward. The monk's white, hairless face and head were like a dolphin's snout twisted in a horrible scowl, and he approached to within a pace of Pianessa, who remained utterly motionless and calm. Amused, Pianessa cut his eyes to Incomel. "Can Noble Corbis not speak for himself?"

"I speak," interjected Corbis in a surprisingly high-pitched nasal tone, almost a whine. "You err, Pianessa."

Pianessa casually set his wineglass to the side, leaned back into his throne. Then he crossed his legs and smiled. "Please, Inquisitor, explain to me why men of God must rely upon men of war for their kingdoms."

Corbis stepped still closer. "You err because you believe you are beyond our power. But not even you are beyond us. Not you, nor the duchess with whom you have had…"

Erupting from his throne, Pianessa instantly towered black and mythic and horrifying, dominating the vastness of the Great Hall by the force of will alone. Corbis cried and staggered as Pianessa's armored right hand lashed out to close on the Inquisitor's thick forearm. His bellow descended with him as his knees buckled and Pianessa's iron fingers dug deeper and deeper, mercilessly grinding flesh and tendon against bone and *still* the fingers closed like a vice, his arm and shoulder immovable as a monument at Corbis's convulsive writhing.

The marquis' teeth gleamed savagely as he bent close over the helpless Inquisitor and whispered, "What happens, Inquisitor, when a man of war resists a man of God?"

Corbis's mouth hung in a silent scream. Pianessa's teeth parted like the fangs of a lion. "*This* is the only strength that matters!" he roared. "By the strength of my *sword* I gained my throne! *Never* think to take it from me! Do you understand?"

Corbis nodded quickly, mutely, and Pianessa turned his smoldering gaze upon the second Inquisitor. Incomel seemed content to ignore what could not be cured. Then Pianessa threw Corbis's forearm back, as if sullied by the touch.

"I will destroy Gianavel without the help of your God, holy man. I will destroy Gianavel with twenty thousand soldiers who will storm his mountain and kill everything that lives. And when the Waldenses are gone from this kingdom, Inquisitor, *you* had best be gone, as well! Remember my words."

Incomel did not blink. With hands folded placidly within his sleeves, he stared unaffected over Corbis, who yet cradled his forearm and rocked mutely.

Not deigning to cast the Inquisitor another glance, Pianessa growled as he mounted his throne and collapsed, as if he'd enjoyed a good laugh. He nodded and smiled. "You are correct, Inquisitor. I am indeed a barbarian, but I conceal it from no one. And you are a whitewashed tomb. But what will you do...what will you say...when the tomb is opened for all men to see?"

Without expression Incomel turned, and with steps cautious and soundless, he walked slowly down the long hall that terminated at the double doors and faded into the gloom.

Moaning, Corbis, too, rose and stumbled slightly as he retreated to a side exit. He made little more sound than a mouse as he opened and closed the door and was gone as well.

Only after the most distant retreating footsteps were gone did the Duchess Elizabeth visibly hover on the edge of shadow.

Pianessa did not turn his head toward her. "You saw?"

In almost perfect silence, she approached. "Priests who worship gold, and not God, are not unique enough to despise, my love. They are certainly not worthy of your wrath."

Pianessa's hands folded before his face, supporting his chin with elbows set solidly on his ironwood throne. His gaze was fixed on some nebulous cell of shadows.

"They are dogs," he muttered. "Holy men who depend on others to do their killing for them. They are not like this man—this Gianavel—who is willing to fight and die for what he believes." After a moment, he added, "A very dangerous man..."

Elizabeth considered the strange comment a moment, then, "Why do you say that, Pianessa?"

"Because...he believes."

"But he is only one man," Elizabeth protested. "How can he win a war that involves thousands upon thousands? This is not like old times, when a brave soldier could change the tide of battle by the strength of his sword. As any other man, he will fall if he is shot. "

With a sigh, Pianessa stood. He gazed upon her from his immense stature. "Even if Gianavel dies, he will win, Duchess. The only way to defeat him is to make him kneel."

The duchess blinked. "But you said you did not care if he knelt before the Inquisitors."

"I didn't," Pianessa agreed, "until today. But now I understand that Gianavel must, indeed, kneel before the Inquisitors. Not because of their Church, which means nothing. No, Gianavel must kneel because if he does not, then his people will fight long after he is gone. If I do not break his spirit, then his children will rise up and fight again. They will use his name for a battle cry. Everything will be an occasion for courage, and I will never know peace."

Silent, the duchess looked away.

Pianessa's dark eyes became opaque, utterly impenetrable and hardened against any light of the world. His face was the purest image of grim purpose. "I must destroy his faith," he said at last.

"But…how will you do that?"

Without removing his eyes from the darkness, Pianessa's teeth parted. "By finding what Gianavel loves with all his heart. Then I will destroy it…and destroy the man."

><><

Despite torches that moved steadily through the village, Gianavel could not help but sense the pale of pain that smothered the spirit of the people.

Although the troops had been repelled before they reached the more heavily populated brick and stone structures that comprised the richest area of Rora, the outlying homes, sprawled across surrounding hillsides and fields, had all fallen.

Gianavel shut down pangs of guilt. He had been forced to instantly select a site to make a desperate last stand against the battalion. He had chosen the bridge because it was the only ground where Captain Mario could attack six men abreast. He could not change what he had done, nor would he have done anything differently. And to lament what he could not have changed would do no good.

The carnage inflicted by Pianessa's troops, though brief in execution, was severe. Virtually every family lost someone, and the death toll was made even more horrible by the means in which they died. Babies had been thrown onto pitchforks, women and children raped, men set afire and dismembered and then set afire again and on and on.

It was shocking that the attackers had been so discontent to merely kill. No, simply killing was not satisfying enough. They had been determined to kill in the most hideous means possible, exhausting their imaginations for cruelty. Not only were the means of murder excessive, they surpassed any law on the Continent.

Even if, as law allowed, governments sentenced a man to die, there were codes of conduct and procedures established by tradition and common moral sentiment. No one, not even the quick-tempered Spanish, tortured prisoners to death en masse. It outraged the common people and achieved no purpose of justice. Even burning, prescribed for witches, was inflicted only because the penitent soul could not achieve salvation if the body were not utterly destroyed.

When Gianavel and his men reached the poorer village after the battle, they found parents and grandparents holding slaughtered children, weeping and wailing. Other children, now orphans, were being taken into the homes of survivors.

After leaving the section where the greatest part of the slaughter occurred, they stripped and loaded the bodies of their attackers into oxcarts, then took the bodies to be burned in a low-lying depression west of the bridge. Bertino, smoldering in anger, suggested spiking their heads along the valley rim, but Gianavel overruled. Being forced to kill a man was one thing, but to desecrate the body was a line he would not cross.

Insuring that his orders were strictly enforced, Gianavel felt both dismayed and heartened at the suffering and the courage of the people. The older generations bore it stoically and wasted little time on words. They knew pain would not fade quickly—experience had taught them that. The best way to deal with a tragic loss was to simply endure and forget what could be forgotten. By their example, those less experienced also set their hands to needful tasks and said little.

When Gianavel turned to the bridge, the dead soldiers, possibly two hundred in number, were gone. But the street was draped in black and heavy with the scent of copper. Angry pockholes scarred the buildings and bridge rails.

Stern with the violent emotion of battle and the heaviness of command, Gianavel approached Hector, whose white hair was now blackened with powder, and asked, "Are you certain we have left no one in the poorer sections?"

Hector nodded. "Oui, we have gathered the dead, and the soldiers are being burned."

"Burn the bridge as well."

Hector pointed to three of his men, who gathered buckets of coal oil and moved toward the bridge. In a matter of minutes, the village glowed and cracked with flames that reached hundreds of feet into the azure night. Heat from the conflagration warmed the streets, blistering them to a black that flaked and swirled at a rising wind drawn by the flames themselves. Then, in another hour it was over, and the bridge was a heap of blackened chunks heaped in the fast-flowing creek that plumed with white geysers of smoke, hissing like a volcano.

Gianavel watched as new gabions were planned and suitable men were appointed to maintain them. He turned into the village again, aware of the fearful eyes and glances that were lifted.

He understood what they were feeling. When the din of battle faded and ragged banners waved drearily over the dead, who even now clutched broken swords, and survivors remembered the fury of the fight against the rightness of the cause, it was difficult to find any meaningful purpose. Even if their cause was just, it did little to lift the horror of the fight, because to fight at all was too horrible.

He turned as a diminutive figure—Jacob—came racing across the square, holding a chunk of bread. He stretched out his arms when he was still far away, and Gianavel smiled as he lifted him. He held him close to his chest as Angela ran forward with the girls.

Her face was wet with tears that she hastily wiped on her sleeve. She embraced and kissed him fervently and then stood back, looking him over for wounds. There was blood on his sleeve—evidence of a cut gained by an action he did not remember—and she gazed into his eyes.

"It's nothing," he whispered and kissed her again. He hugged each of the girls in turn and lowered Jacob to the ground. "Where are you and the children staying?"

"Hector's home," she answered. "His daughters and about fifty more from the valley are with us. But some fled to the caves."

Gianavel's face twisted. "The caves can't be defended as well as the town. How many?"

"About twenty." Angela stood closer. "Should we send someone after them to—"

"No," Gianavel said curtly. "The fields are alive with Pianessa's troops. Even reaching the caves would be difficult. And if Pianessa's men discover them, they'll just build fires in the entrance and suffocate them." He released a hard breath. "There's nothing we can do for them right now. We have to fortify the town."

He gazed around and saw none of his men were close. Then he sat down wearily on a low wall, laying his rifle beside him. The children were close as he checked each of them for injury, but there was none.

Angela allowed the children to be comforted by Gianavel's presence; then she found a small chore that would occupy them for a moment and put them under the care of Hector's wife, known to everyone as far back as Gianavel could remember as Aunt Felice. Finally Angela was alone with him for the first time since the battle.

"How many did we lose?" Gianavel asked somberly.

"We don't know for certain. I know we lost more than fifty children." She paused as he closed his eyes. "I think we lost forty men and women, but some weren't killed."

"Where are they?"

"We're doing what we can for them." She shook her head, a monumental sadness emerging. "But there's nothing we can do. If God is merciful, He'll let them die quickly."

Gianavel drew Angela's head to his chest, and her arm wrapped around his back. There was not so much to say that they could not rest together.

Eventually the children wandered past, each toting an armful of food, wine, and blankets. Gianavel watched them until they entered Hector's house—a large, white one-story structure of poplar and stone—located diagonal to the fountain. It was one of the oldest homes in the valley, having stood for five hundred years.

Lifting her face, Angela looked over the people. "Everyone keeps asking me what is going to happen," she said quietly. "I don't know what to tell them."

Gianavel gazed over the people, aware that some were watching him also. "I don't know," he said. "We beat them back again, but they'll return."

"Tonight?"

He shook his head tiredly. "No."

"Why not?"

Gianavel sighed. "They can't climb the Pelice in the dark, and they lost nearly a thousand men. Yes, they'll be back, but they'll need time to reorganize."

"Meaning…more men."

He nodded, stared. "Yes. When Pianessa attacks again, he'll use his entire militia."

"How many men is that?"

Gianavel paused. "Maybe twenty thousand." He looked across the square at the villagers and shook his head. "There's a chance that I could take us over the mountains—just you, me, and the children. We might make it if we avoid the passes and move quickly. But…but there's no way to bring everyone with us."

Angela stared at him a long time, then at the people. She shook her head and whispered, "No."

They sat together in comfortable silence until Felice emerged from her house and the children sprinted across the square. When they were together again, Gianavel rose and they walked toward a small room off the house that Angela had prepared for them.

"A few hours," Gianavel said as he removed his weapons, laying them on a pile of hay. "Wake me before the moon rises."

"Sleep," she said and gave him a heavy wool blanket that he laid over straw. His hands lifted the trailing of his black cloak as Jacob ran forward and insinuated himself within it. And Gianavel laughed, lying back. Then the girls were there, too, and they piled together against their father.

Together they lay upon the straw, all of them close against Gianavel's chest as the night rumbled with a distant storm like an angry volcano—a force of nature that would soon darken the air with burning ash that would flood black through every home, every window and doorway and room where all the frightened held one another in their fear, destroying all those who lay within its wrath.

∞∞∞

Emmanuel reined his horse at the gate of the castle of Cardinal Fabio Chigi, calling down to the papal guards who stood against him with halberds. Then the gate was pushed open, and in another minute the Duke of Savoy entered a cavernous library that rivaled the secret archives of St. Peters. He saw Fabio Chigi, gray eyes staring without surprise, seated behind a dark desk heaped with opened tomes that were almost too heavy for a single man to transport.

Emmanuel did not remove his dust-caked riding cloak as he entered the warmth of the blazing fire. Cardinal Chigi gestured demurely to a silver platter with two silver goblets and a beautiful canter of red wine.

"Something for your thirst, Savoy," he said distinctly. "It is a long ride from Turin."

Emmanuel uncorked the canter, poured a goblet. "It was," he replied curtly.

"Is your escort also accommodated?"

Heedlessly wiping his mouth with his sleeve, a move more fitting to Pianessa's manners, Emmanuel lowered his goblet. "I brought no escort."

Fabio Chigi's slow smile was rich with amusement. "So, a secret enterprise. Or are others positioned in the alcoves?"

A frown turned Emmanuel's mouth.

Cardinal Fabio Chigi had been Simon's friend since as long as Emmanuel could remember, and when Simon spoke to him in the Great Hall of Turin, Emmanuel knew what he must do. Just as he realized, this visit was not a surprise. Fabio Chigi was never surprised, which is one of the reasons he had risen, in this age of covert alliances and misleading public poise, to the position of cardinal.

No, Cardinal Fabio Chigi had never publicly supported the Waldenses, but what he said in secret was unknown. Emmanuel was willing to risk much for the truth.

With uncommonly imperial bearing—uncommon because he had never felt comfortable as a monarch—Emmanuel stood over the aged priest.

"Not surprised?" he asked coldly.

Fabio Chigi smiled before he leaned back, placing the tips of his fingers before his face in a pyramid. "It is not often that I receive royal visitors in the night, Savoy. But no, it is not a surprise."

Emmanuel removed his cloak and draped it over the chair. He stared with distinct melancholy at the old man. Finally, "Well, if you're not surprised, then you know why I've come."

"Yes, Savoy, I know why you have come." He studied the young prince. "Nor am I surprised that you came by night, as did Joseph of Arimathea— a powerful ruler who also knew the truth but was unable to speak it during the day."

Emmanuel acknowledged the appropriateness of the allusion. "I know I am young, Cardinal Chigi, but—"

"Wisdom is not a benefit of years, but the soul."

Emmanuel paused. "What can I do?"

Fabio Chigi nodded, sighed. "What can you do?" he repeated slowly. "Indeed, Savoy, what can you do?" He rose stiffly and strolled around the desk. "Perhaps a better question, Savoy, is what *will* to do?"

"I want to end this war against the Waldenses."

"Why?"

"Because..." Emmanuel hesitated, "...because they are my people."

"Your people..." Cardinal Chigi repeated with a penetrating stare. "Yes, Savoy, they are, indeed, your people. And that is second evidence of your wisdom."

Emmanuel had ridden nearly thirty miles through a war-torn land without bodyguards. But if he had brought an escort, then word would have spread of his secret rendezvous. And, as Simon had taught, never reveal your mind until it is too late for your enemy to alter your designs. When he looked again at the cardinal, the old man stood before the fireplace.

"It is one thing to claim power over the dead," he mused. "It is another to make bones rise up and walk. A lesson, sadly, that the Church has never learned."

Emmanuel knew his thoughts were as nothing compared to experiences of the cardinal. It was not for lack of subtlety that he had vanquished both despots and tyrants to gain his kingdom.

To some, his alliances might have appeared the dealings of the devil. But Emmanuel knew better—knew that Fabio Chigi had forged the strongest alliance of fools because fools would not have joined him under the banner of wisdom. Or, as Simon had so eloquently put it, even the devil was deceived for the glory of God.

Fabio Chigi continued, "It was within these very halls that I first learned the nature of power, young Savoy. Lessons I learned beside Simon, who has trained you well." His gaze was cryptic. "So you realize things are not as they seem?"

"Yes," Emmanuel said openly. "I know that what you say in public and what you say in private are not the same, Holiness."

"Then you know a great deal more than most," he laughed. "Very well, then speak to me of the Waldenses. And speak freely—half-truths are not worthy of midnight confessions."

Emmanuel settled into his chair; his legs were truly beginning to ache as his body cooled. "I believe these Inquisitors want the land of the Waldenses. I believe that gold and power are their goals, not the glory of God. And I believe that you know these things, too. Just as I think you wanted me to say them to your face before you told me your mind. Now, Cardinal Chigi, with my own words you have cause to either destroy me or help me. I am within your power."

Fabio Chigi laughed. "My dear Savoy, now I understand why Simon had such hopes for you at such a young age. You were, and remain, worthy of his efforts."

Emmanuel did not move.

"Very well," the cardinal resumed, slightly ponderous, "let me explain your peril—it may be greater than you may suppose." He focused on

Emmanuel. "Your greatest threat, at the moment, is that the Inquisitors will not return lands assumed in this war. This would initiate a war with France and would likely destroy Piedmont. So, after removing a sizable treasure, Cardinal Benedict will graciously return all lands to your jurisdiction, insuring Piedmont's political stability."

Emmanuel sipped his wine.

"Next we will proceed with your throne," the cardinal continued. "For certain, your House cannot be deposed as the capital of Piedmont. Nor will the Inquisitors, within any scenario that I anticipate, attempt to establish a new prince. However, they might hope to gain a stronger foothold in your policies and decisions, which would be the same thing." He stared. "You are aware of these possibilities?"

"I'm aware."

The cardinal began once more to pace. "Good, now we will proceed to the third, and most difficult, consideration: How do you end this war against the Waldenses?"

"I don't know," Emmanuel said and sighed wearily. "I only know that I am…tired of watching my people get slaughtered. On *either* side of this war."

"You are no longer a boy, Emmanuel. You have become a monarch. And as a monarch you must accept the responsibility that men die by your commands."

"I accept my people dying for a cause, Holiness. Not for a senseless war that neither side can win."

"Then know that you must kill even more men to end this killing," the old man said calmly. "That is, tragically, the curse of war. To end the killing, you must kill. But you cannot fight like the rest; you must strike at the head." He paused. "Imagine the arms of an octopus, Savoy. The arms are many, and you could very well fight them forever before you were victorious. But that would be foolish. If you wish to end the fight, you must strike an octopus between the eyes. Strike for the brain, and the arms will die. An army is the same. If you wish to defeat a superior force, strike he who commands it—not in the field, but in truth. Strike for the man behind the general. Do you understand these things?"

Emmanuel was frowning. "Yes."

"Good, then let us proceed." He paced calmly, as if the steps improved his powers of reason. "Cardinal Benedict is not the fulcrum of this war."

"Who, then?"

"In time," the cardinal answered. "First, listen, and I will teach you wisdom. For wisdom, alone, will preserve you." He took a moment. "The most powerful player in this drama is Cardinal Guilio Raimondo Mazzarino of France. Only Mazarin can protect you…when you do what must be done."

"But Louis is King of France."

Fabio Chigi laughed. "Louis is only a child, Savoy. Think of what you are saying."

Emmanuel was only five years old when he became the Duke of Savoy, but his regent mother, the Duchess Christina, allowed him to participate in decision-making from the first. Still, he'd made no practical decisions until he was much older.

"Yes, of course. But how much influence does Cardinal Mazarin have in Italy? The Italian cardinals have shut him out of the Vatican. Even his own parliament tried to overthrow him in France."

Fabio Chigi shrugged. "Popular support is not as important as support of the nobles. And support of the nobles is not as important as the support of the military. Cardinal Mazarin has carefully built an extraordinary political machine that merges support from both factions. The common people might yet have dissident bones to pick, but they are not in a position to dictate political policy."

If that was Fabio Chigi's conclusion, Emmanuel certainly had no inclination to debate. Chigi had survived numerous wars during his tenure as cardinal and was intimately familiar with overthrowing old regimes and establishing new ones.

Leaning forward, the cardinal smiled. "Not the kind of games you prefer, Savoy?"

"No, Holiness."

"Nor I, but it is a game you must learn." He cupped his chin. "So, you wish to end the war against the Waldenses because they are under your sovereign and you would have mercy upon them."

"Yes."

"Yes, as I do. But this war will not end unless the Waldenses defeat the army of Piedmont, or the army of Piedmont is withdrawn from the field."

"If the Inquisitors order me to send Pianessa into the field, I cannot disobey without risking my throne. And if I lose my throne I will be no good to anyone, including the Waldenses." Emmanuel paused, shook his head. "I...don't know what to do."

The cardinal nodded compassionately. "It is a complex affair, but let me put it simply: The Inquisitors control your army. But Cardinal Benedict controls the Inquisitors. If the Inquisitors, then Cardinal Benedict, can be silenced, the end is near."

A stunned silence.

"Are you suggesting I *kill* Cardinal Benedict?"

"Of course not, Savoy."

"Oh."

"Competent assassins are far too difficult to find."

Emmanuel blinked at the wall.

"No," the cardinal reproved, "more subtle means must be used to abate Cardinal Benedict's appetite for war. Something beyond your power, and which cannot be traced back to your intrigues. Something…uncontrollable. Something…*English*."

"English!"

Fabio Chigi's gaze was trained on the young prince. "Have you not heard recent reports from England, my son?"

"No. Nothing useful."

"Have you not heard that Oliver Cromwell, that great, imperious, and somewhat unhinged Lord Protector of England is gravely incited over this mistreatment of the Waldenses?" The cardinal appeared surprised. "What of your spies, Savoy? Do they do nothing?"

Emmanuel grimaced. "Well, I have not yet designed a suitable network of reliable—"

"Foolish boy!" Fabio Chigi rebuked sternly. "Have you learned nothing from Simon?" Emmanuel slouched as the old priest walked to his desk and lifted a parchment. "This is a copy of a letter that is to be sent to Louis of France. It passionately pleads the cause of the Waldenses and begs for you to end this war."

Emmanuel could say nothing.

The cardinal did not hesitate: "It is composed by England's most revered poet, John Milton, in defense of Gianavel and his people. I will quote his words; 'In regard to the people of Piedmont, after a barbarous slaughter of persons of both sexes, and of all ages, a treaty of peace was concluded, or rather secret acts of hostility were committed, the more securely under the name of pacification." Cardinal Fabio Chigi turned to Emmanuel. "You know, of course, to what Milton refers?"

"Yes. The ancient treaty with the Waldenses, which grants them freedom of faith."

"Exactly." He renewed the letter: "'The conditions of the treaty were determined in your town of Pinerolo; hard conditions enough, but such as these poor people would gladly have agreed to, after the horrible outrages to which they had been exposed, provided that they had been faithfully observed. But they were not observed; the meaning of the treaty is evaded and violated by putting a false interpretation upon some of the articles and by straining others. Many of the complainants have been deprived of their patrimonies, and many have been forbidden the exercise of their religion. New payments have been exacted, and a new fort has been built to keep them in check, from whence a disorderly soldiery makes frequent sallies and plunders or murders all it meets. In addition to these matters, fresh levies of troops are clandestinely preparing to march against them; and those among them who profess the Roman Catholic religion have been advised to retire in time; so that everything threatens the speedy destruction of such as escaped the former massacres.'"

The cardinal took a deep breath, resumed: "'I do therefore beseech and conjure Your Majesty not to suffer such enormities, and not to permit (I will not say any prince, for surely such barbarity never could enter into the heart of a prince, much less of one of the Duke's tender age, or into the mind of his mother) those accursed murderers to indulge in such savage ferocity, who, while they profess to be the servants and followers of Christ, who came into the world to save sinners, do blaspheme his name, and transgress his mild precepts by the slaughter of innocent men. Oh, that Your Majesty, ver, and who ought to be inclined to use it, may deliver so

s from the hands of murderers, who are already drunk with

blood, and thirst for it again, and who take pleasure in throwing the odium of their cruelty upon princes. I implore Your Majesty not to suffer the borders of your kingdom to be polluted by such monstrous wickedness.

"'Remember that this very race of people threw itself upon the protection of your grandfather, King Henry IV, who was most friendly disposed towards the Protestants when the Duke of Lesdiguieres passed victoriously through their country, as affording the most commodious passage into Italy at the time, he pursued the Duke of Savoy in his retreat across the Alps. The act or instrument of that submission is still extant among the public records of your kingdom, in which it is provided that the Vaudois shall not be transferred to any other government, but upon the same condition that they were received under the protection of your invincible grandfather.'"

Almost reverently, Fabio Chigi laid the parchment upon the desk. Then he clasped his hands behind his back and stood with head bowed.

"Sublime loftiness," pronounced the cardinal. "John Milton sometimes falls to mere eloquence, but his casual nature is the magnificent. He can convince when conviction is needed, but it is his unique power to astonish."

Emmanuel released a breath, unaware that he had withheld it for so long. He required a moment to recover from the soaring eloquence that had dominated the chamber.

"Cardinal Mazarin is not unaware of your plight. You should receive an official transcript of this letter one week after it is accepted by Louis." Chigi paced again toward the hearth. "Your plan should be this; you must silence the most influential and powerful of the Inquisitors. Then you must—"

"And how do I do that?" asked Emmanuel.

The cardinal shook his head. "I don't have the answer to every dilemma, Savoy—use your imagination." As Emmanuel stared, Chigi continued, "Yes, you will silence the Inquisitors. Then you will note the extreme cost of this war to Cardinal Benedict and declare that you can no longer afford such foolishness. You will also reason that, should hostilities against the Waldenses continue, Cromwell will likely invade Piedmont and remove your kingdom from Italy's domain."

In stillness, Fabio Chigi measured the plan. "And *so*…you will silence the Inquisitors and use the excuse of a depleted treasury and the threat of an invasion by Cromwell against Cardinal Benedict. Mazarin will protect you from Benedict. Even Rome cannot remove your kingdom with Cromwell involved, and the Waldenses will be preserved." He was studious. "Quite simple, really, as intrigues go."

"How do you know I will be able to use Cromwell?"

"Because you receive a visitor on the morrow."

Emmanuel's voice was softer. "Who?"

"His name is Sir Samuel Morland. He is an ambassador of Cromwell and, like Cromwell, a Puritan. Morland has recently passed through the territory of the Swiss. He also will bring a petition from Cromwell penned by Milton. But what it contains, exactly, I have not discovered."

"I'm shocked."

Cardinal Chigi lifted a hand. "Unfortunately, my operatives, while dedicated, are not ubiquitous."

Only flames invaded the silence as Emmanuel gazed solemnly out the scarlet-draped window to the starless expanse beyond. It was odd that the sky was so devoid of light. But everything was dense and obscure, blending into inseparable gray.

"I doubt that Cromwell will threaten invasion," Emmanuel said quietly. "He would risk war with the French, and he has not long finished his war against the Irish." He became studious. "No, Cromwell will not invade."

"Perhaps," said Cardinal Chigi, bringing his fingers together in a pyramid, "perhaps not. But you miss the point, my boy."

Emmanuel sighed. "What's the point?"

"The strength of a threat is *not* in whether it will be executed. The strength of a threat is in whether you *believe* it will be executed." Chigi smiled, letting that settle. "Cardinal Benedict's ambitions reveal him, Emmanuel. He mercilessly exterminates the Waldenses, but for what reason? Never in history have these poor mountain people been a danger to anyone—not even to Rome. Indeed, left to themselves, they are peaceful, industrious, and almost utterly devoid of corruption. So what do they possess that others desire? Certainly, not political influence. What else remains?"

"Wealth." Emmanuel shrugged. "Everyone knows that the Waldenses, while they are not rich, are prosperous because of their agriculture. They work hard. Their valleys are fertile. They always have plenty to pay taxes."

"So why doesn't Cardinal Benedict end this war for a large sum of gold coin?"

Emmanuel stared back. "I don't know. Why doesn't he?"

With a laugh, Fabio Chigi bent forward. "There are two means of satisfying a man's greed, Savoy. The first means—give him all the gold he desires. But, as you know, that becomes expensive. The second means is far easier to accomplish."

"Which is?"

"To threaten the loss of what gold he already possesses."

Emmanuel considered it. "Threaten the loss of the gold he already possesses…And how, exactly, do I accomplish that?"

The aged cardinal became more sober. "You are not alone, Savoy. The Waldenses themselves must play a part in his drama. They must frustrate Pianessa's army. They must make this war too expensive—even for you."

Emmanuel seemed as if he'd aged ten years in aspect and tone. "So, even if I wisely play my part, it still comes down to the Waldenses."

Grave, the cardinal nodded.

"Yes," Emmanuel muttered. "And so this man, Gianavel—outnumbered a thousand to one—must hold Rora against Pianessa's army until Cromwell's invasion looms on the horizon. Then I must silence the Inquisitors and pray that Mazarin will protect me from Benedict. And this war shall have an ending."

Fabio Chigi smiled with compassion.

"Now you understand the game you play, Emmanuel.… I suggest you play it well."

10

GIANAVEL DID NOT KNOW from what decimated corners of Piedmont the people came, but they came in great numbers, bearing blankets and clothes and provisions—some with freshly killed cattle, sheep, or antelope, others with weapons. Watching from the second floor of Hector's home, where Angela had moved their belongings to be out of the path of new arrivals, he estimated the refugees at two hundred men, women, and children. Most had fled with what little they could carry. Their pale, haggard faces and bloodied feet testified to what suffering they had endured to reach this place.

The Alpine peaks, even in summer, were unforgiving. The calcite cliffs could easily slice through shoes and even boots. And the huge slopes allowed no place to bind the bleeding, which resulted in long bloody paths that ascended from view, the remains of those who struggled across the crest. The mountain had no allies, and past wars recorded more men killed by the cliffs themselves, caught in a sudden storm or darkness or avalanche, than by cannons and bullets.

In 1554 an entire battalion of French pikemen, intent on destroying the Waldenses, became lost on the face of the Castelluzo and were almost entirely destroyed before daybreak. The story of the horror that befell them as men began to panic, precipitating avalanches of entire platoons, remained a cautionary lesson to all invaders. And since that event, army after army had avoided a direct onslaught against the cliffs, knowing prudence would allow a better occasion.

Watching the arrivals, Gianavel was concerned about a report that criminals, and even select Vaudois, had been handsomely paid to lead a surprise attack upon Rora along the little-known trails. But he could detect nothing overtly suspicious or curious about the stragglers.

Still, as a precaution, he had ordered all those who possessed the knowledge and ability to navigate the trails to serve as scouts. Sent out in pairs, they encircled the valley, each independent of the other. None knew the other's movements, none could take authority over the other, and all were watching the next, insuring that no one betrayed their planned paths of retreat.

Now he had only to organize and train the army God had given him and fight what battle came. Brooding, he turned from the window to Angela and said nothing as he walked to the bed and collapsed onto his back, arms outstretched.

Resting a hand upon his chest, Angela lay beside him. Her voice was subdued. "Are you afraid?"

Eyes narrowing at the ceiling, Gianavel sighed. "Yes…I'm afraid."

"No one believes that you know fear," she added. "They call you the 'Lion of God.'"

Gianavel pulled her closer. "If a commander is afraid, his men sense his fear and lose heart. If a leader fights boldly and without fear, his men take courage from his courage."

"I wonder, sometimes," she whispered, "why it has to be you? Why does the man I love, the father of my children, have to be the one to stand against this...this darkness."

Gently, Gianavel tightened his arm around her shoulders.

"It isn't fair," she said.

Silence lengthened.

"No," Gianavel said quietly. "It isn't."

"I wish I had some answer to all my questions."

He shook his head minutely. "There's no answer to any of this—not that I can see." He paused. "The cause of suffering... If men do not suffer, then they don't know hope. If they don't know hope, then they don't know faith. And without faith they don't come to know God. But the Earth is sufficient for hardship. It doesn't need the assistance of man. So I say that suffering caused by man is evil, because it has no higher purpose than man himself."

A knock at the door.

Gianavel arose. "Come."

The door swung open and Aunt Felice stood with hands at her sides. She smiled. "Boin matin, signore. Captains Laurentio and Jahnier have arrived."

Gianvael nodded. "Tell them I'll be down in a moment."

"Oui." The old woman quietly closed the door. As her footsteps descended on the stairway, Gianavel donned his saber, two flintlock pistols, a long dagger, and ammunition pouch. He slid a long poniard into each knee-high boot and a bellypistol into a leather harness inside his left sleeve. Last, he lifted his necklace—a golden cross suspended on a leather strap—around his neck.

With Angela, Gianavel knelt beside the bed, firmly holding her hand. Eyes closed, he prayed, "Lord, give me lucidity of thought to do rightly.

Guard me from snares laid by my enemies so that I will not dishonor you. Protect my dear Angela and our children from our enemies. And if it be Thy will, bring an end to this fighting. Amen."

"Amen," said Angela and then she hugged Gianavel fiercely and longer than usual. "I love you," she whispered.

Gianavel held her for as long as he could allow and then gently pulled her arms from his neck, cupping her face close with both palms. "I'll always come back to you."

Angela closed her eyes as Gianavel stood and pulled her up, and together they walked from the room and into the rising cacophony of the room below.

The chorus of colliding voices quieted immediately as they appeared on the balcony. All eyes fixed on the captain. Gianavel took his time to gaze over them, seeming to measure the voices and aspects. Then without a word or gesture he moved down the bannister and stepped onto the floor, where he boldly extended his hand to a man with long blond hair and a thick chest.

The man wore the old-fashioned heavy plate armor of a crusader on his chest—armor slightly scarred but well maintained—and stood a half-head taller than the Captain of Rora.

Gianavel smiled. "It's good to see you, Jahier."

Jahier's beard lifted in a hearty smile. "Good to see you too, Joshua." The smile slowly faded. "I heard of yesterday. I am sorry. I suppose there's no need telling you that Pianessa has encircled you from Turin to Carboneri, ten thousand strong. We barely slid through ourselves—not a stunt I'd try twice."

Gianavel didn't even glance at those surrounding them, listening to every word. "It's a long ride from Campignola. Eat first, then we'll talk. How many men came with you?"

"Forty with the will to take part in the suggestion of war and who don't fear the blood," Jahier muttered as they reached the door. "Half have experience with cannon and musket. The others are young, but no younger than you and I when we first wielded a sword."

Their dark silhouettes blocked out the cube of white that filled the doorway, lightened their outlines as if they were stepping beyond the earth—a single step, two, and they were gone.

Emmanuel's servants seemed to retreat from him as he entered his hall, unceremoniously pouring a large goblet of wine and draining it in a long swallow. He refilled the glass, drained it again before pausing and wiping his mouth with his sleeve.

"Prepare a bath," he said hoarsely.

The young girl blinked in bewilderment.

It was Emmanuel's custom to bathe once a month. Only those who had spent time in the Orient, or descendants of those who fought in the Crusades against the Moors, bathed more frequently. But he did not correct his instruction and the girl vanished.

With no one close, yet never completely alone, Emmanuel collapsed tiredly in a tall-backed wooden chair. He lifted a hand to his sweat-and-dust-grimed face. His hand, too, was blackened with dirt and blistered by the reins. Noticing that his legs trembled, he knew he had to move before fatigue stiffened.

He rose and exited the towering front gates to see Simon, hands folded humbly in the sleeves of his robe, standing on the walkway. Incomel, an unfamiliar aspect of anger on his face, had apparently stopped the inferior monk for an interrogation.

Emmanuel almost passed by, his affection for Simon provoking him to look away from this humiliation, but the late-night tryst with Cardinal Fabio Chigi had inspired his fortitude. He slowly sauntered toward the confrontation.

It is much like swordplay, he thought. *Don't plan how you will strike, but strike quickly. Attack is always better than defense.*

He stopped on a step above Incomel and stared down upon the Inquisitor. He had long learned, from no less than Pianessa, that superior height often provided a distinct advantage in these things.

Incomel nodded deeply, face unaltered. "Good morning, Savoy. I was enjoying a pleasant word with my old friend. Am I needed?"

"No," Emmanuel said with a pleasant smile, "not at the moment. I only wanted to observe your ministrations among my servants. As you say, I have much to learn."

Incomel's smile was bitter. "Of course." He turned to Simon with a deep sigh, as if the energetic dispute was now ended. "In any case, Father, I see no reason why you cannot continue your ministrations to the redeemed heretics. Some are in need of medical attention, though some are beyond earthly concerns."

"Yes," Simon said with contempt. "I know well of those, Inquisitor. I believe Corbis's zeal should be reported to the archdiocese so that he might be rewarded for his…passion."

"Corbis is content with God's gratitude alone. I see no reason why the Counciliaries should be made aware of our labors. But should I decide, Father, then I will send reports."

"And just what heresies, exactly, has the good Inquisitor discovered through his labors?" Simon retorted.

Incomel glanced casually at the Duke of Savoy, and Emmanuel understood that Incomel was not unaware of his readiness to intercede.

"Scribes have faithfully witnessed and recorded every word of our examinations, Father." He smiled as a brother. "Over a dozen have renounced their heresies and embraced the Church. They have agreed to shave their beards, to go to confession, to acknowledge the sacraments, to attend Mass—"

"To pay gold for the expiration of souls from hell?" Simon interjected.

Incomel paused. "Yes, that too. In all means, they have agreed to renounce their heresies and embrace what actions will preserve their eternal souls. I'm sure that even you see the benefit of that."

Emmanuel stepped forward. "You have duties to attend to, Father Simon." He calmly held the amused gaze of the Inquisitor. "And I'm sure the Inquisitor has other responsibilities that require his attention."

Simon raised his eyes, but Emmanuel did not blink or acknowledge anything but his sovereignty. The old monk bowed humbly to Incomel. "At your service, Inquisitor."

The Inquisitor nodded and lifted his face to the Duke of Savoy, his gaze as confident and haughty as it had ever been. Emmanuel realized, in the moment, that he would have been shocked if it were otherwise. But there was nothing more to say, so he moved into his tower where a hot bath had been drawn. He was expecting a visitor that might change the entire scope of this conflict—an Englishman who might, at last, shake the imperial Inquisitor.

Nor did Emmanuel intend to meet Sir Samuel Morland dressed in riding clothes and dust. No, when Emmanuel greeted the Puritan, he would appear in every aspect the prince he was becoming.

It was about time.

Jahier unconsciously stroked his beard, and Gianavel rested upon a log, leaning against a stable wall. Surrounded by lieutenants and mayors and the ragged militia, they had already discussed the first two battles. Jahier had asked questions about terrain, ordnance, cavalry, and siege engines until he seemed satisfied with his knowledge. Then he focused long on Gianavel and asked, "So what's the plan?"

Gianavel didn't blink. "We have a choice?"

"No." Jahier shook his head. "Not that I see."

"Then we fight."

"A defensive war? Not a good idea."

"We don't have enough men to meet them on the open field. We have to hold the ravines and the passes."

With a wistful sigh, Jahier rose from his repose. "Very well." He turned to a table spread with hand-sketched maps. "What I say, I say so that you shall not repeat."

The youngest were ordered to leave, and when barely a dozen remained, Jahier began, "On the same day that the five hundred marched against Rora, a group of us, serving as deputies of our villages, were attacked at La Torre. We had gathered for a peace conference, but your village was not represented."

Gianavel sighed wearily, crossed arms on his chest. "I did not allow anyone from Rora to attend."

"Why not?"

"Because I suspected a trap."

"Then you were correct," Jahier confirmed. "Pianessa spoke of the fighting that had occurred during the past weeks. He blamed it on his captains, saying they had misunderstood his orders to pursue a few fugitives into the mountains. He asked politely that we open the passes so that his troops could finish their arrests and promised his own men would guard each village. They would sleep under the same roofs, share the same bread, guard us with their lives."

Gianavel bowed his head as Jahier continued.

"As Jean Leger warned, Pianessa was lulling us to sleep so he could gain the upper passes. And after he had achieved his objective, he struck." A tragic pale passed across his visage. "By some prearranged signal, his soldiers rose from their beds in village after village and slaughtered those who had welcomed them into their very homes. I...I will not describe what followed."

Gianavel was stoic.

"In any case," Jahier spoke to the others, "those of us trapped inside La Torre drew into a tight square and managed to kill the first wave. Then we broke clear of the courtyard and reached the stables. We stole horses and killed anyone who got in our way, but it wasn't by much that we reached the portico." He sighed, as if returning to the exhaustion of that battle. "We evaded their cavalry in the needles of Angrogna and moved east. But as we came closer to Rora we saw entire forests of crucified men, women, and children."

"Pianessa's cunning is equaled by his ruthlessness," Gianavel said without emotion.

Staring a moment at the comment, Jahier asked, "You feel nothing for those we have lost to Pianessa's treachery?"

Almost imperceptibly, Gianavel shook his head. "I feel less for them than for the living, because their suffering has ended." His dark, burning eyes alone hinted at the passion. "What else did you see?"

"Troops," Jahier said brusquely. "Lucerna is only two miles wide, but it's guarded by at least two thousand dragoons. Only a gypsy can crawl through the line."

"Can we fight our way through if we stay in the mountains?" Gianavel asked.

Jahier studied the map. "I doubt it. We'd be too strung out. And there are too many places where the trail can be bombarded with artillery. They could kill a good number of us, or even destroy the trail with an avalanche. Then we'd have to dig in."

None spoke for a moment.

"No," Gianavel said finally, "if we dig in, they'll beat us to death with artillery. And they'll eventually overwhelm a small rear guard, which is all we could manage on a trail." He stared over the village. "How many men do we have today?"

"Eighty, maybe. Some are too young to be counted, but they'll do all right as reloaders, if that's what you're thinking."

"That's what I'm thinking," Gianavel said.

Jahier leaned heavily forward. "Joshua, listen to me." He waited until Gianavel gave him his full attention. "We don't have enough men to retake the passes and secure the valleys. Piedmont is lost. And soon Rora will be lost. Our only chance is to try to cross the Alps, maybe on the lesser-known trails, and make Geneva. The Swiss will accept us. They've always been our allies."

With a quick twist of his head, Gianavel directed attention to the raggedly dressed men and women, the hundreds of children. "And how can we protect all those people with less than a hundred men?" He waited; there was no answer. "Holding a position with the advantage of terrain is one thing. Leading a large group over the Alps is another. We'd need three times as many men to guard a retreat."

Jahier stared, eyes clear and solemn.

"I don't like it either," Gianavel said with faint anger. "But we don't have the men."

Bertino broke in, "Are you saying an army cannot take us as long as we stay in the mountains?"

"Any position can ultimately be taken," Gianavel responded, then gazed over them. "But here we have the advantage of terrain. We don't have heavy artillery, but then they can't really bring up their artillery. And the ravines only allow them to send ten to twenty men at a time."

Jahier was not encouraged. "If they have a commander willing to throw enough men into the slaughter, they will come faster than we can kill them. And, sooner or later, they'll figure that out."

"Yes," Gianavel agreed, "but what choice do we have? Here, at least, we have a chance. If we're caught in the open field, we have no chance at all."

"Gianavel, we don't have enough ordnance to kill a hundred thousand men."

"Then we'll scavenge," Gianavel answered. "We'll ambush their supply wagons and take their ordnance." His eyes burned more fiercely. "The people are willing to endure, and that's the most important thing. And Pianessa's mercenaries might tire of the slaughter."

Gianavel walked slowly down the stable, studying each face, and he wasn't certain they were convinced of anything at all. Yes, they knew they were fighting for their lives—the youngest of them knew that—but he didn't know if they knew the true reason for this war. And if a man was set to die, he did not need to die for a reason unknown.

"This isn't about religion!" he said loudly. "It's about greed! If you can pay enough gold to ransom your life, then you might live! But if you can't pay, then you'll die because your gold is your land! And before the Inquisitors can claim your land, they must kill you!"

In silence, no one moved.

"Pianessa believes he can wage this war in secret." Gianavel's tone betrayed an anger greater than his soul. "He thinks no one will know of his atrocities and crimes! But I believe this war will be shouted from rooftops! I believe the Swiss, the French, even the English will know what cruelties are being inflicted in this valley!"

"And if they do?" Jahier asked.

Gianavel answered without hesitation. "When Savoy and the Inquisitors know that others are watching, they will fear."

"But how long before that happens? A year? Six months? This may be over in days." Jahier was not convinced. "Even hours, Joshua."

"Yes," Gianavel agreed, "it might. And we might well die before intervention arrives. But we know our lives are secure, do we not?" He waited. "I will not yield, because I fear renouncing God will cost me what God has promised to me. I will not renounce my faith—neither I, nor my wife, nor my children. And if we must die, then we will die. There are greater dangers than death."

A pause, and Jahier nodded. "Jeremiah knew of suffering." With a deep sigh he lifted his sword and sheathed it. "Very well, but if we're going to fight, there'll be no chance of an orderly retreat. If we lose even one of the defiles, we will be too scattered to reorganize."

Gianavel walked to the maps and visibly bore the terrible responsibility that was his, and his alone.

Never had so few defeated so many. And even if they were superior in battle, they could still be defeated from within. Morale, spies, and betrayals would play greater and greater roles as the siege intensified. Possibilities and impossibilities rose like waves out of the sea of his concerns, and he shut down the storm entirely. Worse-case scenarios could not prevent him from focusing on the real and immediate.

"Let tomorrow worry of itself," he murmured.

Staring down at the map, he noted three defiles wide enough to allow ten to twelve men abreast. There were seven well-known paths where men could move in single file. But there were only two paths protected enough for a retreat.

First, the larger defiles had to be guarded by platoons—thirteen men each. Second, the seven well-known paths had to be guarded by two pair of scouts—four men who could continue musket fire in tandem. And each man would have three boys reloading.

Men not guarding the defiles and the trails would build gabions—shoulder-high earth-walls with cannon ports that would provide protection from light artillery, which was all Pianessa's troops could haul to this elevation.

Gianavel looked at Hector. "You're familiar with the architecture of the fortress of Metz? The manner in which they built the earth walls of the castle?"

"Oui. Earth works well enough, but there's a problem."

"What problem?"

"Well, when a breach is finally made, the dirt tends to run out, making a right tidy slope for the heathen to climb." Hector's eyes widened—he was glad to be included. "Angled bastions are better, if we can organize the manpower."

"Angled bastions?" rumbled Jahier. "How do they work?"

Hector drew a "VV" image in the dirt. He pointed to the tops of the Vs. "Cannon are placed here so that they can fire along the entire length of the wall. That way, the enemy can't mass at any point without being exposed to fire."

Gianavel appeared impressed. "Very good. How thick should the walls be?"

"As thick as we can make them," Hector said flatly. "Dirt's the best material to stop iron cannonballs, but if the soldiers get close, they can dig out a slope right quick. The best defense against that is thickness and height." He pointed to the pass. "The ledge, there, gives us a good five feet of rock for a sturdy foundation. We can heap another five feet of dirt in a few hours."

Gianavel drew a deep line right behind the Vs. "Dig a trench behind the bastions and set cannon at one end. If they breach the walls, they'll drop into the ditch, and we'll fire grapeshot at close range. Not much of an advantage, but some."

Raising his gaze, Hector responded, "We'll have more advantage than you know, Captain. The only weakness to angled bastions is artillery. And if they can't bring up artillery, we can fire down the wall all day. With deadly effect."

Gianavel nodded and looked at Hector as he lifted his rifle. "You take charge of construction."

"Oui."

"Everyone works, even children strong enough to lift a spade or pick. The rest will minister to the wounded." He turned to Jahier. "Do you want to organize platoons?"

Whatever doubts Jahier may have harbored appeared to have been completely dismissed. "Oui, I'll organize platoons. They can sleep at their stations, leaving a watch. Then, when they return, they'll be able to work on the gabions."

Gianavel stared over the compound. "I'll pick twenty-eight men to guard the trails and assign them three reloaders each. The reloaders can carry food and water."

Throughout the village, peasants bore food, clothing, even the wounded. Several of the barbes were ministering with the disconsolate. Gianavel shook his head and spoke so that only Jahier could hear. "It's an evil thing…but I see no other choice."

"There's not one," the second captain finally confirmed. "You are right. The entire village in a retreat would be caught in the open. Surrender is only rewarded by death. So we either stand our ground and win, or stand our ground and die."

Whatever passed across Gianavel's face was like a cloud blown across the sky on high winds. There was dusk, a slight shading of light or hope, and then it was gone to utter clarity of purpose. His nod was solid. "Let's get on with it."

"Oui," Jahier said.

As he stepped outside the stable, the captain was instantly calling for everyone to arm themselves like men and prepare for the fight of their lives, for wolves had at last come to the door.

✕oo✦⊙✦oo✕

"Riders!" shouted a palace sentry.

Emmanuel raised his face to see the soldier outlined against the white wispy clouds of the late afternoon sky. His arm was uplifted, pointing into the far distance, indicating that whoever it was was not yet close. The Duke of Savoy waited as Captain of the Guard descended and crossed the square in quick strides, bowing curtly.

"Three riders, My Lord," he gasped. "They wear no coat of arms that I can see. What are your instructions?"

"Let them pass," Emmanuel muttered and noticed guards massing along the wall, staring into the distance. He wondered if they thought it was a rogue attack by the Waldenses. If so, they had responded seriously enough.

Word of Pianessa's defeat, down to the finest detail of who was killed and how, had obviously spread through the entire militia so that even a cook could recount the battle in horrendous and dramatic detail. Emmanuel himself had overheard chamber maidens discussing the devilish barbarity of the Waldenses. For it was widely reported that they severed the heads of their victims and made garments from their skins and danced all painted with blood beneath the moon chanting satanic charms to protect them from the forces of the Church.

Emmanuel turned and climbed the stairs, turning his head to a scribe who accompanied his every move. "Find Pianessa and tell him we receive visitors tonight. And order the kitchen to prepare a feast pleasing to an Englishman."

The scribe had already begun to race off when he caught the last comment and fled after Emmanuel. "Did you say an Englishman, My Lord?"

"Yes," Emmanuel said as he entered the Tower, "and summon both of the Inquisitors. They will not wish to miss an opportunity to tell a Puritan what courageous deeds they have performed in their noble service to God."

〉oo◈oo〈

Emmanuel, nobly arrayed in deep scarlet vestment and trousers with Savoy's coat of arms emblazoned in gold upon the breast, stood as the three Puritans entered the hall. Sir Samuel Morland and two envoys bearing passes and letters from King Louis of France had arrived an hour before sunset but had requested a brief respite to clean up and redress before greeting the Duke of Savoy.

Now they came forward in white shirts, black trousers, polished black boots that flared widely at the knees, and two of the men wore black cloaks that opened like wings at each stride. But Sir Morland, in the center, wore a crimson cloak of royal thickness and weight that majestically framed the stark whiteness of his high-collared shirt. With profound gravity the Puritan removed his hat and swept it before his bow. With equal gravity, Emmanuel nodded.

Sir Samuel Morland intoned, "I bring greetings from My Lord, Sir Oliver Cromwell, to Your Majesty, and bid prayers and blessings upon both yourself and your kingdom."

"I am honored to receive such esteemed envoys from the great Lord Protector of England," Emmanuel said, a respectful nod. "My kingdom stands ready to serve."

"Spoken as a true prince," Sir Morland responded as he handed his hat and cloak to a servant.

When the cloak was removed, Emmanuel was intrigued to see that the Puritan was not armed. Not even an ornamental dagger, usually worn among soldiers, girded his wide black belt of polished leather. But Puritans had no quarrel with violence or force. They were, in fact, reputed to be adept at battle when it was necessary. That Morland had consciously chosen not to wear a weapon could mean many things. But Emmanuel had no time to ponder the possibilities. He rose and lifted an arm to a serving table, and Morland fell into stride beside him.

Sir Samuel Morland was a formidable figure. He retained a soldier's bearing, straight and crisp, every crease and edge sharp and disciplined. He was larger than Emmanuel by far with a farmer's strength but not so massive as Pianessa. His face was angled with a long goatee, and his mouth was down-turned at the edges, allowing the appearance of one accustomed to physical pain or emotional hardship. He revealed little in his stoic composure and countenance, and his movements were spare and economical.

Emmanuel presented a table of wine. "I am not certain of your customs," he said with apology. "So we prepared a wide selection of our finest wine and port. We also have water."

"Wine is welcome, Your Majesty." Morland accepted a silver goblet that had been set for the special occasion. "Thank you. It has been a long journey from France, but we were content to sleep in stables often enough, in want of an inn."

Emmanuel wasn't certain, but it seemed the Puritan had wasted no time raising the purpose of his visit. If so, it had been done smoothly and without accusation.

"Yes," the young duke said, accepting another goblet, "I'm afraid the war has interrupted the normal condition of my kingdom." He grimaced slightly. "Hopefully, the fighting is almost over."

Incomel and Corbis, dressed in black with silver vestments that looped behind their necks and descended to the floor, stood placidly to the side, hands folded. Corbis's gaze was directed at nothing the Duke of Savoy could discern. But Incomel, the image of priestly repose, focused on the Puritan as if he were a viper.

Sir Samuel Morland seemed not to notice either the gaze or the Inquisitor at all. He turned his back without a second glance and strolled along a wall lined with the weapons and armor of past generations and dynasties of the House of Savoy. "You are a noble descendent of a noble house, Your Majesty. Your kingdom and ancestry are respected, and I consider myself honored to visit you, even in this dark hour."

"I am humbled, Sir Morland."

"Nay," the Puritan commented, "it is I who should be humbled." He lifted his goblet. "A finer history of courage I have never seen. No wonder that your line has retained its kingdom when so many have plotted to overcome it."

"Yes," Emmanuel said, warming to the Puritan, whom he knew had a purpose and would reach it in time. For the moment he would appreciate the accompaniment of such a man before unwanted matters intruded.

Seldom did he have an opportunity to speak forthrightly with men of gravity and respect, to explore and appreciate their character and wisdom. Most often, he was forced to discern what putrid lies were veiled by flattery, and what use envoys meant to make of him if they could.

Although the Puritans were condemned often enough as emotionless drones of the English Church, Emmanuel judged that Morland would definitely speak in the proper moment and manner, and would not lie when he did.

Glancing over his shoulder, Emmanuel noticed that Morland's attendants stood in quiet conversation with the Duchess Elizabeth, who had chosen, on this occasion, to station herself as a mere adornment—a royal and astonishingly beautiful tapestry behind the regal throne of her cousin. He knew that Elizabeth, with her encyclopedic knowledge of families and national policies, could entertain guests for weeks without a single uncomfortable moment. Listening politely, the two Puritans stood with heads slightly bowed, the backs bent at the waist in something of a deferential bow.

Yes, cultured men…

Sir Samuel Morland noticed Emmanuel's glance. His sudden smile was all the more comforting because the severe face seemed so unaccustomed to the expression.

"The duchess is a remarkable woman," he said. "My envoys were anxious to the point of rebuke for a chance to converse with her." He chuckled, causing Emmanuel to smile. "I thought it prudent to remind them of manners of court."

Emmanuel laughed loudly, drawing the attention of attendants. "You uphold your reputation, Sir Morland. You are, indeed, as intelligent and composed as I was told."

"You are gracious," Morland laughed as they turned to walk along the back wall of the hall, where the greatest relics were displayed. "My Lord Cromwell wishes you good health and prosperity," he added. "I have come to deliver many words of encouragement."

Sir Morland raised eyebrows at Emmanuel's short-lived smile. "I am here also because of the war, Your Majesty," he added. "You know, of course, there are many matters that we must discuss. I have brought a letter from My Lord that is to be read only by yourself...in strict confidence."

Morland produced a folded parchment and delivered it to Emmanuel. The letter revealed little sign of travel, and the burgundy-colored wax was firmly stamped with the impressive seal of Cromwell.

"Not all contained within the letter is suitable for those outside your circle of advisors," Morland added with gravity. "I'm certain, Your Majesty, that you understand the weight of such matters."

"I do." Emmanuel slid the letter into the chest pocket of his robe. "Advise Lord Cromwell that I am thankful for his attention and I will observe the strictest confidence."

Morland nodded, then looked as servants entered the hall bearing platters of grapes, fruit, nuts, beef and bread, and finally an enormous iron tray of roast beef.

"Ah," he said with far greater expression, "'tis far more than I expected, Your Majesty."

"Far less than deserved, Sir Morland."

Emmanuel rested at the end of the long table, with Morland and his envoys on his right, and the duchess on his left, engaging them all in pleasant conversation while Incomel stood apart, watching stiffly.

For the most part Emmanuel enjoyed the meal in peace and almost chuckled when he thought about what would soon happen after the meal when the Puritan and the Inquisitor stood face-to-face, each defending worlds at war in the name of the same God.

And then he wondered of the letter contained within his coat—a letter from Oliver Cromwell that surely petitioned him to cease this suppression of the Waldenses. Indeed, he hoped that the letter did more than simply petition, but Emmanuel was not limited to the dull truth. If the letter did not threaten outright invasion, then Emmanuel's scribes would make it so. It would be yet another reason for him to bring a hard ending to this war.

Suppressing a smile, the Duke of Savoy wished Cardinal Fabio Chigi could have seen how well he was learning to play the game.

xoox◈xoox

He was old. He was alone.

It was an age of sorrow that he beheld, because all his great wisdom was trapped in the blind corridors of his mind—the only place now that his knowledge, memories, words, and thoughts could arise and walk and live.

No one could record what he alone could see. Nor could his hands draw the majesty of that panorama anymore so men might know what God had allowed him to know for so many years.

The black melancholy rose up again within him, a curtain of darkness that made his blindness all the more terrible, and he bowed his head to pray, but he could not pray. He frowned and wondered; why had the Almighty removed the purpose of his life before removing life itself? For now he was useless, utterly useless, though he had avoided that snare from his earliest days.

Before he lost his ability to see, he should have died. For now he was like Samson without his strength—like any other man, or even less, for he had once known greatness. How could he endure this pale existence? Was his strength the strength of stones that he should not long for death? That he should not despise his own flesh?

A knock at the door.

He turned his head, gazing.

Strange that he could still see men, though everyone considered him completely blind. But he could see, though not as other men see. He could see the whiteness of the sun, could sometimes discern shades of letters, sensing the black on white. He could even see the forms of men if the light was sufficient and he was not too fatigued. But he could not see what he wished to see. He could not see the words he would write with his pen, nor those he had once written.

"Enter," he said.

He heard the door open, felt the cold rush of night wind, caught the scent of rain and fog. Although it was not raining, it would rain before morning, and the fog felt like floating wet silk, weightless and ghostly, against his flaking skin. He had become far more sensitive to these invisible things since these comprised his world now.

The door was closed, latched.

Steps approached, the figure still unannounced, and for a moment he felt a twinge of fear, wondering if this was the moment he had come to dread or, sometimes, desire.

"Who is it?" he queried.

"Monsieur Milton, it is I, William Lockhart."

John Milton—hailed as one of England's greatest and, he knew as well, one of her most despised poets—stretched out his hand as the treelike form of Sir William Lockhart walked closer and sat, laying what seemed to be a letter-sized pouch on the table.

John Milton had been waiting three days for Lockhart to arrive with letters from Cromwell, Lord Protector of England, concerning the persecution of the Waldenses. Milton had prepared his own letters that would be included in the hazardous package the Scotsman would bear with much peril to France.

Carefully feeling for the bottle of port, Milton found the glass he had prepared. "Please, Sir Lockhart..." He gestured, hesitated, then, "When are you leaving?"

"Within the hour," answered Lockhart as he poured a glass and drank. "But there are a few more precautions I must take before I cross the Channel."

"Ah," said John Milton, "do you use a military vessel?"

"No, sir, a private contractor."

"Good. Yes, military men have too much ambition to be trusted. And these are opportune times to profit by betrayal."

Sir Lockhart answered, "My journey to reach you was dangerous in more ways than one. By Lord Cromwell's instructions, I avoided both the musketeers and regular militia."

"Wise," Milton nodded. "Yes, very wise. We have too many enemies, both in England and France, who would thwart this plan. But tell me; how is My Lord Cromwell?"

"He is as well as can be expected," said Lockhart. "But I fear his old wounds, body and soul, afflict him. His trembling comes and goes, his fevers grow more frequent." Solemnly, the Scotsman paused. "I fear he has fought his last campaign."

Milton bent his head.

"Yes," he muttered, "all of us, it seems. But perhaps the Lord has delivered to us one last, great task that we must complete—to defend the people of Rora. Do you have the letters?"

"Yes, sir."

"What do they request?"

Even in the vague fogginess of his curse, Milton could discern Lockhart leaning forward. "There are two letters with my personal instructions," the Scot stated. "One additional letter is addressed to Louis, the boy-king. And one letter is addressed to Cardinal Mazarin, written in Lord Cromwell's hand."

"Yes," John Milton nodded, "this is good." He stared a moment, ponderous. "Men may not believe that we took such a part in so great and just a cause, and yet the letters I have written will attest to my hand, if they survive. Nor shall Lord Cromwell's activity on behalf of the Waldenses go unremembered. But, still, this is the age of tyranny, and we do not know what men may say of us after we are gone."

Sir Lockhart was noticeably still, and Milton fell suddenly still, then tilted his head. "You are afraid, boy?" There was no immediate response, but John Milton could hear the deep pull of breath, its hushed depth.

"The task," the Scotsman admitted, "is difficult."

"Describe it to me," Milton said and was immediately struck at how his language had changed and continued to change month by month now. It was the blindness, he knew, that caused him to substitute "describe" for "explain," and had constructed within him a new fondness for clandestine meetings where outside noises and voices, even the whisper of soft footsteps, would not detract from his complete concentration.

"Lord Cromwell has written precise instructions," Lockhart answered. "I am only to approach Cardinal Mazarin at night and by prearranged hours. I am not to venture outside our embassy during the day so as not to initiate suspicions. And I am to make cordial inquiries, then petitions, and if these do not succeed, incentives."

Milton was rapt. "What incentives?"

"An alliance."

"An alliance," Milton repeated. "What manner of alliance?"

Sir Lockhart paused. "My Lord believes that France will be more disposed to aiding the people of Rora if England will support their war against Spain."

Milton chuckled merrily. "An alliance with France to defend the people of Piedmont in exchange for subduing the barbarous covetousness of the Spanish! Yes...generous scales, indeed."

"In any case," the Scotsman continued, "if we can persuade the cardinal to intercede with the Duke of Savoy, then we believe Savoy will have sufficient leverage to refuse the mandates of the Jesuits and these Inquisitors who are so obsessed with the Waldenses."

The old man's lips moved as they did when he dictated his long verse to one of his daughters, his eyes wide and staring, beholding what only he could behold. He nodded his head and said, "Sufficient to stand," he murmured, "sufficient to stand, those possible to fall. How stands Cardinal Mazarin against Parliament?"

"Lord Cromwell believes Mazarin is without any true resistance inside France. But, certainly, the Italian cardinals and noblemen will object to his intervention. The fate of the Waldenses is not a direct interest of France, and Paris has never been kind to Louis."

Milton grumbled, "No, not kind, seeing as they sought to have him starved, hunted down by dogs, and buried alive. No, Sir Lockhart, Louis, though only a boy, holds hatred for them in equal measure of his devotion toward Mazarin, who protected him during the Fronde." He added slowly, "Yes, Louis will have no objections to whatever Mazarin decides, because he is wise enough to love knowledge he does not yet possess. Mazarin, the cunning old man, is our hope. We must intercede forcefully, but wisely, in his court."

Milton's hand finally settled on the cloaked arm of Sir Lockhart. "Are you prepared for this task?"

Accustomed more to a cavalry charge than sinister intrigues and spy games, Sir Lockhart replied firmly, "I am ready. I do not know what may befall me on the way, but if I reach the court of Mazarin, I am committed to doing all that I may do."

John Milton patted the arm. "Good, good. Now I understand why Cromwell chose you for this task. But let me share a few insights, since I have seen divers means in similar junctions." He raised a hand. "Do not be quick to speak, but let others exhaust their ideas and knowledge first, so that they may not later claim your ideas as their own. Do not invite insult, but challenge insolence, especially if it is from a nobleman."

"Why?" asked Sir William. "Is it not better to be discreet and patient when we play these games?"

"If you represent a threat, yes," said Milton. "But your position is one of persuasion and not coercion." He raised both hands to frame his explanation. "Remember, Mazarin is surrounded by men who jealously guard their position and influence. And if they feel you represent a threat to their continued power, they will challenge you. But you must forcefully repulse any indignation, even a haughty gaze or an imperious temperament. If they sense you are uncertain, either with your authority or your resolve, they will attack like jackals that smell blood. Despite what assistance they offer, you must trust no one."

Sir Lockhart paused. "It is tragic that wars are won by such deception. I am not disposed to such deceit."

"If a man's heart is pure, then it will be pure with or without your trust." Milton said the words as if reading from a page. "If they truly want to assist you, and you cooperate not a whit, then they will not cease to help you. But if their motivation is impure, they cannot thwart your actions—they will not know them."

"Yes, I understand."

"Also," the poet continued, "take nothing except what little you will deliver to Mazarin."

"Not my letters of instruction?"

"No, nothing. If you are caught—"

"But I have diplomatic pouch!"

Milton sternly shook his head. "If a man will sell his soul for a loaf of bread, for how much less will he sell the soul of another?" There was no reply from the Scot. "Remember; you must trust no one! Memorize your instructions, burn the letters, and scatter the ashes!"

Sir Lockhart hesitated only a moment. "Very well."

It appeared as if the explosive eruption of emotion had drained the poet's spare energy. He hesitated a long time, lips tightening, curling, as if in debate. Finally he leaned forward, head erect, face set like stone. "Now for the most difficult," he said strangely.

"Yes, sir?"

"Always sin stands against law," the poet began slowly. "Since the beginning, it has been thus. But understand me in this, just a moment, for it will be your aid in days to come. All men sin. The holiest are not immune from the touch of what lies within the hottest heart. Nor are my loftiest thoughts more sublime than the lowliest imagination that ever lifted an iron stylus. One cannot turn to God but that he first turn from what enslaves him, and all men that know God have turned to Him."

The poet petitioned for patience. "I beg you; listen a moment. My meaning is not as clear as I shall make it." He licked his lips, then, "Beware any man that does not confess to you that he has known the blackest sin. If he does not know that his heart also is black, then he will regard yours as less than his own. Such a man will presume himself your master and will subject you to the distribution of knowledge in accordance with his own designs."

"You speak of Cardinal Mazarin?"

"Perhaps," the poet replied. "I do not know this man. I only know his kind, and you venture into regions unknown, where even the smallest mistake can bring an unexpected and violent end. You are not skilled in the means of intrigue, so you must trust what you know of yourself." He paused. "Do you understand me?"

"Yes, I believe so."

"Good, then listen more. You know that you hide these dark vices of your heart because, like a thief that has been caught, you are ashamed. So, too, do other men. They are not different from you. Do not be deceived.

Cardinal Mazarin's cloak covers more than his holy signatures. Whether he knows the humility of repentance and, thus, the true cardinal allegiance to the Lord of All the Earth is unknown, nor can any man know for certain. But the greatest ally you can have in your mission is a man who understands the darkness that presently bleeds on the battlefields of Rora—an ally who has committed such evil acts in the past and repented in ashes, this man is your greatest friend. Who better than their former king knows the mind of these soldiers? Who better, also, to confound their purposes and intents? And who else would know less fear of them, since he was once a king in their camp and has returned, brokenhearted, to the feet of Christ?" As he finished, the poet fell still.

A fog of silence subdued the room.

"Very well," Sir Lockhart said finally, and then he stood and shifted his Spanish blade. "Now, sir, I must bid my leave. I seek to travel in the deepest hours of night when brigands and patrols have chosen to harbor themselves from the cold."

"Anything I might offer?" John Milton asked, and the Scotsman paused at the door.

"Thank you, my friend. But you cannot give courage; I must find that in the night. Farewell."

"Farewell," said the poet.

Reality more alive than sight surged through the room as the door swung and then shut, and John Milton sat alone in the suddenly cold room where a candle yet burned—a candle he could yet see surrounded by a fog and darkness.

And he wondered of it, this candle that did not surrender to the attack of fog and night and cold. And he knew what that candle knew, and gazed upon it strangely, as he could still gaze. Though weak and alone, it burned. Though threatened by the gathering dark, it burned. Though it had no cause for hope—like himself, like Cromwell, like the Waldenses—it burned, refusing surrender.

He nodded his head, words finding themselves out of him, though he did not try to speak.

"May the Lord give us the strength…to endure."

11

APERITIFS WERE ACCEPTED GRACIOUSLY by Sir Samuel Morland and his assistants—both quiet men that Emmanuel had come to regard as solemn, unarmed bodyguards.

Table conversation had quickly spiraled toward the interference of the Catholic Church in the administration of Emmanuel's government, yet Incomel made no effort to approach. Instead, he scrutinized every word and gesture, particularly those of Sir Morland, who moved from vague inquiries into the well-being of the kingdom, to this "wrongful aggression" against the Waldenses, and finally the "murderous intolerance of these Jesuits and Inquisitors."

Pianessa, strangely, had no argument with the Puritan when it came to the subject of military tactics and even religious intolerance. Despite the fact that they were like midnight and morning in justifying war itself, they agreed on strategy and tactics.

In fact, such was their agreement that Emmanuel wondered if Morland was purposely demonstrating to Pianessa that his true battle was not with him. As the conversation progressed from siege warfare to artillery to modern firearms, Sir Morland expressed his respect for Pianessa's perspectives, and more than once proved himself more than his equal.

Both deemed musketeers less than useless against cavalry and agreed that ditches, crosscut like a chessboard, were the best defense against a mounted charge. They agreed that the greatest advantage of modern flintlock rifles lay in mass fire and not with individual soldiers picking off solitary targets. They agreed that artillery, fired point-blank into a square of pikemen, was the best means of breaking the formation. And it was Sir Morland himself who admitted that Berwick was the only English fortress built to withstand modern artillery, as it was the only one built *trace italienne*, and everyone knew that Italians pioneered modern military construction.

Finally they rose from the table and formed a small circle near a tapestry of a battlefield littered with fallen soldiers, the victors little more than dead men themselves. It was, curiously, a damning statement on the madness of war.

"Without question," Sir Morland finished, "all of Europe will soon be constructing cities and castles according to Italy's inventions of angled bastions and sunken battlements. The ancient traditions have been rendered all but useless."

With respect, Pianessa nodded. "But England, I must admit, has the finest gunsmiths with better inventions every day, it seems. I only wish our gunsmiths would more quickly adopt the bored barrels for improved accuracy."

Only by the thinnest presence of mind did Emmanuel not turn when Incomel interrupted the conversation. "It seems the English ceaselessly prepare for war, Sir Morland."

All eyes turned.

Incomel bowed, subservient. "Forgive me. I was only musing that your Lord Protector, Oliver Cromwell, is both respected and feared for his willingness to use his garrisons."

"Aye," said Sir Samuel Morland, and Emmanuel thought he caught a gleam in the Puritan's eye, "in a world where the poor are so cruelly victimized by the rich and powerful, Inquisitor, it is a great thing that My Lord defends the poor."

The Duchess Elizabeth stretched out a slender arm, her gown clasped deliberately at her wrist, allowing the transparent silk to suspend like an angel's wing. "Please, Inquisitor, I do not believe it would violate your vows to be courteous."

With a curt bow, Incomel approached, politely raising a hand to decline an offered aperitif. Then he faced Sir Morland, Pianessa, and the duchess.

Morland's two escorts stood stoically to the side, heads demurely bent, hands clasped behind their backs. Emmanuel subtly turned to have his goblet refilled and did not reenter the circle as Incomel arrived to hover on its edge.

"Allow me to formally admit myself," the Inquisitor said as he bowed. "I am Inquisitor General Thomas Incomel, and I wish to welcome you within these walls. But how unfortunate you would arrive during our efforts to pacify the Waldenses."

"Indeed," Samuel Morland said, inclining his face toward the priest. "But I do not call large-scale murder pacification."

Incomel remained composed. From the utter lack of surprise at Sir Morland's comment, Emmanuel knew the Inquisitor had expected a confrontation and was prepared.

"The Waldenses are a dangerous and uneducated people, Sir Morland. It is best to leave methods of their pacification to those who bravely bear the battle."

Morland's black vestments seemed to suddenly warm the atmosphere about him. "Forests of crucified men, women, and children are not the product of battle, Inquisitor."

Incomel's smile was tight. "I would suggest Lord Cromwell worry himself with England's own pacification of the Irish. The Duke of Savoy has the Waldenses well in hand."

"Does he?" Morland cast Emmanuel a respectful glance, then back upon the Inquisitor.

"I'm not certain what you mean," Incomel stated.

"I mean, Inquisitor, that since I entered Piedmont I have seen atrocities so barbaric that Nero, Genghis Khan, and the late Vlad Dracul would be ashamed that they did not invent them. Heaven surely stands in mute horror, and the universe itself grinds to a halt to behold what monstrous acts of widespread murder you have committed against the Waldenses. What is it that you seek to gain?"

Incomel revealed only cold concentration. He had tolerated much during his reign in the valley, but never had he been addressed in such a manner. The fact that Sir Morland was clearly beyond his reach seemed to add ice to his eyes.

"Is this evaluation of a war that does not, in any manner, involve territories of England the purpose for your visit, Sir Morland? Or did Lord Cromwell secretly send you to scout out routes for an invasion of the Duke of Savoy's kingdom?"

Incomel's words provoked an adrenaline rush in Emmanuel, because if Sir Morland confirmed that Cromwell was, indeed, considering invasion, Emmanuel's station required him to intervene. If Morland denied that Cromwell intended to invade, Incomel would inform Cardinal Benedict and the threat could no longer be used.

But Sir Morland was wise; he would not reveal his cards, whether he truly held them or not. "Does the Inquisitor observe generals at my side?

Does he, per chance, observe navigators? Or does he observe simple men of God pleading for religious tolerance?"

"I have not yet seen a demonstration of tolerance by Lord Cromwell," Incomel answered. "Indeed, I have heard of Catholic churches burned and Inquisitors hunted down like dogs. Even of treasuries looted while English constables watched."

With a thoughtful frown, Sir Morland bent at the waist. "Believe not half what you see, Inquisitor, and none of what you hear. Be assured that My Lord has cast his shield over all the Catholic basilicas of England. None have been burned."

"And our Inquisitors remain untouched?"

Sir Morland shook his head. "Not entirely, no. Some Inquisitors did, indeed, overestimate the patience of their flocks. We had an incident in Dowry where an Inquisitor was himself locked up in the stocks in which he'd punished those not generous enough to his treasury. But after he concluded he may have been too hasty in judging so many guilty of witchcraft, he was released without harm."

"I call it heresy!" Incomel said, unblinking and immobile. "Those who attack an Inquisitor attack Christ. Those who resist an Inquisitor incur the judgment of God."

A dark scowl hardened the Puritan's brow and his mouth turned down. He held his stillness before he spoke. "It is one thing to sentence a man in absentia to death, Inquisitor. It is another to deliver him to the hangman."

Incomel remained passive. "You speak of this heretic of the Waldenses— Gianavel."

"Yes," Sir Morland answered with a hard nod. "I speak of this great prince of the Waldenses."

"Already a tale begins of this man who single-handedly kills thousands to save his poor, defenseless village from cruel Inquisitors." Incomel grimaced. "How romantic."

"No war should be remembered as romantic," said Sir Morland somberly. "But it should be remembered so that it is not repeated."

Subtly drawing attention, Corbis took a silent step forward as Sir Morland continued, "Yes, Inquisitor, I have seen the blackened bones of those surrendered to the flames. You think you have committed your crimes in secret, but all men will know what you have done. Nor does God turn His gaze from the suffering of these people. His hand will yet deliver them from yours."

Incomel turned a step, remembered himself, and faced down the Puritan once more. "You come uninvited into our land. You dare to accuse me of provoking this war. You are fortunate that you are beyond my reach, Sir Morland."

The Puritan's hard gaze cast all illusions of court underfoot. "But I am not beyond your reach, Inquisitor. Order your apprentice, here" —he gestured to Corbis, his hairless lids half-closed— "to lay hands on me. There is more than one way by which a man may meet God."

Incomel blinked as though dazed by an unexpected blow.

Watching closely, Emmanuel did not think it curious that Pianessa only passively observed the encounter. None of the marquis' interests—namely his throne and treasury—were in discussion. And his contempt of the Inquisitor was apparent. Indeed, imbibing a slow sip of wine, Pianessa could have been lazily watching clouds.

Morland was a living, breathing monument to why Puritans were regarded as cold and severe and controlled, but he was not emotionless.

Indeed, the anger that sharpened his countenance was warlike and barely bound. Although he hinted at no physical response, he nevertheless seemed quite capable, in the moment, of seizing the priest and dragging him down the hall to a doom unknown.

"Hear me, Inquisitor," the Puritan said. "The world will know of the horrors you have delivered to these people, whose only crime is refusing to join your church. Which is no crime."

"It is God's war, Sir Morland."

The Puritan winced. When he spoke, his words were grim and restrained. "Hear me, man: The Almighty will not forever suffer you to blaspheme the Holy Spirit."

Baring teeth, Incomel stepped back. His hands grasped the sides of his robe as if he would shake the dust from it. "If this was—" His mouth snapped shut, then he spat, "You are fortunate this is not Rome!"

Morland's countenance hardened as anger flooded over the edge of his control. "Perhaps. But it is not Rome." The Puritan's frown was solemn. "And perhaps it is you who are fortunate."

Trembling, Incomel turned, but some bizarre desire to depart with his dignity intact turned him again toward the Puritan. He did not close upon Sir Morland's space but hovered just outside, like a spider hesitantly testing to see if its prey were indeed dead before it leaped.

"You are a fool to think that you can threaten the Roman Catholic Church, Sir Morland! Nor should you arrogantly presume you could win a war against us!"

Pianessa broke in, muttering as he raised his goblet, "Actually, Inquisitor, with the Vaudois fighting beside them, the English could take Piedmont within a week."

"King Louis would not tolerate such an assault!" Incomel almost shouted and turned fully toward the Puritan. "Is this the true purpose of your visit, Sir Morland? To threaten us? You fail! This war is an instrument of God!"

"Is that how you understand war?" asked Morland more quietly, but also more threatening. "I'm sorry, Inquisitor. I don't see war as an instrument of God."

"And yet you have killed men in war."

Morland nodded. "I have killed men in war, it's true. Sometimes a man must stand against other men. We hope and pray that we are right, but only God knows."

"Were you present at the Battle of Drogheda, Sir Morland, when Lord Cromwell took the city for the glory of God?"

Morland's somber aspect became more subdued.

"Ah," Incomel smiled, "then you were present when your godly Parliamentarians stormed the walls and put five thousand men, women, and children to the sword? You were there when your valiant Puritan soldiers set three Catholic churches ablaze with the congregations trapped within? Burning them alive?"

The Puritan's eyes glazed as if beholding something terrible and haunting. "It was an evil day," he answered, fearfully calm. "Once we breached the walls, the men could not be restrained. They…we…put the town to the sword."

"Even women and children?" Incomel pressed.

Lines in the Puritan's face deepened. "It is a grim rule of war that in battle men sometimes commit acts that they remember with guilt and remorse. And no man, even the holiest, is above it. Flesh is flesh, and flesh will sometimes fail."

With a faint bend of his head, Sir Morland continued, "At Drogheda, the rules of the siege were clearly understood by Sir Arthur Aston, yet he refused to surrender and killed a great number of officers and men. Once we breached the walls, it was too late for him to ask for quarter. The men, including even My Lord Cromwell, were incited to wrath. What happened is a tragedy many good and strong men must bear for the rest of their lives."

Incomel's condemnation was embodied in his stance. "I'm sure the inhabitants of Drogheda appreciate your regrets, Sir Morland." He stared a moment more, then released a hard breath as he turned to the Duke of Savoy. "And now, Your Majesty, I must beg your leave."

Morland said nothing as the Inquisitor walked toward the lesser-lighted sections of the square-stoned corridor adjacent to Savoy's throne and was gone. In the uneasy silence that followed, Pianessa was the only one to move. He lifted a bottle of wine and refilled his goblet, smiled as he raised a toast.

"To war," he said.

✕✕✕✕✕

Staring across the camp, Gianavel turned at the approach of footsteps and saw Jahier's blond hair highlighted by a circle of blazing torches. The captain was sweating heavily and seemed to have completed some kind of grueling run. Jahier's nod was curt and hard. "I have assembled the men."

"Good."

Gianavel moved past him and down toward the stable where a small number of men stood beside the fire. All eyes watched closely as Gianavel came into the shelter. He rested his rifle against an anvil.

"We have defeated Pianessa twice," Gianavel began as preamble. "But Pianessa is no fool. He will attack again and soon. You are here because you have volunteered to be spies, and because you are well suited for the task." Gianavel pointed to an older man. "Pietro, you were in the militia at Turin, so you know the procedures. But you must also be careful no one recognizes you."

"It's been ten years," Pietro replied. "I wouldn't volunteer if this gray beard didn't give me an advantage."

Gianavel turned to the rest. "Remember: When they find you in the field, accuse them of being Waldenses before they accuse you. They will not be so quick to attack when they are defending themselves against the same charge. Then, after the confusion and accusations die down, join them peacefully.

"Once you discover their plan of attack, assume a guard post and desert it during the night. Once you are in the mountains, stay on the secret trails and return to us as quickly as possible. Remember the password and use it. Don't be killed by our own guards." He stared at each of them. "Are you certain you wish to undertake this task?"

Each man nodded.

Gianavel returned it. "Be as cunning as serpents. To practice deceit in war is our duty, and God will honor your courage." He turned to Jahier. "Are they equipped?"

"Uniforms and weapons."

With a last look, Gianavel said, "Push hard to reach the lower level of the valley before dawn. If they see you descending the mountain, they'll kill you no matter what you say."

Without further discussion they lifted weapons and in moments were swallowed by surrounding night. Not even their footsteps could be discerned in the heavy cold of the shelter, and Jahier shook his head.

"It is a dangerous gambit," he growled to Gianavel. "If one of them is captured, they may talk."

Gianavel shook his head as he changed the flint in his musket. "We need information."

"Why?"

"Because Pianessa won't make the same mistake again. Next time, he'll divide his attack and try to make us divide. We need to know where they'll be hitting us."

"True," agreed Jahier, then gazed solemnly over Gianavel. "And what of you, Joshua?"

Gianavel lifted his gaze, said nothing.

Uncharacteristically solemn, Jahier said, "You have responded to this war from the first as if you've waited for it all your life." He paused thoughtfully. "I have been a captain for as many years as you. I have always been prepared to fight, even as you. But it still took me hours to accept the fact that war had come. You accepted it as though you were…expecting it."

There was a long pause, and Gianavel sighed. "I don't know. I've never forgotten the war that almost killed us when we were children. I vowed never to let it happen again—not to my children, not yours." He paused, frowned. "I've always been ready for it."

Gianavel gazed across the camp. "You know, reading the Scriptures so many of those nights…I cannot remember a single night that I didn't pray for the strength to do what I'm doing now. But, even then, I somehow knew that I would." He shrugged. "I hoped that God had not revealed to me a prophecy. I hoped that it was only my mind, or my fear." He looked again at Jahier. "I feared this fight, brother. I have always feared this fight. But I will do what God has prepared me to do."

Jahier did not blink as Gianavel picked up his rifle and walked away.

"It's not by courage that I fight—it's faith."

Hector was hard at work with heavy wads of small round balls crammed into a waxlike mixture that Bertino had lifted from a barrel with a wooden spatula that was as wide as an oar. Faces black and grimy with sweat and soot, they labored with uncommon patience and grace, moving steadily as oxen beneath a plow.

Gianavel glanced at their besmeared visages and said nothing, but his face tightened in a smile because Bertino's eyes were two oceans of white staring from a moon of black. The big farmer leaned forward on his arms, wiped a black forearm across a black face. "'Tis work here, boy, I tell you, for nothing."

Gianavel laughed, studied the short lines of grapeshot, all divided by weight for the demicannon, the ten-pounders and forty-pounders. He estimated no more than a hundred shot. "You're doing well, brothers, but is that all?"

Bertino bent his face. Said nothing.

"The ordnance wagon was loaded with solid shot," Hector said quietly. "We're having to make the grapeshot by hand." He hesitated, lips moving in silence. "We'll have a thousand by morning."

"What about balls?"

"A thousand."

"Hold the grapeshot until they're on top of us," Gianavel said. "And have experienced men on the cannons. How are the bastions progressing?"

Hector nodded, "Well enough. Pianessa's boys won't be able to hide or dig a ramp. If they're going to breach the wall, they'll have to come straight over the top." He hesitated, cocked his head. "I tell you, boy, that'll be butchery."

Gianavel moved to the lip of the ridge and surveyed construction. Fifty men and women were laboring in the dark with shovels and picks and barrels of rock and dirt. Working steadily and strongly without comment or complaint, they had raised the wall ten feet.

Dropping into their midst, where the heaviest stones were being lifted to ring the highest section of the bastion, Gianavel relieved a worn and weary villager. And at Gianavel's smile the man laughed and stepped aside, allowing the Captain of Rora to lift the stones to the rim, where others lifted them still higher, stone upon stone.

With patience and enduring strength they worked, building the defense higher and higher, and then someone began to sing—someone not so distant, but out of sight. It was a woman, her voice beautiful and convinced and strong, and she sang for only a moment before the voices of children joined.

And then almost at once it spread along the line—each man, woman, and child taking up the song that praised their true stronghold, their omnipotent Redeemer who would allow neither demon, nor angel, nor principality nor power, nor height nor breadth, nor any other power to separate them from the love of God which is in Christ Jesus the Lord.

✕◌◈◌✕

Charon, the black-cloaked embodiment of Death who ferried the souls of the dead into Hades, would not have been more cryptic than the silent boatman who ferried Sir William Lockhart across the English Channel.

The shores of France loomed black against midnight blue, a wide expanse of stars that had not been visible as Lockhart exited the heavily guarded corridors of Whitehall, nor the humble abode of John Milton, and Lockport thought he could hear waves crashing against the sandy white shore. Many times he had made this journey, both in war and in peace, but never so alone, or feeling so alone.

He hoped to move past militia posts with his diplomatic pouch and foresaw no violent challenges, since every precaution had been taken to insure secrecy. But inside Whitehall, where Cromwell resided, the perpetual intrigues of Parliament made secrets expensive to purchase, and even then, they were held with questionable currency.

Lockhart lifted his head at the thunderous shore and saw the moonlit foam—streaks of white reaching into darkness above a rushing roar—sooner than he expected because he was almost too keenly registering the most minute stimuli.

The boatman signaled the shore still a hundred yards off, and Lockhart saw a horse waiting. He could not see the face of the man holding the reins, but he appeared to be alone. Lockhart glanced again at the boatsman, static and vigilant in the stern. His eyes were wide and his face alight with the white light of the moon, and still he had said nothing.

Lockhart repressed a mild laugh.

No, he thought, *neither would I say anything if I had been summoned in the middle of night by the Captain of the Royal Guard to ferry a mysterious government agent across the channel, then paid handsomely to forget the journey before dawn. The gold in my pocket and the ominous consequences of careless words would be sufficient stimulus for an indifferent memory.*

Bending his head, Lockhart felt the pouch at his waist.

Cromwell's seal upon an unconcealed diplomatic pouch was his greatest guarantee of reaching Paris unharmed. But it could also attract the greatest danger by inspiring curiosity and suspicion. If an attack came, Lockhart was certain it would come without warning and without quarter because they could not risk letting him live.

His hand slipped upward to the varnished mahogany hilt of his flint-lock pistol. The barrel was fully twelve inches in length and forged from Damascus steel appropriated in Blake's raid at Dunkirk. It was bored for accuracy, as the French did for sporting rifles, and fired a single .50-caliber ball. The pommel of the hilt was capped with a solid steel spike the length of his thumb. An odd accouterment, it was true, but hardly noticeable and perfect for staving skulls in a pinch.

His sword was Spanish—Toledo steel, forged and reforged to lighten the blade and purify it to a point where the steel would bend with an impact and straighten again. He was comforted by the certainty that he was greatly skilled at fencing, but such knowledge was a two-edged sword. When one becomes extremely adept at killing, one also becomes aware of how easily one can be killed.

Fortunately, modern weapons had made hand-to-hand combat almost a thing of the past. Since the invention of guns, it was almost unknown for battles to be settled by blows as in days of old. But this, also, had its curse. Now men kill too often because guns have made killing too easy. No longer did men need courage or hard skill gained from years of discipline and training. Now, with a coward's finger and a ball of worthless lead, a kingdom could be claimed.

Slowly the shore drew closer, and Lockhart reached into his boot, pulling out two small bags of coin. His other boot contained a long dagger and keys of indiscriminate make that would supposedly master all known locks. But, as he was experienced with lock picks, he planned to prudently avoid their necessity. Stalwart courage and an accurate pistol were good—an open window and a fast horse were better.

As the ship grounded, Lockhart took a moment to scan the beach and saw only what he expected—nothing.

He tossed a coin bag to the still silent boatman and went over the stern, seeing the pale, flat slates beneath the white tide. He had time for thought as he descended, and then he walked quickly from the surf to the man holding the reins of a large white stallion. He was pleased, as he reached it, to recognize that it was a full-blooded Arabian, bred for stamina and endurance, the perfect beast to bear him across the road to Paris.

Moving quickly—more from suppressed fear than logical need—Lockhart mounted the stallion and turned it immediately away from England and into the darkness.

EMMANUEL STOOD ALONE ON THE BROAD MEZZANINE that bordered the palace. The evening's dramatic confrontation between the Puritan and Inquisitor had certainly not disappointed. But he knew nothing was over; it had only begun.

The courtyard bristled with more activity than usual for this time of night. One woman was carrying a tightly wrapped bundle of sticks on her shoulder, a few men loitered around the inner wall as if planning a revolt, and the blacksmith shop was fully alight with lantern and torch. The cacophony of voices and the sharp ring of a hammer pounding steel against an anvil reminded Emmanuel that every soldier with a sword had been honing and cleaning his blade for yet another charge against the defiant Waldenses.

In truth, Emmanuel admired this man—Gianavel—and, in general, the Waldenses as a people. They had always served him faithfully and were industrious and diligent tradesmen and craftsmen, renowned for their fastidious inclination to collect coinage. Some even called them misers, but they were not misers. They had simply developed, through the long centuries of persecution, a tendency to seek financial security.

Nothing wrong with that, he mused. Indeed, he wished that all the diverse peoples within his kingdom were so inclined to make his treasury infinitely stronger. In fact, the Waldenses reminded him of the occasional Jew he had encountered.

The Jews, too, were fastidious with a coin and had practically invented the idea of window displays, advertising, regular supply schedules, and specialty shops. Like the Waldenses, they were also close-knit and suspicious and tightly regimented. They had social mores and codes of conduct that Emmanuel found convoluted, complex, and, frankly, somewhat bizarre. But he did not deny that they were both skilled and wise. Nor did he have any disputes with them; they were too profitable to despise. And the wheels of every kingdom needed the lubricant of gold to run smoothly.

Staring toward the blacksmith's, he remembered what Simon had taught him about the unquenchable hatred that seemed to burn against the Jewish people. Monarch after monarch had been set upon their destruction, and monarch after monarch had died, and Israel remained. Then he thought of David, who conquered the fierce Moabites, the Gadites, and the feared Amalekites. And, doubtless, the Hebrew would have conquered the entire world—there was no one left to defy him—if the Lord had not told him to sheath his sword.

Always, among these people, God seemed to raise up a man of obscure origin who was destined to defend them from their enemies.

David…Gianavel, he thought.

Both of them…men who were the most dangerous of enemies, men who embodied a purpose greater than themselves.

Outnumbered thousands to one, virtually alone against armies of incalculable power, nothing to fight with but their sword, nothing to live for but their faith—two men who stood virtually alone against the mightiest military machines the world had ever known. And though Gianavel or David would fall upon their faces before the Lord, neither would kneel to any earthly kingdom, neither would surrender to any foe. Even when their doom was assured, they placed their trust in God, and they defied and fought…and they won.

For years the Waldenses had stood courageously against the Catholic Church. But never had they waged a war of this scope and power, defying the combined might of two armies, that of Piedmont and the Church itself, in a grim and terrible last stand when all hope for victory seemed madness. But now they were, and Emmanuel grudgingly respected them for it.

Emmanuel saw a lantern was set aglow in his cousin's bedroom. He stared for a moment to discern shadows but knew Pianessa was there, that he was always there late at night.

He felt nothing about it. His cousin's life was hers. He did not care whom she chose as a suitor as long as it did not threaten his inherited kingdom. And although Pianessa was indeed a ruthless monarch, he could not inherit the House of Savoy; therefore he was not a threat.

If, perchance, he *did* become a threat, Emmanuel had already set in place certain assurances that Pianessa would not long enjoy his victory. For upon Emmanuel's murder, a faithfully harbored fortune in gold would be paid to an unknown apothecary whose knowledge of poison was almost supernatural. Nor had Emmanuel been slow to insure that the sorcerer was safely in *his* pocket, and not Pianessa's. Such men were necessary allies because they were too dangerous not to be allies.

Emmanuel glanced again toward the blacksmith's. The sounds continued but were not so cluttered as before. Soon all those who had spent the long night sharpening their swords would raise them once more against Rora.

Against Gianavel…who was waiting.

Emmanuel wondered if any of them would return.

><><><

Pianessa set the bottle on the table and stared at the wine a moment before raising the glass for a long swallow.

"I've never seen you drink so heavily," Elizabeth said in a tone neither worried nor condemning.

Pianessa arched a corner of his mouth as he gazed at her. "I am attempting to drown my fears of the Vaudois."

Saying nothing, Elizabeth walked forward as the marquis collapsed on the couch. His eyes were narrow black slits, unfocused and vaguely angry.

"I do not understand this man," he muttered at last.

"This Puritan?"

"No. This man—Gianavel."

"What about him, my love?"

"He…disturbs me."

Elizabeth's hand rested on Pianessa's collar.

"This Waldensian's religion is everything to him," Elizabeth said. "You've seen such men before."

The marquis' brow hardened, as if he could see some terrifying image standing before him—an image with which he was not accustomed. "Soldiers have similar weaknesses—fear, hunger, pain. I know how to break men. But I do not understand…this man."

As the duchess stared in silence, Pianessa mumbled strangely, "I wonder if God raised up this man to defend his people."

There was a stunning interlude in which only the duchess blinked. Her voice was quiet. "I didn't think that you believed in God, Pianessa."

Utterly without humor, Pianessa laughed. "Do you truly think one who has watched so many men die could not believe in God?" He smiled. "No, my dear, I believe in God. It's just that, until now, I believed all His people were sheep. They were not soldiers. They were not even men. But this man...he fights like someone who has spent his entire life preparing for war...I don't understand...."

Watching acutely, Elizabeth touched his arm. "Gianavel is just another man, my love."

Pianessa frowned. "Is he?"

Saying nothing, Elizabeth watched as Pianessa suddenly stirred himself, as if embarrassed, and rose to pure another goblet of wine. His stature was oddly bent.

"Yes," he said with a harsh laugh. "Just a man."

Elizabeth reached up to grasp his hand as he approached. "And he will die. Like any...other...man."

Pianessa's frown deepened.

"Yes..."

Even more morose than usual, Sir Samuel Morland laid his flintlock pistol upon the cabinet of his room. He had carried it during dinner just as his two colleagues, the Reverend Troy Barnes and Virgil Rich, a distant relative of the colorful Puritan Parliamentarian Robert Rich, the Earl of Warwick, walked into the room.

Solemnly, Sir Morland turned to the Reverend Barnes and Master Rich, who were bent over a wide variety of weapons they had concealed. He counted two daggers, three pistols, and what appeared to be a maiden's slender poniard.

Master Rich, with a faculty for flair inherited from his charismatic uncle, suddenly pulled out a palm-sized blunderbuss. Concealed within his sleeve, the weapon most closely resembled a fortified pistol with a flared barrel. The port was almost an inch wide and fired a tightly packed ball of grapeshot.

Morland frowned over the weapon. "How many innocent men, women, children, and, perhaps, elephants did you expect to take out with your blunderbuss, Master Rich?"

The youngest Puritan smiled and bowed, hands uplifted. "Self-preservation is a subject close to my heart, gentlemen." He straightened. "I was trusting Providence that neither of my colleagues would be in front of my weapon when it was, in the utmost desperation, discharged."

The Reverend Barnes who, at sixty, was by far the oldest, grunted, "I doubt I would be complaining about a touch of grapeshot as long as it preserved my life. Not that I wish to witness such an experience."

The smile quickly escaped Morland's face as he went to the open window and stared over Turin. It was only in the plains beyond the city that Morland had been moved to shock, then tears, and then a wrath that he had never dreamed possible as he'd ridden through fields of the butchered Waldenses.

He had not expected the travesty of so many bloating bodies unburied, the innumerable severed arms and legs, and the butchered, unidentifiable body parts strewn like so many tree limbs through grass and meadow. Even more ominous were the wide blood trails that so frequently marked streets and roadways and then disappeared into fields or forests, leaving the witness of torment unknown.

Knowing that he had passed no living human being in that entire great valley was enough to measure the totality of this war, though he twice caught a glimpse of something moving furtively in distant trees. He thought it might be children, probably terrified and starving. And on both instances he had ridden to the wood line, searching and calling gently, but the anticipated pathetic images had not emerged from the gloom. Only silence had hovered beneath the busy hum of the forest day, and he had ridden on.

Morland turned from the window. His two companions were waiting with disciplined patience. Even Master Rich seemed willing to suffer indefinitely—evidence that, beneath the colorful façade, the young Puritan was quite serious.

"We have no choice," he declared.

Glances were exchanged.

The Reverend Barnes' brow raised as he crossed his arms on his chest. "A man might read a hefty tome into that comment, brother. Would you care to elucidate?"

"It means that we must continue to take descriptions of the passes and the valleys," Morland replied. "Clearly, the Inquisitors have a vise on the government, here."

"No surprise," mumbled Reverend Barnes as he poured them three glasses of a rich, red wine. "What did you expect?"

Morland began to pace. "I expected atrocities, but not horror. I thought the age had passed when such things—such butchery—were committed in the name of God."

"There are wars that are regrettable," said Barnes and paused. "And there are wars that are evil. I have never seen a war that was wholly right."

"No," muttered Morland. "Nor I."

"So," Barnes asked, "which is this?"

Morland was solemn. "I call it evil, Reverend."

"Aye," the older man agreed.

"Which means we must proceed with My Lord's plan."

"Which is?"

"Scout out the country." Morland resumed his pace. "Make detailed notes of the roads, the passes. Obtain as much information as we can for an invasion."

Master Rich froze. "You're serious?"

"Of course he's serious, boy," said Reverend Barnes.

"Of course I'm serious, boy," Morland muttered.

Rich took a heavy sip of wine.

"These Jesuits and Inquisitors must be stopped! If not, this war could spread across the entire continent!"

Reverend Barnes mused. "Possible...unlikely, though."

"What men may do in one country with impunity, they will attempt in another with opportunity." Morland stopped in stride. "We have just emerged from an age where conflict with the Church meant instant death. Lord Cromwell has no intention of allowing this tyrannical and unashamed intolerance to spread to the shores of England." In thought, he leaned upon the table. "There are two dangers. One, Savoy may realize we are not here simply to plead the cause of the Waldenses. In that case," he added simply, "we will be murdered. Second, if these Inquisitors consider us a genuine threat to their cause, they might incarcerate us as spies."

"Neither works for me," said Master Rich dully.

With a glance Reverend Barnes remarked, "Don't worry, Master Rich, you're too fond of dancing for the Almighty to throw you in the stockades."

The young Puritan laughed.

"Very well," continued Barnes calmly. "What is your plan, then? Further surveying of the countryside? Do you wish to attempt contact with the Waldenses?"

"That is already being undertaken," Sir Morland muttered. "Lord Cromwell has sent an ambassador to them. A man skilled in covert manners."

"Who?" asked Rich.

Sir Morland waved. "Sufficient to say My Lord is using someone diabolically skilled at subterfuge." He paused, as if stunned by his own admission. "A heathen, actually, of outlandish criminal cunning and unholy powers of deception."

His words assumed the tone of the most reluctant respect. "A madman, in truth, who can scarce conceive of any such thing as decency or morality or—"

"No," whispered Reverend Barnes.

"A reprobate scoundrel, by my word, who would steal his very mother's bones from the grave and sell them to buy flowers for a harlot! A man who would—"

"*No!*"

"Yes!" Sir Morland pronounced.

"It is Blake!"

✕∞✕

Once actually accused of selling cemetery plots aboard a ship at sea, Robert "Blackjack" Blake had no qualms with his reputation—gunrunner, gambler, con artist, or ruffian, he was politely tolerant of those who deemed his chameleon-like profession to be the lowliest of criminals and thieves.

Indeed, he had never actually been convicted of any crime whatsoever, hence he considered himself a businessman. Yes, perhaps a businessman engaged in questionable businesses, but he had no feuds with any government or church, save the uncultured Spaniards and the intolerant Catholics. Besides, he was unfailingly kind and generous to the poor, to orphans and widows and the sick. And, the way he saw it, if you loved the poor, the sick, orphans, and widows—if you made a sincere effort to not overindulge in drink or carnal pursuits, one might stand a chance at the Judgment.

He had never been the least impressed with the Church. He had known more than one Protestant reverend prone to brutalizing the poor sheep of his flock, and nothing could increase the furious retributions of the Catholics when someone muttered disagreement. Hence he found it more expedient to wear a number of hats that he would appropriately tip to the appropriate hat, only to change it quickly enough if winds changed. In an age where a point of view could be punished by death, he found it practical for a man to hold more than one point of view.

Through cunning and generous donations he had friends in every country from his native Transylvania to Ireland and could traverse almost any territory without proper papers simply by relying upon his underground network of safe houses, salaried soldiers, priests thankful for his gifts to the treasury, and equally thankful brothels.

While he was yet a youth, working as a spy in the camps of the Turks, he had learned that loyalty and obedience shared the same portion of the brain. But it was far easier to inspire a man with gold than a righteous cause. A useful bit of knowledge, but it did present problems. Indeed, he had accumulated great wealth on a regular basis, but it was so thoroughly taxed through his system of informants, spies, the usual collection of mercenaries, generals, priests, politicians, and harlots that he rarely retained a substantial piece for himself.

C'ais le guerre...

His current activity involved smuggling the most recently designed flint-lock rifles from France to England, an adventure that had rewarded him quite handsomely until he had been recruited—nay, shanghaied—by three grim and implacable captains of Lord Cromwell. The subsequent "dialogue" held in the catacombs beneath Whitehall was far less negotiation than ultimatum, and before evening he was aboard a ship loaded with military hardware.

As prudence required, he had surrendered choice commodities to speed his travels—namely precious kegs of aged Irish whiskey. He had also reluctantly promised his future services on a stunt of meager profit to a coalition of monarchs. And, in a particularly dire moment in which he stood to lose not only his cargo but also his life, agreed to a temporary treaty with a competitor. Doubtless, posterity would record that lamentable moment as the low point of an otherwise distinguished criminal career, but such were the cosmic vagaries of life.

His instructions, detailed by Cromwell and ominously explained by his captain, were exceedingly precise. He was to smuggle a shipment of two hundred flintlock rifles and pistols as well as swords and daggers through Switzerland. Then he was to "somehow" penetrate the security forces of Piedmont and proceed by any means possible above the Pelice and to the lair of the Waldenses, who were at war with the Marquis de Pianessa.

Presented in his cell with the opportunity to perform the task for the sake of "England and all Christendom," Blake had reckoned it beneath a man of his criminal renown. But upon entering the tightly guarded Alps, he realized reaching the Waldenses with his shipment intact would require a bolt—nay, a masterstroke—of criminal genius. Fortunately, it was not the first time he had been so challenged.

Obtaining the robes of a deceased Inquisitor, whom some say was poisoned, he purchased the cooperation of two comrades to pose as priests. Riding within the "Inquisitor's Coach," as it was known, with the secured firearms under the boards at his feet, they made the journey across the mountains relatively unchallenged by Catholic military forces.

It helped that Blake was quick to suspect "the intervention of Lucifer" at the slightest delay with carefully calculated expressions that hinted of a possible mental unbalance.

Indeed, he learned, there was nothing more terrifying than an unhinged Inquisitor beholding demons whispering in yon ear or one who might abruptly smell the presence of the devil within this man's cloak or that. Who stalked about the campsite alert to "blasphemies," or who, for whatever incomprehensible reason, suspected virtually everyone of being in danger of the fires of hell.

It was not with a little relief that the soldiers abandoned him in the valley of Piedmont after hastily participating in yet another communion, Blake intoning solemnly atop a disguised crate of rifles.

But the journey across Piedmont had been more difficult and involved innumerable changes in direction and purpose to confuse random patrols more than willing to offer him more safe passage. But, no, he pronounced, he would rely upon the omnipotent power of the Almighty, thank you, and would not despise the Most High by trusting in musket balls and cannons and gunpowder and the corruption of the flesh that withered and faded like grass....

By now he could deliver the speech with effortless perfection. Nor could he say that it was the first time he had preserved his life in such a manner. Indeed, this was not even the first time his talents had come into use by England's Lord Protector.

Cromwell usually relied upon an established military man with a flair for friendship to execute covert missions. But his Lordship was not above stooping down to pick up a weapon, so to speak. And Blake had repeatedly proven himself adept at "appropriating" things, as Cromwell so tactfully termed it.

The Pass of Pelice rose toward a huge gray monolith of a mountain, or what seemed a mountain, with a huge cave visible even from the valley floor. And it was there that he first encountered a patrol also accompanied by priests.

Watching from the gun-portal of the coach, Blake quickly donned his Inquisitor's cloak and chanced a quick shout to his two "priests" to halt the wagon. In a flash he decided…

When in doubt—Attack.

He heard a guard. "What is this riot?"

Blake waited, then, "What's *this!*"

He threw open the door of the coach and stood angrily, glaring at an amphitheater of fearsomely armed guards.

"Who is in command of this rabble?" Blake shouted and spied a seasoned sergeant major.

The sergeant bowed respectfully. "I'm sorry, Father, but—"

"But you have *reason* to defy the authority of an Inquisitor General?" Blake challenged. "What is the meaning of this?"

Obviously, the sergeant thought the meaning was clear. The land was at war. Everyone was in danger, and what in the blazes was an Inquisitor doing out here in the middle of—

"You cannot answer?" Blake pronounced. "If you speak the truth, why can you not answer?"

The sergeant was struck. He glanced at the priests, and one quickly spurred his horse forward and dismounted. Blake descended from the coach and extended his hand. The priest, not an Inquisitor, knelt and kissed his ring. "You honor us, Father."

"Yes," Blake murmured. "Rise and speak. What is the meaning of this inquiry that delays my passage?"

The priest humbly folded his hands.

"War, Father, the land is…"

"War!" Blake shouted as he lifted his arms. *"Of course there is war!"* There is *always war!"* He pointed to the mountain that he sincerely hoped belonged to the Waldenses.

"There is the devil!"

Horses shied at the great, enraged voice that suddenly trumpeted with such biblical wrath, and in fear many of the soldiers blessed themselves. The first priest, a Jesuit, reached out to gently pull Blake's arm, pleading with him to not invoke the name of the evil one.

Seizing the moment, Blake raised the scepter taken from the hand of the dead Inquisitor and monumented the posture Moses had *surely* taken at the Red Sea.

"I behold innumerable angels battling with yon dragon!" Blake thundered. Face contorted with Old Testament prophecy, he pointed to the sergeant major. "Do not speak! Say nothing of my journey! For God has hedged me in with angels to prevent the evil one from discerning my location and destination!"

Struck by fear, several of the soldiers hastily dismounted and stood quietly, hands folded. They glanced nervously at one another, as if uncertain whether to stand or kneel.

"Kneel!" thundered Blake.

Even the priests flew from their saddles and hit their knees, and Blake stood over them, his terrible arms stretched in agony, face uplifted to the sky.

"You fight with the hand of God on your shoulder!" Blake bellowed and then paused to listen to "divine instruction." He grabbed the closest priest, who flinched. "Do you have the power to defeat the evil one?"

The priest opened his mouth—

"God has given me the power!" shouted Blake. "And for this reason God has sent me! *Pray!*"

All prayed.

Finally there was only silence, and Blake gazed down, the most sublime of smiles upon his emotion-charged face. His words were barely audible. "Do you understand?"

Blake knew that he did not understand. He was fairly certain the priests did not understand. He was absolutely certain the sergeant did not understand.

"I understand," the sergeant whispered.

Blake held the sergeant's face, weeping tears of joy.

"Yes…"

With a dramatic sweep of his priestly cloak, Blake turned and mounted his wagon and they stood. Then he spun and raised a hand with grave authority, and they knelt again. Blake closed his eyes and almost made the mistake of using his egregious Latin.

"The hour is at hand! Pray God delivers me safely to my destination! Pray for your souls and for all the souls around you! I shall return!"

Blake spun toward his purchased priests.

"Onward!"

With finality he hit the interior wall and then peered narrowly through a gunport to see if his scheme had worked. It needed only to last long enough for him to clear this valley.

The sergeant had turned to one of the priests. His head was turned in the opposite direction, shaking from side to side, and the priest was nodding solemnly. In moments they mounted, and five minutes later Blake felt the first faint tendrils of relief.

If his fortune continued he'd locate the Waldenses before nightfall and his job would be finished. But he had no idea how he would make it out of this war-torn plain. He'd worry about that when the time came.

One catastrophe at a time.

13

EMMANUEL WAS TIRED OF WAKING IN THE DARK, tired of lying in the shroud of shadows for long, dark hours until he felt himself growing dark with them, and finally rose to watch the faintest early dawn.

Watching it as he had watched it every morning recently, he wondered what he was truly thinking and feeling, because he no longer slept peacefully. In fact, he could not remember sleep.

Now, every night was a visitation of familiar images that did not yet have a name and which he did not yet understand. He only knew that they were bloody and horrid, that he was somehow their prisoner, and they would not let him go. He sensed that he was doomed, not because he was guilty but because he could not explain his innocence.

He had hoped, after the first several nights, that they would fade, as most dreams tend to fade, but they did not fade. They returned every night, sometimes the same, sometimes different, but always with the same unknowable message or meaning. Then he would awake half-rested, half-exhausted with his head aching from the ceaseless, unending visions.

He wondered if his fitfulness was somehow related to the Waldenses. His ancestors had warred with the Waldenses, also provoked by the Church to destroy the "heretics." He wondered if they, too, might have been haunted night after night by incomprehensible images of death and suffering that caused them to awake fearful and confused. He wondered if he was simply weak, or if the dreams were more than dreams.

Even as he considered it, he knew he could know no answer. If he could ask Simon, he knew he would receive some cryptic warning about God speaking to men in their dreams. But he did not need old Simon to warn him of that. It was a familiar superstition of the age: Dreams were the domain where both angels and demons battled with men.

He closed his eyes, rubbing his forehead where the headache seemed to reside.

Enough...

He loathed rising early and "administering" to affairs of his kingdom before midday. There was simply something surly about listening to noblemen wax pompous about imagined slights or indulging the cold Jesuits who continuously complained about the evil spread across the land by the Waldenses. He greatly preferred roaming the grounds or practicing fencing or archery. He was, in fact, an excellent archer and regularly defeated Pianessa's bowmen during hunts.

Pianessa was an avid hunter and would often disappear for days, only to reappear with a huge stag or boar that he'd brought down in his unique, barbaric manner. And before he was hardly ten years old, Emmanuel had begun accompanying him. For a time he remained well shielded from the brutality and the blood, but eventually he was drawn into the ritual of the hunt, if only to be accepted by the others, and participated in the kill as thoroughly as all but Pianessa himself. But then no one was so thoroughly involved in the hunt as the marquis.

A true killer, Pianessa despised using a rifle on his favorite prey, the tuskheern—a particularly strong and evil-tempered boar more common to the Black Forest than Italy.

Roughly the equivalent weight of a man, tuskheern grew tusks six inches long that were easily capable of gutting a rider or horse. The animals were also incredibly dense with hard muscles perfectly designed for short bursts of speed. At close distances they could outrun or outmaneuver a horse, and if a rider dismounted he would barely land before he had to whirl into the attack of the beast, spear tight in his fists.

Most men preferred to take the notoriously temperamental creatures from the sanctity of a tree with a well-aimed rifle shot, but Pianessa preferred to use a spear.

Emmanuel had witnessed several of the marquis' legendary battles with the fearsome beasts, but he would not have believed the accounts otherwise.

After dogs ran the boar into a ravine or box canyon, Pianessa would advance upon it alone, spear in hand. Both he and the boar were amazingly quick, and though the boar could spin and strike within its own diameter, Pianessa had the advantage of cunning. He wisely used surrounding rocks to the advantage, stabbing deeply into the beast's side to withdraw just as quick, leaping to a new position as it attacked his last. Then, stabbing behind the neck, behind the shoulder, under the neck, the face, reducing it by blood loss, exhaustion, and fear, he would savage it until it was dead on its feet. Then he would finish it—a plunging thrust that would pin it against rock or tree.

It was not pretty, or pretty to listen to, and Emmanuel had tired quickly of the rituals. He didn't remember when he had first deferred an invitation to the field, but he had never reconsidered. And he sensed that the marquis was instinctively aware of his disgust, but nothing had ever been intimated.

Emmanuel had never seen a man thrive on blood as hotly as Pianessa. And it was not something that came with a season of boredom. Pianessa was addicted to the thrill of combat as some men were addicted to the thrill of wine or gambling or women. If the marquis was not on the battlefield, he was on the hunt. Emmanuel's last hunt also included his first fencing match with Pianessa.

After Pianessa had killed five boar in a single day and called for camp, his blood was still hot and he politely invited Emmanuel to a fencing match, all the known rules of practice—particularly "no blood"—and courtesy, to be honored. Although Emmanuel stood no chance against the marquis, he accepted. If he could not win the match, he would at least win respect.

Squaring off, Emmanuel circled slowly while Pianessa remained relatively in place, neither advancing nor retreating. Obviously, he was confident his extensive skill and experience, as well as his longer reach and superior strength, would be sufficient to nullify any youthful advantage of speed.

Unwilling to be patronized, Emmanuel struck with remarkable quickness. It was a smooth lunge and totally without warning, he thought, but Pianessa parried with casual unconcern before the blade was halfway to the target, and they began to slowly circle.

Not to be intimidated, Emmanuel struck again, but the marquis was noticeably faster with the second parry, striking the blade powerfully aside to instantly return a riposte that caught Emmanuel flat-footed and shocked. Only at the last moment did Pianessa direct the saber so that it plunged harmlessly past his ribs, and Emmanuel knew he would have died then and there.

With a nod, the Duke of Savoy honorably acknowledged the point, as custom required, and Pianessa nodded, equally gracious. Onlookers applauded the noble restrain and respect indicated by the wordless exchange, but to Emmanuel it meant much more. It meant that he understood Pianessa was the true master, and he was only a boy-king—something that could never be said but with swords and in the training arena.

But the contest was not over. In a blinding series of parries, Pianessa repeatedly deflected Emmanuel's blade before lunging, but Emmanuel was prepared for the lionlike speed and parried to riposte.

Almost—*almost*—he caught Pianessa off-guard, but the marquis turned his torso just so and touched the saber with his *bare hand* to direct it perfectly past his shoulder. It was a delicate move executed with hairsbreadth precision and inhuman timing, but Emmanuel could have come no closer in a real duel and would have probably died a second time as Pianessa's blade descended only to the crest of his unprotected forehead before the marquis stopped it in midair.

Although Pianessa was capable of startlingly swift attack—a storming *largeness* of attack when he surged inward with a bear's strength, his huge reach covering immense ground as his saber flashed up-down-*lost*-plunging.

But Pianessa seldom resorted to such mocking displays of skill. Instead, he relied upon an uncanny ability to read the tiny, almost invisible gestures— a tiny shifting of weight, the blade raised or lowered a fraction of an inch, the straightening of one's back, the direction of an opponent's eyes, or the faintest bend of a leg or wrist—that signaled what an opponent was about to do.

In that discipline, indeed, Pianessa's ability was almost supernatural.

Yet by forcefully mixing feints into thrusts, Emmanuel slowly began to force Pianessa to greater speed. Once he even came close to a legitimate hit, but at the last moment Pianessa reacted with a blinding parry that almost tore Emmanuel's saber from his hand. And in that moment, alone, the prince had felt the mountainous might that struck behind that unbending blade, and he had known true fear. It was as if, in the blink of an eye, the Pianessa he had known was replaced by a monstrous force of nature that *would* destroy whatever stood before it.

In the end Emmanuel was soaked in sweat and had come no closer to touching Pianessa than touching the surface of the moon. The marquis had made sport for him—a lion playing with a kitten. Indeed, he had never expected to even appear to be Pianessa's equal with a blade. No man who ever lived was Pianessa's equal with a blade.

Pianessa's renown for hand-to-hand combat, pistol or sword, was recognized far beyond the borders of Piedmont. Indeed, he was feared throughout France and Spain and Germany for his mastery of fencing, his uncanny marksmanship, and prodigious strength. It was common gossip that he routinely entertained others as a youth by bending iron bars with his bare hands, or by taking on all comers in Savate, a savage form of fighting invented by the French.

Taken together, Pianessa's legendary skills and superhuman strength were disturbing. But even more disturbing was Pianessa's inhuman indifference to life or death—including his own.

Perhaps that had something to do with his dreams....

The sun was much higher when Emmanuel noticed it again, and he realized it was time to reluctantly prepare for the day.

His schedule contained a tour of the "pacified" villages with Sir Morland—an expedition Emmanuel had rigidly avoided until now. He had seen butchered bodies before; he did not need to see the Waldenses to know their flesh was red like any other man or that their bones glistened pink like any other man. He only worried what manner of righteous indignation the Puritans would dare to voice and how he would have to respond.

There was a point, of course, where he could not submit to criticism. He was a sovereign and he was not required, nor did he have any compulsion, to satisfy the moral tenants of England's Lord Protector, Oliver Cromwell. But he was also a vulnerable sovereign who possessed neither the militia nor the resources to resist an attack by Cromwell's garrisons. They outnumbered his militia a hundred to one and would doubtless bring heavy cannon and mortar capable of reducing Turin to the ground.

The day had whitened from an orange tint to white, and the sun was blinding, almost painful. He didn't know when Sir Morland and his colleagues would emerge, but he knew Puritans were not known for sleeping late. With a sigh he turned from the day and walked to his wardrobe. His knee-high riding boots and wool trousers and shirt were already selected.

Today he would dress as a hunter, as if he had the desire to ever hunt or kill anything ever again.

✕✕✕✦✕✕✕

There was no dispute.

They would fight because they were doomed to die if they surrendered. But the fact that everyone was in agreement with the assessment did little to settle the angry and even violent attitudes of those gathered in the stable.

There were less than seven barbes remaining. The rest had been caught in their villages or on the roads of Piedmont and murdered outright or tortured to death. And the few who'd managed to crawl through enemy lines seemed angry for having survived the initial conflict. They were not so foolish as to wish that they had also been killed, but their guilt found expression in suicidal plans for revenge.

Seated on a wooden gate, Gianavel listened for more than an hour, waiting while every man spoke, including the most revered of the barbes, Aventius Solomai, who gave an inspiring monologue intended to boost spirits. And he waited until impulsive plans for assaults upon Turin were presented and rejected.

Then a voice erupted near the open door.

"We stand no chance of winning this war!"

Gianavel glanced at the prosperous, black-haired man; his name was Silas. He was a nobleman, one of Rora's largest landowners. Easily, he had enough gold to buy his life from the Inquisitors.

"Gentlemen!" Silas raised both hands. "Think about what you're saying! Fight them? Are you insane? They outnumber us a thousand to one! They have unlimited cannon and cavalry! What good does it do to continue a doomed fight?"

Aventius turned. "And so you will disobey God to obey men?"

"I will plead for mercy!"

"You will die without mercy!"

"And how do you know that?" Silas retorted, stepping forward as if to physically fight.

Aventius stretched out his staff toward the valley. "Six thousand souls slain by the sword tell me that I know!" He pointed at Silas. "Cowardice is a greater sin than violence!"

"Avaunt!" Silas shouted. "You are fool enough to call me coward?"

"I call any man coward who does not defend his family because he fears for his own life!"

One of Silas's men took a single step forward, and then Bertino's low tone cut through the uproar. "Touch him not."

At the quiet words, the man stared.

Silas, surprised that his unspoken wrath was not executed, turned with unconcealed contempt to the big farmer. "First you would insult me, and now you threaten me with base violence? You are twice as wrong as the others!"

Bertino shrugged. "I'm not inclined to be saving toothpicks when my house is on fire, Silas. Right or wrong, you lay hands on that old man, I'll break your arm."

Silas looked at his man, who was already sauntering back to the wall. There had been no growling threat in Bertino's words, just a quiet, unnerving resolve to do exactly what he had said. Men who struck without emotion were to be regarded much quicker and closer than men who struck in anger and fear.

Silas turned to the lofts. "We are fools to throw away our lives like this! What is a promise to their Church? Empty words that mean nothing! Can a man not speak one thing to the devil and believe another thing in his heart? And is the heart not more important? Is not what a man believes in his heart worth more than empty words? Of course it is! So why die for words? Is it not a small compromise to deceive them for the sake of peace?" He turned in every direction.

None answered.

Gianavel watched.

"Well?" Silas demanded. "Is it not worth a vain promise to make peace with these men who will kill us if we don't renounce? What benefit is there in fighting them?"

Aventius turned with an angry scowl. "What does it *ever* benefit a man to defend himself against evil? It preserves his *soul!*"

"Six thousand souls are dead because they resisted!"

"There is a death beyond death!" Aventius pointed with his staff. "Do not fear the One who can only destroy the body! Fear the One who can destroy the soul!"

"So you will throw away your life?" Silas dared to approach the older man. "Did God not make this body? Is this body to be thrown aside for a principle?" He advanced. "How will you minister to others if you're *dead*! Is it not better to lie and continue to live and carry on the work of God in hiding?"

"You do not speak of compromise!" Aventius thundered. "You speak of renouncing God! Bread, clothes, home, and possessions may be renounced! A man cannot renounce the Lord!"

Silas spun. "God judges the heart!"

"Yes!" Aventius declared with equal anger. "God judges the heart! But God judges the heart by what man is required to know! There are many things man does not know! Why is there suffering? Why do the innocent perish when the wicked prosper? But we do know *this*: A man cannot renounce God with his words and preserve God in his heart!"

"You say!" retorted Silas. "Who are you to declare the judgment of God?"

Aventius stood in smoldering wrath. Then his mouth closed, as if in restraint, before he spoke. His tone was iron resounding on iron. "'It is written; whoever believes in his heart and professes with his mouth that Jesus is Lord shall be saved.'"

"You cannot profess to be the last word on wisdom, Aventius!" Silas's frown was bitter. "And there is more than one way to serve God!"

Aventius calmed and spoke with a far more grave tone. "Is serving God your desire? Or is it preserving your skin?"

Silas gazed sullenly upon the barbe, then raised his gaze to the multitude. Finally he shook his head; his anger was dulled. "Then you sentence us to death."

Every head turned down.

Aventius looked to Gianavel. When the silence lengthened and no one spoke, Gianavel raised his head. He looked across those lining the stalls, those seated in the loft. He saw Bertino, stoic and immovable, and Hector and Jahier. They were waiting.

"The question," Gianavel began, "is whether we should fight, or not." He stepped out into the middle of the stable. "Before a man raises his hand to fight, he must know this: Does God require a man to fight this fight?"

Everyone watched, listening.

"It is not a choice to obey the laws of the Lord," he continued. "God has commanded us to obey His Word so that we may live. So how does fighting honor God? That is the question. And I will tell you the answer." He stared. "By establishing justice in the land."

"Justice?" Silas challenged.

"Yes," said Gianavel. "We fight to establish justice in the land. Because without justice…there will be no peace. And God has instructed us to establish peace on the earth."

"How so?"

Gianavel met the eyes of all those staring upon him. "Peace has never been the reward of men who tried to make peace with violent men. Our brothers in the valley tried to make peace. They were murdered, because

these men have no reason to desire peace. We have a duty to administer justice to those who break the law—a duty to instill a desire for peace in those
who would not desire peace."

"An eye for an eye?" the man muttered.

"'It is written,'" Gianavel began slowly, "'tooth for tooth, eye for eye,
piece for piece, life for life.'" He paused a long time. "It is also written: 'If a
man strikes you on one cheek, turn to him the other, also.' And it is written: 'When I was with you, you did not need a sword. But now I am going
to be with the Father, and if you do not have a sword, sell your cloak and
buy one.'

"It is not easily that men shed the blood of men, and God will hold
each man accountable for every thought and every action. Yet there is a
time to establish peace in the land. And if that involves confronting those
who crush down the weak—those would destroy the poor, the widows and
orphans and anyone else in their path, we have a responsibility to take
courage and stop them."

Gianavel continued, "Those who take up the sword do not take it in
vain, and every government is established by God. But men who murder are
not representatives of any government. They are murderers, not soldiers."
He raised a finger. "And the law says that a man shall not murder. Nor shall
a murderer go unpunished. To not punish a murderer for his crime is also
against the law. Yes, men must be punished for murder, or there will be no
justice in the land. And if there is no justice, there will be no peace."

Gianavel became more severe. "This is the darkest hour a man may face.
We have been sentenced to death for obeying the laws of God and breaking the laws of man. But what are we to do? Disobey the laws of God to
obey the laws of men? Renounce God to preserve our own lives?" He

waited a long time, and then longer. No one spoke; many bowed their heads or looked away.

"Each man here must make a decision," he said at last. "I do not expect, nor will I ask, any man to do anything that stands against his conscience, for God speaks to a man through the spirit, and the spirit knows things the mind will never know. But each man must search his heart before God and ask God what is the right thing to do in this valley of death. Should we refuse to defend ourselves against murderers and rapists and thieves?"

Gianavel shook his head. "I do not fight for vengeance. I do not fight to save this flesh that will die soon enough. I fight because God has ordered men to defend the poor, the weak, and the sick from those who would destroy them. I fight because I know that without justice there will never be peace for our children or our children's children. And if I should die fighting to establish justice, what is my loss?"

He took a stance so that all could see him. He spoke so that all could hear him.

"It is far worse to save your life for the sake of life than lose your life for the sake of Christ."

They were words spoken quietly, though all heard easily enough. And no one spoke nor moved, until finally a shuffling was heard in the loft— someone out of sight moving for the ladder. Then more shuffling, once the moment ended, and then more began filing from the barn. Finally all had departed, leaving only Bertino, Jahier, Hector, and Aventius.

Gianavel searched the old man's face; he was simply weary. But there would be no respite from labors now; he would have to persevere. "Aventius, I want you to see to the wounded—all those who need spiritual assistance. Let them know they are not alone—strengthen them."

"Aye," he nodded, too fatigued for further words.

With a laugh, Jahier slapped the old barbe on the back, then looked at Gianavel. "Good speech, Joshua. But how do you think they're going to fare when we're attacked again?"

"The same as any man," Gianavel answered. "Each according to his abilities. Any word from our spies?"

Jahier shook his head. "We're blind as a bat and deaf as a stone."

Together they studied the map. Then Gianavel spoke, almost to himself. "Pianessa is no fool. He won't try a direct assault on the pass again." To Hector: "What do you think?"

Hector sniffed, stepped forward. "Pianessa is cold-blooded, sure enough. But it's not practical to lose men. I'd say he's planning some sort of surprise attack. Probably on three or four fronts at the same time."

Frustration hardened Gianavel's forehead. "Yes...that's what I'm thinking. But from where?" No one spoke, and then Gianavel picked up his rifle. "All right. Let's just keep the guards in position while we wait for one of our spies to return. I don't expect we'll be getting much sleep from now on."

Jahier forced a tired smile. "Like we were?"

✕○○✕◈✕○○✕

When the wagon could climb no farther, Blake pulled it far off the trail and cut branches to conceal it from view. He worked furiously for two hours to conceal every sign of his passing, then used a branch to sweep the wheel tracks and footprints.

He'd paid off his two "priests" long before he reached this high point in the Alps, not trusting them to know the location of his merchandise. Now he had the final responsibility of locating the Waldenses and delivering his cache of rifles.

He was entirely justified, in consideration of the risks he had already undertaken, in heading cross country and reporting to Cromwell that the rifles had been delivered into the grateful arms of partisans that would send emissaries in gratitude for his munificence. Of course, if the "partisans" arrived at Cromwell's door—not unlikely enough—and appealed for an explanation as to why the Lord Protector had not lifted a finger in their defense, Blake's flourishing trade in England would suffer the harshest of blows, along with his neck.

He glanced at the sky. The sun was high, but within these towering cliffs, darkness came several hours before sunset. He reflexively checked his pack for a blanket and provisions, having no intention of returning to the wagon tonight—or ever, for that matter. No, indeed, he planned to simply lead these valiant people to their arms, point, and make a stealthy exit. This wasn't his war and he had no intention of joining it.

As he climbed higher he thought he heard voices in the darkness and crouched beside the trail, listening for a long time. Patience was something he had in abundance, since he was not adept at violence. Of course, he was handy with a cutlass or flintlock when genuine desperation required, but he greatly preferred deception and stealth. Not that he was a coward. He simply thought it foolish for a man to answer every offense with a sword.

Of course, he believed in God. He absolutely believed in God. But he also believed that God was not so easily understood, nor was God disposed to limitations or rituals or walls or organizations or conventional recipes for spirituality. He had met paupers with greater hearts than kings and priests, and he did not think heaven would be rich without them.

Sliding through the forest gloom, Blake mused on his life as he often did in these quiet moments. True, he was a thief. That could not be denied. But he never stole from the poor. He did have a sense of honor, after all. Nor had he planned on a life of crime. It had simply happened, so to speak. When war had taken away his home, he had adapted to his new environment. And it was to his surprise as much as anyone else's that he even found himself remarkably accomplished for the task. Much like men became great soldiers or even kings—fate, destiny, luck, whatever—he was simply a great thief.

He had already determined that this war between the Marquis de Pianessa and the Waldenses would be more of the same—another religious war over the Ultimately Unknowable, with both sides condemning the other for their colossal stupidity amid accusations of heresy, and blasphemy hurled like cow dung until everyone appeared very much the same color. One side would be as vicious as the other, all thoughts of nobility and righteousness flung to the wind as soon as the first bullet was thrown.

Finally convinced of the forest's emptiness, Blake crept from concealment and stepped soundlessly in the open. He searched everything that could be seen, but the trail was winding and narrow. Though he could not see far enough ahead to inspire any confidence, nothing was without risk. Cautiously, he began to work his way up the path, acutely alert to both wildlife and sounds alien to the forest.

He had learned a long time ago that bird and fowl were the best means of determining the presence of others in the forest. A man might not be able to see another man, might not be able to hear him. But fowl had the predictable tendency to chatter and create a general racket when a possible threat was beneath them. By watching the trees, he felt fairly confident that the only threat they observed was him.

That was when he rounded the corner and saw the heads…heads from children no more than twelve years old, all hung from the branches of trees.

Strolling before the table, upon which sat an exactingly detailed map of the Pelice, Pianessa seemed particularly buoyed. He nodded his head steadily as he studied a ridge of mountains that crested the border of the valley of Rora. He pointed to a particularly steep encirclement on the map.

"The Castelluzo is climbable." He nodded. "Even in the dark, we can slip an entire regiment up that face. If they can reach the ridge before sunrise, we can surround Rora during the night and attack at dawn. They will exit their huts to find themselves put upon before and behind. There will be no place to flee." He stood back, distinctly pleased. "Yes...a good plan."

Captain Mario squinted over the map, as if unable to understand Pianessa's plan, as the marquis turned. "Captain Mario? I'm sure you would like another attempt to attack the village. What are your sentiments?"

Mario did not raise his face. "I will lead the attack," he said quietly. "I want this man's head."

"Oh no," Pianessa countered calmly as he poured a fresh chalice of wine. "No, Captain, the great Gianavel's head cannot be taken by you or any of your men. You must capture Gianavel *alive.*"

At that, Mario slowly raised dark eyes. "What?"

Draining half the chalice at once, Pianessa laughed as he wiped his mouth on his sleeve. He gestured to Incomel and Corbis, positioned nearby. "The good Inquisitors have need of Captain Gianavel. They are obliged to save his soul."

Pianessa's laugh was solid with contempt. He smiled at Incomel, who yet seemed moody from his confrontation with the Puritan. "Is that not correct, noble Inquisitor? You must rescue Gianavel's soul before you sever his head from his body?"

"Do not concern yourself with matters beyond your understanding, Pianessa." Incomel's voice was unemotional. "The Church concerns itself with matters far greater than the sword. Perhaps"—he raised an eye—"you will do well simply to succeed in your next campaign."

The barb was not lost upon the marquis, though a challenge was instantly returned. "Perhaps, Inquisitor. Which is why you must escort me into the field."

Incomel's face was as unyielding and frozen as a marble mask.

"You see," the marquis continued as he again took up his chalice, holding forth from his place, "I have decided that perhaps my last two excursions failed because we did not have God on our side. What my army truly needs are the prayers of mighty men of God like Moses who can pray down a great victory by stretching out their staff over the mountain." The marquis waited a moment. "Does God not fight with you, Inquisitor?"

"Of course He does." Holding a cold gaze for a heartbeat, Incomel turned away. "I shall have several of the Jesuits and Inquisitors venture into the field with your army, Pianessa. But forgive me if I am unable to personally accompany you."

"Why is that, Inquisitor?"

"Affairs of the Church, of course."

Pianessa's teeth gleamed. "Of course."

Incomel said nothing more as he walked across the heavily stilled chamber. When he was fully gone, Pianessa leaned both hands on the map, staring down with a slowly settling frown. After a moment he turned his head to a nearby sergeant major.

"Duncan," he said.

Taller than Pianessa himself, but not nearly so heavily constructed, the red-bearded Duncan looked more Scottish than Italian. Yet he also appeared

236

to be a seasoned commander. He seemed neither cruel nor hesitant to be cruel, and equally indifferent.

"Yes, sir?"

"Assemble in the plain southwest of the Vellaro." Pianessa was forced to modify his habit of tilting his head over a subordinate as he addressed the sergeant major. "I want every man equipped with pikes, but I also want one full company of musketeers." He became studious. "These Waldenses seem to be marksmen, and they prefer to hit from the cover of trees and rocks. If we cannot hit them as readily as they hit us, we'll be decimated before we breach their walls."

"Understood, sir."

"Also," Pianessa added thoughtfully, "have the first company comprised mostly of cannon fodder."

The sergeant major grunted. "Yes, sir. We still have some of the Irish. They were not completely killed. And we have a thousand prisoners from El Torre."

"Very well; put Cromwell's criminals and those from El Torre in the first company. We will climb the Castelluzo tomorrow night—there is no moon—in three battalions. The first will be the Irish, and the second comprised equally of musketeers. Once we reach the summit, we'll separate to enclose the valley in the dark. We attack at dawn."

"Very good, sir."

"You are dismissed." Pianessa turned to Mario and stared for a somber, grim moment. "And you will lead the first regiment, Captain Mario. I know you wouldn't want to miss the fiercest fighting! And surely you want to ingratiate yourself once more into the good graces of the Duke of Savoy, whom you have so miserably failed…twice."

Mario's lips came together in a tight line. Finally he managed, "Yes, sir. I will personally take this man prisoner."

"Do that," Pianessa replied, but the faint smile faded with the last word. "You are dismissed."

"Thank you, sir."

Pianessa refilled his chalice and enjoyed a moment of solitude before he turned his head, as he so often turned it in battle, sensing something that only a born warrior would sense. But in the solemnity of his castle, the tilt of his head was far more threatening. He beheld Incomel standing in the shadow of a corridor, staring. The Inquisitor revealed no regret or fear that he had apparently been caught spying. Pianessa lifted the chalice, smiled.

"To your God, Inquisitor."

✕✕✕◈✕✕✕

Dressed as somberly as the night before, the Puritans approached along the parapet with Sir Morland at the tip of the black wedge. But unlike yesterday, they were carrying sabers and flintlock pistols in the style of gentlemen of the crown. Apparently what had not been deemed acceptable by English prudence at a dinner was allowed for a day's excursion on the battlefield.

Emmanuel was similarly armed with a specially forged saber and a flintlock pistol. He wore rough riding clothes more suited for hunting because some half-reflex inspired him to dress in the same dark tones as the Puritans. He had to admit that the grim attire did lend an air of profound and serious authority.

Sir Morland bowed. "Your Highness," he said correctly, not disregarding protocol even though he was here for a dispute, "I pray you rested well."

"Yes," Emmanuel lied and glanced at the old man, Barnes, and the younger one, who was barely older than himself. "I'm sorry," he said, "but we never had an opportunity to converse last evening."

"The duchess was quite fascinating," said the older one with a curt bow. "I am Reverend Barnes and this, as you doubtless remember, Your Majesty, is Master Rich. We want to thank you for your hospitality and graciousness, and I anticipate an encouraging exchange of ideas with you this evening."

At Master Rich's precise bow, his boot heels clicked. "At your service, Your Majesty."

Emmanuel didn't miss the fact that Master Rich declined to venture beyond what was obviously a prearranged comment. Doubtless, he was accompanying the older Puritans to learn how matters of this nature were resolved, not to resolve them.

"We are honored," Emmanuel said and gestured to the courtyard where a half-dozen stallions were already saddled. "I ordered the Master of Arms to have a selection of mounts so that you might choose one suited to your temperament. Please…"

It only required a moment, as they were all experienced horsemen, and Sir Morland selected a fiery young Arabian with huge hindquarters. Shaking its midnight mane against the scarlet run, the stallion seemed to somehow match the black aura of the Puritan. And once he mounted the saddle, Sir Morland was indeed the image of grim doom, black cloak lifting above the glossy blue-black of the stallion, his sword—a long, straight saber much thinner and lighter than Pianessa's—angling with a glint of silver. Even more, Sir Morland presented the clear impression that he was not unaccustomed to bearing weapons upon a steed.

Emmanuel had been the first to saddle and waited patiently until all were ready. He raised his hand to a sergeant and sixty-six mounted musketeers.

The troop opened the gate and rode out of the courtyard, waiting in the field. They would ride close behind the Duke of Savoy through the day.

With a tilt of his wide-brimmed hat, Sir Morland nodded. "At your pleasure, Your Majesty."

As they cantered toward the portico, Emmanuel glanced at the Puritan, who masterfully sat his saddle. "And just what do you wish to see, Sir Morland?"

Sir Morland paused. "An interesting question. But I do not think I shall see what I wish to see, Your Majesty."

Emmanuel did not need to ask. Yet he could not stop himself from commenting, "There is far more to Piedmont than death, Sir Morland. We are not always at war."

"No," the Puritan acknowledged, "you are not." He leaned upon the saddle horn. "In fact, Your Majesty, I believe that, left to your own devices, you would not presently be at war with the Waldenses. Further, I believe you are, at the core, a good and decent monarch, and you are protective of all your subjects. But that does not change the fact that war has come, and that it is a war that should end quickly."

Emmanuel was silent, then asked, "And how would you suggest that I do that, Sir Morland?"

"I do not know," said the Puritan, "but I know God will not be mocked. Not by any army of this age, Your Highness, nor an army of any age to come."

14

LOCKHART WAS GRATEFUL THAT HIS TRIP to Paris had been largely uneventful; not that he'd been exposed to the more barbarous elements of society for it to be otherwise. No, his greatest danger was—and remained—the possibility that the secret purpose for his visit had been discovered, and that he'd been targeted by assassins. He was encouraged by his belief that competent assassins were not as common as many believed and that nothing was more common than incompetent assassins.

Not only did unqualified killers routinely botch the job, leaving the target hotly disposed to retaliation, they inevitably talked under torture and exposed not only their clients but those not even remotely associated with the venture to accusation. In the end, a hundred heads would roll like coconuts for the stupidity of two or three upstarts who lacked the good grace to at least find an assassin qualified for the job. Nevertheless, Lockhart took every possible precaution. It's not that he feared death so terribly; he simply feared dying stupidly.

And yet there had been a disturbing event in a small tavern near Crastel that he still did not understand. It had begun quietly enough; an obscure

argument between two Frenchmen over some imagined slight. But it esca-
lated quickly to blows, and then the tavern lamp was smashed to the floor
and the room plunged into darkness. Lockhart had immediately chosen
escape and had been moving for the rear exit, thrusting others out of his
way, when he sensed rather than heard someone moving directly toward
him with a purpose other than escape.

He had turned to see the man—big, a true manhandler—almost on top
of him with a long dagger low in his fist. Lockhart's hand had immediately
closed around the flintlock at his belt, but in the chaos he wasn't certain that
he would even have time to fire when something else of equal strangeness
happened.

Lockhart caught only a glimpse of a shadow—a man dressed totally in
black and who moved with a panther's sinuous strides—as the man collided
hard against his attacker.

The man who was a mere step from spearing Lockhart through the
heart was flung to the side like a broken treelimb, and in the next breath
the shadow moved into the crowd and was gone.

It happened so quickly that Lockhart was not certain what he had seen.
Then, standing pistol in hand, he slowly became convinced that he was no
longer in danger. The tavern was virtually abandoned, and in the stillness
Lockhart moved forward and bent over the man who had held the dagger.
He had been stabbed through the heart.

No time for questions.

Lockhart had hastily exited the building, found his horse, and vanished
into the night. He did not know if he had seen what he believed he had seen.
He knew only that the big man had moved upon him with a purpose deadly
and certain until the second man entered the fray. And then the second
man vanished as quickly as he appeared, leaving a dead man in his wake.

Never had Lockhart seen a man killed so efficiently. It was as if the night itself had reached out and struck the ruffian and with the silent sweep of darkness vanished again, leaving the viewer uncertain whether he had seen anything at all.

Alone in his room, Lockhart cleaned his pistol and rifle, swabbing out the barrels with warm water while keeping a second set of pistols loaded and primed.

In addition to cleaning them every night, he had long ago adopted the habit of firing them in the morning to insure they were continuously tested and freshly loaded. He'd seen men die dry-firing a pistol they'd loaded only two days before. He had no intention of making that his last mistake on earth.

He turned his mind to more inevitable events and studied the street below his third-floor chamber. Only a few Parisians littered the walkway, not enough to accomplish some riotous stunt even if they wished. Yet he could not shake the—he hated to use the term—"creepy" sensation that clung to his back.

Gazing across the street, he mentally ran through the rudimentary lessons of spying. Never alter your schedule, never do anything out of character, never look over your shoulder, never whisper in the presence of others, never confess to anything, for your accusers may be bluffing, never carry incriminating papers. It was best not to be seen, but if you are seen, then advertise your presence. And Lockhart had invented his own particular technique for deception—it was a measure of true genius to appear far too stupid to be dangerous.

The mostly empty street made it far easier to detect surveillance. There were no elements of militia in sight other than random patrols and official guardsmen. The weather was fair, and the evening was coming apace. From what he could observe, all the basic advantages were present for a covert midnight run to reach the house of Cardinal Mazarin, which is what Cromwell specifically instructed him to do.

He was not, by any means, to attempt to reach the cardinal during the day, because Mazarin was still much hated and feared by too many within his own government. Although Mazarin had defeated his enemies during the revolution, such men do not easily forget defeat. Even now they would execute swift vengeance, for whatever vague cause, if they had enough to call a tribunal. And the French had never been severe about evidence or testimony, which is why so many heads had rolled not five years ago.

Now, at last, there was a sense of permanent government, but governments were comprised of people, and people were not permanent. King Louis, still a child, had the advantage of having survived the revolution, and when he came to manhood he would, doubtless, not forget the reign of lawless terror that almost drove him from the throne, nor those who caused it. Lockhart did not doubt that some battles would be finished only after Louis came into his own, so to speak.

He lowered the curtain and turned into the chamber.

It was opulent and spacious, as everything in Paris seemed to be. He'd decided that the French considered largeness synonymous with grandiosity. But, personally, he was a man of conscript taste and considered it somewhat capricious.

His legs had ceased trembling from the deep fatigue of riding, but Lockhart was profoundly weary. He moved to the thick feather bed and was careful to once again ram the ball home in his pistol and recharge the pan with fresh powder before propping it upright on the dresser. His rifle, similarly charged, stood upright beside the headboard, and his saber and dagger hung from the post. He did not particularly anticipate an attack in the few hours he had to rest. But he was a professional, and there were rules. And once a man began to break the rules, either by complacency or laziness, he was doomed.

As he lay down, Lockhart wondered about this Cardinal Mazarin. Wondered if the intrigue-shrouded priest would see the convoluted political benefits of interceding for the Waldenses, or perhaps do it simply because it was right. Or, then, perhaps the legendary Mazarin would order him shot as a spy.

He decided not to dwell on that scenario. He was in this now, and returning to England with a confession of cowardice was not an option. So, as he had so often done in battle, he considered himself dead anyway. It was for peace of mind but also for survival. The conviction allowed him to sleep and behave without undue concern, which was as dangerous as too much concern.

Sleep descended before he closed his eyes.

✕✕✕◈✕✕✕

It was a depressingly short journey to the outskirts of the valley of Rora, hardly more than an hour's ride, and while they were yet miles away, Emmanuel had detected black plumes of smoke. He knew that the largest measure of the butchery had been completed days before, and that only those "above the Pelice," as it was called, remained. But he still feared what dreadful display of ruined creatures they might encounter by accident.

He'd had the foresight to send patrols ahead of their carefully selected route, insuring that no ghastly displays would be encountered. But such precautions were only adequate for what was here when the patrols passed, not what happened to wander from the forests afterward. He felt slight relief that there had not yet been any events that would galvanize the Old Testament indignation of Sir Samuel Morland.

He glimpsed Morland pointing once again toward the Castelluzo. "These mountains that I have observed for hours—they mark the perimeter of Rora?"

Cantering beside the Puritan, Emmanuel replied, "It's their western boundary."

"Is there a pass?"

"A trail begins on the far side of the River Pelice." Emmanuel recalled the stiff angle of the climb and added, "It reaches the summit after a very difficult ascent, then descends rather comfortably into the valley beyond."

The Puritan studied the mountain range. "Yes…a natural fortress."

Emmanuel admitted, "Their valley is quite inaccessible, particularly when they are defending the pass."

"This pass is the only access to their land?"

"No." Emmanuel pointed to the west. "A ravine, probably no more than four miles in length, but exceedingly difficult to climb. It leads from El Torre and almost immediately enters the mountains. As I said, it's a difficult climb, but it presents a far more difficult descent. More men have been killed descending than climbing."

"Interesting," the Puritan remarked with the gaze of a soldier. "Yes, God has provided them a great defense. I understand why your first two attacks against the village were repulsed."

Emmanuel felt no impulse to defend Mario's stupidity, but neither did he think it prudent to slight Pianessa's capabilities. In this uncertain situation, the fact that Pianessa was indeed a brilliant general was more advantage than not.

"Pianessa did not expect such a spirited defense," he said, attempting to sound offhand. "I believe he has summoned his finest officers to deal with the situation."

It was then that what Emmanuel had dreaded finally occurred—occurred with a stunning white drama that caused his entire reality to change, as if a curtain were lifted on a stage, revealing a wasteland beyond burning with black slag and volcano-like plumes of fire. He heard the Puritan charge his horse, and Sir Morland was riding before him, his right hand descending to spur the stallion forward.

The Puritan's black cloak swept up, blocking the ghastly image of whatever poor creature had stumbled from the forest. It was difficult to determine, exactly, what it was because Emmanuel caught only the briefest glance of a red, humanlike thing emerging from the forest gloom, covered in blood with hands outstretched to the sky, mouth silently screaming in what had once been a face that had once had eyes.

※○○◈○○※

When Gianavel entered Hector's house, he found Angela dressing the wounds of a farmer Gianavel had known all of his life. The man's arms and face were heavily bandaged, and he was calm and silent. Only a slight rising of his chest gave evidence that he was still alive.

Bending, Gianavel kissed Angela on the cheek, and she reached up to take his hand. But she didn't immediately turn to him. Instead, she said softly, "They killed his wife and children. He suffered his burns trying to save them." He gently placed a hand on the old man's forehead. "They're the fortunate ones."

Almost soundless, Gianavel sat on the bench behind her and wrapped his arms around her. He kissed her again, then she placed her hands on his, leaned her head back. He caught the scent of tears and sensed that she was close to collapse.

Movements and sound were subdued within Hector's house, as if any disturbance would only further stress the wounded. Those attending the suffering, including an old woman long known for her expertise in herbal remedies, moved quietly from cot to cot. On the far side of the room a still body was carried into the day, no words spoken.

"He would have been forty years old next month," she said, then looked across the room. "Pavel, there in the corner, was a carpenter. They cut off his hands and cauterized the wounds so he would not die before they could torture him to death. But he escaped and some others brought him here in a wagon."

She sighed, looked over the entire room. "They are not casualties of war. They're people...like us. They love and fear. They suffer pain like anyone else. I think men can only do these things when they no longer think of people as human beings."

Gianavel waited, but she said nothing more. He tightened his arms around her. "You're strong," he said quietly. "You can endure this."

She didn't smile. "Can I?" There was a long pause filled with sorrow. "I wonder what kind of life we will have when this war ends, if it ever ends."

"There will be an ending."

"And how do you know that, my love?"

"There is an end to all things," Gianavel said. "Even war." He took a deep breath, released it slowly, thoughtfully. "There is a price men are not willing to pay for hate."

"I don't see that, Joshua," she said. "I only see these people tortured and killed by other people who have no pity or remorse. They're like animals." She paused. "Is that what life is? Constantly fighting animals to stay alive?"

Gianavel shook his head, silent.

"Promise me, Joshua."

"Promise you what?"

"Don't let them do this to me. Promise that you will not leave me like this." She collapsed back against him. "Death would be better than this. At least in death we will be with God and have peace. This world is not worth this suffering."

Gianavel hesitated a long time—long enough to know what he should say, despite how he felt. "I promise."

"And something else."

"Yes."

"If they capture me or the children, and they use us against you, do not surrender your faith." Her tone had a sense of urgency. "I have seen that this world is suffering through and through. There's no end to it. There never will be. Not while men live like this. And we both know death is not the end. Death is only a temporary change…and a small price to pay for peace."

Gianavel was silent, and she sat forward and turned to him, placing a hand on his face. "Your promise…"

Gianavel bowed his head, and she wrapped it in her arms. He sighed, so tired now, so much more tired than before.

"I promise," he whispered.

※

It was over. As quickly as it began, it was over, and Sir Samuel Morland stood slowly, his cape billowing to a rising nightwind that was closing cold about them. Frowning, he stared numbly over the mutilated man who had collapsed as they reached him, dying in the Puritan's arms.

If the man had had a tongue, he might have spoken of who had done this. If he had had eyes, he might have communicated his pain. But he had no means to reveal what only he knew, though it hardly mattered now.

With Emmanuel's soldiers standing in a passive circle and Morland's friends kneeling beside the dead man, the Duke of Savoy knew he was out of time. If they had not come across this travesty, he might have bought another month from the Puritan, pleading complications of the Inquisitors. But that was impossible now.

There would be no turning the fury of the Puritan, and Emmanuel anxiously braced for an onslaught, not certain how he would deal with it. Expecting an emotional outburst, he was struck even more powerfully when Sir Morland spoke in a voice somber and controlled and utterly void of weakness or pity or the kind of emotional impulse that leads to regret. Rather, it was a voice that communicated quite plainly that he had decided upon a course of action and would follow it through to the end, though it cost him his life.

His words were cold and bitter.

"If it is war you want," he said, "then you shall have war."

✕✕✕✕

It was not that Blake had been particularly shocked by the atrocities he had witnessed while traversing this mountain that still had no name. He only knew that he had seen more than one display of human carnage, or relic, or warning, or whatever these madmen called them, at switchbacks in the trail and spread alongside streams.

No, he was not shocked, but he was moved beyond anything he could remember. He had seen wars uncounted, had seen entire nations destroyed by barbaric invasions that turned entire cities into open tombs. But he had not yet witnessed cruelties so keen, deaths so meticulously executed, nor such passion for blood as he had seen today. In this war, not even the dead had any peace.

But, as distracting as the horror was—made all the more so because the visages were placed where a man afoot would encounter them fully and without warning—Blake couldn't let his acute attention to tactics dull. He forced himself to think of the bloody altars as animal and not human, not a creature like himself, so that he did not stumble deaf and blind into a hostile patrol.

He had rarely seen a mountain range, if that is what it was, so cut with streams. It seemed as though he could not travel more than five minutes without having to cross another stream, and the bulk of the mountain still loomed above him. Not that it was impossibly high, probably no more than a thousand feet, but it was so sheer that it might as well have been ten thousand. In some places he saw where a crack might be climbed to the summit, but he had no intention of hanging on that merciless face when darkness closed, which it would do in less than an hour.

Instead, he had moved toward the village of Rora from the southwest, stoically wading across one freezing stream after another, the price of remaining beneath the snow-striped mountain. The incredible frustration was that he could *see* where he wanted to get. He just couldn't figure out how to *get there*.

He had moved probably less than a mile in the less sparsely covered slope to the east, and his feet were already twisted and aching from the monotony of walking at a slant. He half considered descending lower so he could at least walk like a man and not an ape, but he was afraid he might miss some obscure trail that cut up through the cliff—doubtless there was some secret trail known only to the natives.

The sound of men approaching snapped Blake into action. Instantly descending, he moved for a cluster of trees that seemed impossible to reach before they were upon him. But he picked up speed quickly as he relaxed his knees and found himself fairly flying down the slope. He knew that one misstep at this rate of descent would mean catastrophic injury or worse, but he preferred a danger that was known to one unknown.

He reached out to snatch the first suitable tree, swinging like a door on a hinge before he fell to the ground, and even as he blinked to focus, he saw men walking along the trail. Utilizing what he considered to be the best means for determining friend or foe, Blake watched to see if they moved like criminals or magistrates.

Noisy, confident...not fugitives.

Anyone trapped within Rora, outnumbered and outgunned, would doubtless move like a criminal if they wished to avoid patrols, which he had been informed encircled the mountains. The patrols themselves would be moving with authority—bold, confident. But after watching this group for a few moments, Blake decided they didn't even move like trained soldiers. Rifles slung over shoulders like fishing poles and a lack of flanking patrols indicated a fatal tendency toward sloppiness. If they had gone up against the Waldenses already, they hadn't survived because of soldiering skills.

After they passed, he waited another half hour, until darkness had settled deeper over the mountains and only the daunting cliff above him loomed against the stars over an ocean of black. Only then did he emerge cautiously—much more cautiously than before—and begin a careful tack through the trees that carried him parallel to the trail. Although that had only been one patrol, there would be more, and reaching the Waldenses might be more difficult than he'd anticipated.

From what Blake had encountered, he knew this was unlike any religious war he'd ever seen. There were no uniformed papal patrols, no righteous stumps of holy men exhorting the minions to storm the summit for the honor and glory of God and Rome. No…he'd seen vagabond patrols with a disturbing tendency for dismembering the dead and displaying body parts on makeshift wooden altars as the Druids supposedly did before Julius Caesar wiped them from the forests of northern England.

He heard nothing unnatural as he moved deeper through the woods, staying close to the trunks of trees to avoid the widely scattered sticks that could not be seen. And as he did he suddenly caught a glimpse of a low valley of sparse lights that cut into the mountain above. It was not far off, perhaps a half mile. And if it were what he suspected, he would be within the homeland of the Waldenses before midnight.

In an uncommon moment of hope, Blake wondered what manner of men these might be. Then, remembering the grisly row of heads, he wondered whether there would be any at all.

15

T HE PLAIN OF GIOVANNI—three miles distant from the stronghold of the Waldenses—was black and swarming with a blanket of mercenaries, cavalry, cannon, and the militia of Piedmont. Over a mile in diameter, the field crawled with clusters of the five thousand troops that separated in regiments, battalions, platoons, and squads under the authority of generals, captains, and lieutenants. If France or Spain themselves had been threatening the borders of Piedmont, there could have not been a more thorough preparation for war.

Pianessa strode boldly onto the dais where warlords dressed in armor of chain mail and leather stood patiently. Each of the warriors was a formidable and threatening image, most having earned their position by the strength of their sword, as nepotism did not prolong a man's life or career once a conflict was joined. And yet, as fearsome as they appeared, they were but shades of the Marquis de Pianessa's awesome and powerful countenance.

His armor was solid black, a combination of chain mail and stained leather carefully fitted with straps to conform to his enormous form and to allow vast freedom of movement in the shoulders. It was not plate steel, since no plate armor was reckoned reliable for stopping either a crossbow bolt or a musket round. Rather, it was armor built to withstand random long-bow hits and heavy attacks by sword or dagger. Clearly, the marquis expected a vast amount of the fighting to be hand to hand, and he had caught the scent of blood.

Pianessa was one of the last marquis as they had been in days of old. He considered himself a true military leader and not a pawn of whatever reigning monarch chance had placed in command. After all, monarchs passed at a disturbing rate, but a marquis who could defend his borders and possessed the financial resources to compensate for external threats could remain in power for decades.

His new sword, half again as long as his arm, was sheathed across his back, but it would be switched to his belt when the time for battle drew near. Three flintlock pistols and two daggers completed Pianessa's armament, and his horse bore two rifles. Six servants had reserve armor and weapons prepared. They would also reload his rifles if Pianessa himself engaged in musketry.

Dominating the dais, Pianessa leaned upon the map table. His face reflected an absolute concentration completely devoid of mercy or the cost of casualties for either side. He was in a warrior mode now, and men were as meaningless as chaff. To be concerned about conserving soldiers was an activity appropriate for a war conclave. Upon the field of battle the preeminent interest was victory. A conservation of men set to survive the battle was a base point if the battle was lost.

Nothing was said to interrupt Pianessa, and he continued to study the map, as though disturbed by something he could not understand. His countenance began to harden as if to discern whether there was a weakness to his plans. But he gave no indication of doubt when he turned to Duncan, the sergeant major.

"This is our last attack on these people." Pianessa looked back at the map, and Duncan stepped forward. "This time we will destroy everything. Every child, every babe, every man and woman and old man and woman. Everything."

"Yes, My Lord."

Pianessa lifted his face so that those who dared could look into his eyes. "We climb the cliff of the Castelluzo in absolute silence. We will attack in the morning when all are in position. And if any man reveals our position, I will take his head myself."

"Understood, sir."

Without a shadow of pleasure Pianessa concentrated once more. It was one of his strongest faculties that he never displayed any sign of satisfaction until a battle was absolutely settled. Until then his every word and gesture and glance would communicate only cold will and ruthless determination.

"With night, proceed across the river and begin the climb," he said at last, straightening. "I will ride up the pass with a contingent after the battle begins and their bastions are destroyed. Make certain their bastions are quickly destroyed." He paused, added, "I do not fancy riding into a hail of this man's musketeers. He has trained them well."

"Absolutely, My Lord. I will personally see to the bastions guarding the pass."

With a long look over the warlords assembled on the dais, Pianessa turned away and descended the steps.

No one thought twice about the overworked cook who slipped into the forest to gather herbs for the feast of slaughtered cows cast over bonfires on heavy iron stakes. His every nuance declared that he was in no mood for trifles, and impatient men hungered.

No one noticed when they saw him rooting along the far side of the Plain of Giovanni, searching with a dagger for some unintelligible root that he claimed would cure the stomach ailments of the men and provide long-lasting strength on the steady climb. After all, he had already made massive heaps of the most digestible curry—a meat paste mixed with raw root and assorted leaves—for Pianessa's Royal Guard. And each soldier had a sackful tied to his waist.

No one even noticed when darkness fell, and he could only be glimpsed as he rose and scraped beneath distant, pitch-black heaps of foliage, refusing to return until he had obtained what he sought. But men noticed when, after an hour, he had still not returned. And they took special notice when the patrol sent for him returned shaking their heads, declaring that he had vanished.

✕✕✕✕✕

Gianavel exited the hut to the fervent activity of the makeshift camp high on the Castelluzo. Men were scurrying in every direction to execute his orders and the orders of Jahier. Another captain, Laurentio, had not joined them and was commanding a squad rushing fallen logs to quickly selected ridges.

It would take some work to prepare for the coming event, but there was no time to worry about time. It was a common mistake of men to glance at the sun when they were desperately attempting to beat the sunset. All a man's energy should be focused on what he needed to accomplish, not on what he needed to defeat. All the desperation in the world would not slow the sun's descent, but every extra iota of skill and concentration would hasten the completion of the task.

A man in charge of marksmen rushed forward. Gianavel turned to him as he began speaking, somewhat breathless. "Do we stagger the men up and down the cliff, or do we make a line across the ridge?"

"A single line," answered Gianavel confidently. "No man is to be in front of another."

The man turned as another rushed forward, grabbing Gianavel's arm. "How far down the cliff do we position men with torches?"

"I will position them when I arrive," Gianavel said, and that man also rushed off, almost in the steps of the other.

It was not that the questions were difficult or that the men themselves could not have answered them with common sense. That was not what they needed or truly sought. But with each terse, simple answer, Gianavel provided for each by making himself a strong and fearless general whose strength would flow through the rest, even more contagious than their fear because men would choose courage over fear just as life over death.

It was admirable to make a defiant stand against overwhelming odds— even fearful men could be compelled do such a thing to save their lives. But they would fight like fearful men and flee like fearful men if the battle seemed lost. It was the mark of strong leadership and daunting courage to inspire men to choose for themselves to make such a stand because of a purpose greater than themselves—the only thing that would give a man the ultimate resolve to defend a doomed position with his life.

Yet, even beyond that, he felt a responsibility for the souls of his men that would surpass this battle in either victory or defeat. If his men were to die, he prayed that they might know even a small measure of the confidence he possessed that death itself had been defeated.

Only if a man fears death can death conquer him.

Mario twisted his face to stare into the crystal clear sky, then grimaced toward the private who was hanging so tenuously on the cliff beside him. Together they led the first company of Irish up the sheer face of the Castelluzo, which appeared, at a distance, unclimbable. But at arm's length, a number of narrow hand and footholds could be discerned that would carry a man to the crest. Still, if a man lost his grip and balance, there would be no long, sliding, bruising descent so that he crashed broken and gasping in the river below. No, if a man came loose from this cursed rock, his return to the earth would be non-injurious and, perhaps, reflective, until he reached that sudden stop at the base.

The first company had climbed to nearly five hundred feet—not cloud-crested but high enough when there was nothing between you and the ground but air. The second company was just beginning the ascent, and the third company would follow. Pianessa had issued clear instructions that all companies should not be simultaneously on the face, lest some fool in the leading platoon precipitate a plunge that would tear men from the cliff like ivy from a fence.

Mario, face glistening with sweat, spoke to the private. "When we reach the top...we attack at once!"

The private froze. "What?"

"I said we attack at once!"

The private's trembling said what his words did not. "But the marquis said that we have to wait for the other companies!"

Mario didn't respond.

"Sir!"

"I know what he said!" Mario's words were a hiss, as if it were possible someone might overhear. "But I will not wait for the others!"

"But why?"

"Because no one else will get the glory for this victory!" Mario was grinning now. "I will have Gianavel's head on a pike! And then I'll take it to Savoy! He'll be forced to make me a general!"

Frozen again, the private carefully turned his head to stare out over the valley, as if Pianessa might be spying upon them to understand their words. As if he weren't certain whether to continue or not, he finally said, "Yes, sir. Whatever you say."

"Worry for nothing!" Mario laughed. "I will show Pianessa what a real soldier is!"

xoo⊚oox

Hands behind his back, Pianessa turned toward a sergeant bent over a Galileo-vintage telescope. Although it had been expressly designed for studying the stars and planets, it served well enough to keep the company in sight as they scaled the cliff. Pianessa's face reflected an uncertainty that had been completely absent when he'd detailed instructions of attack to the men.

"Well?" he asked impatiently.

The sergeant hesitated, peering. "Ah…I see nothing, My Lord."

Pianessa didn't move. "Nothing?"

"No, sire." He shifted the telescope a fraction that probably moved its scope two hundred feet on the cliff. "There's nothing at the summit—no movement, nothing."

"No torches?" Pianessa said with a step forward.

"I see nothing, sire." He pressed his eye tight against the optical gold cylinder. "I believe it is deserted."

With a grunt Pianessa resumed pacing, black-gloved hands clasped firmly behind his back. There was energy in his steps, as if hectic emotion could not be contained within subdued movement. As he returned he raised a hand, his mouth opening. Then he shut it as quickly and turned away yet again, bent and concentrated.

"AYYA!"

"What!" Pianessa shouted as he spun.

"My Lord! Fire!"

Pianessa spun to stare at the Castelluzo, where a long line of fire had erupted along the rim, as if a sleeping volcano had suddenly come to life, awakening to angrily search for whatever foolish thing had disturbed its peaceful slumber.

⟡

Mario heard the "whoosh" not so high above, but somehow he couldn't place it until the private shouted in alarm, and Mario followed the wide gaze to see the crest of the cliff ablaze with hundreds of torches. Seconds later, pieces of clay descended over them like dust, harmless and annoying, but gone quickly.

Craning his head back, Mario thought he could observe distinct shapes in the waving light of torches and at first opened his mouth to shout before thinking better. He continued to stare as one of the men walked to the crest, peering down with torch in hand.

The man was tall, middle-aged, and wore a loose-sleeved white shirt beneath a heavy black cloak, and then Mario remembered the face—the face he had seen across the bridge at Rora.

Gianavel.

Then, to Mario's utter horror, he saw that the Captain of Rora was smiling.

xoo{@}oox

Pianessa had not moved. His eyes were fixed on the crest of the mountain as he grated, "What's happening?"

The sergeant shifted, swinging the telescope left to right, an eye pressed hard to the lens. "I don't know, My Lord! They're just standing there! But they...Oh no!"

With three rushing strides Pianessa was at the telescope and flung the sergeant aside like an empty rucksack. He pressed his face against the telescope and froze. After a moment he muttered, "What are they doing? Why don't they shoot?"

The answer came a second later as a huge bonfire erupted with a roar that thundered over the mountain and valley itself, and the sky above the cliff was domed in a hellish glow.

xoo{@}oox

Mario had the distinct impression that the mountain itself had erupted, hurling fire hundreds of feet into the freezing air, and the blaze—logs stacked at the rim—was so hot that Mario felt waves like an ocean of heat flowing down the cliff over him, unnatural and threatening and sentient.

He barely opened his mouth to scream when Gianavel lashed out with his sword and cut something, and then the sky disappeared behind a wall of solid flame that flowed like lava down the face of the Castelluzo. Mario was aware of clawing the smooth rock for a better grip as the fire rushed down over him, and then the world disappeared with men screaming in horror and pain.

><><◆><><

Pianessa came down three feet from the telescope, having leaped back as everything within the view of the telescope disappeared in a roaring circle of white that seemed to travel through the golden cylinder to erupt into his face.

Then across the distance he heard a roar pushed low across the valley by the cold, rumbling thick and heavy with cloud and the latest wisps of winter. The ground trembled beneath their feet and horses reared, straining at the reins, trampling those around them in sudden fear.

Pianessa staggered forward, reaching impotently toward the mount where fire cascaded down the face as if to halt the destruction tearing down over his carefully marshaled troops, wiping them from that rock amid crashing impacts and distant screams that seemed faint and thin beneath the violence. Voices were shouting throughout the camp, and men were running in confusion.

One voice rose above the rest.

"Sire! Sire!"

Pianessa turned with a snarl, fiercely holding control. The sergeant stood close, but not so close that he might be struck down by the marquis in his wrath.

"Sire! What do we do?"

Staring strangely at the question, Pianessa seemed not to have understood the language. He looked again to the mountain to see other huge timbers leaping alive with fire, and then avalanches descended into defenseless troops clinging desperately to the wall, if any still lived. Finally he barked, "Retreat!"

Instantly the sergeant lifted his arm across his chest to drop it, and an archer on the outskirts of the camp fired a flaming arrow in a high arch. In

the distance another arrow was fired, and then another until the arching signal reached the Castelluzo, where horns were heard to sound the call of
retreat. But there was no retreating from that perilous face in the darkness,
and still more fire descended from the ridge.

Then, faintly intermingled within the screams and howls and wounded
cries, echoed the sound of muskets as a hundred flashes erupted along the
skyline of white cloud, illuminated by the flames, each sliver of lightning
reaching down the flaming face of the Castelluzo that had become the face
of war.

xoxⒶxox

Racing along the summit, Gianavel took only seconds to glance at each
platoon to insure they were holding themselves behind cover as they fired
into the motionless troops on the cliff face. He leaped a keg of gunpowder
and glanced down to see a flaming graveyard of men screaming in pain and
fear and almost hesitated.

He did not realize his mouth opened in pain and did not know his face
reflected emotions unfit for a warrior before he turned away, rushing farther. But when he reached Jahier and his men jamming iron into the barrel of a two-thousand-pound cannon, he again looked like a commander
that knew no mercy—no, there would be no mercy tonight.

"Have you loaded it like I said?" Gianavel shouted over the rifle fire and
bellows and conflict.

"Enough powder to level a mountain!" Jahier shouted.

Gianavel threw his shoulder to a wheel and strained to push the cannon to the edge. "Hurry!"

Jahier took position on the other side of the huge barrel. He was straining with a dozen men who fell in behind them. But Gianavel heard his

voice over the tide of moans that rose from the crest. "How long do you want the fuse!"

When the captain didn't respond, Jahier called out again, but by then Gianavel was at the fuse, ripping out his dagger to count silently as he slid his hand down the powdered string. He slashed it and lit it within a heartbeat.

"Now!"

They pushed the cannon down the slight slope to the edge, and then its own momentum took it into the darkness like a whale disappearing into a white flaming sea of trapped souls.

With iron wedged tight into the barrel and gunpowder hard packed the entire length, the cannon would fire, but the expanding force would find no release, so the barrel would explode, lancing the Castelluzo with a thousand deadly missiles of iron that would penetrate flesh or bone or stone or whatever else was in their path.

Gianavel fell to a knee, counting.

"Seven seconds, second company…four, five…"

The explosion tore heated air from their lungs as it threw up a huge layer of sky past the summit, staggering them as it staggered the mountain, and then night took form as the shock wave hit and the carefully positioned barrels of oil ignited on the face of the Castelluzo like the breath of a dragon repelling those who had so foolishly attacked it in its lair. The flame blocked out the sky and the land together before a stunning rush of darkness closed on them and snapped shut like black fangs, and it was only then that Gianavel realized he had never heard the sound of it.

><>◆<><

Mario rolled across a rock ledge, where he had miraculously fallen, and finally stumbled to his feet, trampling down men whose limbs were grotesquely twisted and others who were not there at all as they writhed on the bloody rocks that were black in the darkness and starlight. He saw the slope of a rock and was upon it as he heard the rushing water beneath and wondered how he might descend to reach the holy safety of the flat earth when he sensed a rushing behind him.

He half turned to see wild-eyed men still holding swords rushing toward him and knew they would kill him for this, but they ignored him, shoving him between themselves as they surged past him to retreat from the rock, and suddenly the rock beneath his right foot vanished.

He had time to twist in the air to see the dark water *on fire* beneath him, and then he was descending through the rushing night. He did not feel it when he struck a lower ledge that broke his bones and crushed his organs into jelly, and then he saw the water on fire and watched its approach until he knew nothing more.

Nor would he remember anything later in the night. He would not remember awaking the next day within a wagon bearing the wounded to Lucerna. Nor would he remember his ride within another wagon three days later—a wagon that hauled those killed by defenders of Rora to a mass grave that, five hundred years later, would still not bear the names of those buried there.

✕✕✕◈✕✕✕

The outcry, like a huge wave building at sea and approaching the shore in the darkness of night, swept over the camp before the first stragglers arrived in groups of two or three, supporting each other with staffs and their own shoulders. Almost all had lost their rifles and weapons, and some were still smoldering in the cool evening, even their bare skin creating steam like rising frost.

Bloody wounds had white ghosts hovering over them, the blood warming the air about them, and few spoke as they collapsed in a bivouac that was prepared. But the makeshift field hospital had been designed to handle only a small number of wounded, and in no time all the blankets were claimed. And still they shambled in from the night, sometimes in teams of twenty and thirty, and finally every cot, bedroll, wagon, and tent cover was lined with bodies like the cargo of a slave ship.

Pianessa stalked beside the telescope, ignoring it all. He spoke to no one, answered no questions. Then a ravaged figure, almost utterly black with his face scarred and a red beard half burned from his face, emerged from between torches. Seeing him, Pianessa lowered his arms, staring.

Sergeant Major Duncan was a travesty of the man he had appeared before the battle. His eyes were flat and dead like a man who had seen the depths of hell. He spoke directly to Pianessa. "My Lord?"

With a scowl, Pianessa stared. "Yes?"

"Have you fortified the camp?"

Pianessa cursed quietly and looked away. He voiced disdain born of contempt. "Gianavel wouldn't dare attack my camp."

"This man knows war," the sergeant countered sharply. He did not blink at Pianessa's angry gaze.

"Sergeant, you are wounded. I will deal with the security of the camp." When Duncan did not move, Pianessa regarded him as if he were mad. "Did you not hear me?"

"I heard," Duncan replied in a dead tone. He took several steps forward, his eyes no longer responsive to life. "This man knows war, Pianessa. I have never seen his equal. He ambushed us with torches hidden inside jars of clay."

Pianessa squinted. "What?"

"Jars of clay," Duncan said distinctly. "They were on the cliff the entire time that we were climbing. All of them, waiting with torches concealed within jars of clay. We could not see the flames, but the flames could burn. Then they broke the jars at the same time by some prearranged signal. They waited until we were in their very face, ignorant and exposed, before they struck. This man is wise."

Teeth gleamed as Pianessa muttered, "See to your wounds, Sergeant. That is an order."

For a moment it was not certain whether the sergeant was conspicuously disobeying an order or if he simply could not compel himself to move. Then he said, "Pianessa, use caution. We killed six thousand of these people in the valley and did not lose a single man. But this man has killed six thousand of us in a single night."

For a moment all was still, and it seemed the sergeant would say something more. Then with the same deadness with which he'd arrived, he departed.

Pianessa stared after him immobile, then glanced at a few of those standing nearby. His voice was bitter. "Insure that all those returning are stripped of weapons and arms."

A lieutenant hesitated. "But, sire...why?"

"As potential *spies,* you fool!"

Pianessa stared after the outburst, as if inviting a challenge. But there was no challenge as the lieutenant spun instantly away.

Then an explosion from within the camp itself sent a shock wave to the edge of the great plain itself. The cold retreated at the mushrooming ball of fire that reached incredibly high—a tongue of fire almost instantly swallowed by night—and the distant mountains echoed the surge again and again and again.

"The powder store," Duncan muttered as he rose from a crouch. "This man is wise...."

Pianessa staggered. "Gianavel attacks my camp?"

Even as he spoke, a bullet fired from somewhere in the darkness hit a wagon. It was impossible to tell who had been the intended target, but Pianessa wasn't waiting for the answer. He reached his horse in three strides and pulled the reins hard to bring it about as he shouted to his lieutenants. "Remove the camp to El Torre!"

"In the dark? But, sire—"

"Do it!" Pianessa roared and then thundered off in the night as another shot sailed from the darkness and struck down the lieutenant who had been foolish enough to show himself as someone in command.

><><

Leading a band of men stealthily through the night, Gianavel crouched in the darkness. It had been easy enough to pursue the retreating troops from the Castelluzo, continuously reducing their number with sniper attacks from the shadows. They had not mainly targeted officers because it was impossible to determine who was in command, since everyone was shouting at once for retreat. But those with uniforms that displayed even the faintest semblance of authority had been the first to fall, nevertheless.

Reloading and firing, reloading and firing, thirty men from Rora shadowed the troops for the entire mile back to their camp, and the death toll continued to climb with every step. Finally, even when they reached the relative sanctity of their perimeter, some men had managed to crawl through the line to penetrate the camp and lay into the powder stores—wagons bearing gunpowder and mortar rounds—to destroy them before slipping out again in the confusion.

Bertino and two others came up behind Gianavel, who slid from around a tree where he'd killed another who was speaking to Pianessa. The bullet had been aimed for Pianessa himself, but it was impossible to focus clearly in the darkness because Gianavel could barely see the sights of the barrel.

"Gianavel!"

"Yes…"

"They're retreating!"

Gianavel nodded. "Keep harassing them until they remove the camp from the edge of the Pelice."

"What are you going to do?"

"I'm going after Pianessa."

Bertino grabbed his shoulder. "No! If you die, we're lost! We will have no one to lead us! Think!"

Face glistening with sweat, Gianavel revealed nothing as he took several deep breaths, turning his head toward the camp. "Very well. Keep up the attack until they have withdrawn. Remember: If we let them make camp in the valley, we're lost. Make them retreat!"

"You will stay with us?" Bertino whispered, and fear, for the first time since Gianavel had known him, was unconcealed and pure in the big man's eyes.

Gianavel nodded.

"Until the battle is won, my friend."

✕✕✕✕

Pianessa strode up the steps of Emmanuel's palace in Turin and shoved the guards to either side before they even had an opportunity to salute. He struck one of the huge doors with the palm of his hand so that it swung fully inward. Nor did he hesitate to close it as he stalked through the short entrance and into the magnificent hallway where the Duke of Savoy sat at the end of a banquet table.

As Pianessa entered the chamber, Incomel rose to his feet beside another, smaller table where some heavy tome lay open, the huge pages painted with colorful pictures and imprinted with large Latin text. His two papal guards, pikes in hand, stood to either side and reacted stiffly as Pianessa walked onward without another glance.

Incomel had reached his feet, stunned. He studied Pianessa only a moment before saying with a mixture of frustration and criticism, "Don't tell me you were defeated again!"

With a snarl Pianessa turned fully into the Inquisitor, teeth revealed in savage wrath, and Incomel's guards leaped forward to bar his way. Even as they came toward the barbaric image, Pianessa lashed out and ripped away one of the iron pikes.

Emmanuel stood as Incomel staggered back, and then Pianessa raised the pike over his head in both hands and roared as he bent it into the shape of a horseshoe in one continuous motion that had no pause to shift his grip or initiate a second effort. Then he flung the ruined weapon so that it rebounded wildly from the floor, narrowly missing the Inquisitor, who leaped sprightly to the side.

The marquis did not even cast the second guard a glance as he muttered, "Be careful what you put your faith in, Priest."

"Enough," said Emmanuel.

Smoldering, Pianessa turned from the Inquisitor and walked to the fireplace. When he reached the table, he poured himself a flagon of wine and drank all of it before lowering his head, not bothering to wipe the spilt redness from his face and beard. He leaned upon the table, his face deeply shadowed by the flames.

Emmanuel's voice was calm. "How many?"

In the distance, Incomel took a tentative step, but Emmanuel raised a hand. The priest retained his measure of separation. Finally the marquis said a single word in a chipped, brutal tone that Emmanuel had never heard from him before.

"All."

Emmanuel blinked, wondering if he had heard rightly, knowing at the same instant that he had. He searched the marquis' face and saw nothing there that hinted of a mistake or even anger now. Rather, Pianessa's usually unconquerable visage, or his eyes, rather—staring into the flames as they were—reflected some kind of inner contemplation that was not his nature.

"All?" Emmanuel repeated softly.

Pianessa's eyes turned from the flames and from contemplative to murderous. "I don't have enough men left to count the living," he muttered.

Stunned, Emmanuel said nothing. He knew that Pianessa had taken six regiments—fully six thousand men—to Giovanni. Some of them had been his most tempered troops, men who had seen pitched combat against the Spanish and Germans—men of professional scale who had fought valiantly when the battle was finally joined. Men who, even in the chaos of close combat, had retreated with discipline, holding their formation to reform again at a stronger position. But they had been...destroyed? By a handful of villagers?

"How?" Emmanuel heard himself ask, knowing at the same moment that he could not stop himself, and he truly had no idea what the answer might be.

Pianessa's face lightened abruptly. "An ambush," he muttered and shook his head again. "I have never seen a man like this man. He uses tactics I've never seen. Tactics no one has ever seen."

Silently and with hesitant steps Incomel had begun a slow approach. His guards were wisely wide behind him, lest their presence provoke Pianessa's wrath once more.

"What did he do?" Emmanuel asked, watching closely.

For a moment Pianessa only stared into the flames. "He ambushed them using torches hidden inside jars of clay. When they were directly below the summit, they broke the jars and set timbers on fire. They rolled them down over the men, then…I don't know what happened next. I think they rolled a cannon over the edge with something wedged into the barrel."

No one spoke or moved, and it seemed as though no one would. Finally Emmanuel rose and walked slowly across the room. He was startled when he saw Father Simon, silent and as inconsequential as a statue, standing at the very edge of the light.

At the look, the old priest walked slowly forward, hands covered in the sleeves of his frock, and nodded deeply to Savoy.

Emmanuel said nothing as Simon continued to where Pianessa stood before the flames, still motionless. He had not refilled his wine chalice, a true indication of how deep was his shock. As the marquis saw him, Pianessa muttered in a strange tone, "So what does your God reveal to you now, Priest?"

It was a curious moment; then Simon responded, "Only that Gianavel's tactics have, indeed, been seen before, Monsieur Marquis."

Pianessa's gaze was dead. "I know all the tactics of Italy and Spain, Priest. I have never seen such a thing."

"Gianavel's tactics are far older than Italy and Spain, Pianessa." Simon walked between Pianessa and the flames, the shadow of a ghost passing over his face. "Indeed, they are far older...."

His eyes never left the gray form as Pianessa growled, "You speak in riddles, old man."

Simon halted on the far side of the fireplace, positioned between Incomel and Pianessa. "Gianavel's tactics were taken from men far greater than the kings of Italy and Spain, Pianessa. Gianavel uses the Scriptures to find the means of destroying your army."

"What?" Pianessa snapped, anger in his eyes. "What are you talking about, Priest?"

"I speak of Gideon," Simon said plainly, certainly. "I speak of a king of Israel who ambushed a force ten times his size by having his men come upon them in the night with torches hidden within jars of clay. Men who then smashed the jars at once to give the impression that they were of far greater number and then watched as the army panicked, making them far easier to destroy."

Simon's smile was contained enough to not gloat before the marquis. "To defeat you, Pianessa, Gianavel uses what he knows best—the Holy Scriptures."

"You're a fool," Pianessa muttered. "What do the Scriptures have to do with military tactics?"

"The Old Testament is filled with military campaigns, Pianessa. Those of David, Joshua, Gideon, all the kings of Israel, as well as their enemies. When Israel reached Zion, there were battles upon battles with the Sea Kings—the Moabites, the Amalekites, the Egyptians." Simon's gaze revealed no doubt. "Joshua and Gideon fought a hundred battles against forces of superior numbers and superior strength, and lost only a small number. And then there are the exploits of mighty David, who rose above all those who came before him and all who would come after. David, who defeated the most powerful empires the world had ever known with a military precision and tactical genius that has never been equaled in the history of recorded time. Not Alexander the Great, Genghis Khan, or Julius Caesar overcame the odds that David overcame—defeating so many with so few."

Pianessa was silent.

Emmanuel spoke, "So, since you understand this man so well...tell us; what will Gianavel do now?"

With a deep breath, Simon strolled along the table, passing once more between the marquis and the flames. "He will not let you encamp in his valley. He will use spies. In battle, he will retreat, forcing you to pursue. He will use the terrain to break your army and weapons. He will starve your men, terrify them. He knows that wars are fought in the spirit. So he will strike at their spirit."

Incomel stepped forward. "Fool of a monk," he frowned, "your attempt to frighten us is useless. I don't believe this man is half so cunning as you believe!"

Simon bent his gaze with a smile. "Don't waste your words attacking me, Inquisitor. I am not the one who destroyed eight regiments with a trick of Gideon's."

"Foolishness!" Incomel came swiftly down the table to stand before Emmanuel. "Are you going to believe this madman?"

Emmanuel was stoic. "Is he wrong?"

"Of course he's wrong!" Incomel grated. "I will take him downstairs and make him speak the truth!" He took a single step toward Simon.

Emmanuel stood. "Incomel!"

The Inquisitor spun with a curse, and Pianessa laughed loudly. The pause gave Emmanuel a moment to craft his words. "This is a council of war, Inquisitor. If you cannot control yourself, you will be dismissed."

Stung, Incomel stepped forward. "What do you mean?"

"It means that you will touch no one else without my spoken permission," Emmanuel said distinctly. "It means that your days in my kingdom have almost ended."

"You dare—"

"I do more than dare!" Emmanuel sharply slammed his hand on the table. "If you speak against me again, I will see if two papal guards are enough to protect you!"

Incomel was openly shocked. He glanced at Pianessa, who stared with his dangerous, dark stare that revealed neither mercy nor restraint, then again to the Duke of Savoy.

"My God," he whispered, "you will regret—"

"*Careful,*" Emmanuel warned. "These halls have secrets, Priest."

Incomel took it for what it meant. His face twisted in anger; then he spun and walked swiftly past Simon. In another moment he was gone, and they stood in gloomy silence. Finally the aged priest lifted a hand, gesturing good-night.

"Forgive me," he said, folding hands once more in his sleeves. "I will return to my duties."

Neither the Marquis de Pianessa nor the Duke of Savoy raised eyes as the old priest walked almost soundlessly around the table, and in another moment he, too, was gone in the shadows. They did not hear a door open or close, but they were alone.

Emmanuel sat again into his chair, leaning back to stare blankly at the cathedral ceiling. He did not know what to say; then Pianessa straightened from the table. He turned his head to gaze upon the Duke of Savoy with a look he had never held before—something like respect.

"He will not forget this," Pianessa said somberly. "I will have him killed tonight."

Staring after the Inquisitor, Emmanuel replied, "No, another would only take his place." He paused. "We must find a quick means to defeat the Waldenses."

"No," Pianessa said with a sigh. "It means that we must find a means of defeating this man who leads them. As long as Gianavel fights, Savoy, all the Waldenses will fight. But when Gianavel is destroyed, everything he stands for will be destroyed. Only then will we finish this war."

Emmanuel was silent a long time.

"One man," he said softly, "but his very life gives his people the faith and courage to fight even when all seems lost." He paused. "*That*...is a true prince."

Pianessa's eyes narrowed on the Duke of Savoy.

"True," he agreed. "He is to be admired, in a sense. But if Gianavel is not killed, Rome will give your kingdom to another. So we either defeat Gianavel or lose all that we hold." He glanced to where the Inquisitor exited. "Or worse."

Gazing back again, Pianessa muttered with respect, "You have come far, Prince."

Staring at nothing, Emmanuel sighed.

"Feels like far."

16

NOTHING ATOP THE MOUNTAIN APPEARED as it had appeared before the battle. Even the ground seemed whiter in the starlight, dusted with powder and trampled smooth by the thousands of steps that had raced across it in the fury of combat.

Gianavel stood where they had pushed the forty-pounder over the ledge, staring down into the narrow valley where fires burned in strange formation, consuming what little dry shrub had not been destroyed in the precipitous retreat. He was grateful that the spy's information had come in time for them to rig the elaborate trap.

Pascal, who had been the one to pose as a cook in the camp of Pianessa himself, had overheard the marquis discussing the attack with his captains. But it had been an entire day before sufficient opportunity presented itself so that he could slip out of the camp, and even then, his return to Rora had been dangerous and uncertain. But in the end he had reached the camp and the rest…well, Pianessa could count his dead. Rora had not lost a single defender in the siege.

Using ropes they had rigged at secret sections of the mountain range, he had reached the crest of the Castelluzo in less than half an hour after he left Bertino in the field near Pianessa's camp. When he arrived, he was comforted to see Jahier and Laurentio thoroughly in charge of recovery. They had already regrouped the men and established new listening posts on the mountain and other places where Pianessa might gain entry into the valley. Watching the hectic activity—men moving quickly and methodically but not in panic—he knew all was well in hand.

Which was comforting, since he knew that this battle could not depend upon any man—not Jahier, or Laurentio, or Descombie. Not Hector, with all his experience, or Bertino, with all his great courage, or anyone else. Not even the barbes, with their prophetic declarations and resolution, could the entire nation rely on. And despite what some seemed to believe, this battle did not depend on him either.

He had done everything possible to insure that nothing depended upon him. But he was not naïve, and he knew that men looked to him for courage and strength. It was the way of things in battle, and there was nothing wrong with it. God had made it so that one man sharpens another, as iron sharpens iron.

But no war should depend on one man because, sooner or later, that man would fall. Then those he had inspired would have to take his place and inspire others. So what he wanted to achieve, more than anything else, was a regiment of men who could easily assume his authority and do as he had done. And when he was certain of that, he could die in true peace.

Footsteps—Gianavel turned.

Jahier's blond beard was soaked as if he'd been totally immersed in water. His hair was plastered back from his forehead and dark with sweat. Steam rose from around his neck and sleeves. "Not a man was wounded or killed. We still have one hundred forty-seven."

Gianavel looked over the amazing devastation beneath the Castelluzo. "Incredible…What now?"

The blond captain pointed to the north side. "I've got men stationed in twos and threes so that they can sleep in shifts." He paused to take a large swallow from a waterskin.

"Ah," he wiped his mouth, "anyway, I don't think Pianessa is going to be returning tonight. Not after that."

Gianavel knew that any celebration of victory, however subdued, was dangerous because it broke the mentality of ongoing war. There were more battles to come, and each would be as viciously fought or more. But there was also a time to let men feel relief that their efforts were for something. They deserved to enjoy the joy of victory, however brief. Soon enough they would have to once more bolster their courage and will to make another stand. There was no need to remove what little reward had been won with this one.

"No, they will not attack again tonight," Gianavel agreed, knowing that even Jahier needed some time to celebrate. "Make sure the men eat and drink well. They will need their strength."

"Ola, Captain."

They turned and beheld Hector approaching.

Hector was making the last steps up the steep slope to the level summit. He was pushing up from a knee with his free hand, his right making use of his rifle as a staff. He seemed winded when he straightened, and they waited with faint smiles. "Ayya…I'm getting too old for this soldiering. It's a young man's game."

Gianavel smiled. "How do you feel?"

"I'm alive."

"What of the ordnance?"

Hector placed a hand on his side. "We fired over a hundred shot at the slope." He made a horizontal movement. "We skipped the balls across the face so as to take out more men. No one working the cannons was hurt, though we had some close calls with the gunpowder. We need some more training."

"Tomorrow," Gianavel confirmed. "Tonight everyone must get whatever rest they can. There's plenty of time in the morning to do what has to be done."

"Oui," Hector dismissed himself, "good enough."

"Where are you going?" Jahier asked.

"To get some rest!" the old man called back. "Before I start praying for one of those musket balls to put me out of my misery!"

Gianavel gazed once more down into the valley. There was utter silence, but he wondered how many dead would litter that landscape in the morning. In the distance he could hear flintlocks firing, firing. They would occasionally pause to change positions and begin again. A slow, continuous decimation that would do far more damage to their spirit than numbers. He had ordered his men to keep it up until Pianessa had completely withdrawn from the valley.

Gianavel searched his mind for everything he had ever learned, trying to determine if there was something he had not yet done. They had won the battle, but this victory would mean nothing when they came to the next battle. No, each victory was an obstacle in itself, and the gains of a hundred victories could be wiped out by a single defeat. Which is why he never celebrated. He would celebrate only when the war was won and the fighting was finished. Then, if they were victorious, he would fall on his knees before the people and give the victory to the Lord, because it is the Lord who decided victory, in the end.

"What are you thinking?" he heard Jahier ask and turned to look at the captain.

Gianavel was reluctant that he had been thinking of death after such a great victory. He paused. "Tomorrow—always tomorrow. But that's enough for now. I'll take first watch. Get some sleep."

"I'll relieve you in four hours."

"Take your time."

Jahier descended the ridge, his knees braking hard to slow his momentum, and without much interruption from others soon vanished in a make-shift lean-to they'd raised earlier in the day. Not plush by any stretch, it was filled with cots and sheepskins and wrapped tight with canvas to block the wind and rain.

As men approached him through the night, Gianavel dealt with issues at random. Many were almost inconsequential, but he was patient and attentive, knowing that it was not common sense that they sought, but a leader. And so he wandered up and down the ridge, checking weapons, encouraging and exhorting. He let his character display what simple lessons could not, so that his words had authority.

He neither sat nor displayed any sign of the great fatigue that painfully eroded his patience and will. He ignored his feet that ached and his ears that rang painfully from the cannon. His fingers were swollen and his vision would blur, and he was forced to rub his eyes forcefully so he could see, and still he marshaled meager molecules of strength to continue with an air of unending vigilance, superior endurance, unconquerable will.

When Jahier finally relieved him, fresh from sleep and empowered by a stout bottle of wine that he'd brought along, Gianavel could barely hear the cheerful words as he turned and walked to the hut. Every step was like

a knife driven up from his feet to his spine, for few things were as agonizing as a familiar movement done a million times.

He didn't undress or take off his boots as he saw an empty cot, and when
he arose he did not even remember lying down.

>oo<§>oo<

Contrary to caution, Blake had not slid into a nice, secure cave during
the heated battle he had heard from the summit. Instead, knowing this was
his chance to find the Waldenses, he had followed the sounds along ridge
after ridge, constantly searching for a trail or crevice. The summit seemed
much closer now—it certainly *should* be, he'd been walking most of the
day—but every crack he found in the wall narrowed to nothing within a
few feet, and he was forced to slip back to the ground.

Finally he arrived at a box canyon. Not large, no, actually it was quite
small. A waterfall descended to his right, cascading over a stony ledge
eroded for centuries. And the slope before him seemed to rise almost
smoothly to the crest. So, he mused, this was the end.

At this distance he could even hear voices from the darkness beyond the
thin strand of trees. It was an easy approach; it was also a good place for sentries. Because he'd moved silently, and sentries could certainly see no better
than he could in this pitch, they wouldn't know he was close. But as soon as
he began clambering up the slope, snapping sticks and trampling leaves, it
would be impossible to conceal his position. In that case, they might simply
shoot, or they could call out. Doubtless, there was some kind of password.

He stood in the dark a long time. No scenario that he considered
appealed to him. He did not fancy being shot dead without a warning, nor
did he fancy being captured and hung as a spy because he did not know
the password. Decisions, decisions…

Well, there was only one thing to do.

He climbed a small section of the rise that allowed fairly quiet movement and paused....

Make a decision!

Collecting what courage he still had, Blake cupped both hands around his mouth and shouted, trying his best to sound like someone who did not want to get shot.

"Hello!"

He waited—nothing.

Blake didn't seriously expect a confrontation so low from the summit. But he didn't intend to proceed very quickly, nor did he attempt to make any effort to silence his steps before he called out again.

Strangely the thought occurred to him that this was Cromwell's diabolical plan all along—give him an impossible mission, and if Blake were killed, well, surely the Almighty would have mercy on this scoundrel for the heroism of his utterly doomed last act amen and amen, let's eat....

He did not think any tears would be shed.

⋊∞⧫∞⋉

It was solid dark when Lockhart finished preparations for the evening. He examined the room to insure he had done everything possible to make the staff believe he had turned in for the night. Some might think the embassy staff would be the only ones to trust; he knew they were the last ones to trust. Indeed, he would rather trust his life to some poor beggar he encountered by chance on the street, someone who had nothing to gain from a betrayal. Such practical men were bought cheaply enough and were far safer than one whose profession provided ample opportunities to form discreet and profitable alliances.

Dressed in the black garb of a Puritan, Lockhart slipped over the balcony and descended on a rope he had looped so that he could pull and untie it from the ground. He had hidden a grappling hook in a nearby alley that he would use upon his return, gaining one balcony at a time until he reached his room. It was not a plan that would work indefinitely, but he only needed to keep his mission secret long enough to persuade Mazarin to intercede for the Waldenses, or until he resolutely refused. Yet there was another danger, one more subtle and ultimately harder to anticipate—betrayal from within the cardinal's camp.

The powerful prime minister had a legion of enemies in Paris—most of whom he recently defeated in the Revolution—that had, at first, driven him into hiding, along with the boy-king, Louis. But when the last shot was fired, Mazarin arose victorious. His return to Paris was heralded with unprecedented authority; nor was he slow to dispatch those whose crimes were too great to be forgiven.

King Louis XIV was, of course, the rightful monarch, but he was only ten years old and had not yet assumed full authority and command. So Mazarin, his mentor and surrogate father, was for all practical purposes king and prime minister and pope, tri-scepters he was careful not to publicly display but power he could exercise with inveterate purpose and deeply laid design when provoked.

Lockhart had long thought that the primary weakness of a monarch was a lack of vigilance. It was the curse of a king that he must constantly distrust those who seemed most worthy of trust. But Mazarin was, by all accounts, perpetually alert to betrayal and had crafted such a complex system of spies and informants that not even shambling, nameless lepers encountered by chance in a random field could be considered harmless. In keeping everyone in suspicion, the priest made alliances virtually impossible to initiate and nerve-wracking to maintain. Lockhart glanced across joining streets. No one was visible....

In a light run, careful to avoid limbs and leaves, Lockhart finally reached a nearby street where he began walking quickly but not so quickly as to attract notice. He had brought his cane with a twenty-eight-inch straight saber concealed within the sheath as well as two flintlock pistols beneath his cloak. He also had a number of keys hidden within the folds of his cloak and pants that would supposedly open ninety percent of the world's locks. But his greatest threat was not constables or even French military. The greatest danger was being identified by a mob of citizens who would not wait for a constable or commander to determine his fate.

It took him two hours to make his way to the palace of Mazarin, and it was nearly midnight when he arrived. He studied the sentries at the eastern gate, watching for any sign of betrayal, but there were no extra troops, no wagon nearby. Streetlights were conspicuously subdued, and a long stretch of grass to the palace itself was unlighted. All of it together made this an opportune place to enter unknown, or an opportune place to be murdered without witnesses.

Lockhart made no appearance of stealth, except perhaps for a slightly rapid stride, as he approached the gate. And before he had even crossed the street, a guard turned and unlocked the gate and stepped back, looking quickly down both ends of the street. Lockhart said nothing as he entered, almost at a slight run, and did not stop at the entrance. He let the guard catch up on his own, and they moved steadily through the dark until they came to another door, also unlit.

No guards were visible, and Lockhart entered, feeling the thrill of covert activity, wondering why he had been out of it for so long. He was in his place, here—secret rendezvous in the night, betrayals and conspiracies and plans to topple nations, all executed by men whose wisdom and courage was the rubric of legend. And it was so radically different—and to him, superior—to the battlefield where men displayed such great courage and skill, only to be cut down by a stray bullet.

No, indeed, in this world of shadows and assassins, where the quick-witted and quick were separated from the dead by the most finite edge of intelligence and instinct, a man could change the course of a war if he possessed keen skills and the grace of God. But not even God protected a man from his own stupidity. After all, a man could not blame God if he were shot climbing out a window in broad daylight.

The guard locked the door, causing Lockhart to quickly scan the open doors around him. By reflex, his hand settled on the flintlock at his waist. Then a short, stout woman with quick, busy eyes half emerged and signaled, and Lockhart was led up the stairway to the door of a very small chamber that he suddenly realized was part of some hidden passageway. With an assuring pat on his arm, the woman closed a door that blended perfectly with the wall beyond.

He was alone.

It was one of the moments that came frequently in the life of a spy—alone and in unfamiliar territory, not certain what to do next but knowing every gesture and word would be severely judged. If he appeared inept, they might assume he had little intelligence and thus little bargaining power. If he appeared overly cautious, he would display insufficient character to be considered an equal. Then again, if he did not take precautions, it was far too easy to come to quick death.

He determined it was best to be fairly cavalier about life or death; at least that would establish courage. But he would remain cautious—no reason to tempt fate. And as for appearing inept, he would simply speak little and attentively follow the cardinal.

Holding the cane in his right hand, he boldly opened the door and stepped without hesitation into a gigantic chamber opulently furnished with luxurious scarlet arrangements. The blood-hued satin covered the walls to the height of a man's chest, and above it they glowed white from immense candelabra positioned throughout.

He saw the figure of a man, royal red robe descending to brush the floor, golden crucifix displayed prominently on his chest, his long dark hair immaculately combed. His eyes, even darker and somewhat amused, beamed as he turned. He graciously raised a glass of red wine.

"Sir Lockhart," smiled Cardinal Guilio Raimondo Mazarin, Prime Minister of France and perhaps the most powerful man in Europe. "I was hoping that you would join me."

✦

Although his hands were tied behind his back, a noose was tight around his neck, and his two Waldensian captors were not slow to use their bayonets on his buttocks, Blake wasn't dead yet.

They had asked no questions, and Blake had not yet communicated his intent. Nor had he revealed that he could speak the curious French-German dialect of theirs. Best, he thought, to play no hand at all until he could play one that was decisive.

He raised his face as a tall, heavily armored man with blond beard and long blond hair arrived. With a faintly hostile air, the man—Captain Jahier, they called him—said nothing as Blake's young guards repeated the adventure of capturing this fool who came shambling through the forest like a blind man.

Captain Jahier did not seem persuaded. After studying Blake closely for another moment, he quietly commended the young sentries for their diligence before dismissing them. Then he called for two much older guards to take charge of the prisoner. One of the guards, thick shouldered with a neck like an ox, laughed as he gazed down at Blake. The other, at least sixty with a white beard and soapy eyes, placed a foot on Blake's bench and spat tobacco juice. He wiped his mouth with his sleeve, grinned maliciously.

Blake shook his head and distracted himself by studying the panorama of sunrise, remembering how the sky had been paling for hours. It was amazing, he'd often thought, how a man in the woods could see the sunrise coming for hours and hours before the sun crested the edge of the world.

He was grateful that the air was warming. He'd almost frozen last night, his feet like blocks of wood, as he tried to find some hidden means up the mountain. Now he understood more clearly why the Waldenses were so difficult to defeat. It was always cold in these heights, and men did not fight as well in the cold.

It was obvious to Blake that the Waldenses were stout fighters. Every man he saw was armed with pistols and rifle and sword. He'd also seen a wild variety of older weapons—blunderbusses with wide, flared barrels, dangerous-looking flintlock pistols, numerous crossbows, and curious homemade weapons that he couldn't define and didn't fancy pulling the trigger on, either.

In a moment the captain returned, accompanied by a big man dressed like a catholic monk—Descombie was his name. With a warm smile, Descombie spoke a single sentence in splendid Spanish and waited. Blake shook his head. Descombie spoke grammatically perfect German. Blake shook his head. Descombie raised empty hands and smiled. "English?"

Blake hesitated. He had wondered what he would do when this moment came. Truth seemed like a good idea, but truth had never been his first choice in similar situations, so he was, by reflex, loath to use it. Still, few alternatives came to mind.

He stood dramatically.

They leaped back, lifting rifles.

Appearing utterly fearless, Blake drew himself to his full height. Something told him his only chance lay in boldness.

"My Lord Protector," he projected in the French–German dialect of the Waldenses, "the Prime Minister of England and Defender of Christ, Oliver Cromwell, has sent me here to fight beside the noble Waldenses! And if you be those people, I declare myself your ally!"

Captain Jahier squinted.

Blake's posture put his trust in God.

"Kill him," said Jahier.

Blake blanched. "Wait!" he shouted as hands lifted him from the ground, carrying him toward a wall. "I've got guns! I swear on my mother's grave! I'm a gun smuggler! It's the truth! Dear God, you can't just *kill me!*"

The men carrying him began loudly droning something like an Irish funeral dirge. Blake saw a wall as high as a man, saw more men standing with rifles at port arms.

"Proof!" he shouted. "I have proof! I have rifles!"

Jahier shook his head. "Nay, Pianessa would sacrifice ten crates of rifles to lure us from the Castelluzo."

For the first time in his life, Blake knew true, full-blown panic. He squirmed to escape, but they held him against the wall. Obviously, he was to be shot dead like a dog, and yes, yes—of course he deserved it! *That's not the point!*

They tied him to the wall.

"*English rifles!*" he cried. "Surely this Pianessa has no access to the finest *English rifles!*"

"Yea, he does."

Blake stared in horror.

Jahier commanded the firing squad: "Ready."

Descombie raised his hand compassionately toward he who was about to be compassionately shot.

"Aim!"

Soldiers shouldered their—

"*Soldiers!*" Blake shrieked. "Soldiers! I know where their soldiers are camped! They're inside your valley! I can lead you to them! They have provisions! Weapons!"

The firing squad exchanged glances.

"I can take you to them!" Blake continued quickly. "Surely you want to know where they are camped!"

Jahier's brow was hard in concentration.

Blake attempted to make his eyes and face as transparent as possible. He'd never tried the truth, but then he'd never faced a firing squad. It seemed as if Jahier studied him forever before he tilted his head to a young soldier.

"Gianavel," he said.

The soldier raced up a slight slope and in seconds descended beyond the crest. The rest of the men seemed to relax, and Blake knew he'd purchased a reprieve, if nothing else. He did not know who this Gianavel was, but he was prepared for anything.

Studious, Jahier sat on a stump, arms crossed. He appeared content to study Blake's pale, sweating visage for hours and hours. Oddly, it occurred to Blake that the cold still howled across the peak, but he was not cold at all. He looked at the one called Descombie.

"Priest!"

"Eh?" Descombie grunted, suddenly attentive. "I am a barbe, sir. A pastor, as you English would call it—not a priest. No man stands between God and another man."

"Yes!" Blake gasped. "I couldn't have put it better myself!" He swallowed, trying to calm. "Look at me! Can you not see truth in my eyes? Do I look like I'm lying?"

"No," said Descombie plainly. "You do not look to be lying. But that is not for me to decide."

Blake remembered. "Gianavel?"

"Yes."

Blake searched the slope, but no figure rose on the other side, approaching. He tried to relax, knowing it would do no good to panic. But he'd been in more favorable situations. He tried not to consider the possibility that this was God's justice for not being more circumspect in his life. But if the command to "aim" was given once more, he knew he'd spend his last seconds trying to make a quick and truncated peace with the Almighty.

Then a figure came over the hill.

Tall and powerfully built, the man wore a white shirt with loose sleeves. His chest was wide and deep, and his face was angled and sharp, like a predator. He wore a belt of pistols across his chest and a dagger and sword. But his eyes captured Blake's attention. They were immensely stern and powerful, absolute in their control and confidence. Gray and opaque like a leopard's, they were also intelligent in a way that searched out truth quickly and decided without regret.

The man stopped before him, staring down.

"Speak," he said.

Blake hesitated. "You're Gianavel?"

"I am Joshua Gianavel."

The gray eyes searched Blake's with a purity of thought or purpose or…or *certainty*…that Blake had never quite seen in another man. He didn't know, truly, what to say. But truth seemed to outweigh all other considerations.

"I'm a gun smuggler," he said with eyes of total honesty. "I am not a holy man or a soldier or even a good man. I was hired by Cromwell to bring arms to your people. I smuggled them across your valley! They're hidden in a wagon, south of this mountain. I will take you there. I am not lying! Please! You must believe me!"

The man named Gianavel revealed nothing for, what seemed to Blake, an agonizing long time. As he turned away he cast a look toward the one named Jahier. "Cut him down."

"Yes!" Blake cried. "You believe me!"

Gianavel turned back with that steady, certain gaze. "Make no mistake, sir. I will not shed innocent blood because it displeases the Lord. But if you are lying, I will kill you. Do you understand?"

Rubbing his wrists as the ropes fell free, Blake declared, "Yes! Absolutely! I understand!"

Without another word Gianavel walked up the cliff, highlighted against the rising sun, and was gone.

It was certain that Cardinal Mazarin, Prime Minister of France, was a man supremely learned in diplomacy.

As Lockhart entered through the hidden portal, the cardinal revealed no signs whatsoever of existing tensions between England and France. And Lockhart projected the same air, quietly closing the doorway as if he'd done it a thousand times. He casually laid his coat and cane, which the priest almost certainly knew was a weapon, across a chair. But to demonstrate that he was not a fool or, even worse, an amateur, he retained his pistol.

Mazarin gave no evidence that he considered the pistol any more intrusive to this tryst than his crucifix. He raised his glass in a toast spoken in Latin, and Lockhart courteously repeated the words that he did not understand.

"I take it that your journey was uneventful?" the cardinal said as he gestured to a matching set of plush chairs, allowing Lockhart to select his preference.

Lockhart waited until the older cardinal seated himself, assuring the aged priest that he was not willing to completely abandon protocol. He would respond to graciousness, yes, but would not mistake courtesy for cooperation.

As he sat, Lockhart noticed the chair was of the highest craftsmanship and wondered how much longer such works of art would be readily available in the world. In France, as in every other country of the Continent, the culture of mass production was eradicating this pride in perfectionism.

"I suffered no overt attacks," Lockhart replied finally, "but I wouldn't say my journey was 'uneventful.'"

"Oh?" Mazarin closed both hands on the cushioned arms. "I hope you were not inconvenienced."

Something in the tone alerted Lockhart's combat instinct almost as if he sensed something moving in a faint treeline—not sight, exactly, more of glimpsing a ghost passing in a mist. "There was an incident in a tavern outside Saint Etienne du Rouvray," he remarked while watching the priest closely. "I don't know if I was a target."

Mazarin laughed. "It would be encouraging to say that there was nothing sinister about that incident, my friend. But I'm afraid you were, indeed, targeted for…ah, mischief."

For a moment Lockhart pursed his lips. "Mischief," he repeated. "Then I suppose that was…your man?"

Mazarin nodded.

Lockhart was impressed in more ways than one. "I owe you a great debt."

"I did only what I would have you do unto me."

"The man who attacked me?"

"Is dead."

"I see."

Lockhart was accustomed to treachery—daggers in the dark, the bodies hidden, secrets protected—and he was a bit surprised that he felt uneasy. Hé figured it was because he was so cavalierly discussing murder with a priest. "Did your man happen to determine the identity?"

Mazarin shook his head. "No, I'm afraid not. We know only that he spoke with an Italian accent—possibly Sicilian—and bore French-made weapons. He had no notes, no evidence."

There was a moment as Lockhart appreciated the breadth of what had happened behind his back at the tavern. He felt a soldier's honor demanding him to say, "I have no doubt that your man saved my life. Please give him my gratitude."

Again the cardinal smiled. "He is only a man quietly dedicated to restoring peace to Christendom, my friend. But, sadly, in protecting the sheep, you must sometimes kill wolves."

Reflexively, Lockhart glanced at the curtained balconies. He hoped the cardinal had not noticed his nervousness, but one look into those glistening, obsidian eyes confirmed that the old priest missed nothing at all. "I didn't know these were such perilous times for you, Holiness."

"On the contrary," Mazarin responded, and like a shift of clouds before the sun, his eyes darkened, "these are perilous times, indeed." He peaked his hands slightly beneath his face and spoke carefully, "For instance, consider the purpose of your visit."

Lockhart didn't blink. "Which is?"

"My young friend," the priest said knowingly, "you are here to plead the cause of the Waldenses. Doubtless, you are prepared to offer me a considerable price for my intercession."

Lockhart was absolutely certain that his aspect neither confirmed nor denied.

Mazarin nodded. "Yes—as I suspected. Please do not be surprised, Sir William. I have spent many decades developing my system of spies and informants. If I were a boastful man, I would say that it is second to none. But, in simple truth, I know a great deal about your assignment, including the treaty you're prepared to offer."

"I see," Lockhart replied. "Well, then, I suppose there's not much I can say that hasn't already crossed your mind."

With a warm laugh Mazarin reclined more fully. "I enjoy rendezvous such as this, Sir William. They are far more honest, in my estimation, than negotiations on a battlefield where men often say what they do not mean

297

because the threat of immediate death inspires all manner of half-truths." He laughed. "Yes, here there is just you and I. We are under no pressure to conceal or even distort the truth, so either one of us can simply walk away from any unpleasantness. But let us delay the inevitable. Why don't we simply speak as men?"

"I invite it, Holiness."

"So do I," he laughed. "In fact, it is something I enjoy far too infrequently. Tell me; would you like to know why men fight so passionately for the cause of Christ?"

It was a moment before Lockhart could choose a response. "I've always wondered about it. I assumed it was for love of God, something like that."

"No, Sir William, not for love. It is for fear."

"Fear?"

"Yes," Mazarin commented. "Fear."

Lockhart gazed strangely about the room, then back to the priest. "The fear of what, Holiness?"

"The fear that they are not in control, Sir William—the fear that they never will be."

At that, simply enough, Mazarin settled. "The Inquisitors must target what threatens their power. But they cannot search without hate, for what is more reasonable than to hate what we fear? What is more reasonable than to hate what keeps us from feeling secure in our place?" Mazarin turned his head to gaze toward the empty street. "A man says; 'I am threatened by death—let us kill it.' So he kills the face of death he has placed on someone and considers himself to be enlightened enough to declare that death is, at last, dead. But the truth is this; men kill in the name of God to deny their fear of death."

At least the aged cardinal was not subject to the same base motivations as those who persecuted others for their faith. But Lockhart didn't know if the old man was disposed to bring an ending to such persecution or merely philosophize about it. He waited as Cardinal Mazarin took a slow sip of wine.

"It seems in the spirit of this age men use the love of humanity to mask their fear of God," Lockhart began. "I am...privileged that you speak to me without hidden or selfish interests. But...my mission is dangerous, my enemy is great, and my cause is just. I want to know if you will help me."

Mazarin's brow hardened as he gazed toward the fireplace. His august head, silhouetted by scarlet flame, held a profound majesty that Lockhart had never seen, even in kings.

"Pope Innocent is dying," he began thoughtfully, "and maneuvers have begun for election of the next archbishop. Consequently, the cardinals are striving to outdo one another to forge a united Church—a single Church for a single country. The Waldenses worship according to the Reformation, so the cardinals reason...that the Waldenses must be destroyed."

All of the elements together made a formidable enemy. Lockhart shook his head. "What else?"

Mazarin sighed. "Well, the Church is fast losing lands and titles to the Reformed Church. So, much like a thief caught in the act, it resorts to violence to take what it could not take by deception."

"It's not going to work."

"Oh, certainly it will work to a degree," Mazarin commented. "Tyranny always works to a degree. The sword has its own reason, and it cannot be denied. But the sword also has no friends, and those who trust in it often learn their trust was misplaced." He crossed his legs, pondered even longer.

"This wrongful war against the Waldenses has several solutions. One, England can invade Piedmont."

"Not a good option."

"Second, there is murder."

Lockhart mentally considered possible targets, but, actually, he didn't know who was vital and who wasn't. Only someone intimately familiar with the internal politics of the situation would be able to make that call. "I suppose you have a plan?" he asked blandly.

Utterly relaxed with the question, Mazarin tapped fingers on the cushioned arm of the chair. "Well, in truth I have not given it much thought. There is always the usual—a few generals, perhaps a marquis, an Inquisitor or two."

"I'm not certain that My Lord could be convinced of the wisdom of murdering priests. He has a highly developed sense of personal honor." Lockhart added as an afterthought, "Not that he can't be provoked…to such things."

The cardinal nodded. "The third option, then, is that the Inquisitors are bribed to declare a treaty."

"For how much?"

"I would estimate a value equal to whatever they will gain if they win this war."

Lockhart shook his head. "No, My Lord would not be willing to pay such a price to murderers simply so they will cease murdering. He will invade first."

"As I presumed," the cardinal nodded. "Which leaves you with the last option."

"Which is?"

"The Waldenses," he answered and waited for Lockhart to respond; he didn't. "The only other hope is that the Waldenses make this war so expensive that Cardinal Benedict calls off his Inquisitors and the papal army."

An interlude stretched as Lockhart considered the possibility. From what he understood, the Waldenses, though passionate and determined, were utterly outgunned and outnumbered thousands to one in the kind of doomed last stand one rarely sees. Lockhart knew his face revealed his skepticism.

"I don't think that's a realistic option."

Mazarin's black eyes didn't waver; he spoke with a tone of quiet confidence. "Do you know of this man, Joshua Gianavel? The one these Waldenses consider their prince?"

Lockhart hesitated. "No."

"Yes," the priest continued slowly and pondered for a moment with a suddenly strange gaze. "From what I understand, Gianavel is like those that the Almighty raised up in the Old Testament to lead Israel to victory over their enemies. He fights at the front and is apparently a great general of men. He knows no fear, and his courage has inspired all his people. If Gianavel falls, all of Rora will fall. But as long as Gianavel lives, the Vaudois will fight."

Looking away, Lockhart estimated the potential size of Pianessa's militia. "This man, Gianavel, has no chance." He hesitated. "I don't doubt your words, but there's no way Gianavel can defeat Pianessa's army."

"Not alone, no."

That was the crux. Lockhart saw it easily because Cardinal Mazarin had made it easy. "Explain, please."

For the first time, Mazarin leaned forward, folding hands in his lap. His blood red ring stood out boldly against his olive-hued skin and black cassock. "If you are fortunate, my boy, Gianavel will continue to make this war very expensive for the marquis. Then, once the cost greatly outweighs any potential gain, the Duke of Savoy will be able to legitimately recall his forces. Unless, of course, these particular Inquisitors have the fortitude to accuse Savoy of disloyalty."

"Why can't Savoy deal with these Inquisitors on his own terms?" Lockhart waved his hand in frustration at the window. "Inquisitors die every day."

"It is possible," Mazarin agreed, "but to eliminate an Inquisitor is dangerous and difficult, indeed. And quality assassins are hard to find...as you already know."

Cardinal Guilio Mazarin rose and strolled slowly across the room, one hand cupping his chin, the other arm folded across his black vestment. "Timing," he murmured.

Lockhart looked back. "Timing?"

"Yes, Sir Lockhart, timing." He strolled back with equal gravity. "Three things must converge—a prolonged siege by the Waldensian partisans, an adamant refusal from the Duke of Savoy to sacrifice his treasury and troops to a futile cause, and the elimination of these Inquisitors who demand the conflict. If these facets come together at the same time, it will force an ending. And I can protect Savoy from the wrath of the Church."

"Perhaps, Holiness. But your plan depends on this man, Gianavel, being able to withstand Pianessa's army long enough for the other two factors to come into play. And I find that...doubtful."

Mazarin did not noticeably react. "Perhaps," he agreed. "But I have a feeling that this prince of the Vaudois will not fall easily."

"Why do you say that?"

Mazarin's eyes were suddenly unreadable.

"If God did not fight beside Gianavel, my boy, then Gianavel would have already been destroyed. And if God fights *with* him, then all the combined armies of the earth will not be able to bring Gianavel down from his mountain."

17

HALFWAY DOWN THE MOUNTAIN, Blake ceased to be shocked at the complex pathway of ladders, nets, and ropes that the Vaudois used to traverse the cliffs. But it was an elaborate, even inspired, system. And he became more and more aware of how ultimately resolved these peasants were—as well as how desperate.

Though they hurled themselves across the spidery rope causeways without blinking an eye, Blake had to reckon himself already dead before he mustered enough courage to abandon solid ground. Not only did the bridges and rappels appear sparsely secured, they tended to stretch over chasms of exceeding depth. Indeed, it was an intelligent system of defense along the same philosophy as a moat. Without a bridge, an army was forced to march impotently around the castle walls. With these ladders and hidden ropes, Pianessa was forced to march around this mountain.

As the hours passed he regarded these highlanders, as well as the implacable Gianavel, with more respect. Blake was a veteran of two wars between the French and the heathen Spanish. Even as a child he survived the siege of Romania by the Turks who, to put it mildly, were no better than the barbarous Spanish. And he had fought beside the puritanical Parliamentarians when his facilities as a spy had been required. Indeed, he had seen all manner of soldier from gentleman to knight to the most savage barbarian with human bones woven in braided hair, like the abominable Spanish. But he had never seen such a striking combination of priest and warrior as the Waldensian.

Rarely did Gianavel speak to those following him—there was no need. Through either routine or some kind of highland knowledge passed by blood from father to son, they negotiated cliffs and chasms with little or no instruction or comment. Only when a complex action deviated from routine did Gianavel give step-by-step orders, which they followed faithfully and without question.

Although their captain was obviously not a priest, he somehow seemed to hold a priest's solemn gravity and calm. And the men seemed to regard him as holy or revered, often departing his presence with the slight, deferential bow one might offer a monk. But he was clearly a soldier—a warrior—and the unearthly presence that embodied him was overlaid with a warrior aspect.

Finally they descended into a smooth fissure by means of a rope ladder that was immediately withdrawn, just as most of the ladders and ropes had been withdrawn. Blake stared up as the tethers disappeared beyond the edge, secured by a boy who possessed the disturbing temerity to crawl over the cliff with the agility of a lizard.

When they finally exited the wall by crawling out a very narrow cave-like opening that was all but hidden by low shrubs, Gianavel immediately entered a thick wood line, and no man made more sound than a squirrel as he followed. As always, the captain led at the front, never using scouts or point men as expendable cannon fodder, as every other commander Blake had known did by routine.

With almost preternatural alertness Gianavel guided them unerringly through the forest, tending to move along the lowest ground where the running water and rotting loam covered the sound of the steps. But when fowl or forest denizen raised its voice, Gianavel would stand and study the commotion for as long as it took, insuring himself through some keen wilderness instinct that it was not a trap. Only after being satisfied would he move again; nor did he appear to feel fatigue as Blake felt fatigue. But then he had traveled through the entirety of last night and had not rested except for a short-lived stint before a firing squad.

After an hour of slow progress, Gianavel froze once more. He had reached the section of woods that Blake had described, but Blake was intrigued that the Waldensian could separate—even remember—the details of this section of the forest from those through which they'd already passed.

Silhouetted against a jagged circle of light, Gianavel stood with head bowed, intense and concentrated. He listened, studied the entire scheme of sharply cut hills without studying anything specific, watched the fowl, listened longer. If Blake had not known better, he would have suspected that he was simply afraid to move farther. But he knew this man was not afraid. He had seen nothing in the stalwart Vaudois that even hinted of fear.

In silence, they stood a long time—so long that Blake noticed the sweat freezing beneath his shirt. Then with a slight tilt of his head, Gianavel motioned for him to approach. When Blake stood beside him, he quietly asked, "What direction did they take?"

No question about whether this was the right location. No question about whether Blake was certain. But when Blake thought about it, if he could answer the question that was asked, he had answered the other two, also. With certainty, Blake pointed to a sharp knoll.

As if it confirmed what he already suspected, Gianavel seemed to search the very air for a sign of the soldiers. He began moving forward almost at the same moment Blake caught the scent of smoke—a campfire. Even Blake noted the carelessness.

If he had been the one to lead a group deep into enemy territory, he would have insured that his men were dressed like natives, ate, drank, and smelled like natives. There would have been no campfires smoking, and they would have moved only at night. During the day they would have brushed out their tracks and buried themselves inside a cliff. The cavalier attitude of this group indicated an inexcusable lack of training or a tendency toward overconfidence that was guaranteed to bring doom sooner or later.

With minute hand signals, Gianavel directed the men to disperse and they began to scatter along the edge of the camp. And as they crept stealthily forward Blake learned a few lessons about moving silently in the forest.

Blake noticed the Waldenses never chanced a piece of uncertain ground but would make a wide detour, however inconvenient, to avoid what was dry and brittle. Also, they never stepped horizontally on a stick but rolled their foot from one end to the other, smothering it. And they set down their feet toes first, like Gypsies who, as everyone knew, were natural thieves. But most importantly, they moved with an all-but-infinite patience—*inhuman* patience. Blake could easily imagine them suspiciously studying ten feet of ground for hours—even days—before chancing it. The rule was simple; do not move until you are certain.

It took Gianavel two very slow hours to bring them to the perimeter of the camp.

Crouching in thick rhododendron, Blake saw what he'd expected to see—thirty men with horses tethered, two mobile demicannon, a wagon loaded with mortar and gunpowder, and another wagon for provisions. A tent was established for the captain or lieutenant, and a small war conclave was ensuing.

Resisting the impulse to back away from the camp, Blake barely shifted his weight to move behind a tree where he might not be—

Crack.

Gianavel's head spun at the split second Blake looked down to see the broken branch protruding from both sides of his boot. As he raised his face in surprise, the Waldensian whirled, and a sentry shouted and raised his rifle, aiming.

Gianavel fired from the hip, not bothering to raise his rifle, and the sentry's reflexive shot mushroomed into the trees. Gianavel leaped forward, drawing a pistol to shoot another man, and was inside the camp. Not hesitating to see if the others were following, Gianavel snatched up the second man's rifle and fired it directly into the powder wagon. Blake saw him swing his aim and had one split-second to spin away raising hands over his head. He never heard the rifle as the air about him and the forest itself surrendered to the blast.

Blake was only aware that he had lost his feet and was lying on the ground, coughing and squinting against the blinding sting of gunsmoke and dust. He managed to gain his feet as the captain speared an attacker on his sword and tore it loose to whirl the blade horizontally, slashing another's throat. Before the man hit the ground, Gianavel ripped the pistol from his waist and raised it to fire in the same breath.

Battle erupted with shocking savagery, and Blake leaped desperately aside as unidentified combatants surged past him through the forest, twisting in grotesque embraces with daggers rising and falling, stabbing in crimson collisions until one crumbled with swords, rebounding from sword or stone in scattered whirlwinds of furious howls and curses flung with hissing vehemence and hate.

As one attacker rushed forward, Blake raised his hands to show he was unarmed, but his attacker kept coming. Then a shot cracked at the edge of the camp, and the man staggered away and to the side, holding his neck. Blake spun to see Gianavel hurl the smoking pistol into the face of another attacker before the Waldensian drove his sword through the man's chest.

Already Blake could see that the Waldenses had gained the advantage, having caught many of the men unarmed but for a pistol and sword. But the heavily prepared contingent at the tent put up strong if unorganized resistance as men do when their formation but not their lives have been lost, and Gianavel was in the thick of it, virtually alone and moving quick to make a hard target. Evading and striking, he hit man after man with more than lethal force to kill fast and kill again until a squad staggered over the dead and dying to reinforce him. Other members of the besieged band were isolated in the forest on random errands and hurled waterskins and food aside to flee, but they were cut down by marksmen before they cleared the closest ridge.

Over a red tide of the dead, Gianavel surged into the captain's tent and out the back again, grappling with a man who wore the insignia of an officer. Face-to-face they fought with daggers, each evading and lashing out, only to slip another slash as the opponent's blade returned, but it was Gianavel who pressed the fight, cutting the captain a half-dozen times before his blade disappeared into the chest.

The Waldensian didn't pause before he tore it free again and twisted, his body lengthening into what would have been a lunge with a saber, to sink the dagger to the hilt behind the man's collar. At the huge geyser of blood, Gianavel twisted to the side and drew the blade clear, doing incalculably more damage drawing the knife than he had done with the thrust. His leap carried him to arm's length, where he landed on balance and poised.

Although superior in number, Pianessa's troop was dead within five minutes of fighting that seemed to Blake like hours. At the end, the Vaudois had not lost a single man, and thirty-three of the militia lay dead. In the sudden stillness that followed, *several* Waldenses turned to glare at him, and Blake fully expected to be next.

He had not *intended* to give a warning to Pianessa's troops, but he had. Then Gianavel stood on the far side of the camp. His shirt was vastly bloodied, but Blake knew it was not his own. Although Gianavel had not swarmed across the camp like the rest, his share of the fighting had been decidedly heavier because he had been caught in the open and set upon by the soldiers like a wounded bear set upon by wolves. The fact that he had survived at all said all that needed to be said.

Then Gianavel spied Blake, and Blake felt a thrill of fear. But the angry commander only shook his head and wiped his dagger on a dead man's cloak. He sheathed it with a frown and then paused to catch a heavy breath before moving into the tent.

Strangely, though he was acutely aware of the opportunity, Blake did not seriously consider escape. No one was near him, and he could have, perhaps, faded into the forest unseen. But as he measured what he had seen of Gianavel's mercy against what he had witnessed of his fury, he knew he was not in danger. This man could kill him, yes—like lightning. But he had a reverence and respect for life that seemed profoundly antithetical to his position as a commander.

In a way, the Captain of Rora's honor was not unlike demonstrations of battlefield mercy Blake had seen from the Puritans. But the Puritans were, on the whole, an unreasonable—even unpredictable—lot. For instance, they might hang a man because of a chance remark muttered against the Almighty in the heat of battle that he instantly regretted but *too late*! Then again, they might display casual unconcern, for whatever theological reasoning, at wanton looting and pillaging or even what Blake considered rampant murder.

Gianavel exited the tent holding a handful of papers. Others gathered around him, and then Blake found himself emerging from the forest. As he stood in the sunlight, he glanced at the nearest Vaudois, appropriating new boots from one who no longer required them.

"You!" Gianavel called. "Come here!"

Blake's heart leaped. He saw the captain staring hard at him; his fighting fury had not quite dissipated. "Me?"

"Yes!"

Humble as a beggar without knees, Blake moved to Gianavel and stood before him, hands folded at his waist. Gianavel thrust forward a handful of notes. "What do you make of these?"

Blake studied the letters; they were printed in Ecclesiastical Latin and bore the signature of…an Inquisitor.

Without revealing his alarm, Blake analyzed the notes, translating as best he could beneath the impatient gaze of the surrounding Waldenses. He took pains to *not* raise his face to behold the eyes of these men who had just killed so many and had not yet wiped the blood from their weapons. When he was certain of a rudimentary translation, he looked tentatively into Gianavel's gray gaze.

He spoke slowly, "It seems one of your people has betrayed you, Captain."

Gianavel's face twisted, as if he'd suspected as much. His dark head bent in terrible regret and disappointment. He inhaled deeply, released slowly. His terse response was frighteningly quiet and restrained, but grievous. "Who?"

Blake reread the letter, insuring that he wasn't mistaken. Yes, it was a response written by an Inquisitor to what he assumed was a Waldensian. Apparently, the man had promised to provide the location of hidden trails and caves that the Waldenses were using to evade detection by Pianessa's militia. He focused on the name.

"Silas," he muttered. "Someone named Silas has agreed to lead Pianessa's troops into your valley by a network of secret trails, as long as the Inquisitors will spare the lives of him and his family." Blake scanned the rest of the letter, looked up again. "That's all."

Muttered expletives rumbled from the men, and Blake was uncertain if they were directed at him or not. When he looked at Gianavel, the captain had shut his eyes, as if to avoid a blinding light or something else equally as painful. When he opened his eyes again, he looked at one called Damont.

The old man shook his head slowly, sadly, holding the captain's gaze with an equal measure of grief.

Gianavel closed his eyes, nodded.

He picked up his rifle.

"Let's go," he said.

✕✕✕✕✕

The inhabitant of Rora named Silas must have known the purpose of the men as they cleared the wood line near his farmhouse. Before the band

313

was halfway across a field, a shot was fired from a window and, by Blake's estimation, barely missed either himself or Gianavel, and then they were prone on the ground.

The ensuing fire fight was brief, and then men stormed through the rear door and cascaded through the windows of the farmhouse. Barely twenty seconds passed before Silas was dragged through the front door, his wife and children trailing close.

Immediately, three boys no older than six and seven ran to Gianavel. Together they pulled at his sleeves, his belt and rifle, begging him to not injure their father. And Blake would never forget what he beheld in the captain's face.

Gazing down somberly, Gianavel's gray eyes were like liquid steel that possessed the capacity to be infinitely hard or infinitely soft, according to the fire of his will. The same hand Blake had seen snap a man's neck like a rotten branch gently held the smaller hands, as if it could not, would not, harm a soul. But he remained silent and unyielding throughout, nor did he attempt to console the cacophony of voices that pleaded with him to let their father live.

Still without a word, Gianavel's eyes finally fell away and he turned from the house. He gave no signal as the men fell in behind him, towing the terrified Silas in their wake. But a handful somehow knew to remain at the farm, insuring that neither the woman nor her children followed them into the forest.

Though Silas would not stop pleading for an explanation or to know their intentions, the rest marched in terrible silence, ascending several steep hills and down again for another mile before Gianavel turned and motioned for them to stop.

Turning slowly, Gianavel stared upon the farmer who had not yet ceased to declare his innocence. He glared at them in turn, again to Gianavel. "W-W-What are you going to do?"

Gianavel stepped back.

"Please," Silas cried. "Please… listen to me! I had no choice! They're going to kill us! They're going to kill *all of us!*"

Blake raised his gaze to the side. Each man stood stoic and bitter. Clearly, they were not completely unaffected by Silas's pleas for mercy, but neither did they make any display of quarter. They exchanged narrow glances, none meeting the other's eyes.

It was too much.

Not waiting for a response, Silas turned and attempted futilely to escape, but a handful effortlessly blocked his run.

"Silas!" said Gianavel as a judge pronounces doom.

Trembling, Silas slowly turned to face the Captain of Rora. His head shook back and forth as if refusing a confession that would only assure his death. He fell to his knees, and then, with agonizing, painful slowness, he began to weep, continuing to speak about his family, and Gianavel withdrew his pistol.

Even more frightening than the mask of merciless fury Gianavel had worn in combat was the inhumanly cold control.

No one spoke or moved.

Gianavel leveled his pistol at Silas's forehead. His voice was cold and severe. "What have you told Pianessa?" he asked. "Speak now, man, if you will speak."

Face contorted in tears, Silas could only shake his head.

"What have you told Pianessa?" Gianavel demanded in a louder voice.

Silas glared about as if trying to find his memory in surrounding foliage. "I…I told him I would meet his men on the Bagnol tonight! I told him I would show him the secret trails through the valley! But I've shown him nothing!" He straightened. "I swear before…"

"Do not!" Gianavel shouted. "You have already done evil to your neighbors. Do not do evil to God."

"Y-Y-You can't just *kill me!*"

Gianavel's flashing eyes and fierce frown contained the storm within. "We have no place to keep you in chains! We have no men to guard you! You would betray us to Pianessa!"

"But I'm a Waldensian! I'm one of you!"

"Yes," Gianavel grated, "you are one of us. You have also betrayed us! Only by divine providence, Silas, did we discover your treachery!"

Frantic, vivid hope glared about.

"This is murder!" Silas pleaded. "Look at yourselves! You're committing murder!"

"Only me," said Gianavel. "It is my decision, and I will bear the burden of it as well as the judgment." He shook his head. "Silas…if there were any other way…"

"This is murder!"

"It is justice!" exclaimed Gianavel. "Cursed is the man who withholds his hand from shedding blood when blood is required!" He gathered himself, aimed hard. His words came from gritted teeth. "You will feel no pain."

"But…" Silas began to weep tears of fear and anger, and his words sounded deep as the ocean in their sincerity. "…b-but my children! What will they do?"

316

"You have my word," Gianavel said and nodded long, as if to himself alone. "I will care for your family as I care for my own. Nor will I be alone. All the valley will work together to meet their needs."

A terrified silence and stillness smothered the small group. Gianavel repeated softly, "Pray to the Lord now, Silas, so that you will bear nothing with you to His throne. And worry for nothing in this world. All is cared for."

Silas wept as he closed his eyes, and Blake could not help but watch Gianavel. Minutely, almost invisibly, the pistol began to tremble in his strong right hand. Then his jaw tightened and his teeth gleamed in a terrific grimace, and he pulled the trigger.

The shot hit Silas in the forehead and he tilted forward, not backward as Blake expected. He hit the ground with a surprisingly soft thud, and voluminous smoke from the pistol moved slowly across his utterly still body, spread, lifted, and dissipated like a ghost that slowly enshrouded them all.

Gianavel lowered the pistol to his side. He bowed his head, and for the first time Blake saw fatigue and weariness in everything about him. Now the Vaudois no longer seemed the heroic, larger-than-life figure that overcame catastrophe after catastrophe with prophetic wisdom and courage and strength. Now he seemed only a man—a man who could be wounded like any other man, a man who knew grief like any other man, and who bled like any other man. His face, which Blake had known only to be hard and resolved to defend his people to the death, was no longer fixed with the stoic, inhuman control that characterized him.

The silence that followed was the most dreadful Blake had ever been forced to endure.

Gianavel stood, head bent, eyes tight. Then, slowly, he removed his powder horn and reloaded and recharged the pistol. He did it mechanically and dutifully like a man that, by force of will and discipline alone would not break the rules of war no matter how terrible the rules of war might injure him. Finally he rammed the ball home in the barrel, stoically reset the rod.

Then, inexplicably, he stared at nothing as if expecting, or hoping, someone would speak to make what had happened easier to live with or even…right. But no one had any words and nothing was spoken, and with deep weariness Gianavel turned and walked softly into the mountain's dark mossy silence and gloom.

✕✕✕✕

Emmanuel entered the large chambers that Pianessa had secured for planning his next invasion. Maps of the entire valley drawn in the finest detail, though the Duke of Savoy knew no map could match the memories of the Waldenses, were carefully spread on a large oak table. At least twenty high-ranking members of the militia stood nearby, some joined in quiet conversation, others idly sharpening swords or daggers.

As Pianessa spied the young duke, his face lifted brightly. "Enter, Savoy. We were just finishing preparations for the next, and last, attack on this valley." Pianessa's smile twisted sardonically. "Perhaps you can find a weakness in our plans."

Emmanuel shook his head politely as he stared down at the table and almost instantly understood the flags and wooden markers strategically placed beside the Castelluzo, the Bagnol, and the Vellaro. It was a three-pronged attack with a crafty sense of design by Pianessa. Clearly, he valued depth of length of line and was pouring heavy troops reinforced by artillery into the three weakest points of defense. Emmanuel studied the notes but saw no indication of how many men would be required for the attack. He had not forgotten the pardon for prisoners he had signed at Incomel's request.

"I suppose you found quality soldiers in my prisons?" he asked mildly.

Pianessa laughed gustily as he sliced a huge red slab from a roast. He sheathed his dagger without cleaning it, wiped his fingers on his chest. "Indeed, Savoy. We have almost twenty thousand eager recruits ready to storm the bastions of Rora. A full pardon from the dungeons of El Torre can inspire amazing loyalty in even the most miserable and wretched of murderers, rapists, thieves, and traitors." He raised a hand for indulgence. "Worry not, Duke—a special regiment of the very worst are assembled to charge the cannons. I doubt you will be troubled by their lives when the battle is done."

Studying the map another moment, Emmanuel saw the details of the attack. Approximately ten thousand would cross the forests from Bagnolo and climb the mountain range on the east of Rora. Another three thousand would once again try to force the Pass of the Pelice, where they had been twice repelled. The last eight thousand troops would climb the trail that led upward from Lucerna, a deep-cut ravine with a steady enough path for ascent but bordered with bluffs high enough to cripple or even kill if a desperate last handhold was not gained.

Three distinctly separate attacks—the Pass, the Bagnol, and the Lucerna. Almost twenty thousand soldiers trying to take a valley more than fifty miles in circumference defended by less than two hundred men. The aspect of what manner of battle this would be was horrifying.

The Waldenses would not surrender, neither would Pianessa's troops give them the opportunity. Once the battle was joined in that jagged chessboard of hills, it would be dagger or sword to the death, no quarter asked, none given. Neither side would know how well the battle was faring because no man would be able to see more than a few feet; so none would fight less fiercely even if their forces were already defeated.

Emmanuel had a vague vision of blood running the depth of that valley as high as a horse's bridle, covering the Earth. His expression must have caught the eye of the Marquis de Pianessa.

"Savoy!" He slapped Emmanuel on the back. "Is this not what you wanted? Victory?"

Emmanuel heard the sound of cavalry in the courtyard beyond and turned to behold hundreds of dragoons. Clearly, Pianessa intended to overrun Rora's perimeter with a mass of bodies, hurling men into that hell until they were simply too innumerable to kill.

Pianessa pointed to the map. "This is the Pass where Gianavel has defeated us on two occasions. I am certain I don't need to remind you." A smile. "But I think I have discovered a weakness in our earlier attack. Although it appears sturdy enough, it will be far less defensible if we crawl over the ridges in groups of three or four. That will force them to disperse their cannon shot, and several of the teams should be able to slip through." He stared down, pondering. "We should lose no more than a third of our forces to storm their bastions. After that we will be inside the valley, and they have no stronghold to retreat to. We'll go farm to farm and village to village until we've killed them all."

Incomel appeared in the doorway, always with the facility of appearing when Pianessa's gusto reached a peak. But he had taken to not appearing without a cadre of minor Inquisitors, as if to make a show of force. It revealed weakness, but Incomel obviously saw the changing tide. It was lasting too long and becoming too expensive in terms of both men and money. It was one thing to endorse the inexpensive destruction of a small village. It was another to provoke a war that depleted Savoy's sizable treasury.

The marquis lifted an arm as if the priest were an old comrade-in-arms. "Inquisitor!" he boomed and Emmanuel knew now why Pianessa was so animated. The marquis staggered slightly and took a long swallow of wine, then bowed to indicate the Inquisitor's noble rank and station. "We have royalty among us!"

Unaffected, Incomel approached until he stood over the map. He seemed to understand well enough, then looked to the marquis. "So this will be the last contest with these peasants?"

The black gleam in Pianessa's eyes glinted. "Aye, Inquisitor, nothing but death before you. Imagine all the souls you'll have rescued from the flames of perdition!"

"Insolent fool!" Incomel snarled in a startling display of emotion. He moved around the table until he stood face-to-face with Pianessa. He raised his hand to stop his guards from approaching, but Pianessa never cast them a glance as he laughed silently.

"This will not end with this war, Pianessa! You have tested the patience of my office long enough! There will be rights to wrong when this is over!"

"Indeed?" Pianessa smiled. "I look forward to that tryst, Inquisitor." He laughed recklessly. "Indeed..."

With a curse Incomel spun and moved from the room in a ghostly, silent sweep that seemed disturbingly unnatural. When he was fully gone, Emmanuel looked placidly at the marquis.

He laughed again. But the cold, deathly gleam in his dangerous gaze had darkened with anything but laughter.

18

BLAKE FELT AN AMAZING LIGHTNESS as he crossed the final rope-bridge to reach the highest part of the mountain. Although the ascent was much easier this time, it didn't much matter because he had been moving for two days and a night, and at this point, everything was difficult. His fatigue was so great that he felt himself floating on his feet.

He was glad that he hadn't been required to help carry the rifles and ammunition from the wagon. He wouldn't have made it a quarter mile with anything heavier than his head. Even unburdened, he was assisted by the Waldenses at crevice and ladder as he stumbled or leaned upon knees, catching his breath.

Although the air was not noticeably thinner, it seemed to have a distinct effect. But the highlanders didn't seem winded as they hiked mile after mile, and Blake began to wonder if he was getting too old for this. He was not old by any means—some of the men almost tripled him in years—but, then again, age could not be completely measured in years.

Gianavel was certainly in his fourth decade, though he seemed younger in the suppleness of his stride and his seemingly endless endurance, for he revealed no more fatigue when they finished than when they began. He also seemed to have an older man's stoic patience and calm, for he was neither irritable nor critical, despite the physical obstacles they had overcome and the traumatic events of the day. The battle itself would have been disturbing enough, but the death of Silas was almost too much for Blake himself to handle. He could only imagine what emotional distress Gianavel had suffered and still suffered.

He had learned quickly that the Waldenses were an uncommonly courteous and kind people. Almost to a man, once he had been accepted, they shared their food or water with him. And after they arrived back at the ridge, the old man, Hector, had handed him a bottle of wine, bread, and cheese.

The English flintlocks he'd smuggled into Piedmont were noticeably finer than the French muskets, so Blake took a moment to explain the double-set triggers and the rifled barrel. He also explained elevation and windage screws, loading weight, and provided a good estimation of accuracy and range.

In the last case was a uniquely beautiful flintlock apparently custom designed for someone of royal rank. Exquisitely plated with antique blue steel, it had a patchbox emblem of England on the oak stock and had an adjustable sight marked to three hundred meters. Blake did not even think rifles could throw a round so far, but the maker of this firearm had high hopes.

Gianavel tested it on the side of the mountain and was openly impressed that it did, indeed, reach almost a quarter mile with the right load. A quick inspection revealed that the rifling was twice as tight as the rest, immensely improving accuracy, and also immensely more difficult to forge. Whoever had ordered the rifle had spent a considerable sum on its construction. And Blake wondered if the weapon had been crafted for

Cromwell himself. If so, Cromwell had certainly known of its delivery to the Waldenses—another hidden key of his passionate endorsement of their cause.

The sun had almost completely descended when Gianavel handpicked forty men and told them to acclimate to the rifles until they lost the light. Within moments the mountainside echoed with a cacophony of blasts, and smoke flowed lazily from the jagged arena of rock to the waving green sea of foliage below.

Blake watched curiously as Gianavel walked a distance apart, finally rising on a slope. Following the captain, he watched as Gianavel knelt alone on the side of the slope, nearly hidden in the shadow of a giant oak with boughs that bent somberly in the dusk like one weeping with the grief of another, mourning with he who mourns. And he watched the cold hillside until the sun was gone and solid dark separated one man from another, and still the captain had not come down from the hill.

Others ate and drank, and by twos and threes began to retire, and then Blake began to feel sleepy and warm beside the fire and lay on a comfortable bed of furs. When he awoke the next morning the hillside was bright and the tree was alone in stark light. Then he looked beside his bed and saw that the rifle with the ornate patchbox emblem had been stood carefully beside his bed in the night.

And Gianavel was gone.

)oo⟨⊙⟩oo⟨

Angela awoke and knew not why.

It was morning outside, but it was yet early, and she had worked almost through the night, not able to rest until it was almost dawn. She shouldn't have risen so early, but she thought of Gianavel.

As if she could see the ridge of the Castelluzo from the window, she wrapped a shawl around her shoulders and stood. She saw him before her mind could realize what she had seen and lifted an arm in sharp exclamation. But instantly she fell silent, staring in horror at the man who led Rora.

Motionless, Gianavel sat in a cushioned chair against the wall. His shirt was blackened by blood and soot. Blackened hands rested upon his knees against his black trousers. His head was bent with profound melancholy, his hair swept back carelessly from his forehead. He stared at nothing, yet he stared. He did not move, save for the soft shifting of the folds of his shirt, and the whole of him inhabited a tragic desolation of spirit that seemed beyond human consolation.

Angela took a hesitant step. "Joshua...?"

Gianavel blinked once, then inhaled deeply and released. He didn't look up as he wearily shook his head. Angela rushed to his side, falling to a knee to stare up in the dark, tragic gaze and saw the kind of pain that broken men know. His eyes softened as she grasped his hand, and he blinked. Angela had never seen him like this and hid her shock. And she knew that no words would be adequate to quell whatever gloom his spirit had not been able to defeat.

Finally he lifted his face, shook his head slowly. He seemed to search the room as he whispered, "Such things must be done...in war. The people need someone...to defend them. And not all have the power to do the things that must be done."

Angela listened, waited, watched.

"I...have power," Gianavel said bitterly. "The power to change the scope of this war...to do what must be done. It would be easy to say that I don't, but that would be a lie. So I decide between good and evil, and enforce my will. And men die."

For a long time he paused.

"If there were only someone to tell me...that I am right."

Angela looked at the hand upon hers. She turned her palm over and held it, placing both hands over his. Holding it tightly, she said, "I have seen this hand touch with such gentleness. I have seen it wipe away the tears of a child. I've seen it work day and night to feed your family." She paused. "I have never seen it do wrong."

Gianavel hovered on the words. "It is hard, sometimes, to know what is wrong. And I wonder...how severely the Almighty will judge us for what we cannot know."

Gently, Angela reached up to touch his brow. "Not as hard as we judge ourselves, Joshua."

He said nothing more as she embraced him. Then she helped him to the bed and removed his boots and shirt, and he lay back on the feather mattress, and she lay beside him.

Almost immediately he was asleep, and she didn't remember falling asleep with his arm around her shoulders as the street below them began to shuffle and clatter with those who yet lived.

✕◦◦◉◦◦✕

Pianessa had the bizarre air of hunger, as if he hungered for war as substantially as other men hunger for bread and meat, as he strolled amid the cavalry in the courtyard. He jubilantly greeted Emmanuel with an upraised hand. "Savoy!" he hailed. "I hope you're prepared for a few days in the field!"

"I'm ready," Emmanuel replied with far less enthusiasm. "Did you see the Puritans last night when they departed?"

"I can't say that I did." Pianessa dismissed their departure as cavalierly as their arrival, but Emmanuel knew better. The marquis had monitored

327

every movement, every word of the Puritans. What he did not personally observe, his spies reported to him.

Emmanuel looked over at least two hundred heavily armored horses and dragoons armed with rifle and lance. All commanders had plans at the onset of a battle, but a good commander—like Pianessa—would quickly abandon such plans if they weren't working. If Emmanuel had learned anything from the marquis, it was resourcefulness.

"We'll camp seven regiments at Giovanni," Pianessa said. "It's close enough to Lucerna and the Pass. Another thousand will camp east of Bagnol. We'll move mortars within range during the night and attack at dawn." His teeth gleamed in a wild smile. "Are you ready for a bloodbath, Prince?"

Emmanuel pulled on his gloves.

"Let's get on with it, Pianessa."

Laughing, Pianessa walked back into the courtyard and within moments was shouting for his commanders to take charge of assigned battalions.

As the day warmed, Emmanuel rode toward Giovanni, both amazed and disturbed by the thousands upon thousands of soldiers spread across the countryside like locusts, all gathering at the indomitable mountain that seemed to be held by one man.

True, Gianavel had many behind him—he was not alone. But he was their prince, their champion, and Emmanuel had never seen, or even heard, of a man leading such a small number to victory over such odds. Even if Rora finally fell to this overwhelming force, the Duke of Savoy was certain that history would bequeath upon Gianavel the victory.

Nor would men ever believe that it actually did require twenty thousand soldiers to defeat one hundred peasants who chose a tiny village in the Alps to fight one of the most heroic and defiant last stands in the history of the world.

There was no mistaking the alertness that had galvanized the camp above the Castelluzo. The air hummed with hectic details of troop movements, and everyone with sufficient strength rushed to and from the barricades, building the walls higher or piling cannon shot and powder. Several had descended down the Pass itself and were chopping trees to fall across the trail.

Blake had seen the adrenaline surge of battle before and walked to the stable where the blond captain, Jahier, was speaking to a small group. When he was done, the men loped into different directions. Blake spoke from his place beside a stall.

"Have you seen Gianavel?"

Jahier's brow lifted at the question. "Oui, mon ami. He left before daybreak. I'm in charge until he returns." He set to sharpening his sword. "What are your plans, English? Perhaps Pianessa would let you leave the mountain, if you tried."

"I wouldn't bet on it," Blake muttered. "What I saw coming up the mountain tells me that Pianessa isn't taking prisoners."

Although Jahier said nothing, the look in his eyes revealed that he wouldn't, either. He spoke with a touch of dread. "If you're going to stay, you might want to be armed. I don't think Pianessa's soldiers will be asking friend or foe if they breach the walls."

All the grisly war stories Blake had ever heard in smoky taverns rose to the fore—dark scenes of blood and fire, of butchered bodies that would not die and heads spiked on swords and lances. Some of the scenes were so horrible that Blake could not reckon them to reality because he could not imagine men doing what they claimed to have done. But they would, and they did, and the captain was right. He might as well fight.

Within a stall Blake saw an armory of weapons and stepped into it. He already had a rifle, but he selected several pistols, insuring that they were all the same caliber. Then he found belts, a sword of adequate quality, and four daggers. He'd carry two on his belt, one in each boot.

Blake was profoundly realistic. They stood no chance against the full Militia of Piedmont joined with the entire Catholic army. If they killed a man with every bullet, they wouldn't have enough bullets to kill every man. And it made him think again of Gianavel; what could compel a man to take such a defiant yet also such an utterly doomed last stand? What could Gianavel possibly win?

He thought of the rifle that had been laid beside his bed during the night. Imagined the captain descending the hill, moving silently, leaving it…for what reason? To show Blake that he was trusted now? To, perhaps, inspire him to take courage? Against *Pianessa*?

There was no knowing, and it didn't matter. Before tomorrow night this mountain would be bathed in blood—dark rivers of it that would flow like water beneath the moon. It would be alight with fire—spiraling cones that lifted human ashes into the night, consuming all that could be consumed. Men would be fighting through the dark, swirling in lone conflict as if battle on a larger scale did not exist, not knowing if they were winning or losing, killing to the last.

Anyone who chose not to take up a sword would die the same as those that did.

Fights like this did not leave survivors.

xoo⬦oox

Alone in a stable, Gianavel turned up a bucket of frigid water and let it drench his entire form. He was not shocked. He had often removed his clothing and bathed with cold water in the strongest winter wind that would dry his body before he could don his clothing once more, as it did today.

He had bent to lift his rifle when he saw Hector bearing a basket load of trays and plates. The old man seemed little diminished by the long days and even longer nights of battle. He nodded curtly as Gianavel donned his belt and blade and set the bucket beside the stall. With a low groan, he rubbed his back, staring at Gianavel. His words were low.

"I heard, Joshua."

Gianavel notched his belt and adjusted it so that his pistols were in convenient reach. When he did not reply, Hector continued, "Let me ask you something, Captain."

With a sigh, Gianavel raised his head. "What is it, Hector?"

"You ever heard the term 'dead reckoning'?"

Gianavel squinted. "A mariner's term." He frowned, thinking. "Yes, I've heard it."

"Know what it means?"

"No."

"It's a term that navigators use," Hector said and nodded with a solemnity that caused Gianavel to pause. He watched carefully as Hector added, "When a man is lost at sea—when he ain't got no compass to steer by— when he can't see no stars, or sun, or even the sky—then that man's just about as lost as lost can be."

Unblinking, Gianavel held his gaze.

"When a man is in a situation like that," Hector spoke more firmly, "the only thing he's got to find his way home is a 'dead reckoning.' Without the sun or the stars, he doesn't know north. But he knows he has to make a decision, so he trusts what's inside him." The old white-haired man thumbed his chest. "What's in here. And so he lays a course by dead reckoning, not knowing if it's the right way, but trusting God that it is. He don't know if he's right, but he prays he's right...and sets his course."

Gianavel didn't move.

Hector shook his head.

"Ain't no man that can tell you that you're right, Joshua. All you got is what's inside of you—dead reckoning. You follow it, boy. Trust it. And see this thing to its end."

19

N O WAR ENCLAVE EVER EXISTED more terrible than the one gathered about Pianessa the night before what was certain to be the last battle for Rora, thought Emmanuel.

It was the third day of their encampment in the Plain of Giovanni—four days since the Puritan had departed Turin—and Pianessa was clearly growing impatient as he stalked through the gathering of warlords, each a rival to Pianessa's barbaric image, barking terse orders. Each of the mercenary commanders bore weapons from a hundred years past and weapons of the current age, and the Duke of Savoy was almost amused that a Celtic battle-ax did not seem incongruous alongside a pewter long rifle or bandoleer of silver-plated pistols. Some also bore painted faces as warriors did in old days—black visages streaked with red or yellow—and some had braided their hair with occult symbols and human bones that went conveniently unnoticed by the Inquisitors. Emmanuel saw two others who wore bear skulls as helmets as well as necklaces of claws and fangs. One had red ribbons tied in his beard with black marks to indicate the number of dead he had left in his wake. Another had a belt ornamented with beads and paint—some kind of cultural medal of honor.

The Duke of Savoy had seen some on the battlefield and knew the awesome fury of their slashing brand. He was also familiar with their animal cunning and their brutal philosophy of war—attack, attack, always attack. Others he knew by reputation alone, but they held the scorched earth mentality of the vanished Vikings. They burned church and home alike, left no one alive.

Pianessa's warlords were not esteemed commanders in any sense, but conquerors without a continent to conquer. In another age they might have led marauding bands across the land, destroying village after village, sustained by pillaging and slavery. But times did not allow for such wanton savagery, so they found sustenance on a more limited scale. It did not change the fact that they survived and thrived on war.

Though any single one might have given Pianessa a hard fight in single combat, they were reserved and quiet in his presence. Nor did Pianessa give any hint that it would be otherwise. Emmanuel wondered what might happen if a coup were attempted for the marquis' position. Without bothering with details, he was certain enough how it would end—Pianessa would be victorious.

The marquis was far too dangerous to underestimate, and those who, because of pride or spite, or whatever foolish sentiment, refused to accord respect where respect was due, did so at their peril. The Duke of Savoy had never deemed it wise to despise a dangerous foe. Which is one reason, he supposed, why he was one of the few who did not underestimate Gianavel.

The Vaudois had thrice proven himself Pianessa's equal in cunning and his superior in generalmanship, causing this to become much more than a battle for a simple village. Pianessa intended to destroy the Waldenses with such brutality that every nation on the Continent would know how securely he held his land. No longer was this only Incomel's war against the heretics. This was Pianessa's war to convince every nation that he was not to be challenged.

Watching Pianessa detail exacting instructions, Emmanuel knew he was not needed or ever desired here. He turned in the direction of his tent and pondered whether he should examine the troops or horses or, perhaps, inspect the cannons and mortars. But his commanders were competent—any inspection would be mere theatrics.

And, remembering the Inquisitors, he decided there were already quite enough theatrics.

><><@><><

Blake somehow found himself atop the barricade at the Pass of Pelice. He had not actually been assigned to it, but no one had instructed him to go elsewhere, so he had stayed where he was.

Staring at the gap where six thousand men would be attacking within a day, he imagined wave after wave of Pianessa's soldiers charging this wall. He blew out a soft breath, shook his head—he could imagine the carnage that was to come but didn't care to.

An eruption of voices made Blake turn.

Gianavel was at the barricade, and for the briefest moment, seeing the captain's bold visage, Blake did not deny the inspiration. The Waldensian, if he knew fear at all—and Blake was not certain that he truly did—never revealed it.

"Gather around," Gianavel called out.

Thirty men gathered quickly as he laid his rifle on a table. Blake descended and joined them. He didn't know what the captain was going to say or do, but there was no denying the courage his presence inspired within everyone, including him. It was as if Gianavel's very presence diminished the threat of death. Not that it made death ultimately less likely, but that death no longer held its sting. No one spoke as Gianavel gazed.

"Remember what I'm about to tell you," he said with authority—like one who has *done these things* and not merely read of them. "If a man is confused, he is no good in battle. He'll be thinking about what the enemy is doing and not what *he* should be doing. So if you become confused, look for me, and do exactly what you see me doing." He held up a finger. "Remember that one simple thing: If you become confused, look for me. Do exactly what I am doing. Do you understand?"

Heads nodded and Blake found himself joining.

Gianavel pointed to a secondary wall. "When we retreat to that wall, don't panic and don't make a show of it. Remember to hit the officers and not soldiers, and take an extra second to aim. Don't worry about being the last to pull the trigger, just shoot accurately."

The captain turned his attention noticeably to the younger men. "If you are hit, *get up.* Do *not* lie there and think you are going to die, or you *will* die. I've seen a man shot in the hand and die. And I have seen a man shot three times in the chest, and that man lived." Gianavel leaned farther forward, speaking intensely. "If you are hit, you must make up your mind that you are going to live. Fight to live. Use your anger. Use your hate. Use your love. Use whatever you can find inside your heart to hold on to life. Don't let fear kill you."

A young man's voice was so hesitant the question was barely audible. "What does it feel like…to get shot?"

One farmer, obviously a veteran, grumbled, "Like getting kicked by a mule."

"You won't feel nothing for a bit," said Bertino.

"I didn't feel nothing for three days."

"Don't worry 'bout it, boy," another piped in. "It'll be your first chance to taste some whiskey."

They laughed, but the mood remained somber.

Gianavel waited, then stood. "Remember that they are only men. Don't think that they are stronger than you are—they're not. They're not braver. They're not smarter. They're only men, and they'll die like men. How do you fight a hundred men?"

"One man at a time," said a young man.

Gianavel smiled. "Right—one man at a time."

The implacable Vaudois hesitated for a long moment. "Do not fight because you're afraid of death. Fight because you do *not* fear it. Do as I do, and God will be with you."

Upon a nearby ridge an exuberant battle cry erupted. They turned their heads, staring. In the distance Jahier could be seen atop a barricade gesticulating wildly to his detachment of men.

Beside Blake, a man muttered, "It seems Jahier uses a more jubilant speech for his men, Captain."

Gianavel laughed again, lifted his rifle. "All right; they've been gathering men and arms for almost five days now. We don't know exactly when the attack will come, but probably tomorrow or the next day. Stay alert. Man your position. Stick to your routine. Check your gear and recheck it."

They began to disperse and Blake found himself staring at Gianavel, who smiled when he saw the rifle with patchbox emblem. "I thought it was a commander's rifle."

Blake studied the Waldensian carefully. "What makes you think I'm a commander?"

"You took a big risk bringing those rifles," Gianavel commented easily. "Maybe you were drafted for it, maybe not. All I know is that you're here, and these rifles give us a better chance."

"Still not much of a chance."

Gianavel mildly shook his head. "That's not what matters, monsieur."

"What matters?"

"Whether our cause is just."

Staring a moment to see no trace of doubt in Gianavel's gray eyes, Blake said, "You really believe, don't you?"

Gianavel smiled faintly, nodded.

"Yes, monsieur…I believe."

"And you're willing to stake your life on that," Blake said; it wasn't a question.

"A man stakes his life on it, anyway, Monsieur Blake. You are welcome to the Militia of Rora. Or you are free to leave, and no man will bar your way." Gianavel paused, staring keenly. "But if you fight, Monsieur Blake, fight for the right reason. Or don't fight at all."

Simple as that.

Blake didn't move as Gianavel had walked past him to the barricades. Not missing a beat, the captain began encouraging and instructing. In another moment he was teaching a young soldier how to tie a tourniquet above his knee.

Gazing across the valley, Blake saw fortresslike bonfires and smoke rising, much like their own bonfire was sending spidery wisps of flame into the cobalt sky. And though orders had been given for each man to claim whatever meager sleep he could claim, Blake knew with absolutely certainty that he wouldn't sleep.

He wondered how someone who had worked so assiduously all his life to avoid conflicts like this could have become locked in the most colossal conflict of them all.

Along with everything else, he thought, God almost certainly had a rich sense of humor.

✖✖✖

Sir Samuel Morland had ridden hard in the four nights and five days since he departed Turin. He had killed three horses and left his fellow Puritans in villages far from Paris, aghast and amazed at the merciless pace demanded by the loyal aide of Lord Oliver Cromwell.

By prearranged agreement Morland arrived in Paris and barely took a moment to discard his dust-caked riding clothes and don similar apparel before storming into Lockhart's private chamber, quickly and unceremoniously spreading maps on the table.

After truncated introductions—they were already familiar with each other by reputation—Lockhart bent over the papers. Detailed passes and plains and critical ravines and villages were all drawn with exacting precision. Clearly, anything relevant to troop maneuvers had been painstakingly recorded.

Lockhart required little time to determine that an invasion of Piedmont by English garrisons was certainly possible, even unstoppable. But the same terrain that made the Waldenses so formidable an enemy also made them a difficult ally to support.

While an army could attack any place that a soldier could march, it was far easier to coordinate men on an open plain than the side of a mountain. And mountains completely surrounded the Vaudois.

"So," Lockhart pondered out loud, "you're saying that the Waldenses could hold off Pianessa's forces indefinitely if they had fresh arms and provisions?"

Sir Morland was silent, then responded with a distracted air, "With suitable arms, they could hold out as long as their food stores were restocked. But there are not enough of them to survive more than three or four major battles. Even if the Vaudois kill five times their number, they will be defeated."

"But this man—this Gianavel—you say that he has already defeated Pianessa three times?"

"Yes," Morland nodded. "But they were not battles on the open plain."

"They were fought in the hills?"

"Fought in a pass that leads to Rora."

Lockhart considered it carefully. Yes, he could imagine that. But, still, it had been no mean feat. "This man, Gianavel—he must have been highly trained by Savoy."

"I don't believe he is trained at all."

"Really?" Lockhart raised his face. "Then how does he know to do all these things? To fight so brilliantly?"

Morland stared at the map. "I don't know…'Tis strange, for certain. I only know that he is gifted in arts of war. He has never been taken by surprise. He is eternally vigilant. He never wastes his men or resources. He always kills commanders, channels his artillery into ravines and narrow passes for maximum effect, retreats brilliantly." He paused. "He possesses a more brilliant understanding of war than any man I have ever seen, including My Lord Cromwell."

Lockhart raised a gaze. "Could Gianavel conceivably win this war, Sir Morland?"

"No." The reply was chipped. "Never in the history of the world have so few stood against so many and won."

"Then what are you going to suggest to Lord Cromwell?"

Sir Morland sighed heavily. "I suppose that will depend on Cardinal Mazarin. I do not want to suggest that we invade through Switzerland, which the Swiss would certainly allow. It would provoke a reaction from France, and we're already at war with Spain. My Lord does not wish another."

Lockhart waited patiently.

Suddenly the Puritan's right hand tightened in a fist. "There is no good option," he said with frustration. "If we invade, we plunge the entire continent into religious war. But if we do *not* invade, the Waldenses will be murdered like dogs." He grew angrier—fiercer. "But if men *do not* fight for the right to believe and honor God, then *what else* do men have worth fighting to keep?"

Well spoken, thought Lockhart, but added nothing to the words—he didn't have to. If the Puritan were utterly alone in the world with his conviction, he would ask no one to join him.

Evening had faded to dark, and Lockhart found himself following the growing sounds of traffic. Paris had the unique quality of being far more alive during the night than the day. But the thought reminded him that he would soon be venturing through those busy streets for another nocturnal tryst with Cardinal Mazarin.

Before attempting to convince that great mind that even France would be served by a treaty with the Waldenses, he needed a stone-solid, point-by-point argument. Mazarin was far too wise to use his political power rashly. The cardinal understood that power was a precious commodity—something to be used sparingly and with the clear understanding that, once used, inevitably created either a new ally or a new enemy. Worse, neither may be desired, even though the purpose of the power is accomplished.

It was growing late. Sir Morland had served his purpose and then some. He had reconnoitered Piedmont and learned all that needed to be known to launch an invasion. But things would not take that route if Lockhart could succeed in his task.

Without question, Mazarin *could* bring the full force of his office to bear on the war and probably bring an end to it. But Lockhart had not yet found the proper combination of elements to compel him to do so. Perhaps, he wondered vaguely, because they did not exist. Or, perhaps, because he simply was not realizing them.

He looked hard at the Puritan. "What will happen in the next few days?"

Sir Morland's mouth turned down. "From everything I observed, Pianessa will mount a massive attack against the valley. He will probably divide his forces and spread the lines of Rora. Then he will simply pour more men into a gorge than the Waldenses can kill." He paused. "The only advantage the Waldenses have is that they have not yet lost a pass. When that happens..."

Abruptly falling silent, Sir Morland became grim. "When that happens, Pianessa will kill them all."

Lockhart turned from the map and table. He walked slowly across the room, arm folded across his chest, one hand over his chin. He halted with his back to the Puritan. "How many people have been killed thus far?" he asked finally.

Sir Morland took a moment. "Six thousand or so. It is impossible to know for certain. Some say two thousand—some, four. All I know is that the population was about six thousand men, women, and children, and only a few remain alive." His face hardened. "You do not want to know what I have seen."

Lockhart spun back. "Indeed! I want to know *exactly* what you have seen!" He walked forward with discovered purpose. "In fact, I want you to tell me the worst of what you saw in Piedmont. Withhold nothing. That is an order."

"What I have seen would make Nero weep," said the Puritan stoically.

"Precisely," Lockhart said as he sat and raised hands before his face. "And those are the atrocities I must know."

"Why?"

"Because Cardinal Mazarin has no political reason to save these people, my friend. So I must offer him a different reason."

"You think horror will compel him to intercede?" Sir Morland's eyes darkened. "Very well. Then I will tell you of horror. I will tell you what monstrous acts have been committed against these people under the Inquisitor's banner and in the name of God. And when it is done you will certainly command me to never speak of it again."

And Sir Morland spoke of the unburied dead and the crucified, of bodies hung in trees and heads stacked like coconuts, of torture and mounds and dunes of ashes where souls were surrendered to the flames because they would not deny the Lord. And as he spoke Lockhart expressed nothing. Not because he was not shocked, and not because he wished to hear more of death and mutilation and torture of astonishing cruelty. No, he listened and expressed nothing because he did not want to lose the desolate and terrible melancholy welling within him more powerfully with each descriptive word—a melancholy he would bear with him to the palace of Cardinal Mazarin.

Yes, he would repeat this evil tale word for word. And he would see if somewhere within the breast of the aged priest still beat the heart of a man of God.

><><><

Staring down over the valley, Gianavel was not surprised at how clearly objects could be detected in moonlight. He had long ago learned that moonlight was equal to daylight as long as you could determine shading and size, and since sound seemed to travel so much better in the cold, distance was easily learned.

Studying the shadowed trail, he estimated that it would be almost impossible for Pianessa's men to steal upon them in the night. Not only were scouts positioned along the pass with torches hidden within clay pots, which would be broken at an attack, but the last half mile was littered with gravel and broken stone. Anyone who climbed it during the night could be heard a half hour before they arrived.

This site, at least, was secure. And Gianavel had full faith in Jahier and Laurentio, who were every bit as competent, though they had radically different styles. Jahier was boisterous and daring and inspired his men with enthusiasm. Laurentio was more of a strategist and insured a hundred times over that each man understood the simplest instructions. Jahier was creative and would quickly seize the narrowest opportunity. Laurentio was by far the best in preparing for every contingency.

He longed to descend into the valley to check on Angela and the children. But he would be unable to leave this summit for days or, perhaps, weeks. But he couldn't allow himself to feel emotion in it. He turned his mind to tasks at hand.

The bastion was fully ten feet high and thick enough to withstand rifle fire and perhaps even cannon fire for a while. The walls were angled to provide shots along the wall, killing men in platoons. Stakes were set at the crest and base. A ditch angled in a "V" with cannon at each high point had been dug behind the wall. If Pianessa's men breached the wall and entered the ditch, the cannons would be discharged, killing along the length. Nor was there a danger of hitting one another in crossfire.

Gianavel studied every facet of the defense. He could think of no way to improve it, but he resisted the sudden anxiety that shot from his heart at thoughts of the coming conflict. Once this battle began, there would be no retreat. Even if they managed to kill five thousand of Pianessa's men, the marquis would not withdraw.

His plan of attack would focus on pouring more men into this ravine than they could kill. Pianessa's reputation, perhaps even his kingdom, was imperiled, and men were ultimately expendable to preserve it. Also, when the Waldenses were destroyed, Pianessa would inherit the treasure bequeathed by his late wife, and that fortune would more than rebuild his shattered army.

Gianavel spied the Englishman—Blake—teaching a few of the younger men how to tie their gear so they could move more quietly. Gianavel felt chagrined that he had not taught them, himself—it was certainly a needed lesson. But he had been distracted with many preparations and had trusted and prayed that others would pick up what he lost, would fill in the gaps he had forgotten.

A sense of peace settled as he watched them adjusting their canteens and powder horns and pistols, moving them so they wouldn't clatter against one another.

Always God will provide a way....

Winter wind moved heavily on the ledge, and Gianavel half turned his face at the biting cold. As always, the mountain froze during the night, only to thaw at late morning.

It was Pianessa's advantage that his men would pass the night in relative comfort in the valley near Pinerola that even now burned with innumerable bonfires. Gianavel and his men would have to fight off the cold till morning, burning energy and strength.

As Gianavel stepped down from the ledge, he felt a premonition—a sensation of the future—that seemed to come more and more often these days. He did not know if it was the Spirit or his own fears, but he thought he glimpsed a terrible darkness before him—a darkness where the dead were piled in mounds and dunes with lifeless arms frozen outstretched toward a sky as black and soundless as the grave, eyes forever open and forever unseeing at the base of some sharp-edged dusky ravine that drained endless blood from some higher place.

Gianavel frowned at the sensation.

Thirty against three thousand…

In his heart he felt rising words from which he took comfort: "Have I not commanded you? Be strong and courageous. Do not be terrified; do not be discouraged, for the Lord your God will be with you wherever you go."

If the words had been sufficient for Israel's Joshua…they were sufficient for Joshua Gianavel.

No, he thought, as he gazed somberly over the pass, that he fought would not be his eternal witness among men…but that he fought without fear.

◦◦◦◦◦◦

Lockhart had repeated all that the Puritan had described, and Cardinal Mazarin had listened patiently, not even moving, until he finished. Now they gazed upon each other in stillness, and Lockhart could not say what he beheld in those obsidian eyes.

With an expression of deep-felt but restrained grief, Mazarin slowly lowered one hand, rubbing his chin with the other. He stared across the chamber toward the blazing logs in the hearth, but did not seem to see them. "And so," Lockhart finished, "now you know."

Mazarin did not respond, nor did he avert his gaze from the flames. Lockhart felt a wave of concern that he had overstepped the priest's tolerance, but he had seen no other option.

France had no political interest in Piedmont. Quite simply, Cardinal

Mazarin would interfere because he decided it was the right thing to do, or not. Nor was Lockhart anywhere near so foolish as to assume he could persuade the old man. Mazarin was far too intelligent, and his morality was far too complex for Lockhart to debate.

Finally the older man spoke, "You have given me cause for great grief. Yes, I agree—a hard end should be brought to this persecution. But what you ask…is difficult."

Lockhart said nothing.

"I have fought many battles in my career," Mazarin added. "Some within the church, some without. I have battled kings and prime ministers, the Citié del Vaticano, my fellow cardinals…even the people." He released a heavier sigh. "I have never challenged the power of the Inquisition."

The power of the Inquisition itself was a blind zone for Lockhart. He decided to keep his responses as mild as possible. "Does the Inquisition have the authority to resist you?"

"Oh yes," Mazarin laughed without enjoyment. "Indeed, the Inquisition has the power to arrest me and kill me if the local government cooperates. But I made proper arrangements some time ago to insure that that would not occur."

"What kind of arrangements?"

Mazarin gestured. "Oh, the same as with a king or an ambitious general. You simply make relevant parties aware that dramatic actions have dramatic consequences. Yes, they may kill you, but they will certainly not live long enough to enjoy the victory. No man is quick to take a stand if it guarantees his doom."

It was a moment before Lockhart spoke, curious as to why it occurred to him. "Except Gianavel."

At the name, Mazarin looked fully at Lockhart, nor did it seem done by decision.

"Yes," he nodded. "Except Gianavel."

Lockhart had learned to reach the implacable cardinal's eyes. And when they focused on him steadily, like twin black suns, he knew the old priest was deep in a complex process of thought that was impossible for him to communicate. It was more than two minutes before Mazarin spoke; Lockhart had not looked away.

"My friend," he began with an air of genuine charity, "allow me to speak freely."

"Please."

"In the beginning, the Inquisition had a good and noble purpose," Mazarin commented, much like a history professor. "I will not go into specifics; noble intentions crushed underfoot for power are not rare enough to be tragic."

Mazarin rested both hands on the arms of his chair and spoke with a presence he might have held thousands. "A tree is known by its fruit, so the end of a thing is greater than its beginning. The Inquisition began in light but was overcome by the night. It does no good to lament ruined opportunity. One must make a new opportunity and not repeat his mistakes. Fortunately, all things are possible with God." He paused, then laughed. "Doubtless, you wonder where I am proceeding."

"The thought did cross my mind," Lockhart admitted.

The cardinal smiled, folding his hands beneath his face. "You enter this fray for the sake of the Waldenses, Sir Lockhart, or because of your loyalty to Lord Cromwell?"

For a moment, Lockhart pondered his true reason. "I've seen enough killing in the name of God, Cardinal."

If Lockhart had been forced to guess, he would have said that the cardinal was pleased. "Your eyes do not lie, which is good. Heroic moral fortitude will make your task easier."

Lockhart didn't blink. "My task?"

"Yes," Mazarin nodded, "a task that you will certainly undertake if you wish to save the Waldenses."

"You're the only man with the power to save these people, Cardinal." Something within Lockhart prompted him to tactfully imply that his nerves might not be fortified enough for more covert intrigues.

Mazarin laughed, genuinely amused for the first time during the night. "As I told you, Sir Lockhart, neither I nor any other man can bring an end to this war. But a combination of circumstances may provoke the young Duke of Savoy to defy the Inquisitors. Your task will be to provide Emmanuel with sufficient reason and motivation to risk not only his throne, but his life, to do so."

Realizing he had not breathed for the entire sentence, Lockhart inhaled and cleared his throat. "I see. And what, exactly, did you have in mind?"

Mazarin folded his hands once more, which Lockhart realized as a signal of masterful scheming. "The act is upon us, and it is time for the players to act their roles. Those who have trained themselves and waited patiently in the shadows can at last emerge to defend the children of God, and you shall be among them." The priest nodded slowly, certainly. "I will explain my plan to you, Sir Lockhart. And if you agree to risk your life to save the Waldenses, then you shall have your chance."

Lockhart silently measured his life and personal beliefs against the almost certain death of physically intervening in an unknown war between unknown enemies with unknown allies.

It occurred to him both strange and somehow appropriate that peace-makers were forever forced to act with more courage than warriors in order to end wars.

There was really no choice to make.

"I agree," he said.

✕✕✕◆✕✕✕

Emmanuel walked slowly among the warlike legions gathered on the fields of Giovanni. There were thousands beyond thousands of them, and they seemed to ebb and flow, swirling and gathering and lifting forests of pikes far into the night in barbaric rituals abandoned by more civilized nations.

But Pianessa had not been discriminate in recruiting men for this army. Pardoned prisoners stood the field in full battle regalia beside barbaric Turks in front companies that would doubtless be horribly reduced by the Waldenses' cannon. Pianessa's personal militia and papal forces comprised rear regiments that would trample across the slain to finally gain the summit.

Pianessa's entire plan depended, quite simply, on whether he truly possessed the bloodless soul to pour men into the ravine faster than Gianavel could kill them.

It was more easily said than done—Emmanuel had read of more than one commander who, at the last, could not stand watching thousands upon thousands of his men butchered like dogs and called off the attack. But Emmanuel knew Pianessa would not cringe. He would not even blink as he watched his men blown to bloody rags and ground into pulp as others charged over their dead bodies.

Doubtless, Gianavel was prepared to kill men as long as they threw themselves at the battlements, but in the end Pianessa's troops would simply be everywhere at once, flooding through the ravine like a dam burst. Then the Vaudois would effectively retreat, killing as he fell back to secondary and tertiary positions, where the massacre would be repeated again and again.

Not for a hundred years had any great battle been decided by legions locked in physical combat. The invention of the cannon and long rifle made such contests unnecessary. But this battle would surely go house to house and room to room with men fighting dagger and sword to the last. Even when all hope for victory was lost, the Waldenses would not surrender—they had no reason.

As Emmanuel strolled toward his tent, surrounded by mercenaries and Turks, his six formidable bodyguards gave him comfort. But it was an unfortunate thought, because it reminded him of Gianavel, who needed no bodyguards at all.

✕✕✕❖✕✕✕

If it had not been night, Blake would have thought the air was dark with war.

He saw Gianavel standing atop a battlement and left his warm place beside the fire. He climbed the short ladder to the top of the wall, and Gianavel was smiling at him.

"You should get some sleep," he said.

Blake tightened a blanket around his shoulders. That, and a sheepskin coat, a gift from one of the Waldenses, was more than sufficient to repel the cold wind. He was aware that Gianavel wore only a long black cloak that was voluminous enough to wrap his body.

"I don't think anyone will sleep tonight," Blake grunted and then looked closely at the captain. "Just tell me one thing…. Do you think it was worth it?"

Gianavel's gaze froze on the pass. Then he took a deep breath and released it slowly, frostily into the night. He was in no hurry to reply. Blake was in no hurry for an answer.

"Yes, monsieur," Gianavel said at last and looked steadily at Blake. "I think it was worth it."

The greatest things are said with the fewest words.

Blake didn't move. "I suppose the outcome would have been the same either way."

"And if they told you, Monsieur Blake, that you could live if you renounced God, do you think a few more years here would be worth eternity?"

"I don't know if God would judge a man so harshly, Captain."

Gianavel lifted his face toward the sky where millions of crystalline lights burned steadily in the dome of night. Wind moved over the parapet—cold, bitter, and stronger than the world.

"Whether we live or die is not the greatest importance," Gianavel said finally. "If I am not killed in this battle, then there is the next. Or the next, or perhaps even old age. The truth, monsieur, is that the Lord is greater than death." Gianavel stared. "Only if a man fears death can death conquer him."

Blake stared into the gray eyes that never seemed to look away or even blink and knew Gianavel was allowing him to search for truth behind the words, and Blake saw it was there. Finally he sighed and looked down through the long ravine. His thoughts turned toward tomorrow.

"You think we have a chance?" he muttered.

Gianavel turned his gaze to the pass, nodded faintly.

"Yes, monsieur…I do."

20

DAWN BROKE TO THE DOOM, doom of drums as the ground trembled at their feet, and Blake turned to behold a thousand pikemen marching steadily up the narrow Pass of Pelice. And behind them rolled a black sea of helmets, shields, harnesses, pikes, and rifles that swelled like waves from men massed shoulder to shoulder in the ravine. And although the length of the line disappeared beyond the far bend of the Pass, it was clear enough—it stretched all the way to the valley below.

Blake glanced at Gianavel. The captain was staring stoically at the attackers. He revealed nothing at all.

Pianessa's men were proceeding cautiously but would doubtless charge when the first volley was fired. They had no place to hide from rifle or cannon fire and knew their only hope lay in overrunning the wall. But they were obviously not in a hurry to attack, wanting to know what direction to avoid when they closed.

Blake muttered and bent to lift another bandoleer with four flintlock pistols. He settled it over his shoulder, adding to the four he already carried. He had cleaned and loaded them all in the last hours before dawn, insuring that the powder was dry at first light. With the rifle, he had nine shots before reloading, and he had been assigned two young boys to reload for him as he fired.

Still, he felt unarmed.

Gianavel was dressed as before with a heavy bandoleer of four pistols. He carried his rifle in his hand and his saber and two daggers on his belt with a pouch for ammunition and powder. He'd discarded his cloak just as Blake had discarded the sheepskin coat. They'd be warm enough when the fight started.

Hector manned one pair of cannon on the left of the wall, and the big farmer, Bertino, manned two more on the right. It gave them a total of four huge forty-pound grapeshot rounds before reloading, but in this ravine the scattered rounds would be devastating. Blake hoped the dead would pile up so quickly that those in the rear wouldn't be able to crawl over the bodies to reach the bastions.

The bellow from deep inside Pianessa's regiment made Blake turn, and he glimpsed Gianavel raising his rifle as those in the front suddenly lowered pikes and charged, unable to wait further for the display of cannon fire that they would surely face.

Gianavel fell to a knee and placed the rifle on the edge of the wall to steady his aim, and everyone duplicated his stance. Yet no one fired because the captain had instructed that no one was to fire, not even cannon, until he did. The stampede of men closed furiously on the wall, almost bounding over the last steep section of slope with the furious charge of wild boar, and Blake glanced nervously to Gianavel. The captain held a steady aim, unwavering and calm.

Blake saw Gianavel's hand tighten as he began to look away, and his shot threw a wide blast of white smoke along the bastion. Then the rest opened up, cannons erupting only a split second behind rifles with deafening roars that buried the entire ravine beneath a cloud of swirling white. Almost immediately Blake retrieved another rifle as the boys reloaded the first, and Gianavel had already shot again before Blake leaped back to the port.

As the smoke flooded down the ravine, another bellow erupted and Blake saw...*hundreds* of dead men were strewn across white boulders splashed and gory with blood, and bodies and then Pianessa's men were thundering over the carnage, rifles firing.

Blake fired and grabbed a third rifle, and then the cannons opened up again—huge blasts that threatened to collapse the wall itself, and the militia was hurled and shredded once more by what seemed the fists of God that struck with the power of meteorites to vaporize men and blast arms and legs and bodies through the air so that blood rained through the white mist in a surreal, scarring sight.

Blake had no more time for thought as the living charged over the bodies of the slain, not betraying fear or doubt or even concern as they fired a hundred bullets that struck like hail, rebounding from stone to stone and cutting the air with a howl as they sailed cleanly over Blake's head. He ducked reflexively at the first enfilade and then ripped out a pistol and shot a soldier that reached the wall.

The man fell back, but others replaced him as Blake found a rifle and whirled to the wall, unable now to hear separate rifle fire amid the unending roar. He glimpsed Gianavel gain his feet and watched as the captain ran swiftly down the battlement. He leaped from the wall as he reached the cannon and instantly disappeared into the wall of hardwoods at the ridge.

If Blake had had the time, he would have wondered what Gianavel was doing and where he was going—he didn't need to wonder whether he was retreating. Then he sensed something to his left and turned as one of Pianessa's soldiers appeared in the portal.

Blake leaped back, narrowly evading the wild swipe of a sword, and as he crashed into the boys, he saw that the soldier held a pistol in his hand, having drawn it in the confusion. He fired and heard the howl, and when he scrambled back, the man had disappeared.

Drawing a pistol in each hand, Blake found himself shooting one and then another as their attackers climbed the battlement. The cannons erupted in an endless volley, and the wall thundered with smoke and the roar of rifles and pistols, and men beneath were heaped thigh-deep and still they kept coming.

Blake traded pistol after pistol and rifle after rifle, killing one attacker, only to kill another, and another, and another, and still they flowed to the wall, a wave of men with rifles and swords and pikes howling for blood without end.

And somewhere in the rush of bleeding bodies and stabbing blades, Blake fell into the furious heart of killing—a hot fellness of purpose that knew neither right nor wrong but only the full horror of war in the round so that even the horror of war was no more and only war remained.

∞∞∞

Ducking bullet-blasted limbs that would have taken off his face, Gianavel ran swiftly through the forest in a line parallel to the ravine. He expected them to chance a flanking attack on the wall, and he was right. Then there was no time to think as he collided with four men rushing through the treeline.

Gianavel struck first, firing point-blank into an attacker before throwing his shoulder into another. The man's musket shot went high, and then

Gianavel's sword slashed in a backhand blow that speared the third man in the chest.

Whirling back and drawing his pistol, Gianavel fired to hit the second man as he rose from the loam. Then the fourth was behind him, and Gianavel twisted sharply to avoid the slash of a saber. As the man stumbled forward off-balance, Gianavel's sword descended—a hard, straight blow that caught the man in the back of the neck.

Instantly Gianavel stuck his saber into the ground and kicked a wide sleeve of bark from the port of a cannon positioned on the ridge. As the next group came hurtling over the hill—not twenty feet away—he struck the wick, and the discharge devastated the hill and everything upon it, blasting tree and rock and flesh into shreds. The third group, barely cresting the ridge, saw the cannon and turned as a single man back the way they had come.

Knowing he had beaten the attack, Gianavel reached the moss-blanketed log that concealed the barrel of gunpowder he had hidden. He didn't need to check to see if the troops were below his position. The howls and cries told him where they were.

He held the flint at the wick and struck it with the butt of his pistol. Sparks jetted in streaks, widely missing. He tried again, and again, badly missing. The battle raged beneath him, and his thoughts strayed to the wall, wondering if they'd breached. Panic and heat were overcoming, billowing out from him in waves, and he forced himself to pause, steadying the flint where the sparks were tending to fly.

Aim, strike.

Caught!

Burning!

Gianavel threw back the moss and rolled the barrel clear, watching the fuse, feeling the timing of it as it burned, and when it was less than three seconds from the barrel, he pushed it down the slope. The short run cast it into the air, far above the bottom of the ravine, and it barely disappeared beyond the edge when the explosion lifted moss and rocks from the wall, lancing the trees around Gianavel like grapeshot, tearing bark off trees and sending limbs pinwheeling in a tremendous silence that smothered everything at once.

Gianavel never knew he'd fallen sideways at the blast, never knew that his face was bleeding and torn. But he knew he'd reached his feet and was stumbling past dead men toward the wall. Then he'd made it through the trees to the battlement.

The wall...

It was clear.

Dead men heaped down the pass like islands in a sea of blood that stretched from the wall to the distant militia, which had withdrawn. And the dunes and mounds at the base of the battlement were already beyond counting, but it was as if here were the gates of hell, and here all the dead of the earth must come, and pass, to enter.

✕∞◈∞✕

Stunned by the inexplicable explosion that had struck the wall like a hurricane, Blake groaned as he staggered to his feet. It took him a moment, scanning the ravine, before he realized what was different.

Seconds ago, the pass had been filled wall to wall with hundreds of Pianessa's troops charging over their wounded to reach the wall. Now there was only a blackened space between the upraised pikes in the distance and those heaped at the wall.

The last mushrooming trace of a black cloud was vanishing above the summit of the Castelluzo, the most visible sign of whatever had descended into the ravine from above, for little else remained where it had struck.

A tremendous rotunda of scorched earth now marred the pass, and men were scattered on all sides, still and unmoving. Blake stared over them in awe; never before had he seen such carnage, never had he seen such a grim battle. In this there was no place for retreat, no place to hide. It was face-to-face from first to last—the bloodiest part of battle that only came at the last of a siege or ambush. But this had hit the apex in the first moment and remained there—it was inconceivable that any flesh could stand.

He saw Gianavel running toward him on the battlement. His face was cut, and blood ran freely off his chin and cheek. He seemed stunned or partially blinded, then he squinted to study the militia regrouping outside rifle range.

Bertino released another shot on the right, and they ducked reflexively at the discharge. When they straightened, Gianavel scanned the numbers around them, apparently checking for wounded.

"None," said Blake and became aware that he was shouting. Doubtless, he had lost a fair amount of hearing. He was also aware he shouted the word with unusual stoicism. He didn't attempt to understand it—perhaps this was the way a man became when he knew he would shortly die. And, indeed, death had less fear for him now. Whether from the fury of battle or something more, he didn't know. Nor did he have the time or inclination to wonder as another thunderous bellow swelled against the wall, and the pikes and muskets were lowered once more, and the black sea rushed toward them.

With little expression they knelt behind the boulders, and Blake reached for a rifle. He didn't insure that it was loaded as he aimed, and it discharged sharply at his touch. Then he reached for the next and the next, timing it so his shots hit solidly, and then their attackers reached the battlement again.

In seconds the Turks scrambled up the ravaged wall, now torn and pitted to provide a host of hand and footholds, and he glimpsed Gianavel standing at the very edge, arms encircling his legs and waist as he struck down men with his sword, the blade rising and falling, rising and falling as he also stabbed out with his dagger to kill and kill, heaving man after man after man from the wall.

With a shout Blake turned his musket like a club and raced to take a place beside the Waldensian captain. And standing shoulder to shoulder they held the middle of the wall, beating back the rising tide of knives and swords and pikes and muskets that had no end. Blake's chest heaved for breath like a blast furnace, his face tight with the strain of killing, and still they came—endless, tireless, unstoppable and unmerciful, dying in droves, and still they came.

The world faded beyond this as Blake knew, somehow in the rising and falling of his musket, that some part of him had joined this battle for something more than life. It was a thin realization beyond the enclosing red haze of violence and death, but it was there, nor did he question it or even care for the why of it.

Faintly he glimpsed Gianavel almost submerged in a sea of knives and swords, eyes blazing as he roared and struck like a lion torn by jackals, killing every one that rose against him and still they came and still he killed, and killed, and killed....

〇〇〇◉〇〇〇

Pianessa reined his mount hard as the battle ebbed and flowed along the Bagnol. The entire ridge pounded with cannon and rifle, and the mountain itself was hazed in a white cloud that rose and fell unnaturally, sound following moments later. Emmanuel, riding beside the marquis, was stunned at the resistance mounted by the Waldenses. Despite being over-whelmingly outnumbered, they had fortified their positions well and were excellent marksmen.

They knew when to shoot, when to move, and had extra stores of can-non and ammunition at each fortified retreat. Every yard of ground that Pianessa gained cost him thirty men, but one glance told Emmanuel that Pianessa cared nothing for the loss. He would drive his entire militia off a cliff if it would force his victory.

With fierce, bellowed commands the marquis rode up and down the ascending troops, threatening soldiers and commanders alike with death if they did not accomplish his instructions swiftly and completely. He shot one soldier who hesitated with a ruthlessness that both inspired and terri-fied. Men charged up the mountain for blood or fear, but they charged, and at the summit the war heated until the cliff itself could not be seen but for the long streaks that Emmanuel glimpsed starkly against the face, wonder-ing vaguely what it was until he realized it was blood.

>οο◉οο<

With broken blades they beat them back till crimson ran the wall, Gianavel and Blake fighting savagely against the tide, but it was only a mat-ter of time. Then Blake sensed rather than saw frantic movement at the end of the battlement and heard the warning.

He spun to see Bertino angling the huge cannon so that it would blast full length along the wall and knew the reason why. They were overrun— all was lost. There was nothing to do but blast the artillery along the wall and hope they survived.

Gianavel, too, heard the cry and turned his head for a frantic moment as Bertino paused the torch above the fuse, himself beset with Turks and regular militia storming the wall.

Blake killed the last man before him and leaped back, dropping from the wall, and as he hit the ground, Gianavel landed beside him, still locked in combat with an attacker, but only one rose. As Gianavel gained his feet, the wall above them seemed to heighten in shadow—the cannon erupted without sound.

Blake did not witness what happened, but the sun disappeared in a roar that shook stone and earth. And when they scrambled back up the wall, all was red and white with flesh and bone and blood. What had been men innumerable, there was not a single cry or moan—all had been killed.

Bertino had survived and was swinging the cannon toward the remnant as even more of the militia surged forward. There was no time for anyone to prepare, and they picked up whatever weapons they could find as the cannons took advantage of the respite.

In a rhythm of rifle and cannon and rifle and cannon, they kept the militia at a distant of a hundred feet. And while they had the advantage of stone to cover themselves, Pianessa's troops had no cover at all from the enfilade launched down the ravine that shredded stone and flesh alike in a continuous resistance.

It seemed that they would never stop coming. They would charge and retreat, only to charge again to be turned at the last moment by point-blank cannon fire that should have won the day but didn't, because there were just so many.

Just...

So many...

>oo<❖>oo<

In blood-soaked boots Emmanuel reached the heights of the mountains guarding Rora. He saw the human carnage that littered the crest and wondered how many men had died already. It was surely thousands, and the day was young. He knew they would fight all day and through the night if necessary. Whatever the cost, however grisly the price, Pianessa would not stop until the last man, woman, and child were dead and no home stood in this valley, consumed by the same flames.

Twice errant shots had ricocheted off Emmanuel's iron breastplate, sending small pieces of lead into his chin and upper arm. He didn't know if it was friendly fire or purposeful hits from the Waldenses. But only a glance confirmed that Pianessa's forces were decidedly less in commanders and sergeants than when the battle began.

Emmanuel understood the wisdom of selecting commanders for rifle fire, almost ignoring the troops. Yes, Gianavel was wise. He had trained his people well. But all the training in the world could not overcome such superior numbers. If for no other reason, the Waldenses would eventually fall because they did not possess the strength to endlessly kill the mass of humanity Pianessa was hurling at them.

Like a flood rising from the valley below, Pianessa's troops stormed upward, swelling over rise upon rise, moving in hundreds and thousands. Everywhere Emmanuel turned there was blood—stones, bush, tree, and slope. Rivulets and streams of blood flowed past him like lines on a map revealing a thousand white roads bordered by thousands of scarlet streams. In all his life the Duke of Savoy had never imagined carnage on this scale; such total, defiant war where death was reduced to something no more important than a breath, and dead men were passed without a glance or thought or care.

And there were so many of the dead now that Emmanuel could not begin to count. Long flat slopes were filled with them, and sometimes ten or twenty of them would slide past him in an avalanche of blood of viscera and human remains, an entire platoon destroyed at once by some close cannon blast.

But like ants swarming over an anthill, they came, and there was no end to them, no end....

Gianavel's last shot had been calculated and proved critical. Blake had sensed that the captain held aim an amazing long time before he fired, then he understood why. The incredible shot killed a commander of unknown rank in the very midst of the maelstrom of attackers, and for a moment Pianessa's troops faltered, uncertain.

"Fire!" Gianavel roared.

Twin blasts from either end of the battlement erupted into Pianessa's troops once more, and then riflemen dropped those closest to the wall, turning again. Blake felt no relief as he emptied rifle after rifle and then his last pistol at their backs, and finally they reached the far bend where further shooting was futile.

Ears ringing painfully, skin burned again and again by powder and cuts and slashes, Blake stood.

Thousands of men littered the ravine, piled like carpet for three hundred feet. Bodies and arms and legs protruded into the air like rolling hills seen from a height with broken pikes and rifles and the banner of Pianessa, somehow erect but torn and shot through and through, waving drearily in the overheated air.

"Reload!" Gianavel shouted, and frantic movement began along the wall—no words, no complaints.

Each man had been hit, and Gianavel worst of all with at least a dozen cuts, but no one uttered a word. Working mechanically, they quickly positioned their rifles, and within two minutes Blake had reloaded his pistols. He shoved one after another into the twin belts across his chest, careful not to slam them too hard and dislodge the ball.

He looked up to see Gianavel approaching.

Stalking the battlement, Gianavel visually checked each man for wounds, not trusting their words. Several had been hit by grazing shots, but none were seriously injured.

At the far end of the wall, leaning heavily on the forty-pounder, Hector was completely blackened by soot. He made no complaint as Gianavel approached.

"Reloaded, Captain."

"Good." Gianavel examined the remaining rounds. "Next time, fire before they're so close. Try to take their momentum before they reach the wall."

"I'll give them something to dance over."

At the other end Bertino was quickly scraping out a bore, inserting another fuse. He raised his face, and only his white eyes were visible in the black. "We've only got thirty more grapeshot, Joshua."

"How many do we have at the second wall?"

"Fifty for each cannon." Bertino scowled and rubbed his face with his blackened forearm—it did no good. He leaned on the huge cannon for respite.

Gianavel looked down. "Load the second cannon with grapeshot and all the remaining powder. Jam the barrel and put in a twenty-second fuse. If they overrun the wall..."

"I know what to do. Just make sure you're behind that second wall when it goes off. It's going to kill everything on this side of the wall and everything on the other."

"You make sure *you're* behind that second wall," Gianavel said sternly.

"Worried about me?"

"I can't afford to lose a good soldier."

Bertino turned to his support. "Give me that sledgehammer and grapeshot, boy. Have it ready when I need it."

In a moment Gianavel was back beside Blake, and at the far bend of the ravine they saw Pianessa's troops slowly pushing a huge forty-pounder into the gap. They were straining to roll it free of the slope so that it could be used to reduce the battlement.

Gianavel spun to Hector as the old man cried, "Help me swing her around!"

Together they lifted the cannon hitch, tilting it forward, and Gianavel shouted, "Enough! Fire!"

"It'll go wide!" Hector shouted.

"Fire!"

The old man touched a torch to a thimble full of powder, and the cannon thundered. The ball hit to the right of the distant forty-pounder, but Gianavel had foreseen the effect, and a dozen men were struck with sliced stones that spun through the air like knives. They writhed on the ground, some rolling pitifully back down the slope, leaving the cannon unguarded. And at that moment Gianavel made a decision that set Blake's heart racing. He moved to edge of the wall and looked at Blake.

"Come on!"

In such a situation, Blake would realize later, a man makes a decision by what he has brought to the battle, by what he decided within himself long before the first blow was thrown. Men do not become heroes in a war; they are heroes before a war. War is only the place where their heroism is most easily seen.

Blake saw the ground and dropped from the edge. He knew Gianavel intended to race to the cannon before replacements could reach it. What Blake did not know is what Gianavel intended to do when they arrived, and then they were there.

Anticipating the worst, Blake got off a quick shot at the startled troops, staggering and shouting only twenty feet away. They had not expected or seen their approach and were wildly surprised at the attack, but surprise wouldn't last. Instantly Blake dropped his rifle and fired a pistol and then another, casting one aside as quickly as he fired to draw yet another. He didn't take time to what Gianavel was doing.

"Come on!" Gianavel yelled, and Blake didn't need encouragement. He flung the last pistol aside and ran the scant three hundred feet back to the wall as shots hummed past them. Then the ravine exploded in an earth-shaking roar that knocked Blake from his feet. He hit the ground assuming he was dead or dismembered and didn't thank God or anything else when he realized he was not.

He scrambled up the slope ahead of Gianavel and cascaded over the lip of the wall, figuring that one of these maneuvers was going to result in a broken neck. Gianavel landed on top of him, and they separated fast to remount the wall.

In the distance, it looked like a meteorite had hit the mountain. The ravine itself was enlarged, as though the fist of God had struck the earth, annihilating stone and flesh and iron, leaving a compact, crusted scar of black. No one lived.

Gianavel's face was intense.

They heard no sounds, glimpsed no movement.

Blake looked at the captain. "What is it?"

"They're just stunned." Gianavel bent and groaned as he heaved a series of deep breaths. Blake was watching, himself barely able to breath: "You all right?"

"Yes," Gianavel whispered. "I'm okay."

"You're hurt."

Blood was flowing heavily from Gianavel's arm. Blake noticed it had not been there before the blast and knew the Vaudois had caught a piece of cannon or rock. But Gianavel could not have cared less. If it were mortal, he would know soon enough.

"Here they come!" Bertino shouted.

Blake saw them surging around the bend and knew instantly their intent. They were coming full force without cannon or cover fire, intent to surge over the wall like a river surging its banks.

"Fall back!" Gianavel shouted.

Racing side by side they reached the secondary wall at almost the same time.

"Get down!" Bertino bellowed as his boots pounded the gravel behind Blake. On top of the wall, Blake took a heartbeat to catch a glimpse that he would never forget—three hundred men swarming over the wall like locusts, all raising rifles and pikes. Their howls and cheers sounded like a river roaring up the ravine.

"Get down!" Gianavel shouted and colliding hard with Blake to carry him completely over the wall.

The Vaudois shouted some indistinct warning, and before they hit the ground, the ground rose up to hit them—a concussion caused by whatever great force had just moved the mountain. Then the sky again vanished in a cloud of dust and smoke that flowed over them like an ocean, smothering and soundless.

✕✕◈✕✕

Pianessa's rage knew no bounds. Though they appeared to be gaining ground on the mountainside of the Bagnol, they were paying a terrible price. And as bloodless as the marquis was, he knew he could not win the battle if *all* his troops were killed.

They had ascended to the very crest, but the fighting had still not come to blows. Along the ridge, the Waldenses had positioned a series of cannons in cavelike indentations, like a honeycomb. None of the cannons could be attacked from the flanks, and though each cannon had a limited scope because of the walls of the cave, they had positioned them so that they criss-crossed. Each cannon had only to fire upon what was directly in front it. If it was not in front of one cannon, it was in front of another. But every inch of the slope was scarred by grapeshot that had the lethal tendency to skip across the downward sloping cliff as rocks skip across a smooth lake.

To Pianessa's further irritation, many of the balls didn't even kill his men but simply blew off a foot or a few toes. They could scarce climb with half a foot, so they remained crippled and uselessly alive. But more than once Emmanuel saw Pianessa pause long enough to kill the wounded, an action that inspired those around the traitor to rise on mangled feet and stumble forward.

Emmanuel turned at footsteps that raced up behind him. Drawing his sword to kill, he saw a runner who stumbled breathlessly into Pianessa's back before the marquis hauled him around with a burly arm and shouted, "What is this?"

The runner was so out of breath he could not speak.

Pianessa struck him. "What is it!"

"Gianavel!" the boy shouted and pointed. "The Pelice!"

For a moment Pianessa scowled. "Gianavel is holding the Pelice? He's not on this side of the valley?"

The boy's head shook.

Teeth bared in a snarl, Pianessa hurled the boy away and advanced without a word. Doubtless, Pianessa had wanted to personally defeat the captain in combat. It would have done great repair to his marred reputation as a military commander.

For, despite what was said openly within Pianessa's castle, even throughout Piedmont, Gianavel had become the prince of his people. It was competition the marquis neither desired nor needed. And now, even if Pianessa won this war, he would never reclaim his fearsome reputation unless he himself defeated the captain.

More than anyone else, Pianessa knew the security of a powerful military reputation. It was the central truss in his kingdom and, if removed, might precipitate a domino effect that could collapse the rest. For if others followed the Waldensian's example, they could, for certain, harass Pianessa from Piedmont, regardless of his militia and papal endorsement.

Walking boldly up the cliff, Pianessa dared the thickest onslaught of cannon and rifle fire, but Emmanuel was not surprised. While Pianessa was a beast in human form, he was also a soldier of dauntless courage. And when he took the field, he acted as if he were impervious to the death that struck on either side, killing hundreds. Emmanuel understood—Pianessa's very fearlessness was the heart of what made him so feared.

And, now, the summit was within reach.

><o<◇><o<

Six hundred feet of blackened earth, broken stone, and broken men lay in flame and smoking blood and splintered weapons along the Pass of Pelice. It was as though a volcano had erupted to send a firestorm along the ravine, destroying what could be destroyed and burying everything else in the dead dust of an open grave.

Rora's defenders rearmed with prearranged weapons. The second wall had been equipped so that they would have to carry nothing from the first. Each man grabbed a loaded rifle, and Blake donned two additional belts of pistols. His reloaders were miraculously uninjured and settled behind him, trembling.

Blake looked back at them. Both of the young boys were frightened as they should have been frightened. But they had courage—great courage. He understood deeply why these Waldenses were so willing to the death to defend their children, not to mention their way of life.

Pausing, Blake smiled faintly. "We'll be all right, lads. Just keep doing what you've been doing."

They nodded, almost in tears.

But some commander within Pianessa's militia was no fool. He knew what they had done, just as he knew they probably did not have a third wall to fall back to.

Even now, dim shapes could be seen advancing through the foglike shroud. Then silhouettes emerged, rifles leveled at the waist, and fired as soon as they saw the second wall—fired in a long, cascading staggered volley that sent hundreds of rounds over their heads or rebounding futilely off stone.

Then Hector and Bertino opened up with the last cannons, and the entire militia of Piedmont charged. Within seconds they were before the wall, and Rora's defenders rose up, aiming and firing, killing as fast they could pull the triggers. Men fell before their faces and were instantly trampled down by others who climbed with hysterical fear and haste over the dead and wounded alike, caring nothing for another man, and the battle was eye to eye and to blows once more.

Gianavel, dagger and sword in hand, took a position upon the wall and struck only once before a man fell back. Then Blake began pulling pistols from his belts and firing them as fast as he could pull the triggers. He could not kill them all, but he could kill one with each shot, and he had ten shots.

Blake fired, and fired, and fired.

And fired his last.

><><>><><

Emmanuel summited only seconds behind Pianessa, but when he looked down into the valley, he did not witness the massacre he had expected. Rather, the long slope into the valley of Rora was deserted except for the exhausted militia of Piedmont that stumbled, drunken on blood, toward level ground.

At the last moment the Waldenses had fallen back from their fortified positions. They had probably reached the valley in seconds and disappeared into the trees, taking unseen trails or perhaps one of a hundred narrow ravines that crisscrossed the floor.

It was stunning and disheartening that they had charged into the very face of death to finally gain victory and not find a single dead man or even wounded. But Gianavel would leave none of his wounded and would probably even carry off his dead to make Pianessa believe they were unsuccessful in either an attack or defense. Or, Emmanuel considered, perhaps the Waldensian, out of honor, would simply not leave a man behind.

For either purpose, the effect was the same.

Distant fires cast a long column of smoke into the air, and Emmanuel could see from a well-worn path they were near a village of some sort. He saw Pianessa staring about, as if counting how many of his men remained. Although six thousand troops had attacked the slope, less than two thousand reached the summit. Many if not all had been wounded, but they continued to advance, fanning widely and without pattern into the wood line. They fired into every crevice or bush that might have held an enemy, pausing only long enough to see that they hit nothing before moving forward again.

Emmanuel proceeded almost casually, almost gravely, knowing that the rest would unfold as it would unfold. Even if he tried, he would not be able to restrain Pianessa's wrath. The marquis had already paid too heavy a price for this battle.

Distant shots—surprisingly distant—echoed through the thick trees, and Emmanuel knew that the Waldenses were attempting to maintain a guarded retreat. But no retreat was as safe as an attack, and those still capable of fighting would eventually be forced into desperate last stands where they would certainly die or fade into the caves and trails where they would be hunted down like animals.

Either way, it was over.

Rora had fallen.

21

B LAKE STAGGERED THROUGH THE WOODS killing every man he met who wore the coat of Pianessa. He had fallen back from the wall with the rest when Gianavel had called the retreat. But in the chaos he had lost the boys and the captain and, now, even himself.

He knew only that he was somewhere in a forest and that it was swarming with forces, and he was considered hostile. His mind should have been focused entirely on escape, but he could not deny himself a strange, and even comforting, thought.

That he was caught in this war by accident was no longer a cause for regret because his decision to stand beside Gianavel had changed him on a profound level that men search for but rarely reach. For the first time in his life Blake did not consider himself a thief or a drunkard or a vagabond. He felt that he was more, and that he had always been more, and he didn't think that even death could turn him from what he now knew and held.

Yet he knew that death was inevitable if he continued to run blindly through these trees. But he didn't know where he was going or where the others had gone. He searched for—

"Blake!"

If they knew his name, they had his allegiance. Blake stumbled forward and threw himself headlong into the dark entrance of a cave barely larger than a man.

He didn't care if he was diving into a stone wall. He hadn't a moment to spare. He was instantly caught in strong arms and recognized Bertino whispering, "Close it! Close it!"

Sunlight faded from the side, and Blake glimpsed a large rock dropped over the tunnel. He knew that above ground the entrance was hidden and had his first thought of safety.

Then he thought of Gianavel.

◊◊◊◊◊

Gianavel reached the village of Rora to see Pianessa's militia swarming through homes and buildings, exiting with prisoners only to kill them in the streets.

No one was spared.

Rushing across the small space behind Hector's house, his mind was only on Angela and the children. He heard shouting and crashing inside, and Gianavel burst through the back door, leveling a rifle in each hand at his waist.

A soldier of Pianessa, wearing a gleeful smile, turned at the intrusion. The smile vanished as Gianavel blasted him backward across the room. Instantly Gianavel shot a second man, slamming his dead body into a cabinet. Hurling the rifles forward, Gianavel charged to smash his shoulder into a third man. Catching him across the face with his elbow, Gianavel ripped out his pistol and fired point-blank. The man had not even hit the wall as Gianavel turned and scrambled up the stairway.

"Angela!" he cried, stumbling hard to automatically tear a dagger from his boot. He reached the crest and was searching by sound and sight at once.

Empty.

They had fled.

Relief flooded through him, but he had to find them. Racing down the steps, he met three soldiers in the front who sighted him instantly. No time to think or evade, Gianavel hurled himself into the first man. At the last second he twisted the rifle barrel aside, and then they were bunched in the corner as the other two rifles erupted.

Gianavel drove his dagger into the first man's chest, and as his hand released, he tore the man's pistol from his own belt and killed the second. The third actually dropped his rifle and shouted for mercy as he threw up his hands in surrender—Gianavel showed none.

With a pistol in each hand Gianavel charged into the street. The fighting was chaotic, but soldiers already outnumbered villagers. Everywhere homes were burning, and the dead lay in the street, killed indiscriminately. It was clear that Pianessa's orders were to kill everything, man or animal. And they were.

Gianavel could think of only one other place that Angela might have taken the children and ran into the stables, quickly searching, shouting. He was moving along a wall when he saw a shadow moving parallel to him on the other side of the wall, outside the stable itself. And with the unearthly combat sense that comes wide awake when a man is fighting for his life, he knew every detail.

Taller than Angela…shadow of rifle…in clear view of the street but moving…not afraid of being seen.

In the same breath Gianavel cocked and raised and leveled the pistol at the head of the shadow. Without hesitation he instantly placed the barrel flush against the thin board and fired and heard a man fall to the ground. He was out the door as quick and lifted the dead man's rifle. He began to . . .

"Gianavel!"

Spinning and dropping with the rifle raised, Gianavel instantly recognized Descombie. The priest staggered through the battle, holding Jacob in his arms. The boy was crying and screaming for Gianavel.

As Descombie collapsed, Gianavel caught Jacob from his arms. He didn't listen to his child's cries as the priest struggled for breath, bleeding profusely from the chest.

"Descombie!" Gianavel shouted, knowing there was nothing that could be done to save him. "Where's Angela! The girls!"

"Pianessa!" Descombie shouted painfully and fell forward with a groan. "Captured!"

Gianavel's face twisted in pain and rage.

The priest pushed Gianavel. "Go! Go!" He coughed fitfully, surged up to his knees to grab Gianavel's shirt. His voice was coarse. "Go! If you live, we live! Hurry!"

Without a word Gianavel stared in horror over the village. What had been dozens of soldiers were now over a hundred, with more streaming in like locusts from every trail and path. In seconds the village would be completely surrounded and conquered.

"Hurry!" Descombie cried and slumped to the ground.

Gianavel lifted Jacob and turned from his friend, whom he knew would be dead in seconds. He snatched out his dagger and instantly slashed a piece of cloth from the stable wall.

He quickly hooked Jacob with an arm and pulled the small boy onto his back. Then he threw the cloth over Jacob and tied it across his chest, securing the child in the makeshift harness. Even if Jacob released his tight hold on Gianavel's neck, he would not fall.

A last second, Gianavel searched the streets, not to insure that Pianessa was victorious this day but for any sign or hope that Descombie had been wrong and his wife and children might be free in this swirling maelstrom of battle.

No…

Turning swiftly, Gianavel loped down the alley between two homes when another soldier emerged at the end. The man had time only to raise his rifle before Gianavel's outstretched hand touched it with the barest end of a single finger, turning it mere inches to shoot past him and his son. In the next breath Gianavel crouched and his dagger found the man's stomach, and Gianavel twisted it hard as he drew it free.

The man was dead on his feet.

Ripping out his sword and last dagger, Gianavel raced along the homes toward the thickest wall of forest that might give him a fighting chance to get his son to safety. Jacob was screaming, but he didn't have time to respond as a titanic image in black armor mounted upon a black horse erupted before him.

The Marquis de Pianessa thundered darkly into Gianavel's path as if forces beyond this world had ordained this battle.

Their eyes met.

Pianessa roared, "Take him!"

Gianavel's eyes blazed.

Within seconds a half-dozen soldiers raced around the close edge of the building, and Gianavel killed the first with a lunge of his sword before the man could even identify the threat.

Gianavel attacked, lunging into the second man.

He did what they did not expect, what they were not prepared to deal with. They knew a dozen tactics to wear down a man in retreat, slashing his legs or arms, surrounding him, taking him a piece at a time because he fought to survive.

But Gianavel was in their face, killing the second one and then pushing another into the wall before killing a third, only to step from the wall and stab again, dropping the fourth. The other two had used the moment to recover and might have retreated before the fury of Gianavel's rage but for the presence of Pianessa.

They paused, then attacked, and Gianavel took them one at a time, parrying one sword with a powerful slash that threw the man off-balance and twisting to avoid the other saber. Gianavel's backhand slash caught the other in the neck, and the last man gave a respectable but short fight before he fell back with his throat pierced.

Gianavel registered everything at once...*No soldiers close...Pianessa, still here...Jacob secure on my back, and he hasn't been hurt yet...Rora is lost...*

Spurring his horse for quick distance, Pianessa gained a space on the prince of the Vaudois and swung his broadsword in a circle, shouting for more soldiers.

Gianavel saw the forest—only a few steps. He saw a dozen soldiers racing to answer Pianessa's call—coming fast. He spent a single second to raise his sword, pointing directly at Pianessa, who beheld the movement and backed away.

Before the soldiers were close, Gianavel stepped behind the wall and shots rang out. He raced quickly to the wood line and was within it before clear shouts could be heard, and in another ten minutes he was deep inside the forest.

A few soldiers encountered him as he erupted from foliage or forest in a full run—an inhuman thing who turned into them and not away from them in retreat. No, no, it *purposefully* came for them like some unleashed beast, murder in its eyes.

An hour later Gianavel reached the Cave de Casette located south of the Roc de Duc, where more than seventy of Rora's defenders had already taken refuge. They greeted him with wild cries of relief and concern, and Gianavel collapsed across the cold stone.

He knew that hands had lifted Jacob, who was still screaming and crying from the ordeal. Gianavel, kneeling on his knees, gasped, "Leave him with me."

Instantly Jacob ran back into his arms, and Gianavel held him for a long time. Held him until the shooting faded in the area of the village and the air grew gray and then black with homes and fields burning. Held him as the sound of angry patrols faded and natural night blanketed the night that had lasted through the day.

><><><

Blake was accustomed now to not knowing where he was, where he had been, or where he was going. At the moment, he knew he was traveling through some natural tunnel system that ranged cavern to cavern in this valley. It was incredible what use the Waldenses had made of them. It was extensive and well supplied with food, blankets, and weapons much like an underground home—indeed, a village.

It took little to recognize that these caverns had been prepared for days, even years. In fact, moving steadily through them, Blake had the distinct impression that they had been prepared for centuries. Some of the shelves where candles burned had been carved out of the calcite walls, and the tunnels were well stocked with extra torches and candles so that no one would be without light regardless of the journey.

An entire nation could subsist down here for as long as food stores lasted. And from the volume of stocked wheat, dried fruit, jerky, and the thick red jelly these Vaudois seemed to put on everything they consumed, that might be a while. But Blake also knew the tragic history of these caverns.

As Gianavel had explained, the caves were safe only so long as the fugitives remained undiscovered. But, if discovered, the caverns were a death trap. It was simply too easy to build a bonfire in the cavern entrance and suffocate all those within, or pile stones to block escape. Although the tunnels were well stocked, the food stores were not unlimited. Or, as Gianavel had put it, better to risk the forest, where there are always paths of retreat, rather than a fortified position. Because no fortified position can withstand a prolonged attack.

But today there was no choice.

Pianessa's soldiers were riding down those caught in the open field and tracking down those who had escaped into the trails. Without the faintest human sentiment they were raping, murdering, torturing, and burning both homes and bodies. Those who were killed in battle were far more fortunate than those captured.

Then, with surprising swiftness, Blake found himself in the exit of the tunnel. It seemed incredible that they had left a gigantic cathedral chamber moments earlier.

"I see nothing," Bertino muttered, staring out the entrance. "We should leave quickly."

Blake turned his head. "Leave for what?"

"The Cassette is only a short distance."

"The Cassette?"

"Another cave." Bertino looked at the rest. "Stay in the trees. And if you're caught, don't run for the cave. Better to take your chances in the open field than lead them there."

No disputes were offered, and they began to slide from the cavern entrance. Soon after true dark, Blake made the journey beside Bertino, neither of them making more than a whisper of sound, to finally reach a narrow sliver of utter black in a rock wall. Even in the day, the cave was difficult to detect.

Blake entered the cavern to see nothing, but there was unnatural warmth to the air. The last cave had been noticeably cooler, and Blake pondered that it perhaps had been the exiting breeze or even his fear. Then he realized that the warmth was the body heat of a dozen men standing in pure darkness just inside the entrance.

Tenderly and without words or sound, Blake slid through them and five minutes later rounded a corner with Bertino leading by torchlight to see Gianavel before a fire. Burning deep within the cavern, the flames could not be seen from outside, neither would the smoke from the dry wood leave much trace even in the day.

Almost immediately, Blake noted the fallen countenance of the great champion of the Vaudois. Gianavel did not raise his face, and his eyes reminded Blake of the eyes of a trapped wolf he had once seen. Caught in a snare, the wolf had been unable to chew off its leg and had simply sat in the snow, eyes dead, alive only in the physical sense. Whatever was life in it was at a dead center that felt no pity for itself. There was only knowledge of a grave injury stoically accepted, as if death were simply the meaningless end of life.

Yes, they had lost the village, but Gianavel's spirit seemed struck by more than that. But Blake did not possess the emotional energy to contemplate it further or even ask. Exhausted, he sat on a blanket and leaned sideways against the wall. Surrounded by this shocked and shattered group, he thought about what he had been a lifetime ago—before this war.

What he could recall was a gray, faceless, soundless panorama of lies and deceit. Yes, he was guilty of lies and deceit, of theft and betrayal, and exchanging his integrity for whatever seemed easier. But none of that wounded him as much as what he knew had been the greatest sin of all—that of a wasted life.

Until today.

✕✕✕

The illusion of some gigantic black curtain descending from heaven enclosed the village of Rora, the village itself bright as day with burning buildings and bodies. True to his word, Inquisitor General Thomas Incomel had spared no one. Not the oldest nor the youngest, neither the very few who did renounce their faith, in the end, nor those who refused. All had shared the same fate with a handful of prisoners taken for the sake of appearance and posterity.

Incomel wore a grave and serious air, as if his task had been somehow regrettable. Flocked by a dozen additional Inquisitors, he moved from body to body, gesturing with his crucifix as he intoned in solemn Latin. Watching him, Emmanuel could not help but feel fear of someone whose conscience was so cold.

If a man could do this, he was powerful in a manner most men never knew. Even the worst men had vestiges of guilt; no one was completely evil. But a man who was so absolutely beyond the self-imposed restraints men exercised even in war was dangerous, indeed. That kind of bestial indifference gave a man a black advantage.

Emmanuel knew he did not possess it. He had never known a man that possessed it. Despite Pianessa's blood-thirst for war, he was, for the most part, simply greedy. He did not run around crucifying people on a whim or setting them ablaze to wager how long they might live. Pianessa was a killer, it was true, but he was first and foremost a soldier, and even Pianessa respected the rules of war.

The rules of a siege were clearly understood. If a castle or village were attacked, terms of surrender were customarily offered. If those terms were refused, then the ensuing battle, as long as it was not too severe and no beloved commanders had been killed, could be terminated by a later acceptance of amended terms. However, if the attacking party was forced to suffer terrific losses before they finally stormed the wall, then no one was spared and nothing was sacred.

By the rules of war, Rora certainly deserved no mercy. They had fought to the very last, even brandishing sticks and bottles in the street, a resistance utterly futile and even sad. Not that Emmanuel had felt any particular compassion; he had paid a great price for this victory. Although Pianessa led the Militia of Piedmont, he was merely a general in Savoy's army. It was the Duke of Savoy's treasury that recruited men, trained them, equipped, and paid them.

Not that they could not be replaced, but Gianavel's last stand had been particularly devastating to the rank commanders. No less than two hundred above the station of sergeant major had been killed, and experienced men were far more difficult to find. Despite what Pianessa openly admitted as he finally stood inside the village, saying it was doomed from the beginning,

Emmanuel knew the peasants had come within a hairsbreadth of winning. If Rora's defenders had not lost the Vellaro, Emmanuel might well have run out of men before they ran out of rounds. Which, he discovered later, was the only reason the defenders were forced to retreat. Pianessa had simply thrown more men in front of their cannons than they possessed the ammunition to kill.

Emmanuel saw men loaded with stolen goods flee a burning house. Sad that his soldiers were not intelligent enough to at least pillage before they burned.

He wondered what manner of people these Waldenses had been. From what he could discern, they were excellent craftsmen and artisans. And even though they were part of the Reformed Church, they were not dour and stoic like the Puritans. He saw no chapel and thought it curious that there was no recognized place where they convened for their cherished worship services. Upon inquiring of it, he was informed by an Inquisitor that the heretical Vaudois believed that a building was not needed to worship God, because God heard every prayer offered from a sincere and contrite heart.

Emmanuel pondered the thought and almost regretted that he had never journeyed above the Pelice before—after all, it *was* his land—to learn what manner of people these Waldenses had been. Too late for that now....

When the Vellaro fell, word must have spread quickly, because the other two passes were abandoned, and Rora's defenders tried to retreat into the better-fortified section of the village. But Pianessa's troops were following too closely and broke the perimeter before the peasants could secure it with marksmen. Not that it mattered. It was impossible for the Waldenses to forever hold Rora against such superior numbers. That they had endured so long was miracle enough.

Laughing, Pianessa came forward, seemingly energized by the atmosphere of flame and blood. If he held any regret of the carnage, it was only that there was not more of it. The marquis slowed the final steps, then stood utterly still, measuring Emmanuel with that implacable gaze. His smile did not lessen. "What think you, Prince? Do you like the sight of victory?"

Emmanuel looked away.

"Have your patrols captured Gianavel?"

Pianessa's smile faded the faintest degree. "No, Savoy. But the victory is mine. And Gianavel cannot hide forever."

The moment was strangely still, and Emmanuel resisted the fleeting impulse to smile. It was not often that he had seen Pianessa frustrated, and never in battle. Still, it wouldn't do to express pleasure, not in these dark burning ruins where Emmanuel could be found with his skull split by an "unknown Waldensian."

"Very well," he said and actually backed away from Pianessa before realizing there were far too many witnesses. He mounted quickly and reined his stallion in beside the gigantic marquis.

"As long as Gianavel lives, the Waldenses will fight," Emmanuel said with utter certainty. He waited for a reply; Pianessa offered none. "I will await word of his capture at Turin."

Surrounded by bodyguards, Emmanuel took the pass that had been held by Gianavel, toward Turin. Mercenaries had been clearing a trail through the bodies since sunset, but the horses shied and bolted during the long apocalyptic journey through dead men piled in smoking black heaps and dunes and mounds that lined the road into the darkness. The atmosphere so reeked with the coarse stench of burning human flesh and boiled blood that Emmanuel was certain that soon the entire world would be aware of it, if they were not already.

Nor would it ever forget.

No patrols had been sent from the Cave Cassette, though many had pleaded with Gianavel to at least try to determine if Rora had truly fallen. Yet Gianavel only shook his head, said that Rora had indeed fallen, and ordered them to remain quiet and still. He did not have to stress that they were not safe, hiding in a cave in a forest swarming with the marquis' soldiers. They were not even in the mountains, where they could use the terrain against their pursuers. And, even worse, many of them were unarmed, having lost weapons in the frantic retreat.

Blake judged that Gianavel's analysis was correct—these caverns were a regrettable refuge. If discovered, they were dead men. But they were also anything but defeated. Yes, they had lost Rora. They had lost loved ones and their homes. They were hiding in a cave now, outnumbered and unarmed. But they had not lost their spirit, and spirit, Blake knew at last, was enough.

Strange that the Inquisitors would openly declare intentions to imprison the Waldenses so they could not spread their poisonous beliefs through the land. By the very means the Inquisitors professed to destroy this people, the lie was revealed. It was power the Inquisitors sought to achieve, and not truth. For any man that enchains the body enchains the body alone.

What chains can hold belongs to man.

The rest is God's.

22

E MMANUEL DISMOUNTED IN THE COURTYARD of the palace and moved with a sense of confrontation for the cell where he'd ordered his guards to imprison the wife and children of Joshua Gianavel.

First, he wanted to question the woman to determine if she might persuade the valiant Vaudois to cease his resistance. For, despite Pianessa's contemptuous boast, Emmanuel did not think Gianavel would be so easily captured. Second, he wanted to see for himself what manner of woman she was. It would reveal something of the man.

The guards opened the door before Emmanuel arrived, and he moved downward toward the holding area. It was not a dungeon in the classical sense, but it had the same ambiance with torches and scattered straw and chains bolted to the wall.

Emmanuel saw the black-clad Inquisitors standing before a woman wearing a pale blue dress. The woman was on her knees, her hands chained to the wall, as she gazed sullenly at the floor. One side of her face bore a huge welt, and she had smaller cuts and abrasions on arms. Beside her were three young girls, also chained and bloodied.

Incomel's tone was the tone used for last rites, but he was apparently attempting to persuade her of something.

The Inquisitors bowed deferentially as Emmanuel waded quietly into the circle. Almost immediately the young Duke of Savoy saw that the woman was beautiful, as he'd expected, but her face was badly bruised. He thought briefly of inquiring of her injuries but knew she would not talk. She did not even reveal that she was in pain, though he knew she was suffering.

Incomel did not seem to care for either the woman or her children. He nodded politely to Emmanuel as he continued in a dulcet tone, "Your husband can hide forever. Within hours, probably, he will be captured or killed. Why do you resist cooperation? You only injure yourself…and your children."

Gazing down, Emmanuel anticipated that she would not speak, and he was not disappointed. With a soft blink she shifted her gaze to her children, who were staring intently, terrified and trembling. The mother shook her head sadly, and one of them began to cry. Emmanuel could not deny his pity, though Incomel seemed glacial and alien to the least human sentiment.

The Inquisitor spoke loudly, "If you refuse to renounce your faith, you will be burned." He waited for an effect; there was little.

The woman was already beyond fear. And the children, perhaps, did not fully understand the implication. Bowing her head, the woman closed her eyes.

"Where will he hide?" the Inquisitor questioned. "You can at least say something to reduce your suffering. Speak, and I will be merciful. Refuse and you will burn."

The children clutched at one another and began to cry with choking, restrained sobs. With her head bowed, the mother was the semblance of a white marble Madonna.

Nothing.

As Incomel stepped forward and opened his mouth once again, Emmanuel spoke somberly, "Leave her be, Inquisitor."

Stunned, the Inquisitor turned to stare at the Duke of Savoy, but Emmanuel cared nothing for the wrath blazing in those imperious eyes. Making little sound, he knelt before what he now knew was a great woman—a woman of dignity and grace and, most of all, of courage and a kind of strength the Inquisitor would never understand.

Her face was angelic, though her eyes revealed the first faint signs of the harsh wind and cold of the Alps. Her long blond hair was unique for a Waldensian, and though Emmanuel could not determine the color of her eyes, he imagined they were the palest shade of blue.

Still, she revealed nothing, and Emmanuel sensed that she was utterly exhausted. But neither she, nor her children, could sleep as long as they were chained. Emmanuel half turned his head to a guard.

"Unchain them."

Incomel took a step. "What!"

"They cannot escape," Emmanuel said calmly. "Unless your intention is to torment them, Inquisitor, I see no reason for them to be kept in chains."

"Torment is a trusted means of questioning heretics, Highness."

"She will not reveal where her husband is hiding, Incomel. Quite probably, she doesn't even know."

"Perhaps I should be the one to decide what she does and does not know," Incomel said tightly. "The children will eventually talk, I assure you. They are not as uncooperative."

Gazing upon the woman, Emmanuel shook his head. "I think there's been enough killing for the day, Priest. If Pianessa doesn't capture Gianavel, we have other prisoners you can question." Emmanuel paused. "This one will not betray her husband."

Incomel projected the same cold gaze he held during interrogations, and Emmanuel saw nothing human in it—no patience, no mercy, no compassion. It was like a glacier come to life to look upon fragile human flesh with nothing but eons of frost and frozen rock behind it, and there was nothing to connect the two.

Angela Gianavel's hands fell to her waist, and the chains collapsed with a startling clang. Then the children were free, and they crawled quickly and silently into their mother's embrace. She held them close, and they wrapped their arms around one another.

To the young Duke of Savoy, it was a tragic sight. Slowly, Emmanuel stood and gazed down a moment longer. He spoke to the guard without looking. "See that they have blankets and hot food—whatever they require. I do not want them to suffer."

"Yes, My Lord."

"She is a prisoner of the Inquisition," Incomel said tightly. "What gives you this right?"

Brow hardening, Emmanuel turned a gaze upon Incomel. The priest revealed no fear. It was a moment that Emmanuel could easily lose with so many witnesses, for as he well knew, his person was not above the power of the Church.

"My throne gives me the right, Inquisitor. In case you have forgotten, only the government, and *I am* the government…has the right to kill. You may condemn, and that is all."

Incomel's chest fell as he released an angry breath. If he had dared to speak, he would, doubtless, have condemned Emmanuel.

Without another challenge Emmanuel mounted the long steps to the tower door, where he paused to look back. The Inquisitors were standing in a close circle, apparently discussing something of grave importance. Emmanuel surmised it was probably a protest. He didn't care. It was enough for now that they did not openly defy his authority. And he knew something else.

No matter what his woman said or did, she and her children would be dead within days.

✕✕◈✕✕

Standing in the darkness of this tower inside this castle located somewhere inside Piedmont, Lockhart mused over the bizarre chain of events that had brought him to this uncanny situation.

It had been four days since the climactic meeting with Mazarin, and upon leaving that tryst, Lockhart had been in the company of a grim, dark man who said little, expressed only courtesy and kindness, and was uncannily adept at avoiding militias. As he led Lockhart from one desolate, mysterious country manor to another, where they received fresh horses from equally mysterious attendants, they were confronted with not a single challenge, finally entering Piedmont.

That alone was incredible. But what Lockhart found even more incredible was Victor's knowledge of patrol patterns—the time, place, number of troops. When Lockhart, unable to contain his curiosity any longer, asked what Victor's profession happened to be, he said only that he had once been a priest. But no more needed to be said; Lockhart knew enough to guess the truth.

He did not doubt that Victor had once been a priest any more than he doubted that the scars he bore on his wrists were from the racks of the Church. So, yes, Victor had been a priest and, like hundreds of other priests, had voiced disagreement with the hierarchy. He was then tortured, recanted, and was now in the secret service of the formidable Cardinal Guilio Raimondo Mazarin for a purpose unknown. But Lockhart was far less inclined now to doubt the existence of the Assassini.

For hundreds of years legends had been told of a secret sect of priests within the Catholic Church silently dedicated to protecting the Church from its enemies. Although the Church had repeatedly denied the existence of the Assassini, the legends had never quite assumed the dusty mantle of history. For every few years, it seemed, an unexpected death or inexplicable change in national policy would once again save the Vatican, and whispers would begin of shadowy agents of God who simply came and went, and someone died while they were here.

If Victor had not already saved his life inside France, Lockhart might have well refused this stunt on the grounds that it was the height of insanity to travel through a war-torn land with a consummate assassin to a destination unknown.

It was one thing to slip through the night to nocturnal meetings with Mazarin. It was another to attempt to penetrate the very heart of this land and convince the young Duke of Savoy of the dangers he would encounter if this war continued. Quite probably, Savoy would not even care to entertain the conversation. For all Lockhart knew, the young prince was far too terrified of the Inquisitors to risk disobedience, which is what made this war possible.

But, as Mazarin had said, wars are won in the spirit. If critical elements changed, then perhaps Emmanuel would find the purchase to defy the monumental powers he had not yet defied.

Victor emerged in utter silence from darkness, but Lockhart was by now accustomed to the spectral comings and goings. Always the priest moved with a black ghostly air that was wholly unearthly. Not even the folds of his cloak made any sound as he would shift or slide in a new direction without warning and apparently without reason. But, as Lockhart had discovered, there was always a reason. Inevitably after Victor moved into or out of shadow, some guard or peasant or soldier or someone else would eventually pass the way. Of course, they would not see Victor standing so close, nor would they hear him when he moved away.

Often Victor appeared to move with startling speed, but he never moved physically fast. And it was a while before Lockhart understood the nature of his stealth. Victor would move as he perceived the movements of another so that he already took a step in the proper direction before they stood or turned. He did not have to move physically fast because his ability to anticipate oncoming movement or read some faint intent of another was so highly attuned. He seemed to know what they were going to do before they did it, so he moved ahead of time to deal with it. The overall effect was that he seemed to fade in and out without ever risking a quick step that might reveal his presence.

Lockhart did not attempt to be so perceptive. He simply followed the priest with as much stealth as he could manage, not even attempting to mimic his smooth, soundless strides. The moccasin-like boots he had been presented were more than sufficient to muffle his steps. In truth, he was afraid that if he altered his steps too much, he might lose balance and consequently expose their presence. With the thought, Lockhart wondered how Victor would deal with it. The answer—he'd probably kill him and leave him there—was unsettling.

Finally they reached a section of the corridor wall that was thinner and smoother than joining sections. As he had done at several earlier junctions, Victor removed a small vial from his cloak and smeared oil on four cobwebbed iron hinges. After rubbing them tightly for a full minute, he then lifted the dusty latch. As the priest pulled the portal inward, as Lockhart anticipated, the Scotsman saw a richly furnished room burning brightly with candelabra.

As Lockhart moved into the room, after the priest, he beheld a young man asleep on a large feather bed. His saber and pistol belt hung over the iron bedpost, and he wore the clothes of a huntsman.

Lockhart felt that he should have been amazed that he had been brought almost entirely across this land within a period of four days, or that they had slipped unseen and unheard past hundreds of guards and Inquisitors and servants. But he had watched and learned too much from Victor to doubt the priest's cunning and skill.

Nor was he amazed that Victor had brought him, without a single incident, into the bedchamber of Charles Emmanuel, the Duke of Savoy, Supreme Lord of Piedmont.

XOO◈OOX

With Gianavel in the lead, some seventy survivors of the battle of Rora climbed higher into the Alps. They moved in single file, each bearing a load of blankets or weapons or provisions, and none complained or even seemed to weaken as they walked through the night.

As usual, Blake did not know where he was, but, strangely enough, neither did anyone else seem to know this area of the mountain. Only Gianavel, moving without hesitation, held an aura of confidence as he selected narrow ledge after narrow ledge, carefully picking a path along the Castelluzo.

Nor was it difficult to guess why this area of the mountain was avoided. After glancing off the last ledge—a sheer drop of six thousand feet to the valley floor—Blake determined to look no more.

Finally they rounded a corner, and the huge mouth of a cave gaped before them. Although immense, Blake did not think it could be seen from the valley. And even if it could, a half-dozen men with rifles could hold off a thousand on this trail, since only one man could approach them at a time, and even then he would need to be as surefooted as a mountain goat and possess nerves of steel.

Within a half hour they were inside a gigantic cathedral cavern where they laid blankets and built fires to cook deer they had killed on the way. The flames could not be seen this deep in the cave, and the smoke could not be detected against surrounding clouds.

It was only then that Blake finally approached Gianavel, sitting quietly beside a fire, his boy, Jacob, asleep on his chest. The captain did not raise his gaze as Blake knelt, nor did he speak.

Blake duplicated the solemn air, for he had learned the reason for the captain's grief. He spoke slowly, "I'm sorry about your wife and children, my friend."

Gianavel nodded tiredly.

Blake waited, then, "Perhaps we can still rescue them."

Finally the Vaudois responded, "Perhaps…but to reach them we'd have to fight our way through Pianessa's entire militia."

"Then we will fight," Blake heard himself say and was instantly aware that he included himself in this war.

He had never included himself in a war—not even for England, not even when he had been a critical element in the war. Yes, he had fought. He had fought for profit or to escape prison or, even, sometimes for the sheer excitement. But he had never fought with his heart and had never cared for the outcome. But now he cared so much he could not restrict his concern to mere words.

Gianavel was pensive. "I will not throw away any man's life to save my own, or even…for the lives of my family. If there were any chance I might rescue them, I would dare anything, I would endure anything. But we do not have the men to assault Turin."

That was indisputable, but Blake searched. "Perhaps we can find some secret way into the fortress."

With a nod, Gianavel considered it. "Doubtless, there is some secret passage we do not know about. But to discover it we would have to risk a standup fight. It is one thing to make a stand where you have even a slight chance of victory. It is another to invite a fight when you have no chance at all."

Tilting his head tragically, the patriarch of the Vaudois gently caressed his son's head. The boy's breaths were heavy. "I have a child that I must protect, and I cannot protect him if I throw away my life in a doomed attempt to reach my wife and daughters." He was silent, then, "But for him, I would fight my way inside Turin or die in the attempt. But I cannot abandon him."

There was no doubt in Blake's mind what Pianessa would do to them. Just as he knew that the marquis would first use them, if possible, against Gianavel. Although he did not reveal it, Blake was stunned by a future far too terrible to contemplate.

Gianavel would not—could not—surrender because everything in his life would be proven a lie. The hope and faith he had fostered in his children, his wife, and his people, would be worthless, and so his life and their lives would be worthless.

If Gianavel were right, and if God did, indeed, require a man to embody what he believed, then even death could not win in this dark hour. And if Gianavel were wrong, if God did not require a man to live as he believed, then those who judged and those who were judged were meaningless alike, and God was not God. If life with God did indeed overcome death, then death did not ultimately matter. If death did indeed overcome all life, then life did not matter, because death was then the end of all things.

No, Blake shook his head, no...that is not the truth. Everything within Blake told him that that was not the truth. Man was not born to incalculable suffering only to be conquered, in the end, by death. That was *not* the life he sensed within himself—even when it had been a life barely worth living. And he knew he was not alone.

For the first time, Blake truly understood that all of life hinged on this one single question. Why endure a life of incomprehensible suffering only to die a meaningless death? If that was reality, then suicide was the only rational decision.

And he didn't see people standing in line for that.

✕○○✦○○✕

Standing silently at the foot of the bed, Lockhart stared in fascination as Victor moved up to Emmanuel, the Duke of Savoy, and touched him gently on the shoulder. Only when Savoy rolled over with a gasp did Victor place the keen silver dagger at his throat.

Emmanuel said nothing as he stared at Lockhart, unwilling to look within the cowl of the man holding the dagger. He genuinely surprised himself when he refused to reveal fear. Apparently, some part of his mind had prepared for this, nor did he expect to survive. But he would at least send a message to Incomel or Pianessa—it didn't matter which, arrangements had been made for both—that they, also, were not long for this world.

"Tell your Inquisitor General that I have already made arrangements," the young duke said with remarkable hate. "He will not live long enough to enjoy his victory."

Unmoving, Lockhart stared down from shadow. "Do I look like the accomplice of an Inquisitor, Savoy?"

Emmanuel's eyes narrowed. He took a sharp breath as the knife moved slowly away from his neck. "Then speak," he said at last. "What do you want?"

"Your life, Savoy." Lockhart stepped to the very foot of the bed. Emmanuel's eyes flared, then settled as Lockhart continued, "You are engaged in an evil war against the Waldenses. We are here to petition you for an ending."

"To petition?" the Duke of Savoy glanced at Victor and did not seem to like what he saw. "A wordless phantom holding a dagger is an unusual petition."

"We wished for you to understand our sincerity." Lockhart waited for a reply; there was none. "We will speak to you for a few moments, Savoy. Then we will leave you in peace. If you do not heed my words, then we will return. I hope you understand."

Emmanuel's jaw tightened. "Who are you?"

"Who I am is of no importance," said Lockhart. "What is important is that you find some means of ending this war against the people of Rora."

"It's not my war."

A hard tone—the young prince had courage.

Lockhart nodded once. "I know—you are obeying the Inquisitors and the Jesuits."

"So why do you threaten me?"

"Why?" Lockhart's face bent forward. "Does the Duke of Savoy, Supreme Lord of Piedmont, not have the strength to disobey a handful of Inquisitors?"

"It's not the Inquisitors I fear," Emmanuel answered. "It's Rome and Spain. If I move to protect the Waldenses, I will undoubtedly be invaded, and my throne will be taken. How can I protect the Waldenses then?"

"You will be invaded in any case, Savoy!" Lockhart moved forward. "Cromwell is prepared to send ten garrisons into Piedmont if you do not desist from this persecution! Sir Morland has already designed the invasion!"

The words noticeably disturbed the young monarch, but he did not seem surprised. "So, if not Charles of Spain, then Cromwell…" His frown was bitter. "Either way, I am doomed."

"No," Lockhart said firmly. "You are not doomed, Savoy, because Mazarin has vowed to protect you. And when you move against the Inquisitors he will—"

"Move against the Inquisitors?" Emmanuel almost rose. "Are you insane? How can I move against the Inquisitors? And how could Mazarin protect me? Incomel would kill me!"

"*Fool of a child!*" Lockhart came down the edge of the bed and grabbed Emmanuel by the hair. "Do you think we will *not*? This isn't about kingdoms, Savoy! It's about life and death! For as surely as the Waldenses have died, *you* will die if you *don't do as we say.* To defy the Inquisitors is *possible* death. To defy us is *certain death!*"

Emmanuel's voice trembled. "You would be murderers."

"Yes! And I accept that! And don't think we cannot reach you!"

Emmanuel grimaced at Lockhart's grip. Then Lockhart released him and stepped back. "This is your only warning, Savoy. Find some means of ending this war."

"How?" Emmanuel grated.

"Change those who command the army and you will change the army. If you change the army, you change the war. Who is most critical to his fight?"

"The Inquisitors."

"Which Inquisitors?"

"His name is Incomel. He is the Inquisitor General. A second one, Corbis, also has great authority."

With only a slight turn of his head, Lockhart looked at Victor. The Assassini nodded.

"What will happen if we eliminate these Inquisitors for you?"

"Then there is only Pianessa."

Lockhart looked at the Assassini once more, but Victor did not move. "Pianessa is a more difficult matter," he muttered. "I don't know if we can reach him."

"You *have* to reach him," Emmanuel said. "I cannot restrain Pianessa now."

Silence lengthened.

"We'll see," Lockhart responded as he began to back away. "How much time will you require?"

"If the Inquisitors are killed, perhaps very little. I won't know until I try."

"Then we will kill your Inquisitors, Savoy. After that, you have three days."

"And Pianessa?"

Startling Lockhart, Victor whispered his only words, "God will see to Pianessa."

The comment, seeming to come from darkness itself, froze Emmanuel. His entire form solidified in a fear beyond trembling. He did not look at the priest.

Lockhart finished, "Do you have any questions?"

"Just one."

"Speak."

"How did you get in here?"

Lockhart lifted a hand, and Victor's hand closed the black rag instantly over Emmanuel's mouth, his other hand holding his head. The young Savoy struggled for only a few seconds before his hands fell limp, and Victor laid him gently back upon the bed.

The priest reached Lockhart's side, and Lockhart asked, "Will he remember?"

Victor nodded once, and then Lockhart followed the dark priest through the doorway and into the shadows.

23

BLAKE TURNED AS TWO EXHAUSTED SCOUTS emerged from the thin trail that led to the cavern. One fell before others could support him, and the other rushed to wineskins hanging beside the entrance as Gianavel watched, stoic and silent. Selected because they had been skilled enough to penetrate Pianessa's camp earlier, they'd departed in the night to see if it were possible for Gianavel and a small team of men to attack Turin and rescue his wife and children.

The incredible tension held until one finally lowered a wineskin, gazing long at the Captain of Rora. With sorrowful eyes, the man shook his head. Blake watched Gianavel's expression. There was only the faint tightening of his jaw. His eyes remained grim.

The second scout managed to catch his breath. "We might be able to slip across the cliffs and evade the patrols. But Pianessa has pulled almost his full militia back to Turin. A snake couldn't crawl through."

Gianavel's concentrated, then said, "What if we were in Pianessa's uniforms?"

The scout shook his head. "No one, uniformed or not, is getting through the portico."

It was as if Gianavel expected the news. Still, he was not defeated. He paced back and forth, shaking his head.

Bertino grimaced angrily and growled, "Let us take someone that Pianessa values! Then we can threaten him in the same means he intends to threaten us!"

All eyes turned to Gianavel.

The patriarch of Rora stared at the big man a long time. Clearly, he was considering it. Then the anger seemed to fade. "No," he said. "We will not shed innocent blood."

There was a curtain of pause like an act closing.

"If we were to shed innocent blood even in battle, the Lord would be displeased." Gianavel's face and tone were tragic. "How much more will He be displeased if we shed innocent blood for our own purpose?"

No one answered, but Bertino's fists clenched as he stepped forward. Still, seeing the certainty and command in Gianavel's gaze, the big farmer did not challenge. He turned away, muttering.

Without any expression of pain or frustration or even regret, Gianavel walked to the edge of the cliff. Nor did he make any display of bitter disappointment or even grief.

But no one approached him to find the truth.

✕✕✕◈✕✕✕

Impressed that he had arisen much like usual, only later, Emmanuel was sedately consuming a plate of cooked almonds as Pianessa strode into the Great Hall. The marquis appeared clean and remarkably refreshed in body and soul and wore the same armor as the day before, but it had been polished and oiled.

Pianessa laughed as he poured himself a flagon of wine. "It is a good day, Savoy. I don't think that a single Waldensian remains in the valley." He winked. "Alive, that is."

Emmanuel didn't deign to ask about Gianavel. Obviously, Pianessa had not captured or killed the Vaudois. If so, he would have walked into the hall carrying Gianavel's head in his hand. He was also curious to see if the marquis would bring rise to the subject on his own.

Pianessa swallowed a long drought of wine, gazed unblinking upon the Duke of Savoy. "Do you not wish to know about the great Gianavel?" he asked mildly.

Emmanuel shrugged, chewed more almonds.

"He has escaped us," Pianessa said flatly. "Our best reports indicate that he is somewhere in the Alps."

"It will be hard to capture Gianavel in the mountains, Pianessa. He was raised on those paths."

The marquis refilled his wine. "I don't intend to pursue the Waldensian into the hills, Savoy. I have his wife and children—Gianavel will come to me now."

"And why would he do that?"

"Because I have sent a message to him." Pianessa lifted his chalice. "I believe we shall see Gianavel before tomorrow evening."

Emmanuel was not convinced of anything but Pianessa's ruthlessness. "You truly believe this man will surrender?"

"If he wants to preserve the lives of his wife and children, then yes, Gianavel will come down from his mountain, Savoy. He will come in order to save their lives, but I've also given him...other incentives."

"Indeed," Emmanuel mused. "What kind of incentives?"

"What all men want, Savoy. Gold, land, the title of a prince."

Emmanuel was amazed that Pianessa did not understand this man. No, Gianavel would not come down from his mountain for gold, or land, or the title of a marquis. For, in Gianavel's mind, there was nothing on this earth greater than what was beyond it. Emmanuel's words were calm, certain, and quiet.

"Gianavel is already a prince, Pianessa. He will always *be*…a prince. Nor is his kingdom something you or I could ever bestow upon him, for it is not of this world."

With the bark of a laugh, Pianessa cast the rest of the wine in the flames. He set the chalice down sharply on the table and did not look at Emmanuel as he turned away.

"We shall see, Prince."

Angela raised her head as the monk bent, silent and unassuming. He did not look into her eyes or attempt to gain her attention. Instead, he began to lay soft white gauze wet with some unknown herbs on her cuts. He finished shortly and then repeated the same procedure with the girls, asking them gently if they hungered, if they were cold or uncomfortable. He nodded repeatedly, listening more than speaking.

Angela watched him closely, always aware of the guards who had allowed this one captor to approach. Finally she began to speak and found her voice dry and cracked.

"My husband…"

The old monk paused, head down, his cowl covering his face. He did not lift his gaze and spoke with such softness that even she could barely catch the faint reply.

"Lives…"

Angela closed her eyes, leaning her head back. She breathed deeply and then lowered her face again. She somehow knew that communication was not allowed, but only a few words…

"What will they do?" she whispered.

The monk shook his head.

It was all she could gain, and she smiled as she looked upon the children. They were terrified, yes, but they were striving to be so very brave. She had to look away again before tears came into her eyes, because she knew their fate.

Then the monk finished and carried the bowl of bandages and ointment with him. But before he left their presence he turned back and slowly blessed them with his rosary. His next words were clear and distinct, as the guards could not un-ring a bell once it was rung.

"Fear not the one who can destroy the body, but the one who can destroy the soul."

Angela bowed her head.

✕✕✕✕

The spies whom Victor used to hide them within Turin amazed Lockhart not only by their scarcity but in their wordless, emotionless reactions to their comings and goings.

When they had finally entered the stable of a blacksmith after hiding in a half-dozen safe houses, the burly, balding man had simply reached out to grasp some hidden lever, and a concealed portal opened, then closed silently behind them. Victor said nothing as they entered the stable and nothing as they departed, and then they moved down a long stairway to some underground chamber that had yet another door on the far side. Lockhart noticed that a massive iron bolt secured it from within.

So, they were well hidden, and not without an escape route, if necessary.

With a mild flourish, Victor discarded his cloak. He hung the black vestment upon a hook and removed his sword belt and pistol. Last, he shed the thin black gloves and turned to the cold hearth. He began piling dry straw and twigs as he spoke over his shoulder, "The smoke will be channeled through the furnace above. In a little while someone will arrive with food and wine."

Lockhart could not help but ask, "The man upstairs?"

"Condemned by the Inquisition," Victor replied, undisturbed. "The charges were as false as the witnesses, but he was sentenced to death. Fortunately, we managed to smuggle him from Calais before his execution, and now he assists us."

Contemplative, Lockhart nodded. "I see why you do not doubt their loyalty. They have nothing to lose but their lives."

"It not the Assassini that they fear." Victor tossed a larger stick on the small blaze. "Their lives, as they knew them, ended because the Church wanted their land. They had two choices—to suffer death by burning, or accept our help and begin new lives. We provided them with new identities, new homes. We do not ask their assistance. They provide it freely."

As the blaze gathered strength, the Assassini stood and moved across the room. It seemed very much as if he began the fire for Lockhart's benefit and not his own.

"Only someone who freely gives his loyalty can be trusted," he added, briefly pausing to insure that the door was secure. "In this, as in anything else, if someone is forced to fidelity, they will betray the first moment no one is watching. Or, as Cardinal Mazarin says, character is what a man is in the dark."

Lockhart laid his cloak across a chair. "Yes, My Lord Cromwell says the same. He also tends to say that your revered cardinal is an effete snob."

Victor laughed. "The cardinal says your Lord Cromwell is a well-dressed basket of fruit."

"Mutual admiration," Lockhart mused. He was surprised that he had not noticed his fatigue until now. "My Lord does respect the cardinal. I just don't believe that he likes him."

The priest understood. "It is a curious thing that great men agree on values while disagreeing on personalities." He poured two chalices of wine. "And it seems a particular malady of the great."

The wine was deep, rich, and heavy—almost intoxicating by its sheer aroma. Lockhart studied the chalice as if it were responsible. "These people make fine vintage."

"The Waldenses," Victor remarked, "are renown for their winery as well as their orchards and crops. They are farmers, mostly. But they make excellent clothing and embroidery."

There was the trace of familiarity in the priest's voice as he spoke of the Waldenses. Lockhart had not noticed such a tone before and studied the severe, angled face.

"If I may ask," he ventured, "how is it that you came to be a quiet defender of the Church, Father?"

Victor revealed nothing—did not even reveal that he had heard the question. Then he released a deep breath, blinked tiredly. It was the first sign of weakness or fatigue Lockhart had observed.

"Does it matter?" He smiled wanly. "My story is no different from the blacksmith's, or even the Waldenses'. I was condemned to burn after refusing to testify against another priest. He burned, and I was only saved by my own village, which rioted, much like Waldenses, and drove the papal guards out before they cut my ropes. Cardinal Mazarin encountered me during the Fronde, and the rest..."

He shrugged, then actually laughed—a strangely comforting tone. Lockhart could, all of a sudden, imagine that Victor had once been a much beloved priest. He pondered how many hundreds—nay, thousands—of innocent people had been convicted of witchcraft or heresy and imprisoned or killed over the past century. And yet the power of the Inquisition was finally fading. Indeed, it was virtually eradicated in England, where Cromwell had imposed severe penalties for the condemnation of English citizens by any church or assembly. In Piedmont alone the Inquisitors ruled with an iron fist that broke all civil laws, even the laws of the Church.

He thought of the Duke of Savoy, who had been so remarkably reasonable and even calm during their unexpected visit. Without question Lockhart had expected a more dynamic response. But Savoy had retained admirable composure, considering guards were stationed just outside the door. A young man of lesser intellect might have easily panicked and chanced a quick cry, his fear overwhelming his judgment. But Emmanuel had handled himself in a manner worthy of respect.

Lockhart passionately hoped his drama had persuaded Savoy that they would indeed return to make good on their threat. But Lockhart had no spirit for killing the young prince. Even what little he had said and done had required his full cold measure of control. He did not know if Victor would carry through on the promise.

Somehow the priest seemed to read his face and spoke with a mild smile. "You think of Savoy?"

Raising his eyes, Lockhart did not deny it. "What will you do if he does not obey?"

Victor solemnly shook his head. "That is not my decision. My mission was to deliver the warning."

"But surely you have some idea," Lockhart said with more force. "You have done this before."

"I have killed, yes, but never in revenge. It is not my purpose to kill men, Sir Lockhart, but to save them. But in a land where murderers outnumber victims, a man must be as cunning and as deadly as a serpent."

Lockhart could not deny that much. "How many like you are sent on missions and never return?"

"Many," the priest said simply.

"I would imagine."

"It is an ancient Order," the priest continued. "It was forgotten for centuries, and even now would not exist but for the fact that the Church is being destroyed from within and without by rampant butchery and corruption. Rome had become a den of thieves and murderers, and until it is reclaimed by men of God, it must be restrained."

He took a deep breath. "Make no mistake, Sir Lockhart: I am a priest. What I do, I do for my Church. But my Church is not a church of butchers and thieves. It is my mission, if God allows, to return peace to Christendom."

"By any means necessary?"

Victor did not blink. "No…not by any means necessary. Nor do I operate without accountability. Cardinal Mazarin and others know all my actions and judge them." The dark eyes stared upon Lockhart with hypnotic effect. "And I know that I, too, will be judged by the Lord for my actions. It is only with reluctance that I use force. But sometimes force is necessary to remain among the living."

A knock at the door broke the trance, and Victor moved quickly to it, listening. There were two more knocks, then three. He opened the door, and a woman entered bearing a plate of cheese, meat, and bread. She carried two bottles of wine beneath her arm. With profound reverence she bowed to the priest before departing almost as quickly. Victor closed the lock behind her and returned.

Staring at the plate, Lockhart was surprised that he was famished. Like the fatigue, he had been unaware of it until he saw the food. Victor began to slice pieces from the roast. "Eat well," he said graciously. "You will need your strength tonight."

Lockhart raised his face.

"What's tonight?"

"We will visit a priest."

∞⊚∞

Alone upon the bluff before the cliff, Gianavel held the note from Pianessa. No one approached him, well aware of the almost palpable aura of sadness. He opened the letter—

Captain Gianavel,

I exhort you for the last time to renounce your heresy. This is the only hope you have of retaining the pardon of your prince and thereby saving the life of your wife and daughters who are now my prisoners, and who shall be burned alive. But if you come down from the mountain and renounce your faith, your family shall be freed and you will receive the land and gold and title of a marquis. Yet if you refuse, such a great reward shall be placed upon your head that even your closest friends and family will finally betray you. And when you are finally brought living into my presence, there is no torment that you will not suffer before you die.

—Pianessa

Utterly alone, Gianavel stood on the mountain.

He slowly crumbled the letter in his hand, stared below the summit over the valley now dark with evening and the dusky horizon where the sun had gone.

Wind, deep but close, gently lifted his cloak, and clouds moved serenely over the face of the cliff. He stood alone until the last light of the distant day was gone and forgotten. Until only stars blazed high in the dome of night like eyes from another universe peering through the night, watching to see what he would do.

And when the invisible cold rose, embracing him in a chill-like death, he stood. And when the rocks about him turned white and soft with frost, he stood. And when the sky grew wet and moist and the moon disappeared behind a deep night, he stood.

But when the night wind began to weep with snow and ice and a misty, mournful tone, Gianavel turned and walked to the summit to stand in the full measure of the cold that kills and the winter that forever binds bones in the grave.

※

Blake tossed a stick onto the fire and did not look as Bertino entered the cavern entrance, irritably shaking ice and sleet from his heavy sheepskin coat. The big man knelt beside the fire and warmed his hands, rubbing them fiercely.

Looking up from where he had been drawing a dagger across a whetstone, Blake asked, "Where is he?"

"He has gone up to the summit," Bertino rumbled, his eyes black pinpoints in his swollen face. "He will, perhaps, not return tonight. I don't know."

"Do you know what the letter contained?"

Bertino nodded. "If Gianavel does not renounce...Pianessa will burn Angela and the girls alive at the stake. Pianessa has given him one day to answer."

There was no means for Blake to truly measure what he experienced at the words. It was not shock or astonishment; he had expected such. Nor was it grief or even sympathy; it was beyond all familiar sensations.

Blake only understood it when he glanced down to study what wetness spread across his wrist. The dagger had run off the stone and sliced open his hand.

He was not curious that he felt no pain.

24

AFTER A QUICK TRIP through the catacombs, Lockhart found himself again inside the Duke of Savoy's palace following Victor, once more attired in complete black, through cobweb-curtained tunnels that faded to black as soon as their lantern passed. But it wasn't until they finally entered a hallway susceptible to random patrols that Lockhart felt vivid fear at possible discovery. He was grateful when Victor found a discreetly located doorway and led through it.

As Lockhart quietly shut and bolted the door, he saw the tall figure of a monk standing with his back to the entrance. Then, when the latch closed, the man turned without surprise and moved forward to embrace Victor. He stared at the spectral priest a moment, holding him firmly by the shoulders. "You are well, my friend?"

Victor nodded. "What have you learned?"

The monk, seemingly for the first time, saw Lockhart standing in shadow. His eyes opened slightly, and he smiled. His tone was pleasant. "And who is this bravado?"

Victor gestured for Lockhart to approach, and he did so with faint caution. The monk raised his empty hand in the air, folded it back within his sleeve. "I am Father Simon."

"I am Sir William Lockhart of England. I come on a mission from My Lord, Oliver Cromwell, to do what can be done to stop this persecution of the Waldenses."

The man named Simon did not express surprise. He sat at the table, as if he were dreadfully weary. His placed both hands flat against the roughhewn wood and spoke in a low tone, "This is the situation as I understand it, my friends. Rora has fallen. Many have been killed on both sides. Pianessa apparently lost as many as seven thousand of his men. Virtually all those holding the village were killed. The wife and children of Captain Gianavel were captured."

"And Gianavel?" asked Lockhart.

"He cut his way through Pianessa's troops and escaped into the mountains carrying his infant son. Pianessa has sent him a letter, indicating terms of surrender."

"What terms?" responded Lockhart.

"Gianavel has one day to come down from the mountain. If he refuses, then his wife and daughters will be burned alive at the stake. Also, if he comes down, he will receive the title and the land of a marquis."

Victor spun and glared. "They have not even been formally tried by the Inquisition!"

"These Inquisitors are not willing to wait for trials," the monk responded. "They want the head of Gianavel. They are willing to break any laws, civil or ecclesiastical, to gain it."

Victor took a single quick step across the room, moving like a phantom. His cloak opened like huge black wings. "Where are the woman and her children being held?"

"In the dungeon," was the reply, and then the old man shook his head. "There are no passages, Victor. You would have to attack a contingent of guards."

"You are certain?"

"Yes."

For the first time since Lockhart had known him, the priest seemed to shudder with anger. His teeth parted in a snarl. His black hair rose in hackles like a wolf. His voice was hoarse and cold. "Is Incomel responsible for this slaughter?"

"The same who condemned you at Languedoc."

Once again, Lockhart deemed Victor's silence, his stillness, far more terrifying than his actions. His piercing gaze beamed upon the old man. "Is Corbis with him?"

"Where the dead are found," Simon said bitterly, "there the vultures will gather. But be wise, Victor. It is not your place to exact revenge for what they did to you."

Victor's words were terse. "It is not revenge."

Simon looked without surprise upon Lockhart. "And so, Cromwell himself, intervenes. I did not think England's Lord Protector would be able to remain aloof. Not when the peace of all Christendom was threatened."

"He is not alone," said Lockhart.

"No, I did not believe that he was. But neither Cromwell nor Cardinal Mazarin can openly interfere in this war without also risking war with Spain."

"We're here to insure that does not happen." Lockhart looked again at Victor. "What else do you need to know?"

Victor seemed to return from where he had been. "What precautions does Incomel take?"

"Every precaution."

"Guards?"

"No less than six." Simon stared upon the Assassini without fear. "It is impossible for you to reach the Inquisitor General, my friend. Even together, the two of you would stand little chance. Once the alarm is raised, all of Pianessa's guards would respond."

Victor did not move. "What about Corbis?"

After pondering it, Simon answered, "Corbis is, perhaps, within your reach. He spends most of his time in the dungeon, torturing the Waldenses. But he is vulnerable when he returns to his room." He sighed deeply. "Even demons must rest."

"For the final time," Victor muttered and moved forward. "When do they burn this man's wife and children?"

"If Gianavel does not surrender? Tomorrow."

Victor swept past Lockhart and listened closely at the door. He gazed once more upon the old man. "Spend tonight in the company of your enemies."

Simon nodded. "Worry not. I will be engaged in a debate with Inquisitor General Thomas Incomel when Corbis is sent to defend himself before the Almighty."

Without another word or glance or gesture, Victor slipped through the door, and Lockhart pulled it shut quietly behind him. In another thirty seconds they were again hidden, and the Englishman felt the distinct thrill of fear as he followed the phantomlike specter of Victor quickly through the corridors.

Silent and black and spectral, the priest moved with a sense of doom and dark purpose—Death stalking the world of the Living, come to claim what was his.

"You're insane," said Emmanuel.

His words were equal parts fear and rage, but he knew the fear was hidden well enough. Nor would it do well for the Inquisitor General to know it existed at all.

Having taken to inhabiting the castle only in the presence of six or more Inquisitors and papal guards, Incomel no longer indulged surreptitious conversations. He did not allow anyone to approach him closely enough for a whispered threat, nor did he say anything that was not faithfully recorded by scribes in one of the large, leather-bound tomes that were to become the official record of this "pacification."

Emmanuel felt confident that he knew what was recorded within those pages, just as he was fairly certain that it had no more relation to the truth than fairy tales or the eyewitness accounts of the blind.

Incomel, chin on hand, stared placidly at the Duke of Savoy from his chair. He had remained still and silent since Emmanuel entered, berating him for his obviously illegal decision to burn the woman and her children alive at the stake. Not only was it impossible for Incomel to have organized a tribunal to hear any witness accusations of Angela Gianavel, there had, in fact, *been* no accusations and no witnesses. Further, to sentence someone to death for heresy or witchcraft was the right of a tribunal. But to actually execute the punishment of death was the solitary right and power of the governing civil authority.

Emmanuel had not approved such an action, yet four stakes in the courtyard were being heaped about with loosely tied armloads of dry brush and planks. A glance at the place of execution lent the impression that they were preparing to burn Satan himself.

"Well?" Emmanuel leaned forward. "What have you got to say for yourself?"

Incomel lifted his chin from his hand, then gestured at a scribe. "Please read for the Duke of Savoy the confession of Angela Gianavel, as well as the unanimous judgment of five Inquisitors that she is to be purified by flame."

Emmanuel did not have the heart to hear it. It was one thing to know that hundreds, even thousands, had been killed in this war. It was another to look one in the eyes before she was burned alive for what was not a crime.

"No," Emmanuel shook his head as the scribe began to read, yet the scribe did not cease bleating words. Shocked, Emmanuel turned upon him with. "Are you a fool? I said *No!*"

Incomel was vividly alert to anything that might condemn Emmanuel— words that would remove him from his throne as surely as a sword cut. Frowning, the Duke of Savoy stared into the Inquisitor's eyes.

"This war nears an end."

Incomel smiled. "Yes, Savoy, it does. Because now Gianavel will come down from the mountain. He will come for love, for mercy, and for the lives of his wife and children. But he will come. And when he does, this great prince of the Waldenses will be defeated."

Without another word Emmanuel spun and snatched a water bowl and slammed it upon the Inquisitor's desk. The violent movement actually startled Incomel, though he recovered quickly enough. Slowly, the Duke of Savoy pushed up his sleeves. He dipped his hands once into the water and then cast it intentionally across the pages of confessions and witness statements, running the ink like blood. Staring Incomel in the eyes, he said, "This blood is on your head."

The Inquisitor would not condescend to rage in the presence of others. But his breath was strained, and his eyes glowered as Emmanuel spun and departed the chamber, his own guards falling in closely behind him.

Just as Incomel had taken to prowling the castle only with armed protection, Emmanuel had done the same. He had even considered placing them within his chamber to prevent another visit from the priest. But he had a premonition that guards could not ultimately protect him from the man who knew more about this palace than Emmanuel himself.

Emmanuel's face opened in surprise as he encountered Simon in the doorway. The old priest had an armload of books and documents and appeared ready to stay awhile. It was not simply unusual. It was shocking, and Emmanuel had suffered enough shocks.

"What are you doing here?" he asked sternly.

Simon did not forget their customary demonstration of courtesy and respect. "I have scheduled an inquiry with the Inquisitors," he replied humbly and bowed. "I am certain that I will occupy them long into the night, as is my right."

Emmanuel did not understand, but he sensed rather than saw something concealed within the priest's intention. Simon did not look him directly in the eyes—unusual—nor did he seem angered to be in the presence of the Inquisitors, also unusual. Whatever his true cause, Emmanuel knew it was not to debate make-believe testimony cast at make-believe trials.

It was none of his concern.

Emmanuel moved past the old priest toward where Pianessa was stabled, enjoying the bacchanal delights of victory.

If only to understand the true depth of his dilemma, Emmanuel would know his mind.

)oo(⬦)oo(

Corbis, his utterly bald head and hairless face greased with sweat, lovingly shoved the heated iron into the brazier. His eyes were alight, as if he received vivid pleasure from being so close to the white-hot steel. His voice as a whisper as if he spoke only to himself.

"Is that all of them, Sergeant?"

Corbis received no answer and turned his cannonball head toward the ashen guard. "Sergeant? Is that all of them?"

The sergeant's mouth opened in an effort to reply. His eyes did not move from the ghastly carnage before him—carnage that glowed incredibly red and white beneath the torches.

Once it had been a man, yes. What it was now, after attempting to escape the patient, thorough interrogation of Corbis through the entire day and night, could not be easily determined.

The guard managed, "Yes, Inquisitor."

Corbis calmly cast his blood-soaked harness aside and washed his arms, face, neck, and chest with a bucket of steaming water. Then he moved carefully, almost daintily, through the grisly aftermath of the long afternoon.

"Have your men clean this up," he murmured, lifting his skirt to pass over the blood. "I cannot fancy such filth."

"Of course, Inquisitor."

The Inquisitor tenderly treaded a high path over the remains of what had been human beings and ascended the wall-anchored stone stairway. At the portal, two guards fell in behind him, and the door was quietly, almost solemnly, shut.

)oo(⬦)oo(

Pianessa was not nearly so drunk as Emmanuel expected when he finally gained entrance to his chambers. But the marquis was enlivened enough to respond inappropriately to the Duke of Savoy's unexpected intrusion. Reclining upon a chair amid a roomful of harlots and drunken military commanders and badly trained musicians, Pianessa focused on Emmanuel with distinct contempt.

"So…the boy-king would confront me on the eve of my victory celebration." Pianessa gave no indication that he noticed Emmanuel's equal contempt. He bowed without rising, arms outstretched. "Enter, My Prince, and join the festivities."

Emmanuel looked across the assortment. "No, thank you, Monsieur de la Marquis. I have already visited the stables."

Pianessa's laugh was an eruption of madness and some kind of unquenchable wrath that fueled his aimless, endless hate. He recovered quickly enough, leaned back. "And what is the purpose of this honor by the Duke of Savoy?"

Although Emmanuel was no monk, he did not descend to Pianessa's level of debauchery. "I do not wish to linger in your presence any longer than necessary, Pianessa. I came only to ask this: Do you know what Incomel intends to do to Gianavel's family if he does not come down from his mountain?"

The question did gain Pianessa's attention. He nodded, "Yes, Savoy, I know the Inquisitor's plan. Just as I know that there is nothing you or I can do about it." Strangely, his tone seemed almost wise. "It is not our war, Savoy."

Emmanuel stood an alarmingly close step to the monstrous form of the marquis. "You are a man of war, Pianessa. But even you have a sense of honor in combat."

If Pianessa wished, he could have snapped Emmanuel's neck before one of Savoy's bodyguards could lift a finger—his cautious stance revealed that the prince knew the danger. Emmanuel added, "By the rules of war, Pianessa, those of noble heritage should be given the opportunity to ransom themselves! It is not only traditional; it is practical! My treasury has been reduced and my lands depopulated without so much as a by-your-leave from the Inquisitors! It is your duty to help me recover what this war has cost!"

Emmanuel expected Pianessa to erupt from his throne at the affront. But Pianessa only opened his eyes wider and listened patiently until the Duke of Savoy finished. He stared upon Emmanuel a long moment, shook his head.

"Savoy," he said pathetically, "how tragic it must be, for you have a conscience in this. You are not a practical man." As Emmanuel stared sullenly, Pianessa added, "The Inquisitors will burn this woman and her children at the stake, Savoy. They will burn them even if Gianavel comes down from his mountain."

Emmanuel's frown was bitter.

Sadly, Pianessa shook his head. "You are a monarch, Emmanuel, and still you do not understand these matters."

"Understand what?"

"That you are the tool of fearful men, Emmanuel. You think the Inquisitors are certain in their knowledge. You think that they know each other's mind, and that they stand together from strength." He laughed. "They stand together from fear, Savoy, and they have no power but what you give them. The only person who can truly end this war is you. All you have to do is defy the Inquisitors."

No one moved, and Emmanuel asked, "And what does that say of you, Pianessa?"

Pianessa smiled, refilled his chalice.

"I am a practical man, Savoy. I war with Gianavel, quite simply, because I am not the Supreme Lord of Piedmont. Because I do not have the power to defy the Inquisitors. And when the time comes that I do not have to obey them..." Pianessa shrugged. "I would just as soon fight beside the Vaudois."

Emmanuel's gaze projected contempt and reluctant respect. "An ultimately practical man."

"Yes," Pianessa replied, and his eyes gleamed like polished obsidian orbs. "Ultimately."

∞∞◆∞∞

Corbis's attendants made no display that they were quick to depart his presence as he dismissed them from his room. In fact, they moved with solemnity and patience as they assisted the porpoiselike Inquisitor with his nightgown, then backed slowly out the door, bowing deeply and reverently before disappearing. He did not see after they turned away, blessing themselves with trembling hands.

The priest hummed tonelessly as he paraded about the small cubical warmed by the small hearth fed with coals. And already the room was almost too warm for clothing. His white face glistened like dew upon polished ivory. He nudged the hearth with an iron and settled back upon his bed, staring into the flames.

He did not see the shadow that moved silently through the window located two hundred feet above the courtyard. He did not hear the shadow as a boot settled upon the floor. He did not sense the shadow as it walked up behind him and stood. But the sudden presence of an unexplainable cold provoked a curious scowl.

Corbis turned.

A strong hand clamped upon the Inquisitor's neck, shutting off his scream. The phantom stared upon the Inquisitor's trembling lips, the flaring white eyes. The phantom shook his head sadly.

"You will terrify no more," he whispered. "I give you a moment...to seek forgiveness for your cruelties."

Corbis's mouth twisted in terror.

With a flash of a black robe, a long silver dagger appeared in the phantom's other hand, the blade poised at the Inquisitor's fat neck.

"I would be quick," he whispered.

✕∞∞✕∞∞✕

Gianavel reentered the cavern shortly before dawn. He was soaking with cold and sheathed in broken garments of ice. His hair was drenched and frosted with sleet and snow, and ice cracked as he laid his cloak beside a fire.

Without expression he came near to Blake and knelt beside the fire, holding his hands to the flames. He blew upon them, rubbed them, and his face was perilously pale. Blake said nothing, intended to say nothing. And Bertino was much the same, leaning against the wall, staring dully into the flames.

It was Gianavel who broke the silence.

"I have sent my reply to Pianessa," he said, intoning nothing more than that. "Now we will pray."

Bertino's eyes shifted as they shifted when he spied enemies moving stealthily along a wood line. He did not blink as he studied the captain. Blake watched and then looked away. It was not his right to even speak in this uncanny hour.

"If Pianessa intends to make good on his threat?" Bertino asked, reflecting Blake's own thoughts. "What will we do then?"

"What chains can hold belong to man," Gianavel said and bowed his head. "The rest is God's."

Blake knew that to attack Turin with less than fifty men would be suicide. To attempt to sneak through the lines was no better. To capture another monarch or noble person and use them as ransom was beyond what Gianavel knew as righteous defense—beyond what he believed God allowed him to do in war.

So they would pass the night and then the morning, and then the afternoon until the evening. And when they heard word from Turin again, they would hear that Gianavel's wife and children had been burned alive and were now dead.

Strange, Blake thought all of a sudden, that it had never occurred to him that Gianavel might surrender.

✕◦◦◈◦◦✕

It was still early morning when Emmanuel arose, not surprised that he had slept little and fitfully. He had been expecting another visit, but none had come, though he felt certain his palace had been disturbed. For a moment he wondered who was ushered to judgment last night by the grim, silent man, then cast the thought aside. It had not been him, and that was all that was important.

The sun had barely edged the palace walls, angling orange and glowing through the crystal windows of the hall, when Emmanuel entered to see Incomel hedged by bodyguards. The priest was reading a letter, and Emmanuel did not have to ask whom it was from.

Incomel's face was anything but pleased with Gianavel's response. He barely noticed Emmanuel's presence, then spoke, "It seems Gianavel has relieved us of further inquiries into this matter." He presented the letter to the Duke of Savoy, who studied the words written boldly and without hesitation.

My Lord Marquis,

There is no torment so great or death so cruel, but what I would prefer to the abjuration of my religion; so that promises lose their effect, and menaces only strengthen me in my faith.

With respect to my wife and children, My Lord, nothing can be more afflicting to me than the thought of their confinement, or more dreadful to my imagination than their suffering a violent and cruel death. I keenly feel all the tender sensations of husband and parent; my heart is replete with every sentiment of humanity; I would suffer any torment to rescue them from danger; I would die to preserve them.

But having said thus much, My Lord, I assure you that the purchase of their lives must not be the price of my salvation. You have them in your power, it is true; but my consolation is that your power is only a temporary authority over their bodies; you may destroy the mortal part, but their immortal souls are out of your reach; and will live hereafter to bear testimony against you for your cruelties. I therefore recommend them and myself to God, and pray for a reformation of your heart.

—Joshua Gianavel

With a deep sigh, Emmanuel lowered the letter, not looking again at the Inquisitor as Incomel spoke. "They will burn at midmorning. And by evening, our victory will be complete."

In a triumphant march, Inquisitors and priests and papal guards exited the long hall. Not a word was spoken, and when they were gone, Emmanuel looked upon Pianessa.

The marquis was leaning against the hearth, head bowed. He may have been staring into the flames, or his eyes may have been closed. Emmanuel could not determine, but he could read the defeat etched in every line of the marquis' body. He asked, "Why so depressed, Pianessa? Is this not the victory you sought?"

Pianessa's slow reply was bitter. "Savoy...you are such a fool." He released a heavy breath. "By refusing to come down from his mountain, even to save the lives of his wife and children, Gianavel has won his victory.

"And today, when his wife and children are burned, thousands more will join him. They will come from England, from France, from Geneva, and they will never stop coming. They will never stop fighting." He straightened. "You have never seen war like you're about to see war, Savoy. And we will not be hunting Gianavel this time."

The Marquis de Pianessa turned and stared. "This time, Gianavel will be hunting us."

Seeing Emmanuel's reaction, Pianessa laughed.

"Why the pallor, Savoy? Did you expect to live forever?"

✕✕✕✦✕✕✕

In the depths of a dark, soundless, subdued day in May 1655, as thunderclouds hung oppressively in a dead sky that seemed to cast a curse across the land, Angela Gianavel and her three young daughters were led through a strangely silent crowd at Turin and burned alive at the stake.

25

GIANAVEL, SURROUNDED BY WHITE STRANDS of snow and ice that lay across the Alps even in the warmest months, but even more so now, stood upon the pass that led downward to the city of Geneva sprawled across the fields below. Here his son would be safe with friends and family, protected by the army of the Swiss.

He had traveled across the Alps alone after the death of his family, bearing Jacob, wrapped warmly in sheepskins, upon his back. He had evaded Pianessa's patrols by traveling at night and hazarding only the most treacherous trails, and now his journey was at an end.

Gianavel stared over the city, listening to Jacob's soft breaths while he slept. Here, if Gianavel wished, they would be safe—they could begin again. Never again would he have to fight for freedom of conscience—such a grim fight that had already cost him so much that he loved.

Slowly, he began to make his way down the pass.

✕✕✕❖✕✕✕

Deep in bitter defeat and untold personal grief, Jahier tossed wood upon the fire as if it hardly mattered now. Surrounding him, Bertino, Blake, and Laurentio gazed dully into the flames.

No one spoke prophetic words. No one recited the Psalms—most often the fifteenth Psalm—as Gianavel had done in both victory and defeat—in hours of joy and in hours of sorrow.

No one commanded them to continuously prepare for battle, to sharpen dagger and sword, or eat so they might have strength to resist the dragon. No one cautioned them to pray and be vigilant and to guard their hearts, for no one spoke of victory.

✕✕✕◈✕✕✕

Lockhart watched the heavy, continuous rain descend outside the palace of Cardinal Guilio Raimondo Mazarin and felt a disturbing sensation of standing upon a small piece of heaven drenched in blood, floating upon the sea.

Frowning, he bent his head to watch Mazarin as he had watched him for hours, sitting and staring morosely into the flames, his rosary moving lightly through his fingers.

When Lockhart himself had delivered word of the death of Gianavel's family and the apparent escape of the prince of the Waldenses to Geneva, the cardinal had not expressed either grief or relief. Instead, he had fallen into a close silence that excluded all from his mind, though Lockhart knew that whatever was within that great mind might well be beyond the rest of them anyway.

✕✕✕◈✕✕✕

Sir Samuel Morland stretched out his hand to Lord Oliver Cromwell, who stared out the window of Whitehall, despondent and churlish at this strange, endless summer rain.

When word arrived that Rora had fallen, and word that Angela Gianavel and her children had been executed, the Lord Protector of England had almost mobilized the entire English army for a full-scale invasion of Piedmont for a "truly righteous war to defend Christendom." Only a letter from Cardinal Mazarin, who begged him to wait only a little longer, had dissuaded his lionish wrath.

The cardinal, as was his custom, revealed nothing of the covert actions underway, but he did imply that forces were secretly at work in Piedmont, and that the final moves were yet to be made in this very deadly game. But he had passionately pleaded with Cromwell to not provoke a continental war. And so England's Lord Protector had temporarily relented, though for how long was uncertain.

Standing somberly to the side of England's uncrowned king, Sir Samuel Morland pondered what colossal forces were even now colliding in that tiny region in what might be the greatest battle ever fought for religious freedom in the history of the world. He also knew that if England, France, Geneva, and Austria joined the fight, the battle would become so terrible that no nation would escape without profound injury. The principle—that every man, and woman, and child has the right to worship God according to their freedom of conscious—left little room for compromise.

To the steady drone of moaning water and the fevered trembling of Lord Cromwell, Sir Samuel Morland remembered the words of the horribly wounded peasant he had found in the forest. He remembered the hope that he beheld in the man's bloodied face—a hope somehow above physical suffering. He remembered the expression of peace that found full freedom even in the face so ravaged by torture—a peace that even death could not overcome.

And he wondered why such peace forever escaped the living.

Standing outside, watching snow falling in long waving clouds that blanketed every rock and patch of frozen ground in frosty silence, Blake wondered how he came to be here. He had once been a thief, a man who lived by his wits, by lies, and gifts. He had never felt compelled to make a stand for what he believed. Indeed, he had never believed in much of anything at all and wondered if this—this fear, this sense of grief and pain, this hope—meant that he believed.

He knew only that he was standing on a mountaintop, heedless of the snow the heavy, cold wind that smothered everything about him, knowing that it was warm in the valley below, and that he no longer cared for that warmth.

What was next?

It was only a vague thought, and he knew the answer enough because it did not matter…as long as he remained here.

※

Strolling along the battlement of his palace, Emmanuel pondered that the land had been strangely silent since the execution of Gianavel's family two weeks past.

Initially alarmed by Pianessa's evil foreboding, he had fully expected a full-scale invasion by England or France within days, but no word moved from the west, and envoys continued to be sent by Cardinal Mazarin, openly petitioning the Inquisitors to cease their persecution of the Waldenses. It was, on the whole, completely without effect. The Inquisitors had no intention of answering to the cardinal and prime minister of France. They were not subject to his authority, nor did they care to mend torn ecclesiastical ties. After all, Mazarin was despised and hated by the Italian cardinals, who fully supported the war.

After Corbis had been discovered, his throat cut as cleanly as a sheep's, there had been an escalation of security around the Inquisitors, particularly Incomel, who rarely ventured outside his chambers now. But after the initial shock faded, the tension lessened to something tolerable, and the dead Inquisitor was not mourned. Only Pianessa, with a black aspect that seemed to laugh at all of them together, persisted to utter vague and incomprehensible comments of foreboding doom. He had ordered the entire Militia of Piedmont to the field and had not recalled them. And when Emmanuel cautiously questioned the marquis about what might be an overly pessimistic dispensation of the future, Pianessa only laughed, swallowed more wine, and "begged" the Duke of Savoy to have patience.

"I am evil, Savoy; I am not a fool," he rumbled. "All good things come to those who wait."

Incomel dismissed the cryptic words as the overt symptom of irreversible mental disease brought about by excessive wine and wanton debauchery. His kindly offer to hear Pianessa's confession was laughed to scorn, and Pianessa had informed the Inquisitor that God would hear all their confessions soon enough.

Glancing across the land, Emmanuel saw only peaceful merchants entering Turin as they had done for two weeks. He witnessed no foreboding army amassing on the plain, beheld no alien banners pronouncing a siege. There were not even rogue bands of Waldensian peasants resisting in the mountains. Nor had there been another terrifying visit by the Englishman and the dark man. In fact, it was if they had never visited Emmanuel during that night which now seemed so distant—a nightmare from another life.

No other Inquisitor had been found with his throat cut. And Emmanuel did not think that the sickness that plagued them—the strange malady that had taken the lives of so many of Pianessa's military commanders and Inquisitors in the last two weeks—could be linked to violence. It was totally natural that, in a land ravaged by war, men inevitably became sick and died from all manner of scourge, even if it was an inexplicably high number of priests.

He was so deeply involved in his reasonable dismissal of events that he did not see the lone rider approaching fast from the east. A commander of Pianessa's militia, bloodied and weaponless and riding a pale horse dying with exhaustion, pressed to the portico. But he heard the cry at the gate and found himself leaning tensely over the wall to see the commander fall into the arms of guards. He did not hear what the man must have gasped before his death that came almost immediately, but he did, indeed, see the guard as he staggered back in horror, turned, searched, and saw the Duke of Savoy clutching the wall.

The guard's face was more ghastly than his scream.

"He's coming!"

26

WAR, ENDLESS AND MERCILESS, raged over the bloody plains of Piedmont, and thousands were crushed by the army of Gianavel that rose from the borders, the mountains, and the ground itself that seemed to release hordes of rebels who fought each battle as their last and to the last, refusing surrender.

At the Battle of Crusol, Gianavel and three hundred men who returned with him from Geneva, where the story of Angela had been told, only to arouse the wrath of a sleeping lion, utterly destroyed the Royal Regiment of the Marquis de Pianessa, ten thousand strong, and delivered the store-houses of food and munitions to dwelling houses and prisons of Piedmont.

Then, after taking the mountains pass by pass, Gianavel began reclaiming Piedmont village by village and town by town, sparing those who vowed to throw down arms forever and live in peace with the Waldenses, and killing those who continued to fight. Entire battalions were destroyed and fortified cities and prisons reduced so that stone did not stand upon stone—Lucerna, St. Secondo, Cavors—all fell as Gianavel's army advanced and then camped openly in the field of St. Giovanni, sending a messenger to the Duke of Savoy.

Accepting the challenge, the Marquis de Pianessa engaged the outnumbered Waldenses in a stunning, whirling battle that raged over the plains of Giovanni, where tactics and troops changed minute by minute as Pianessa and Gianavel battled each another on a titanic scale of hundreds and thousands.

Pianessa's regiments took hill upon hill, only to behold another fortified retreat of the Waldenses from which the cannons of Gianavel reduced the place where he stood, rock and flesh, to fragments. And on and on the battle spun in a maelstrom of constantly changing strategies and attacks of men and rifle and swords that beat down flesh and blood, only to attack again until the sprawling, burning fields were littered with ten thousand of Pianessa's dead, conquered by Gianavel.

Then Captain Jahier, surprised and caught in the open field with only forty-four men, was attacked upon the plain at Ossac. Unable to retreat and unable to improvise a defense, it was full combat without quarter, and Jahier's platoon killed the attacking commander in chief, three captains, and fifty-seven infantry before they fell.

After the battle, Jahier's severed head was sent to the Duke of Savoy at Turin, who said nothing at the grisly prize before he rewarded Captain Rodriguez with one hundred pieces of gold.

Upon hearing of it, Gianavel took four hundred men and attacked the same battalion in the open field—no defense, no cover, no artillery or cannon fire, or passages for retreat, but no retreat was needed. Before the day was done, six thousand of Pianessa's soldiers were strewn across the field like butchered sheep, and Gianavel took the head of the great Captain Rodriguez and returned it, along with the one hundred pieces of gold, to the Duke of Savoy.

And then, the Battle of Angrogna...

Incomel raised his face as the Duke of Savoy halted in his doorway. It was not surprising that the young prince was visiting him so early in the day. Indeed, Incomel had come to expect such visits. He straightened from his battle maps and smiled pleasantly.

Without returning the expression, the Duke of Savoy approached. He glanced at the maps, detailed with the scribblings of prelates and scribes and priests who truly commanded his army.

"I understand that Gianavel is encamped at Angrogna," he said without inflection. "What are your plans?"

Incomel's smile turned down as though he were weary of Emmanuel, and he reclined into his throne.

Across the table was another priest—an emissary from Emmanuel's old friend, Cardinal Fabio Chigi, now destined for the Throne of Rome. Though Emmanuel could have never met the emissary before, the dark-haired priest looked strangely familiar.

"Gianavel is at Angrogna," said Incomel, "and commands less than three hundred men. Pianessa departs this afternoon with three thousand of his strongest troops. He intends to finish this war, at last." He sighed, smiled. "I foresee no difficulties."

Emmanuel took a few slow steps forward and gazed down at the map. Angrogna was a lonely place, well isolated and suitable for a final battle to end this war that had already gone too long. If Pianessa descended on it without warning, he would easily be able to take Gianavel's small detachment. There was no path for a retreat and no battlement fit to resist a siege. He looked again at the Inquisitor, silent and defeated.

"Why so depressed, Savoy?" Incomel laughed and gestured as if these were the inconsequential matters of life. "Tomorrow we should be troubled no more by Gianavel and his rebels, and you may resume the life of a prince."

"I will never be prince of this land, Inquisitor." Emmanuel's words held an accusation, a condemnation, a sneer. "You slaughtered the Waldenses, it's true. But they'll return, Inquisitor—they always return. And they'll endure— they'll endure like the mountains that are their home. And you and I will be forgotten, and Gianavel will be remembered."

Emmanuel stepped back, laughed tragically. "We were doomed from the very first, Inquisitor. You fought for money. I fought for fear. Pianessa fought for himself. Only Gianavel fought for God."

Incomel's face tightened in hate.

Emmanuel shook his head, "Whether Gianavel wins or lives or dies tomorrow doesn't matter. He will die victoriously, Priest. Because Gianavel never...he *never* dishonored his God. He never surrendered his faith, his freedom—not even his words."

Emmanuel waited for the Inquisitor to reply, but Incomel didn't and wouldn't.

With a slight bow to the dark priest, Emmanuel felt a distinct memory as if he had seen him, perhaps, in a dream. He walked toward the doorway when he remembered the face—a glimpse caught in darkness—*the face of a phantom*. Slowly he turned, staring at the dark priest—yes, the phantom— who did not look at him.

An open bottle of wine stood upon the table.

Emmanuel knew, nodded. "Aren't you afraid of being poisoned, Inquisitor?"

Incomel released a merry laugh and gestured to the mysterious priest whom Emmanuel remembered now. "But then the noble ambassador from

Rome would die as well, Savoy! We have both shared the bottle that he brought from the archbishop!"

The nameless priest did not blink, and Emmanuel nodded faintly. He did not look back as Incomel made an indistinct comment to the priest, and they began to speak of loftier things than war.

Yes, loftier things…

Such as judgment…

✕∞✕✦✕∞✕

Blake lifted his sword after teaching the newest, youngest recruits to parry and thrust, checked it for notches, resheathed it. He had discovered, quite to his surprise, that he was an able teacher of both fencing and marksmanship, a quality that inspired Gianavel to muse that he might have found his true calling.

During the past months, Blake made good use of his extensive nonpartisan experience in battle to become one of Gianavel's most trusted advisors. And he would be certain to put these boys far to the rear, so as not to shed innocent blood.

As he turned, Blake saw the silhouette of Gianavel standing upon the broken wall of the gate of St. Bartholomew. Gianavel stood with his back to the sunset—a classic profile of the man, rifle in his hand, sword at his waist, watching, always watching.

Blake lifted two mugs of steaming broth from the fire where Bertino had filled them and walked slowly to the wall, lifting them with a smile. Seeing the approach, Gianavel had dropped to the ground, and together they rested side by side upon the wall, enjoying the heftiest meal they'd had in several days.

Their supplies were exhausted, but for a few bushels of wheat. Their ammunition was almost depleted, save for a few hundred cannonballs and grapeshot. And, after taking so many villages in so short a time, even their musket balls and powder were running low.

In a last-ditch effort to slow their advance, the marquis was wisely leaving nothing for them to salvage. Even unused food and blankets had been put to the torch in what seemed a spiteful denial of the inevitable. For despite the fact that Pianessa's men still retained the ability to retreat, they no longer had the strength to advance.

In battle after battle Gianavel had outplanned and outfought the main Militia of Piedmont, and now they were defeating isolated battalions, steadily closing upon Turin. Although they were less than three hundred, Gianavel's hit-and-run tactics combined with his stalwart courage and tactical genius had enabled them to leave field after field heaped with the dead from battles that had already become legend. Stories abounded of Rocappiatta, Lucern, El Torre, and though Blake knew that some exaggerated the exploits of Gianavel, they were true in essence.

Time after time the Waldenses had been outnumbered and outflanked, only to turn the tide of battle by an unexpected tactical maneuver, a well-fought retreat, or an ambush that caught Pianessa unaware. In more than one battle, Blake had deemed victory all but impossible, and yet Gianavel had found a way, sometimes by something so simple as building a bullet-stop for his men to advance beneath and take a town room by room until the day was won.

Most military leaders, Blake knew from experience, did not possess the ultimately practical and even brilliant understanding of tactics that Gianavel brought to battle. Most military commanders saw a large battle in a large sense—entire hectares defended or lost, an entire border possessed or surrendered. Yet Gianavel saw battles in both the large and the small scale. He did not think of a village as won or lost. He thought of a single room in a house, or a single house in a village. And he would fight inexorably to take that room and then the house, then the next house and the next until the village was won, careful to secure one village at a time while not forgetting the larger perspective.

It was the day of small victories—room upon room, house by house, village upon village—that comprised the molten core of Gianavel's philosophy and tactics. And that was a way of thought that Pianessa could not understand. He saw no defeat in losing a single field or house or village. But these small, inconsequential victories, which had no value alone, had great value when combined.

"Do not despise the day of small things," Gianavel told Blake once. "Great things are made with them."

"Which means?" Blake asked.

"Which means that any fortress can be taken if you take it one piece at a time. Go slow and steady and secure what you gain. Then move to another street, another room, another building. In time, you will take the city."

Blake studied the field before them now and said, "Well, can't say I'm thrilled about your choice of campsites. It's comfortable enough, but retreating will be difficult."

"Yes," Gianavel agreed. "The problem now is that there will be few retreats. We can't hold the ground we've already taken unless we keep advancing."

"Why's that?"

"Because time is not on our side," the captain said. "If we give Pianessa time to fall back and regroup, he'll eventually gather as many men as he had at the beginning of this, or more." He gazed in the direction of Turin.

"We've got one chance to take Turin and end this war. Then we will give Savoy a final choice."

"What choice?"

"To make peace with us," Gianavel answered without emotion, "or die."

Blake didn't care to ponder the political consequences of destroying Pianessa and then the Duke of Savoy. It was clear enough what would be the fate of the Inquisitors. Those that lacked the good, God-given common sense to run when they saw Gianavel approaching were too stupid to live, anyway.

Still, Blake felt that this war would be over soon. It was simply not possible that the Duke of Savoy and his forces could fight with the tenacity and passion that motivated these people. Savoy's soldiers fought in the day and complained at a lack of food. Gianavel's men fought day and night and subsisted on dirt.

What Gianavel had said at the beginning had proven true; wars are won in the spirit. True, superior numbers and armaments were an advantage, but only for a while. Artillery could not hit what it could not find. And continuous, nagging attacks that sometimes did no more that create inconveniences eventually destroyed the moral of those who fought for money and not principle.

The mistake of everyone from Pope Innocent to the Inquisitors to Pianessa was that they thought overwhelming numbers would win their war. They had placed their hope in guns, and not men, and they were wrong.

From the very first, in every word, in every battle, in everything he had done, Gianavel had remembered the value of small things. How does one man defeat a hundred?

One at a time.

Emmanuel sensed that it might be the last time he would see Pianessa, but as he sauntered into the command area beside the palace, the marquis barely acknowledged his presence.

Fitted with a brand-new set of chain mail and leather armor, the Marquis de Pianessa looked every inch the warrior. His black and gray Goliath-form was imposing enough to win a battle by appearance alone. His sword, which had slaked itself on enough Waldensian blood in the past two months to float a ship, was strapped across his back.

His horse was heavily armored against musket balls and even sword attacks. It was also equipped with two rifles and a bandoleer of flintlock pistols that Pianessa would use one after the other in the heat of close conflict, not troubling himself with recharging. Despite the fact that the great army of the marquis had been reduced one platoon at a time, Pianessa had accounted well of himself in combat. He'd killed every man he had encountered with the wrath of an angry god.

But hate does not endure like love; it is the awareness of pain that destroys, not pain itself.

Emmanuel commented mildly, "So you meet Gianavel in the morning?"

"I meet him if he is not warned that I am coming," Pianessa commented as he cinched his sword belt. "I do not fancy chasing the Waldensian across the countryside. He retreats far too brilliantly."

The Duke of Savoy had noticed that Pianessa's thirst for battle had lessened somewhat in recent months. As the tide of the war inevitably began to change, so had Pianessa's love for it. And as he saw Gianavel increasing and himself decreasing, he had become almost contemptuous of more battle. Not that Pianessa openly admitted any inevitability at all. He did not comment on his defeats, but neither did he comment on Gianavel's victories.

"I understand you'll have the captain outnumbered by at least ten to one," Emmanuel said.

Pianessa waved off the comment as though it was an irritation and not encouragement. "Gianavel has an uncanny way of neutralizing superiority of numbers."

Sensing the marquis' severe mood, Emmanuel mused it was not a good moment to comment. So he watched as the marquis finished preparations and stood in silence a moment, head bowed as if studying the exacting map of Angrogna. It seemed that Pianessa would say something more, then the marquis turned and simply walked out of the tent. Emmanuel heard him calling orders to commanders, mounting his horse.

There was nothing more for Emmanuel to do. The war was playing out before his eyes, even if no one else could see.

He meandered slowly through the now quiet castle and indifferently watched a group of Inquisitors rushing in something like panic to where Inquisitor General Thomas Incomel and the dark priest had been enjoying that last bottle of wine.

Emmanuel didn't have to ask the reason.

27

THE SKY WAS A FLAT, GRAY BLADE as far as the eye could scan. A sunrise the color of blood made the morning right for battle and for killing. The entire world was violent and dismissive—a good day to die without regret of anything lost.

Peering narrowly over a chunk of ground, Pianessa studied the ground, noting that last night's rain would muffle footfalls for a hundred paces. With this water-soaked sod, they could march into Angrogna without a hint of their approach. It would be an advantage—the last advantage he needed to defeat Gianavel's meager force.

Inside the walls of St. Bartholomew's, Gianavel's men could be seen moving in the early morning haze. The captain himself was not visible, but the sentry appeared bored and frustrated. It was the break Pianessa had been awaiting; he would not neglect it.

Slowly, quietly, Pianessa slid down the mound until he was solidly shielded from view. Beside him rested two commanders and three captains. He whispered, "Attack fast through the gate. Once we are inside, we should finish them within a few hours."

They nodded tensely, and Pianessa added, "No matter what, give no warning. Charge only when you hear the trumpet sound from my area. Understand?"

Again they nodded and then slid off into separate directions. Pianessa removed a canteen and drank heavily. It might be the last chance before the end of the fight.

He searched narrowly over the rise once more; yes, they were unaware— completely unaware.

It was all he needed.

Setting a freshly prepared pistol on a wooden case that doubled as break- fast table and gun rack, Blake noticed Bertino. The big man was noticeably slimmer than when they began three months ago, but he retained his implacable aura of strength.

At the moment he was boiling acorns to remove the bitterness. Blake knew that, for some reason, a man who ate the unboiled nuts starved to death no matter how much he ate. Blake didn't try to understand why; one lesson he had learned from Gianavel was to always "grab things by the smooth handle," meaning men usually had a good reason for doing things the way they did.

"Where's Gianavel?" Blake asked absently.

Bertino raised the wooden spoon he was using to stir the pot, and Blake turned toward Gianavel, who was only a few steps away. He laid two legs of a sheep on the table.

"That's the last of it," the Captain of Rora commented. "We'll send out scouts in a little while and march on Turin."

Bertino, wordless, removed his dagger and began filleting the leg for soup that would be mixed with fruit berries and vegetables to be shared equally by all. Gianavel sat upon a bench and removed a tight coil of leather line that he used to make everything from bivouacs to wooden racks for air-drying beef jerky, which, Blake had also learned, was far more effective than smoking it.

"We'll herd whatever sheep or cattle we find on the way," Gianavel continued as if to himself. "The more we— "

All of them spun at the signal of war.

✕∞◈∞✕

Staring at the location where the trumpet sounded, Pianessa cursed and instantly ripped his sword free. Whatever fool inadvertently sounded that alarm would die. He pointed in the direction of St. Bartholomew and bellowed to those around him.

"Fire!"

Cannons opened up almost at once, blasting sections from the walls of the tiny village. Then musket smoke erupted from along a section of wood line, and battle was the day.

"Who blew that trumpet?" Pianessa strode fiercely to where he'd heard the warning. He saw the sergeant majors standing over a dead soldier. The sergeant grimaced with fear.

"I told him to wait for your command, My Lord!"

"The fool!" Pianessa spat before striding back to where three thousand men were plummeting the walls of the village with tens of thousands of shots, knowing they could do no damage at this distance. He mounted his horse, grabbing his rifle.

"Take the gate!"

As if erupting from the ground itself, three thousand men rose and charged, rifles and pikes lowered. Half were musketeers and half were spearmen, and it was more than enough to force the small gate.

Pianessa led them across the field down the throat of returning rifle fire and sensed rather than saw the black blunderbuss that appeared in the entrance of the village.

He reined his mount hard as it erupted.

Bertino hit the wick of the four-pounder almost before they leveled the barrel, and hundreds of musket balls sailed across the field, raining flesh in a long continuous storm back over muddy footsteps. Mists and geysers of crimson erupted uncountable from men who'd hoped the unexpected suicide rush would carry them to the gate. And truly, if they had gained the perimeter, they might have found a defense along the wall. But they never got that far, and the first blast of grapeshot, and then another, and another, twisted hundreds in their steps, where they fell writhing in agony, blasted to shreds, howling.

Gianavel raced along the wall separating men and scattering reloaders so that a random cannon shot didn't disintegrate the lot of them. And within seconds the wall boomed with rifle after rifle.

Within the charge, those in the rear saw the carnage that ripped and shredded those before them like so many sheep. Many hesitated, and in hesitating they encouraged one another to hesitate even further, and within seconds half the battalion stalled.

Even Pianessa had angled past the front gate where death thundered in the cannon smoke, apparently searching for a more vulnerable entry, and Blake hoped there was none. For the moment, he knew, they had the advantage. And unless Pianessa's artillery reduced the wall, they would have to force the gate.

Pianessa also understood the situation, and in a moment he was racing along the wood line commanding men to charge through the murderous musket and cannon fire while he searched for an easier point of attack. And in the steady, booming rhythm of the cannons, Blake witnessed a massacre in the naked and bloody glade beyond anything he had ever imagined. Those in the center flank were ripped apart like paper silhouettes. Those fortunate enough to be on the flank were sliced with musket fire, and it was only then that Blake realized he was no longer hearing the cannons, though the glade erupted with geysers of crimson.

Gianavel separated the men into zones to keep up continuous fire as they'd been trained—slow and methodical, waiting until their shot was certain. As Gianavel had said, it didn't matter how close a man came as long as he died with his last step.

Within twenty minutes, five hundred of Pianessa's men were cowering in the field, unable to retreat and unable to advance as they awkwardly returned rifle fire. There was no time to be astounded, but Blake knew he should have been amazed at the carnage before him.

In every war, before he had joined these people, he had gazed with pity at the dead and even at the living, wondering what madness men delivered to men. But he knew now that there was far greater evil than fighting, and that evil was what he was fighting to defeat.

Then Blake heard a sudden roar at their backs and whirled and saw a black image on a black horse—Pianessa—and a hundred men racing through some unknown and unguarded back gate. Something—it didn't matter what now—had been overlooked.

A rare mistake for Gianavel...

And perhaps his last.

><<◊>><

Pianessa's sword swung back and up again at the first man, severing the arm like paper. He kicked the dying man with his boot before leaping from his mount. In such close quarters, a horse was more of a handicap than an advantage—maneuverability was not important when your silhouette made you a readier target.

Pianessa struck down two, three, four men, working his way through the shocked Waldenses like a butcher too long denied the pleasure of his profession. Then a rifle erupted close, and the marquis twisted at the glancing impact that tore a plate of leather armor and bruised his shoulder beneath his chain mail.

With a growl the Marquis de Pianessa stalked forward, and as the man threw away his rifle to withdraw his sword, Pianessa's descending blade split the man's sword and head together. And the blow continued to the ground, crushing what remained into a ghastly thing that seemed as if it could have never borne human form. With barely a glance, Pianessa hit another man and another and became aware they were backing away from him to engage his soldiers.

Man to man, he could, without question, wade through the camp and kill them all one by one. Flies were more of a hindrance than their futile attempts to fight. Then the marquis spied a man who fought with greater skill than the rest—a man who appeared strangely different from the Vaudois.

"You!" Pianessa roared as he stalked forward. "Who are you!"

∞∞∞∞∞

Blake knew the identity before he turned and knew he could not defeat Pianessa. The marquis was too strong, too fast, and too heavily armored.

Revealing nothing, Blake repeated a gesture he had witnessed by an English colonel who had known his death was certain. He raised his saber, pointing at Pianessa, who released a barking laugh.

Launching himself forward, Blake slashed to take out the marquis' knee.

But, incredibly, Pianessa had already stepped to the side, and the huge sword he wielded lightly as a saber cut through the air toward Blake's head. The fight would have—probably should have—ended there, but for Blake's good fortune.

A figure collided with the marquis before the blow met Blake's neck, and Pianessa staggered forward, roaring and enraged, as if he had been insulted. He turned into the form wrestling with him, and Blake saw *Bertino!*

The big farmer swung a tight, hard blow that caught the marquis in the chest, and Pianessa's wrath was prehistoric. He lashed out with a backhand that sent Bertino sprawling. Then, before the big farmer could gain his feet, Pianessa's blade fell thunderously, and Blake knew that the big man he had come to admire, respect, even love, was dead.

Yes, Bertino would live for a moment, hovering between this world and the next, and then whatever was him would leave the broken chest that could no longer protect the heart. Just as Blake now believed that he would see the farmer again…and possible sooner than he knew.

He turned as Pianessa whipped his blade through the air, scattering blood. The marquis laughed as he came forward again. His teeth gleamed like a beast's crouching before a kill.

"Where is Gianavel!" he shouted.

Blake shook his head. "I don't know…." He raised his sword again. "But I won't disappoint you, Pianessa."

Bold words worth nothing, Blake knew. He had never spoken before in combat, didn't know why he did now, except perhaps because this might be his last chance.

Pianessa's face twisted in anger and frustration, as though he did not consider Blake worthy his steel. But as the marquis strode forward, his lips parted in a snarl. Then the huge sword hummed over Blake's head, sending him sprawling.

So quickly had Pianessa moved, Blake had not even seen the blow begin. Rather, it had appeared from nowhere and in the next second he was rolling across the ground, sensing the long black strides of the marquis approaching.

Blake threw up his blade as Pianessa roared, and the huge blade struck solidly. Blake never even felt his saber shatter but realized it had as Pianessa's broadsword continued through empty air. Reacting instantly—anything was better than nothing—Blake hurled the broken shard at the marquis, who evaded it without effort.

Once again, Pianessa raised his sword. "I tire of you Waldenses.... Now you will die."

Staggering, Blake rose and spat.

Pianessa laughed, drawing back.

"Pianessa!"

Pianessa whirled with a snarl, clutching the long hilt of his sword in both hands.

Emerging from a storm of bloody roars and colliding bodies, Gianavel surged forward. His eyes were fixed on Pianessa; his face was grim. He held his sword low in a single hand and struck men aside like wheat as he closed.

Swirling his great blade in a quick circle, Pianessa stepped into a bloody arena that left the two of them virtually alone, to decide this war. And the marquis seemed to enlarge in the moment, his arms and shoulders swelling with barbaric strength. The black hair along his head and neck rose like the hackles of a wolf.

"At last!" Pianessa whispered, eyes gleaming. "The great prince of the Vaudois! I've already made the acquaintance of your wife and children!"

Gianavel said nothing, made no display of courage or cunning as he came forward. Blake half expected some words—some act of defiance, something said in hate, but all that was said was said by Gianavel's clear and remorseless purpose.

With movements as pure and deadly as his aspect, Gianavel closed the final stride. He made no display of preparing for complex swordplay but at Gianavel's first move his swordplay was complex beyond anything Blake had ever imagined.

Gianavel lunged terrifically, almost fully committing himself to a direction of attack—almost. But his right foot dragged, keeping him in contact with the ground.

Pianessa did not catch the last move or didn't have time to doubt the attack, and his broadsword was flung on a course to intercept the saber. But as the blade rose, Gianavel bunched, bringing his hilt close to his body so that the blade fell short of Pianessa's block, and Gianavel straightened in a second lunge. His saber flashed beneath the block and speared Pianessa in the shoulder.

Shouting with rage and surprise, the marquis swung his blade in a backhand blow that would have killed—any of his blows would have killed if they had connected—but it was too late. The Captain of Rora had already leaped outside striking range and watched almost with contempt as the blade sailed through empty air. Then Gianavel lunged forward again and slashed down, striking Pianessa's knee.

The marquis turned into the blow and leaped to close the gap, and it seemed to be what Gianavel had expected. Almost before Pianessa had committed himself to the move, Gianavel had pinned Pianessa's sword arm and blade against his body.

Face-to-face they struggled, neither willing to be the first to retreat because the first to retreat had the disadvantage of retreating *and* avoiding a blow, whereas the one who held his ground only needed one quick twist to hurl his sword.

Both Pianessa and Gianavel knew the rule. Neither would be retreating from this contest of pure, brute strength. Both held the other's armor, keeping his opponent close, their other hands wrapped around their hilts.

Straining, Gianavel bent forward, preventing Pianessa from using his superior weight. Pianessa surged, attempting to throw the Vaudois off-balance. But Gianavel turned *into* the twists, hurling Pianessa's weight much farther and harder than the marquis expected or wanted, removing him of any advantage.

Suddenly Gianavel's boot slipped on the wet ground soaked even wetter with blood, and Pianessa seized the advantage. His sword rose a mere six inches, enough to clear his hand from Gianavel's hold, and he tried a hard shortcut.

The Captain of Rora knew it was coming and surged forward, his shoulder colliding with the marquis, and the blade hit a glancing blow from Gianavel's cheek. Instantly blood erupted from the cut, and Gianavel didn't care to wipe it away. He retreated just outside contact range of the blade and bent, breathing heavily.

Pianessa laughed and swept out with his sword, flinging blood in a wide crescent. "Is this the man who defended Rora in their fight against persecution?" he cried.

Blake saw that Pianessa, too, had somehow been cut in the last exchange—blood flowed from his lip and cheek.

Pianessa frowned, circling slowly. "You certainly fight like a man, Captain. Let's see if you die like a man."

Gianavel's eyes were dead. He said nothing. His concentration was complete.

Pianessa's hate was as heavy as the heart of a star. "You should have watched your family burn…as I did, Captain. Your children screamed for you."

At that, Gianavel's mouth turned in the faintest frown. Minutely, his hand shifted on his blade. Then Pianessa's hand tightened on his sword—he saw the signal of an attack. Blake wanted to break the moment, to warn the captain of Rora he was being goaded into a trap, forsaking his skill and cunning.

Gianavel lunged, fully committing himself to a line of attack, and Pianessa read every movement, every direction of the eye, every shift of weight however small, and his sword flew outward in a lunge that blasted Gianavel's sword aside and plowed across Gianavel's ribs, plunging out his back. They stood face-to-face.…

Gianavel's teeth were clenched in pain and…control.

Upon the face of Pianessa was shock—even surprise—and then blood erupted from his mouth. He caved inward—into his armor, it seemed—falling slowly, like an avalanche in black, to his knees. And then Blake saw Gianavel's left hand—the hand he had *not* seen—release the hilt of a dagger buried deep in Pianessa's guts.

On his knees, Pianessa stared at the blade as if his mind had not yet realized that he was defeated. He gazed dumbly at the dagger, then reached up slowly to grasp it. Then, even more slowly, he raised his face to the Captain of Rora.

Almost invisibly, Gianavel's shook his head. And for the fraction of a second, Blake thought he beheld tragedy there, in his face. As if this war had been so much waste—as if even *this*…had been so much waste—at such a precious price.

Like a tree the Marquis de Pianessa fell forward, leaning against Gianavel's stoic form. Then he slid off the Captain of Rora and to the side, landing facedown in the mud. Groaning, he curled into the posture of a man who was ultimately defeated—a man who was defeated in spirit even more than he was defeated in the flesh.

Across the compound, the marquis' soldiers were dead or dying. Those who'd survived were fast disappearing into distant trees, unarmed and wounded. And the Waldenses, who seemed as numerous as when the battle began, had secured the gate.

Gazing across the compound, Gianavel's eyes revealed neither victory nor defeat. With the end of this battle, as with the end of every battle, he would command the men to kneel. And then he would recite to them the fifteenth Psalm, and they would stand.

Frowning, Gianavel sheathed his sword.

Blake felt so much that he felt nothing at all.

It was finished.

✕✕✕✕✕✕

Emmanuel raised his face as a terrified monk stood in the open front doorway of his Great Hall. The monk did not enter and would not unless the Duke of Savoy bid him come.

The Duke of Savoy waited, finding some manner of cryptic pleasure in the monk's obvious terror. He glanced toward Father Simon, who revealed nothing at all.

"Come," Emmanuel ordered at last.

The monk came quickly, as if he would be relieved to deliver the words and be as quickly gone. He halted before Emmanuel and bowed. "It is…Noble Incomel, My Lord."

Emmanuel waited.

The monk whispered, "He is murdered!"

The monk stared as if expecting some violent reaction from the Duke of Savoy, if not at the surprise, then possibly at whatever consequence this might deliver to his kingdom. It was not often that an Inquisitor was killed inside the palace and never without some dangerous inquiry from the Citié del Vaticano.

With a gesture Emmanuel remarked, "And has this murderer been apprehended?"

Confusion flushed the monk's face. "No, My Lord. Not yet. But the second Inquisitor is dead, also. The one from Pope Alexander." His hands locked. "What will we do?"

Emmanuel said mildly, "Call out the Sergeant at Arms. See that everyone is detained and questioned. Have the Inquisitors record the answers in their records."

The monk stared. "The Inquisitors, My Lord?"

Emmanuel actually laughed out loud as the monk backed away in confusion. The man hesitated and then turned and ran down the long hall and out the guarded portal. Leaning against the mantel, the Duke of Savoy looked upon the old priest. "You knew?"

Somber, Simon nodded. "He was…my friend."

That was…a curiously tragic note to mark a victory.

Emmanuel cast his wine into the fire, turned, and walked silently across the hall, past his throne, and to the open courtyard. Slowly he mounted the stairway of the battlement and searched the city and forest that surrounded his palace that was finally his in truth.

So much death…

Though ravaged by war, he knew greatness would return to Turin, and then the people, though it might require years and years for them to rise up and repopulate the land. But they would bear more children. They would rebuild what had been destroyed. They would plant new crops. They would pray together and work together. And he hoped that both tyrant and hero would be remembered by the world, because what had happened here was too great to not be remembered.

Here, one of the mightiest military machines the world had ever known had been defeated by the power of faith and courage—by the faith and courage of a man who had inspired that same faith and courage in his friends. And, gazing over the war-torn land, Emmanuel knew that Simon, from the very beginning, had been right.

"Slaughter the Waldenses until the hills are bleached by their bones, Savoy. Slaughter them till your hand freezes to your sword and you cannot let it go, and the Waldenses will number like locusts. Because you cannot destroy their faith, Savoy, and their faith is their life.…What is created by the spirit cannot be destroyed by flesh."

Emmanuel nodded. "Yes…"

Wisdom learned too late.

He wondered if the world would remember.

⊚ EPILOGUE

QUIETLY LOCKHART CLOSED THE DOOR and entered the room where the old poet worked—even now worked on what would be his masterpiece.

Paradise Lost, he called it.

Lockhart knew the old man heard him, though the pen did not hesitate, nor did John Milton raise his head. With a faint smile, the Scotsman walked forward, stared down.

It had been years. Cromwell, whose stout courage and spirit had helped still the massacre of the Waldenses, was dead. And Cardinal Mazarin, whose faith and love for all people of all faith, was gone. There were few now who knew what had happened in Piedmont. But the poet would not let it go; he would make the world remember.

To always remember…

As Lockhart smiled, John Milton tilted his head. He gazed at the pages as if he could see them. "They believe I am a foolish old man," he said and then laughed. "Perhaps they are right…. I write in darkness. I cannot even see…what I say."

Still smiling, Lockhart pulled a chair and sat. "The world would be fortunate to be so foolish, old man."

Though Lockhart was gray now, he had become what he had been destined to become—a noble man.

For a moment John Milton shut his eyes, as if in earnest prayer, then spoke. "Who will ever believe that the Waldenses secured their future in a manner more worthy than kings?" He laughed gently. "Who will believe that Gianavel, that great Patriarch of the Waldenses, defeated the mightiest army in Europe with only a handful of men? Perhaps no one...? But so that men will never forget the power of his faith and courage and his own resolute will, I have written these words."

The old man needed no eyes to read what he had written with his own hand and his own passion. As he spoke, his voice grew strong.

"'Avenge, O Lord, Thy slaughtered saints, whose bones lie scattered on the Alpine mountains cold. In Thy book record their groans, who were Thy sheep, and in their silent fold slain by the bloody Piedmontese, that rolled mother and infant down the rocks. Their moans, the vales redoubled on the hills, and they to Heaven....'"

John Milton took a heavier breath and smiled faintly. "I pray those days will be remembered when men must once choose whether they will stand for what they believe. I pray that Joshua Gianavel, and those great heroes of the faith who stood beside him, will be taken for an example.... And the saints of the Lord will know that any battle can be won...if they believe."

"I believe," Lockhart said quietly as he leaned forward, placing a hand on the old man's arm. "Tell me the rest."

As his eyes saw something that was not yet before them, John Milton leaned back. "Pardoned by the Duke of Savoy, Joshua Gianavel was, henceforth, exiled to Geneva, where he and his son lived the rest of their long years in peace and prosperity. But yet another great massacre was to follow, a massacre that left virtually no Waldenses alive in their valley."

The poet's voice was no less than prophetic. "And as the castaways were fleeing toward Geneva—naked, starving, and hunted—word reached Gianavel, who yet lived. And the Prince of the Waldenses gathered with him six strong men, as in times of old, to meet the refugees in the wilderness.

"Pursued by ten thousand soldiers of the Duke of Savoy, the wounded Waldenses reached the border at last. Their strength was as nothing. Hope was a ghostly veil before their graves. And, caught only moments before they would have reached safety, they would die as the rest had died. And then…"

Lockhart didn't move. "And then?"

John Milton's eyes opened even farther, seeing what no one else had yet seen. "And then seven men appeared on the horizon." He stretched out a hand. "Only seven men, child. But the entire army of Piedmont saw the man who stood in the center of the crescent. He was old, white-haired, and surely his strength had diminished, though his greatness had not. And as Gianavel stared upon the beast, ten thousand strong…the beast stayed his hand from killing. And those who had been persecuted…were set free."

Lockhart stared upon the old man, whose face shone with such light.

"And then the commander of the army of Piedmont looked upon the low hill where Gianavel had stood. Looked once more to see the silhouette of that great warrior whom God had used to defend His people. Yes, looked for the man who by faith and courage defeated what no one believed could be defeated."

Rapt, Lockhart whispered, "And then?"

With a smile, the poet bowed his head.

"And then...Gianavel was gone."

Old and gray, now, Blake turned and watched the children playing, free and happy. It was a simple thing, he knew, but such a price had been paid for this freedom. He watched them arguing over a piece of coal, over who had actually won it. He laughed.

As an Elder of the Waldenses, Blake could have stood and settled the matter without dispute. But life was not so simple, and children must learn. Yes...they must learn that the world is a place forever filled with conflict and confusion. But it can also be filled with courage and wisdom and faith and love—and victory—if they seek the Lord with all their heart.

He raised his face and closed his eyes and remembered all that had passed, as he often did now with the weight of his age settling heavier upon him. For more than half a century had passed, and Gianavel, his great friend, old and full of years, was dead.

Shoulder to shoulder and against the tide they had stood and won a victory greater than any one of them could know, though he often prayed that the world might understand one day. For what had been won was far greater than villages or valleys or kingdoms or even the now silent bones of heroes lost to time.

With a sad smile Blake remembered the words of Gianavel—words spoken in that dark night so long ago as Gianavel's wife and children, cruelly bound by chains, were sacrificed to flames. For, from the very beginning, Gianavel had been right.

What chains can hold belongs to man.

The rest is God's.

⚘ ACKNOWLEDGMENTS

THE STORY OF JOSHUA GIANAVEL and the War of Piedmont is very briefly described in *Foxes' Book of Martyrs*. However, the account lacks important details of specific events. Therefore, I attempted to build a cohesive account by researching the individual lives of Oliver Cromwell, Charles Emmanuel II, John Milton, Sir Samuel Morland, Cardinal Jules Mazarin, and others who played important roles in the Waldenses' struggle for freedom of faith.

Yet after reconstructing events from a wide range of personal letters, official petitions, papal testimonies, and eyewitness accounts, I found a disturbing lack of agreement. So I chose to weigh the testimony against the personal interests of the witness. I quickly decided the official records of Inquisitors were of dubious merit, as I did the accounts of those who most zealously defended the Waldenses. Each side, to polar extremes, apparently wrote to color history, so the engineering of an undisputed conclusion was not possible.

I decided the letters of those who had the least personal interest in the War of Piedmont to be the most reliable. However, they were also the most lacking in detail. Some events cannot be denied, but neither can others be fully explained. And in those cases, if a realistic analysis of the political-religious activities of the time period provided logical possibilities, I followed where evidence led.

As with names, I used rules that seemed most appropriate. Joshua Gianavel and all the leading characters, some quite famous in their time, are accurately identified. However, the particular Inquisitors who most fervently promoted the war against the Waldenses were impossible to identify with any certitude. I did not believe, and still don't believe, that an exact identification of Inquisitors is necessary. It is clear enough that the Inquisitors of Piedmont forced the Duke of Savoy to launch an unprovoked war against the people of Piedmont. In such matters, I decided that the most vital element is how the office of the Inquisition was misused, not the guilt of the man who misused it.

I have also included, for purposes of narrative technique, imaginary personalities who, placed in the center of the story, allowed me to recount events of the war without intruding unduly into the minds of the more prominent participants. Where it was possible, I did not "create" thoughts for Cromwell, Mazarin, or Milton beyond what their personal letters and memoirs allowed and was consistent with their character and efforts during the war.

The second great struggle I confronted was crafting an accurate description and sequence of battles. There is no question from any source that Joshua Gianavel and the people of Rora were outnumbered hundreds to one in battle after battle. Nor is there any dispute that their ultimate victory for religious freedom was anything less than miraculous. There were, however, conflicting accounts of certain engagements, and I was forced, in the end, to simply build as accurate a portrayal as evidence allowed.

Without question Joshua Gianavel was a brilliant military tactician. His inexplicable but comprehensive understanding of physical and psychological warfare was respected and publicly recognized even by his enemies. The indisputable fact that Gianavel was offered the land and title of a marquis if he would only cease his resistance to the Inquisition is testimony to that. But he was also a man of profound faith and sincere devotion to God who found physical resistance to religious persecution an option only when all other options had failed.

If you are familiar with my work, you will recognize some names and elements from my first novel, *A Wolf Story*, where I placed these characters in an allegorical setting. I suppose it is a story that has lived with me for many years—a story I was destined to eventually write. I hope that it will not disappoint.

I want to thank John Peterson of Koechel, Peterson & Associates for his friendship and support. I thank my editor, Lance Wubbels, for his exacting craftsmanship in editing and writing, for his wise judgments, and for making the story much better than I could have alone. I want to thank Terry McDowell and Helen Motter for their scholarship and attention to detail, and Diana Nortowicz for her expert research. C. Michael Dudash's illustration for the cover was exquisite, and David Koechel did a masterful job on the design. I also want to thank Daniel Stoecker, Cliff Ford, and Pat Matrisciana.

I believe the story contains themes of courage and moral conflict that become more relevant to our lives each day—questions that have no easy answers or any answer at all sometimes. But I am convinced that in the coming age, advancing so quickly upon us, now, we face the same questions and conflicts, and we will also be forced to choose. And perhaps, when that day comes, we will take those who fought beside Gianavel for example.

AUTHOR'S NOTE ON TRANSLATION

Endless difficulties concerning the correct spelling of names and places were confronted during the writing of this book. Even the correct spelling for the name of Joshua Gianavel—Josia Janavel, Joshua Gianavel, Josia Gianovello, according to the records of various languages—was uncertain.

The extreme discrepancies in the spelling of names and places arise from the fact that during the late Medieval Period and Early Modern Period the region of Piedmont in Northern Italy was more culturally aligned with France, while politically aligned with Italy. And when English scholars translated documents from the primary language of Piedmont, a combination of French and Romaunt, English equivalents to the unfamiliar and unique dialect were indiscriminately elected.

Both layman and scholar have variously adopted the liberties, therefore contemporary readers must deal with the frustrating task of deciphering who or what is referred to in respective documents. For the sake of consistency I settled upon primarily using the English derivatives. But some disputes, such as the name of the wife of Joshua Gianavel, had no practical solution, and so I elected the name from a French document that seemed most reliable. Any mistake in selecting a various translation is mine alone.